WINNER OF THE 2007 PACIFIC NORTHWEST BOOKSELLERS AWARD
FINALIST FOR THE 2007 LOS ANGELES TIMES BOOK PRIZE
BEST BOOKS OF 2006, *Washington Post, Seattle Times, Kirkus Reviews*

"Walter is a gifted writer with unusual breadth. And among the already proliferating and formulaic body of film and fiction grappling with September 11, *The Zero* is a standout."

—*San Francisco Chronicle*

"This is political satire at its best: scathing, funny, dark. And the actual mystery rivets. . . . Grade: A." *Entertainment Weekly*

"It has taken years for black comedy to assume a salutary role in puncturing what very quickly became a spectacle of opportunism, bathos, and bad faith. It does so brilliantly and ingeniously in *The Zero.* . . . The surreality of Walter's novel pretty much matches that of our own world. Except the book is far funnier." —*Boston Globe*

"A brilliant tour de force . . . the breakout novel of a brave and talented young writer." —*Kirkus Reviews* (starred review)

"[With] its deadpan truths, its insider smarts, and its everyguy hero . . . [Walter] elevates *The Zero* above mere satire to Kafkaesque parable."

—*Wall Street Journal*

"Walter's irreverent take on the 9/11 attacks ultimately renders *The Zero* more moving and honest than any of the books bursting with patriotism and pieties on the subject. As Joseph Heller did for World War II with *Catch-22*, Walter expertly captures the absurdities that ensued from the tragedy of the terrorist attacks, and in doing so has written one of the best books of 2006." —*Boulder Daily Camera*

The Zero

ALSO BY JESS WALTER

FICTION

Citizen Vince
Land of the Blind
Over Tumbled Graves

NONFICTION

Ruby Ridge: The Truth and Tragedy
of the Randy Weaver Family
(originally released as *Every Knee Shall Bow*)

The Zero

a novel

Jess Walter

HARPER PERENNIAL

NEW YORK • LONDON • TORONTO • SYDNEY

HARPER ● PERENNIAL

A hardcover edition of this book was published in 2006 by Regan, an imprint of HarperCollins Publishers.

P.S.™ is a trademark of HarperCollins Publishers.

THE ZERO. Copyright © 2006 by Jess Walter. All rights reserved. Printed in the United States. No part of this book may be used or reproduced in any manner whatsoever without written permission except in the case of brief quotations embodied in critical articles and reviews. For information address HarperCollins Publishers, 10 East 53rd Street, New York, NY 10022.

HarperCollins books may be purchased for educational, business, or sales promotional use. For information please write: Special Markets Department, HarperCollins Publishers, 10 East 53rd Street, New York, NY 10022.

FIRST HARPER PERENNIAL EDITION PUBLISHED 2007.

Designed by Kris Tobiassen

The Library of Congress has catalogued the hardcover edition as follows:

Walter, Jess.
    The Zero : a novel / Jess Walter.—1st ed.
      p. cm.
    ISBN-13: 978-0-06-089865-6
    ISBN-10: 0-06-089865-8
    I. Title.

  PS3573.A4722834Z47 2006
  813'.54—dc22

               2006044346

  ISBN: 978-0-06-118943-2 (pbk.)
  ISBN-10: 0-06-118943-X (pbk.)

07 08 09 10 11 RRD 10 9 8 7 6 5 4 3 2 1

To Brooklyn Walter

AUTHOR'S NOTE: THIS HAPPENED.

Could I, I thought, be the last coward on earth?
How terrifying! . . . All alone
with two million stark raving heroic madmen,
armed to the eyeballs . . .

CÉLINE,
Journey to the End of the Night

PART ONE

Days After

THEY BURST INTO THE SKY, every bird in creation, angry and agitated, awakened by the same primary thought, erupting in a white feathered cloudburst, anxious and graceful, angling in ever-tightening circles toward the ground, drifting close enough to touch, and then close enough to see that it wasn't a flock of birds at all—it was paper. Burning scraps of paper. All the little birds were paper. Fluttering and circling and growing bigger, falling bits and frantic sheets, some smoking, corners scorched, flaring in the open air until there was nothing left but a fine black edge . . . and then gone, a hole and nothing but the faint memory of smoke. Behind the burning flock came a great wail and a moan as seething black unfurled, the world inside out, birds beating against a roiling sky and in that moment everything that wasn't smoke was paper. And it was beautiful.

"Brian? Is everything okay in there?"

Brian Remy's eyes streaked and flaked and finally jimmied open to the floor of his apartment. He was lying on his side, panning across a fuzzy tree line of carpet fiber. From this, the world focused into being one piece at a time: Boots caked in dried mud. Pizza boxes. Newspapers. A glass. And something just out of range . . .

The flecks in his eyes alerted and scattered and his focus adjusted again: sorrow of sorrows, an empty Knob Creek bottle. They were both tipped over on their right sides on the rug, parallel to one another, the whiskey fifth and him. In this together, apparently. He told himself to breathe, and managed a rusty-lunged wheeze. He blinked and the streaks and floaters ran across his eyes for cover. Outside Remy's apartment, Mrs. Lubach yelled again. "Brian, I heard a bang! Is everything okay?"

Remy had heard no bang himself, although he tended to believe literalists like Mrs. Lubach. Anyway, a bang of some sort would explain the muffled ringing in his ears. And how it hurt to move his head. He strained to raise his chin and saw, to his right, just past the bottle, his handgun, inert and capable of nothing but lying among the crumbs and hairs on his carpet. If he waited long enough, a rubber-gloved hand would pick it up by the butt and drop it in a Ziploc, tagged and bagged—and him too, as long he didn't move, a bigger bag, but the same—thick plastic the last thing he smelled before the last sigh of the reefer truck door.

Mrs. Lubach's voice came muffled from behind the door: "Brian? I'm going to call the police."

"I am the police." His own voice was tinny and small inside his skull; he wasn't sure the words had actually come out of his mouth.

"Brian?"

He sat up on the floor and looked around his studio apartment: collapsed futon, patched plaster walls, paint-sealed windows. He put his hand against the left side of his head. His hair was sticky and matted, as if he'd been lying in syrup. He pulled his hand away. Sure. Blood.

Okay. Coming together now.

He called to the door, louder: "Just a minute, Mrs. Lubach."

Brian Remy stood, queasy and weak, trying once again to find the loose string between cause and effect—long day, drink, sorrow, gunshot, fatigue. Or some other order. Steadied on the stove, he grabbed a dish towel and held its fringed end against his head. He looked back at the table and could see it all laid out before him, like the set of a student play. A kitchen chair was tipped over, and on the small table where he had been sitting, a self-determinate still life: rag, shot glass, gun oil, wire brush, note.

Okay. This was the problem. These gaps in his memory, or perhaps his life, a series of skips—long shredded tears, empty spaces where the explanations for the most basic things used to be. For a moment he tried to puzzle over it all, the way he might have considered a problem on the job. Cleaning oil might indicate an accident, but the note? What lunatic has ever written a note before . . .

Cleaning a gun?

He picked up the note: "Etc . . ."

Et cetera?

Well, that was funny. He didn't recall being so funny. And yet there it was, in his own handwriting. Okay. He was getting somewhere. Whatever had happened, *whatever he'd done,* it was funny. Remy stuffed the note in his pocket, then righted the chair and bent over to pick up his nine, wobbled, set the safety, and laid the gun gently on the table.

"Brian?"

"I'm coming." He followed the path to the wall and put his finger in the fresh hole in the brick behind his chair. Then he stepped away from the wall and held the dish towel to his head, braced against a slithering jolt of pain, and when it passed, walked to the door. He opened it a crack on the hallway outside his apartment, Mrs. Lubach's orange face filling the gap between door and jamb.

"Brian? Is everything okay? It's three o'clock in the morning."

"Is it?"

"There are noise ordinances, Brian." Her voice echoed a split second behind the movement of her mouth, like a badly translated movie. "Rules," she continued. "And that *bang*. People work. We have jangly nerves, Brian. If you're not hurt, then it's inconsiderate, all that noise."

"What if I *am* hurt?"

Mrs. Lubach ignored him. "Just *imagine* what we thought that noise could have been." She was small and lean, with short straight white hair and wide features; her heavy makeup was painted on just a fraction off-center, giving her the look of a hastily painted figurine, or a foosball goalie. Before, she had been an accountant. Now, he thought he remembered, she wasn't sure what she would be. Would people just go back to the same jobs? As if nothing had happened? "For all we know the air might be combustible," she said now.

"I don't think so." Remy shifted the towel against his head.

"Jennifer-in-6A's boyfriend says that we'll all be in trouble when the wind shifts. Do you think that's true, Brian?"

"I don't know." Remy had no idea who Jennifer's boyfriend was, or who Jennifer was for that matter, or who lived in 6A or which way the wind had been blowing before.

"They don't tell us what's in the smoke. Do they tell you, Brian? Have they told you what's in the smoke?"

"No one has told me anything."

"Would you tell me if they had?"

Remy wasn't sure how to answer that.

"I didn't think so." She leaned in and whispered: "Karl in 9F said it's only a matter of time. He says we're wallowing in carcinogens. Soup of our own extinction. Those were his exact words. Matter of time. Soup. He's atheist. Very scientific. Cold." Then she looked over her shoulder. "I have a friend at the hospital. There are birth defects. Pocked gums. People without legs. I don't like to be in crowds, Brian."

Remy felt blood trickle down his neck and pool in the triangle of his collarbone.

Mrs. Lubach craned her neck to see. "Spontaneous bleeding," she said.

"No. I was just cleaning my gun, and . . ." She stared at him as if he knew how to finish the sentence. "*Et cetera,*" he said.

But Mrs. Lubach seemed to have lost interest in Remy's head

wound, in the bang that had brought her to his door. "I won't go down-town anymore," she said, "or on the subway, or to any building taller than ten stories. I think we might leave the city."

Remy rearranged the towel against his head. "I'm gonna go clean this up, Mrs. Lubach."

"I was in the shower," she said, as if he'd asked. "I was in the shower and sometimes the water slows to a trickle, and it did, maybe ten sec-onds before, and then when I got out, the phone rang, and it was my sister and she told me to turn on the TV. She lives in Wilmington. Her power went out at that precise moment." Mrs. Lubach's eyebrow arched. "In *Wilmington*. I don't understand any of it, Brian."

Remy pulled the towel from his head. "I need to go clean this up, Mrs. Lubach."

"When do you think it will get back to normal?"

Normal. The word itself seemed familiar and strange, like a re-pressed memory. At one time there had been a *normal*. "You know," he said. "I guess I'm not sure."

"Your friend said things will be better when all the paper has been cleaned up."

"My friend?" Remy asked.

"The young man who was here looking for you this morning. The paper guy."

"Paper guy?" Remy asked.

Mrs. Lubach opened her mouth to answer but—

REMY SAT alone in the emergency room, across from a dew-eyed Vietnamese girl holding a washcloth around what seemed to be a burned hand. She was nine or ten years old, and she was wearing footed pajamas. She was staring at Remy. Every few seconds she would close her eyes and sigh. Then she'd open them again, stare at Remy, and squeeze them shut, as if he were the thing causing her pain. She appeared to be here by herself. Remy looked around, but there was no one else in the ER except a senior volunteer sitting at the check-in desk, reading a hardcover book. After a moment, Remy stood and walked up to the senior volunteer, a shell-eyed man with a dusting of white whiskers on his cheeks. The man refused to look up from his book. Peering over, Remy saw he was hiding a ratty paperback behind the hardcover. At first Remy thought it was a blank book, but then he saw that he was merely at the end of a chapter and there were only a few words on the page: *nothing more hopeless, than this freedom, this waiting, this inviolability. . . .*

Remy waited but the man didn't look up, didn't even turn the page, just sat reading over and over: *nothing more hopeless . . . this waiting . . .*

"Excuse me," Remy said finally. "But that girl—"

"I told you, Mr. Remy, it will just be a minute," the senior volunteer said. "Please sit down. The doctors know all about you." The old guy stared at Remy and refused to break eye contact, until finally he turned the page and Remy read the first line of the next chapter: *"And he tore himself free . . ."*

"But the girl—"

"They are aware," the man said, "of your condition."

Remy tore himself free and returned to his chair. The Vietnamese girl sighed again and then her eyes snapped open and she stared at Remy evenly, as if she were waiting for the answer to some question. Finally, Remy had to look away.

His eyes fell on a small television bolted to a pillar in the center of the waiting room, flickering with cable news. Remy felt a jolt of déjà vu, anticipating each muted image before it appeared, and it occurred to him that the news had become the wallpaper in his mind now, the endless loop playing in his head—banking wings, blooms of flame, white plumes becoming black and then gray, endless gray, geysers of gray, dust-covered gray stragglers with gray hands covering gray mouths running from gray shore-break, and the birds, white—endless breeds and flocks of memos and menus and correspondence fluttering silently and then disappearing in the ashen darkness. Brian Remy closed his eyes then and saw what he always saw: shreds of tissue, threads of detachment and degeneration, silent fireworks, the lining of his eyes splintering and sparking and flaking into the soup behind his eyes— flashers and floaters that danced like scraps of paper blown into the world.

DAYS AFTER—with everything sun-bleached and ash-covered, with a halo of smoke still hanging over the island—Remy's partner Paul Guterak announced that he'd never been this happy. Paul and Remy were driving one of the new Ford Excursions that FEMA had sent over—"beautiful fuggin' truck," Paul said, white with tinted black, bulletproof windows, bumpers and back window plastered with stars and stripes, a tiny plastic flag fluttering furiously on the antenna. People lined up all along the West, waving signs and flags of their own, crying, holding up pictures and placards: "God Save . . ." and "Help Us Avenge . . ." and "We Won't Break."

Broken—that's how they looked to Remy. Busted up and put back together with pieces missing. They stood on roadblocks and behind barricades on the street, in flag T-shirts and stiff-brimmed ball caps, animated by Paul and Brian's passing like figures on an old Disney ride, grinding and whirring buccaneers from the Pirates of the Caribbean. A boy in a long-sleeved rugby jersey waved a yin-yang painted skateboard over his head near a woman holding a Pomeranian to her chest. Two women in jeans and heels, a bearded guy in a wool coat, and hundreds more, great bundles of open faces, until, after a few blocks, Remy could no longer look and he had to turn forward. And still they cheered and called out, as if desperate to be noticed into life. They cried. Saluted. They yelled for Remy to acknowledge them, but he stared ahead until they blurred together, the picket faces sliding by, the voices blurring together as he tried to place their longing.

"This is what I mean. We're fuggin' famous." Guterak said it the way someone might admit to being alcoholic. Maybe Paul was right, in his way—this was what it was like to be famous, to have people desperately reflected in the glow of your passing.

Paul pulled the truck off West Street before they reached the tunnel and the line of double-parked dinosaurs—the sat-news trucks and flatbeds, the reefer meat trucks. They stopped for coffee at a corner deli with an American flag taped to the corners of the window. There were flowers again, in pots and in window boxes, freshly misted, bleeding dirty water onto ashy sidewalks. That was something, anyway: For a day or two afterward, Remy remembered, there had been no flowers in the shops. At the deli door, an old couple smiled and gave them a thumbs-up. Brian adjusted his ball cap, which was clamped too tightly against the rough stitches he'd gotten in the ER the night before.

"Listen, I ain't sayin' I'm *glad* it happened," said Paul through his teeth. He was built like a bowling pin, wide at the hips and narrow at the shoulders. He spoke out of one side of his mouth, a gambler giving a tip. "Nothin' like that. But you gotta admit, Bri . . ."

"No, I'm not admitting anything, Paul." His head hurt.

"No, see, what I'm sayin' . . ."

"I *know* what you're saying," Remy said, "I just don't want to hear it."

"I ain't a fuggin' moron here, Bri. I know this ain't politically correct. I ain't gonna say this to anyone else. But come on . . . for you and me . . . I mean . . . we're alive, man. How can we help feeling—"

"I don't want to think about it, Paul. I don't want to talk about how you feel."

"No, you're not understanding me." Paul rubbed his neck.

They lined up for coffee, but the people on line parted and let them move to the front. As they passed, a woman in fur came to life and reached out to pat them on the shoulders of the new Starter jackets the bosses had gotten for everyone. Remy reached for some gum, but his hand went left a few degrees and he bashed his knuckles into a box of Snickers. No one seemed to notice.

When Paul tried to pay, the coffee guy waved them off. "Heroes drink free," he said, and the people on line applauded and Paul tipped the guy three bucks.

"Thank you, sir," Paul said, and he swallowed that thing that kept trying to choke him up.

"God bless!" said an older woman pushing a dog in a baby stroller.

"Thank you, ma'am," Paul said. "God bless *you*."

The dog stared at Remy, who finally had to look away.

Back on the sidewalk, Remy looked over his shoulder to see if people were still moving in the deli, but the sky's reflection glinted off the glass doors and he couldn't see inside. Clouds coming. Jesus, what would the rain do to the dust and ash? And the paper, the snow banks of résumés and memos and reports and bills of lading—what would rain do to all the paper? He knew there must be meetings taking place right now, officials preparing for just that possibility: that the vast paper recovery efforts would be complicated by rainfall. Paul and Remy climbed back in the truck. "That's exactly what I'm talkin' about, what happened in there just now," Paul said. "You can't tell me that ain't the best feeling, them people treating us so good like that. That's all I'm saying, Bri. That's all."

Remy closed his eyes.

"See," Paul pressed on, "before, no one said shit to us, except to gripe about a summons they just got or bark about why we didn't catch the mutt who broke into their fuggin' car, you know? Now . . . free coffee? Pats on the back? I know you been off the street for a while, but Jesus, don't it seem kinda . . . nice?"

Remy hid behind his coffee.

Paul whipped the Excursion back into traffic. "I mean, the overtime. And the shit we get to do. Taking the Yankees on a tour a The Zero. The fuggin' *Yankees*. Look at what we were doin' before this. Picking up The Boss's dry cleaning, runnin' his girlfriends around the city. Sitting through meetings with morons. You can't tell me you'd rather be doing that. And it ain't just that . . . it ain't just relief. It's something else, maybe even something . . ." He leaned over, and for a moment Remy thought he looked completely insane. ". . . something *bad*. You know?"

Remy stared out the window, down a deep canyon of dusted glass and granite, at palettes of bottled water stacked along the street and crates of donated gloves and granola bars. And then the rows of news trucks, two dozen of them queued up for slow troll, grief fishing, block after block—Action and Eyewitness and First At, dishes scooped to the sky like palms at a mass, and beyond them flatbeds burdened with twisted I beams, and then, backing up traffic, the line of expectant refrigerated meat trucks and the black TM truck, the temporary morgue where Remy had taken—

"See, what I'm sayin' . . ." Paul wrestled with his words.

"I know . . . what you're saying," Remy said quietly. "And maybe you're right. But there are things we can't say now. Okay? You can't *say* you've never been this happy. Even if you think it, you can't say it. Everything is . . . there are things . . . we have to leave alone. We have to let 'em sit there, and don't say anything about 'em."

"Like the scalp."

Remy rubbed his mouth and remembered it. Second day at The Zero, he'd found a section of a woman's scalp—gray and stiff—in the debris. He hadn't known what to do, so he put it in a bucket. They searched all afternoon near where it was found, but there were no other body parts, just a six-inch piece of a forehead and singed hairline. An

EMT and an evidence tech debated for ten minutes what to do with the scalp, before they finally took it out of the bucket and put it in one of the slick body bags. Remy carried it to a reefer truck, where it sat like a frog in a sleeping bag, a slick black bump on the empty floor. At least five times a day, Paul brought up the scalp. Whose scalp did Remy think it was? Where did he think the rest of the head was? Would they simply bury the scalp? Finally, Remy said he didn't want to talk about it anymore—didn't want to talk about what a piece of someone's head felt like, how light it was, how stiff and lonesome and worthless, or about how many more slick bags and meat trucks there were than they needed, how the forces at work in this thing didn't leave big enough pieces for body bags.

"See," Paul continued, "you ain't hearing me right, Bri."

"I'm hearing you."

Paul drove to the checkpoint, where two nervous-looking National Guardsmen in sunglasses and down-turned M-16s flanked a short foot cop, who stepped forward and leaned a boot on the running board of the Excursion. Paul reached into his shirt and came up with his ID tags. He held them out for the cop to read.

"Hey, boss," the street cop said, breaking it into two syllables: *bu-oss*. "How's it goin'?"

"Goddamn tough duty, you know?"

"Fuckin' raghead motherfuckers."

"Yeah. That's right. That's right."

Paul put his hand out. Remy removed the tags from his neck and put them in Paul's hand. Paul showed Remy's tags to the street cop, who wrote something down and then gave the tags back to Paul, who handed them back to Remy.

The street cop patted the Excursion's hood. "Nice truck, though."

"Freddies gave it."

The foot cop jerked his head toward the two guardsmen. "All they gib' me was these two stupid fuckers. And I know one of these Gomers is gonna shoot me in my leg before this is over."

"Maybe they got rubber bullets."

"In a perfect world, huh? Hey, you gib'm hell in there, boss," the cop said. He patted the hood of the Excursion again and stepped back, waving them through.

Remy watched the street cop, watched with a certain wonder the way that word, *boss,* was tossed between the two men, connoting everything of value, the firm scaffolding of reverent loyalty that promised each guy below the chance to rise to heights: his own crew, driver, office, parties, and budgetary discretion and security details, a shot at being boss someday himself. Wasn't this the ladder Remy had patiently climbed *before*? But now . . . what? Remy vaguely remembered thinking it was a corrupting and cruel system, but he had to admit . . . it lived for days like these.

Guterak drove through the checkpoint, to a cascade of applause and waving flags. He chirped the siren, then touched two fingers to his forehead and pointed. "Wish I could do something for these people," he muttered. "Anything. Mow their lawns." Remy leaned back in his seat and tried to breathe through his mouth. The smell never left him now. It lived in the lining of his nose and the fibers of his lungs—his whole body seemed to smell, as if the odor were working through his pores, the fine gray dust: pungent, flour of the dead. Remy was surprised at the air's ferocity down here, acrid with concrete dust and the loosed molecules of burned . . . burned everything. It was amazing what could burn. We forgot that, Remy thought, in our fear of fission and fusion, radiation, infection, concussion and fragmentation. We forgot fire.

"You see Durgan's kid on TV?"

Please be quiet.

"Big. I hadn't seen his kid since we all played softball. That's what

I'm talkin' about . . . seeing Durgan's kid. I mean . . . honestly? Better him than me. Right? Come on. Admit it. Better his kid crying on TV than mine. Or yours. Right?"

Remy stared out the window.

"But here's Durgan . . . dead as an eight-track, never get to see his kid again. And that could have been me, right? Except that, instead a bein' dead, I ain't even injured . . . or bankrupt. Or outta work. I got overtime comin' out my ass. I got backstage passes to Springsteen, right? Durgan's in pieces out there somewhere and I can't even get anyone to let me pay for a fuggin' cuppa coffee no more. All because I was standin' here and he was standin' there. See? I'm just sayin'—"

"I know," Remy interrupted. "Please. Paul." Remy took off his cap and rubbed the stitches on the side of his head.

Guterak looked over. "Hey, you got your hair cut."

"Yeah." Remy put the cap back on.

"What made you do that?"

"I shot myself in the head last night."

"Well." Paul drove quietly for a moment, staring straight ahead. "It looks good."

THE ZERO was humming. A raccoon-eyed firefighter had heard something, most likely the shriek of shifting steel, and was convinced that someone was calling his name. Rescue workers in respirators and surgical masks scuttled around the southwest corner of the pile, putting their heads in crevices, rappelling down cracks, furrowing between beams. Remy had watched as the ground began to shift beneath them, but even as they managed to pull away one husk of steel they just found more, *turtles all the way down*, bent steel shells as deep as anyone could imagine, and below that, seams of liquid fire, which they dug toward frantically, in the hopes of purifying some rage.

"Ants on a fuggin' hill," Paul said as they walked, too loudly, always too loudly, and Remy grabbed his partner by the wrist. It was as if Paul had lost whatever filter used to separate his mind from his mouth. He said whatever came into his head now.

"No, don't you think?" Paul asked. "Don't we all look like ants out here?" Remy couldn't remember if Guterak had always been this way or if his Touretic insensitivity was new. He turned to Paul to tell him to be quiet, but just then the soot-eyed firefighter held his hand up and the bucket brigades froze in place, eyes on the smoking fissures, everyone stone quiet, like some children's game, desperate to hear over the generators and construction equipment and the low buzz of conversation. The firefighter was staring at them—no, right *through them*. Goddamn.

"You know what? I can barely stand to look at these fuggin' smokers now," Paul said at his elbow. "I used to hate those lousy, pampered mopes. You know? *Bravest*, my ass. The old ones are lazy fat fuggs and the young ones spend all day working out—"

"Paul—" Remy began but his partner just kept talking.

"And they get all that tail. For what? Let's see one of those lazy-ass work-two-days-a-week assholes foot a beat on the Deuce, right? Let's see one of those steroid-suckin' probies make a buy in some hooch in the Heights.

"But I can't begrudge 'em now. Sons-of-bitches just walked right in. You know? I mean, damn. They can get all the blow jobs, all the cooked meals. Fuggers walked right in. Half of 'em off duty, and they walked in. I can't say I would've—"

"Shut the fuck up!" The poor smoker was still running around the edge of the pile, yelling at people who were already staring blankly at him, until he was the only one making any noise. "Please, shut the fuck up! Why can't everybody just be quiet? Why can't everyone shut up?"

Paul and Remy drifted back a block. They were supposed to meet

Assistant Chief Carey at the southern entrance of the vast stadium of debris, beneath B-Trust, what Guterak called "the holster," its face pierced by a steel javelin, just to the south of The Place That Stunk. Everyone knew that it stunk especially bad here, and everyone knew what the smell had to be, but no one could find the exact source. An elevator bank? A stairwell? A fire rig? A few years ago, when he was still married, Remy had kicked his kid's jack-o'-lantern underneath his porch and this was how it smelled in the spring. It drove people crazy, smelling that at the south end of The Zero, and not being able to find the thing that was deteriorating. And now that the smell was getting weaker, the fact of it was even worse, like they were losing whoever was down there. He'd see guys wrinkle their noses, raising their faces to the sky, as if they just needed to try harder. And that was another thing you couldn't talk about. While the slick bags sat piled on sidewalks and the meat trucks sat empty and you took apart the piles one goddamned bucket at a time, like taking pebbles from a mountain, you knew what was happening below, you could smell what was happening, the quickening decay and dissolution, like paper burning in air.

The bucket brigades started up again: only six today, and the bosses were trying to get even these to stop, so they could bring in more heavy machinery to get at the rubble. The machines tested the edges of the pile, nosing their way in, sampling the surrounding buildings, yanking twisted I beams like horses grazing at deep-rooted grass. Eventually, the smokers and cops and hard hats would have to give way to the machines—they all knew this—and the order would be forever reversed, people pushed to the edge, snacking at the corners while the machines ate to their fill from the center.

"Fuckers took your sweet time." Ass Chief Carey strode over to Remy and Guterak, wearing a hard hat and one of the new satin jackets. The jackets made them look like a slow-pitch softball team. "I was trying to call you on the Nextels."

Paul shrugged. "I gave my Nextel to Kubiak two days ago. He said we was getting new this week."

The Ass Chief's eyes bugged. "You gave your Nextel to Kubiak?"

"I thought we was getting new, boss."

"What? You didn't get new walkies?"

"No!"

"And you gave yours away?"

"Come on, Chief. Why you bustin' my balls here? I . . . fuggin' told you."

The Ass Chief wrinkled his long forehead, all the way to the hard hat perched on his black brush-cut hair. He turned to Remy. "That true? You didn't get new Nextels?"

"I don't know," Remy said.

Carey turned and snapped his own walkie-talkie out. "Pirello! Where the fuck you at, you piece of shit? Where the fuck are my Nextels? My guys got no radios."

Ass Chief Carey stalked off, shouting into his hand, and Remy turned back to the pile. Water was being pumped from three angles, from ladder trucks on the fringe of the massive smoldering jungle, while fire raged in its roots and hot shoots jutted from the pile. Up close, you didn't really get any better idea what the smoking leaves and vines were made of, except a few things like window blinds. Everywhere, window blinds. How many window blinds could there be? A billion? Everywhere Remy looked he saw hoary window blinds, hung over bent beams like casual summer wash. He longed for the cool comfort of raw numbers. What percentage of the pile was steel? What percentage window blinds?

And paper. What percentage paper? Much of the paper had made a dramatic escape; that's what Remy recalled, watching the paper flushed into space, a flock of birds hovering over everything, and then leafing down on the city. That would help, somehow, knowing what percentage of the pile was paper. And people. Most of the pile was steel and concrete and window blinds and you became grateful for these because they mostly stayed put. You could figure out how much steel and how many window blinds; you could account. It was a simple math problem. But the people were different. And the paper. The people and the paper burned up or flew away or ran off, and after it happened, they were considerably less than they had been in the beginning; they were bellowsed and blown, and they scattered like seeded dandelions in a windstorm.

This seemed to upset everyone, not just him, and he supposed this explained the new agency, the Office of Liberty and Recovery, with its two independent bureaus: the Remains Recovery Department, the R&Rs—former military coroners, forensic specialists, top medical and EMS people—and the even more secretive Documentation Department, the Double-D's, the Docs, comprised mainly of retired military intelligence officers and some handpicked librarians and accountants rumored to have Special Forces training. The very difficulty of the Docs' job was what made it so essential, as The Boss had testified before Congress and later on the morning talks and prime-time panels, his words adopted by the administration and repeated every few minutes on cable news: *There is nothing so important as recovering the record of our commerce, the proof of our place in the world, of the resilience of our economy, of our jobs, of our lives. If we do not make a fundamental accounting of what was lost, if we do not gather up the paper and put it all back, then the forces aligned against us have already won. They've. Already. Won.*

Staring at the massive ribs, the shattered steel exoskeleton in pieces as far as he could see, smoldering bones draped with gray, like a thousand whales beached and bleached, rotting in open air, it was hard for Remy to imagine that they hadn't won. But the thought ebbed away as he stepped over thick bands of electrical cord and fire hoses and made his way to the pit, which was the hardest place for him, because it was the same endless, shapeless debris as the pile, but concave. Sunlight sparked off the helmets of rescue workers as they dropped down into voids, drawn by the enigmatic pull of gravity; one after another, like strings of pearls, they went in one hole and came out another. Those holes, he thought, were made by something beyond even fire, by a force that could push a half mile of vertical steel and life into a banked pit fifty feet deep. Maybe, he thought, there are *gray* holes.

Remy squinted his eyes, trying to make himself comfortable with the view, imagining a high mountain lake surrounded by acres of smoldering iron forest, the smoke not smoke, but warm autumn fog, a floating memory of some misted morning at camp when he was a boy. It was familiar, not like an actual place he'd seen before, but like a postcard committed to memory, a sharp pit of regret that he couldn't quite locate. He told himself it didn't mean he was deadened; a person could grow used to anything.

It occurred to him then that he had kept a pretty good line on this day so far. He hadn't lost track of it, and in this he felt a small measure of pride. Maybe he was getting better. Maybe the gaps were going away, the crack in his mind—or wherever it was—was sealing itself. Maybe his thoughts were coagulating. And that's when something on his waist vibrated. Remy took it off his belt and stared at it, not sure when he'd gotten a pager. He pressed the button on top and a single word appeared on the little screen: "NOW."

Remy stared at the pager. Now? Now *what*? Something about the message chilled him and he backed away from Guterak, who was watching the bucket brigade intently. Remy stuffed the pager in his pocket and moved south, edging down the street toward a familiar storefront—his favorite ghost bar, windows broken and jagged, dust covering everything. He pushed open the busted door and stepped in.

Just inside was a small round table waiting for a busboy who would never come: two martini glasses, one still holding a gray olive, a highball glass with a stir stick. The chairs that went with this table were dumped, as if its owners had leapt up and run off. Remy had come here the second day and noticed three bills beneath one of the gray martini glasses. Every day he expected someone to take that tip, but the rescue workers only added to it—for luck maybe, or more likely, irony—until a flower of twenty or thirty singles fanned out beneath the dusty glass. Steal the booze; leave a tip. Remy pulled a dollar from his own wallet, lifted the glass, and slid the money beneath it. He patted the table. *Now* . . . what to have? Behind the bar, the top-shelf bottles were gone; the guys had begun going down-shelf to the well booze: empty Canadian Mist and Gilbey's and the like, although there was still a bit of Bookers. Decent gin, just what he wanted. Cool, clear, unambiguous. Remy looked beneath the counter for a clean glass. Beautiful ghost bar.

When he looked up, a slender man in a dark suit was standing in the doorway, holding a briefcase. He was younger than Remy, but about the same height, with a short, military haircut. But his exact age was hard to determine because he had the youngest face Remy had ever seen on an adult, as if a ten-year-old's head had been grafted onto the body of an adult lawyer. He wore a name tag ("Markham") tucked into his lapel pocket, the way Feds did it, but if he was a Freddie, the tag didn't identify which agency. Markham smiled and set his briefcase on the bar, sliding a dusty highball aside. Remy thought about pretending he was just a bartender, a holdover who hadn't fled that day. He thought about offering this baby-faced Markham a drink, and for a moment he flashed on what a nice life that would be, the simple transaction of warm comfort for cold money, glass clinked on a counter, the long pour, a bar rag to clean off the dust, and what else could you possibly need? What ghost bartender ever had gaps in his memory, or woke with a gunshot to his head? What ghost bartender ever lost track of days, or had to convince his partner to stop talking? What ghost bartender ever suffered temporal streaks and floaters?

"I see why you wanted to meet here," the baby-faced man said. "Appropriate."

Remy didn't know what to say. Had he wanted to meet there?

"I should begin by saying that we're all thrilled," the man said, "to get someone with your experience to help us"—he smiled slyly and thoughtfully—"expand our responsibilities. Obviously, we don't have the institutional history of other investigative agencies." The man leaned forward. "To tell the truth, we're all eager to show the bureau and the agency that we're not just some kind of clerical service. And, if I may add a personal note, may I say that I'm looking forward to—"

A cell phone rang and Markham held a finger up to Remy while he took the call. "No, no problem at all. Yes. In fact, I'm here with him now." Markham looked up and met Remy's eyes. "I'll ask him." He covered the mouthpiece of his phone and asked Remy: "Is there anything else you'll need?"

Remy looked down at the glass. He needed this gin, but that didn't seem to be what the boy-man was asking. He lifted the dusty glass but it slipped out of his hand and with it slipped the moment, Remy reaching for the falling glass and finding—

TWO YANKEES, it turned out, were all that showed up to take the tour that day, much to Guterak's apparent dismay. Remy looked back and recognized a big second-year relief pitcher and the bullpen catcher in the backseat. Looking down, he saw he was still cradling the glass that was no longer there. He hoped at least he'd gotten to drink his gin. He shook his hand and looked back at the marginal Yankees. "I guess The Boss took most of the big-name guys down," Paul said. He was pissed. Remy recognized the players: a young reliever everyone was hoping would develop a curve and the stones to become a setup guy, and a backup catcher who'd once given The Boss's kid some pointers on hitting. It didn't matter to Remy which Yankees they got, but Paul was clearly angry, and seemed to wonder what it meant—if they'd fallen out of favor, somehow. He told Remy that he heard Bannerman and Dooley were taking Bruce Willis around, and that Lopez and Dunphy got the cast of *Sex and the City.*

Paul was furious. "What I'd give for an hour in a car with that goddamn Sarah Jessica. Fuggin' Carey . . . he knows how I feel about Sarah Jessica. It's disrespect."

Remy looked around the truck. *Be quiet, be quiet, be . . .*

"It ain't a sexual thing, either. I think she's got style. I like them little skirts and she wears a lot of . . . what would you call it . . . *flouncy* stuff." He turned to face Remy. "I wish Stacy would wear more flouncy stuff."

Remy stared out the window.

"You think Stacy's too fat for flouncy stuff?"

"I . . . I don't know, Paul," Remy said.

"You think my wife's fat?"

"No. Of course not."

"Aw, I'm just fuggin' with you, man. 'Course she's fat. I know she's fat. Krispy Kreme knows she's fat. White Castle, Schwann's, Burger King knows she's fat." Paul turned back to the road. "I'm just sayin' . . . you and me, we almost die in here and all we get are a coupla scrubs—" He looked in the rearview mirror. "No offense."

The pitcher shrugged. The catcher, who didn't speak English, smiled and gave them a thumbs-up.

Paul looked over at Remy again. He spoke more quietly. "It just pisses me off . . . fuggin' Lopez takin' Sarah Jessica around."

"Paul—"

"What the fugg is he gonna show her? Here's the building where I hid under a desk and shit my pants?"

They drove down the West for the second time that day, the gray cloud drawing them down, passing beneath people on banisters and fire escapes, leaning out windows, cameras following them. The Yankees were staring out the windows in the backseat, quiet and respectful. Every few minutes, Paul chirped the siren to clear the traffic but Remy could tell he wasn't into it.

"Something else," Paul said to the car, and Remy sensed danger and closed his eyes. "You notice how the number keeps dropping? Eight thousand. Seven thousand? Six. It's like the swelling going down. I was thinkin', maybe it'll go back to zero. You know? I mean, where are the bodies? Maybe it'll turn out that everyone was at home that day. Maybe we'll actually *gain* people when this is all over."

As usual, no one knew how to respond to Guterak, so he just kept talking. "How would they explain that? More people than we started with? Wouldn't that be some trick, huh?" As they approached The Zero, Paul began to fidget, the words struggling to get out. Remy could see him getting ready. Everyone who took tours had his own version of this place, names for different landmarks. Remy saw a firefighter and a welder get into it one time over whether the deep part was called The Pit or The Hole. Among the guys who took tours—and especially on The Boss's detail and staff—it was acknowledged that Guterak's names were the best. A few of them had even become standard: *The Ribs, Cathedral, Spears, The Void, Big Peach, Dry Falls.* Maybe this was Paul's art: He couldn't stop talking about the things that so many others had trouble talking about. Guterak always started his tours on West Street, where he and Remy had come in that day. He'd circle below to east, then north, and finally back south, and always end right across from the hole, where Remy's car was still visible, its windows shattered, up to its axles in grit and paper. Even though they'd only gotten two Yankees and no Sarah Jessica, Remy knew that Paul would set aside his disappointment and do what he always did. Talk.

"So this is where we came in," Paul said to the Yankees as they approached the West Street checkpoint. "I was on a mission in midtown for The Boss—there's this frozen yogurt he likes—when I got the call. Brian was on his way down, so he stops and gets me and we run his car down the West just like we're going now, smoke everywhere, and we get down here, on the south end, and we're just standing around, watching all this shit, and *bang*, the second one comes in, and then we're running around—and here's what you didn't get on TV, it was so *far up there*, it didn't seem real, not until someone jumped, arms flapping crazy like they could change their minds, but of course, they couldn't . . . and you'd watch 'em grow as they came down . . . hitting like fuggin' water balloons, but deeper, you know—thumping and . . . and . . . bursting . . . and then Brian wanders off and I'm alone, just walking along, lookin' at all these people and this kid firefighter, I'll never forget his little face, some probie starin' up at the sky and I don't even have to look at what he was seeing because I hear this groaning noise and this pop and then it's so quiet—*eerie* quiet, you know, just for a split second, not even long enough to think, Oh shit, it's quiet—but I can tell by the look in this kid's eyes that it's not good, and then comes this horrible grinding and a roar, like thunder in your head, ten fuggin' seconds of hard thunder as the floors pancake, and as soon as it starts, this firefighter does the crazy bravest thing I ever seen, he starts running *toward* the thing, as I start goin' in the other direction, toward Brian's car, and throw myself against the car and then it's like we're in the middle of a hurricane of shit, and this wave crashes all around us, black and thick, pushes me under Brian's car and all the way through to the other side and I know I'm gonna get buried with all this shit that's flying around and I can't breathe or see and the wind is still blowing hot shit—see on my arm here, this burn came from some shit blown against me, and this cut, four stitches there—I'm crawling on my hands and knees until I bump the corner of a building and I crawl through a broken window and over people and I can't tell if I'm inside or out—it's all black—except the floor beneath all the dust is marble, so I think, I must be inside and it seems like I crawl forever, and then I get up and walk, and all of a sudden there's a hundred of us, ghosts, gray and choking, and we come out of this cloud one at a time, like little fuggin' kids waking up on Christmas morning, and no one says a word, not a single word, and we're walking toward Battery Park, like someone threw a switch and we couldn't speak no more. All we could do was walk. Just walk."

The Yankees stared.

Paul blinked it away. "But I'm getting ahead of myself. I'll cover all of that once we get inside. Any questions so far?"

Nothing.

Then Paul had a thought: "Oh, oh, oh! Look at Brian's eyes."

Remy rubbed his temples.

"Come on, man. Show 'em."

Remy turned in his seat and opened his eyes wide. Paul liked to make sure people saw the broken blood vessel in Remy's right eye.

"He's got that muscular vicious disintegration. You know what that shit is?"

The Yankees didn't know.

"*Macular degeneration*," Remy corrected. "And *vitreous detachment*." He'd told Guterak ten times that his eye condition had nothing to do with the burst blood vessel in his right eye, and therefore with that day, that he'd had escalating eye problems for years. But Paul insisted on making it part of the tour.

"What it is, see, is his fuggin' eyes are flaking off. From inside, is what that shit is. Creepy, huh? I mean this is some serious shit we went through here."

The relief pitcher winced. "That sucks."

"Yeah," Remy said to the genial reliever, and he thought about how nice that would be: relief, a guy in the bullpen waiting to take over when you run out of gas. Go to the left-hander. Life would be much easier if we all had a coach watching us, looking for any sign of fatigue or confusion, specialists waiting just down the foul line to stride in and save our work, to salvage what we've done so far, make sure we don't waste the end of a well-lived life. A good reliever might've saved his career, his marriage—what else? That's all Remy wanted: someone to save him.

They eased up to the checkpoint, third on line.

"What are those?" the pitcher asked.

"Those?" Paul looked out his window. "Reefers. Refrigerated meat trucks."

"For . . ."

"Bodies."

"Jesus, are they . . ."

"The trucks? Nah, they're empty." He leaned back conspiratorially between the seats. "Look, don't tell no one, but the truth is . . . we can't find the people. Little pieces. A body here and there. But mostly the people are . . ." Paul held up his fingers and rustled them like a field of wheat. Then he began driving again.

They pulled up to the checkpoint and a street cop stepped forward. "Hey, boss. How's it goin'?"

"Goddamn tough duty, you know?" Guterak said.

Remy wondered, wasn't I just here? Didn't I just hear this conversation? Were the gaps moving him backward now? Skipping like a record? Maybe he'd get to go back and drink that gin, or find out what the guy in the ghost bar had wanted. He felt a vibration, put his hand on his waist and found the pager again.

"Fuckin' raghead motherfuckers," the street cop was saying.

"Yeah. That's right. That's right."

REMY'S EX-WIFE Carla lived out past Jericho with her new husband Steve in a grand new house—four bedrooms, three dormers, two baths, something called a great room, and a lovely brick façade—and that's where Remy found himself, sitting on the couch, drinking weak coffee from the good china. About six months before the divorce, Carla had declared that she needed to *start living my life or else go crazy*, and the next day she'd opened the big oak cabinet and begun using their good wedding china for every meal; that morning, Remy came downstairs to find little Edgar eating Cap'n Crunch in a shallow, hand-painted bone bowl. Six months later, Remy and Carla were separated.

Steve pried his lips from the rim of a Bud Light. "Personally? I don't see that it matters *who* we bomb, long as we do it while we still got the upper hand. Line 'em up. Clean house. But I don't need to tell you that, right?"

"No. You don't." Remy looked up at a triptych of school portraits above the mantle: brilliant Edgar at six, at ten, and now at sixteen, long black hair parted on the side and swooped in a spit over the front of his lineless forehead. He was wearing a rugby shirt and sticking his bottom lip out in this latest picture, not defiant, but like someone contemplating the workings of the camera. He didn't look much like Remy anymore, not like when he was little, when Remy would look at Edgar and fight the urge to feel for the pieces that had been taken from him to make the boy.

"See, we're never going to have a better excuse," Steve continued. "I'd use the *Times* as my guide. Go to the UN and say, 'Let's make a deal. If your country shows up on the front page of the *Times* for anything other than a travel feature, you're toast.' We should've had the Stealth bombers in the air before the smoke cleared."

"The smoke hasn't cleared," Remy said quietly.

"My point exactly!" Steve swallowed a big mouthful and pointed the neck of the beer bottle at Remy. "See? You know what I'm talkin' about. Don't waste time separating guilty from innocent. Let them sort it through later."

Remy cleared his throat—*start living my life or else go crazy*—and leaned forward. "Steve? Do you think you could tell me what I'm doing here?"

"That's exactly what I mean!" Steve sat back on the couch. "If we ain't gonna make the assholes pay . . . what are any of us doin' here?"

"I mean . . . could you tell me where Carla is?"

"Well . . . I think she agrees with me on this, but you know how women are, Brian. A little squishy when it comes to actually pulling the trigger."

"I mean where she is *physically*, Steve. And Edgar?"

Steve laughed. "That's good. You're so funny, man. I tell people that. You're hilarious. I tell people, if I was Carla, I might've stayed with you. You're a hell of a lot funnier than me. You could even make an argument that you're better looking, although, classically, I'd probably be considered more handsome. And younger. Obviously. And I make more money." He waved his hand around the house. "I'm taller . . . more of a man's man, probably, athletically . . . although you, being a former cop and all, could probably kick my ass if you wanted . . . at least back in the day . . . are you losing weight?"

"I'm not sure."

"What size pants you wear?"

"I don't know . . . thirty-two."

"What about the length?"

Remy looked down. "Thirty-three?"

"Thirty-two, thirty-three? No shit?" Steve stood up and lifted his shirt, patted a wide stomach. "I'm a thirty-five, thirty-four now. That's when it starts getting messed up for guys, when our waists get bigger than our inseams. No shit, right?"

Remy took a drink of coffee and closed his eyes, wondering if he could induce a gap, open his eyes and find himself somewhere else. He watched the marionettes dance behind his lids for a while, tracking their drift across the vitreous. When Remy opened his eyes, Steve was still there, watching him intently.

Remy heard footsteps on the stairs and nearly cried out in relief as

Carla came up the stairs, lips drawn tight, followed closely by the loping Edgar. Carla wore thin, tight, low-waisted teenager jeans, a big,
wide-necked T-shirt, and tennis shoes. The older she got, it seemed, the
younger her clothes became. They sat on the couch next to Steve, across
from Remy.

"Sorry," Carla said. "He was in the middle of a video game."

Edgar wore a black armband over his gray T-shirt. He smiled patiently at his mother. "It's not a *video* game." He looked up at Remy.
"It's called Empire. It's a communal computer experience . . . like an al-
ternate world. It's character-driven and action-reaction oriented. Just
like the real world."

Yes, Remy thought, the real world is action-reaction oriented. He
needed to remember that.

Carla smiled. "More coffee, Brian?"

"No," Remy said. "Thanks, though."

"So . . . would *you* like to start?" she asked.

"Uh . . . why don't you," Remy said.

Irritation broke on Carla's face. As if she'd grown hot, Steve removed his arm from her shoulder. "I'm gonna get another beer." He
winked at Remy. "Let you-all talk."

Carla took a breath. "Well . . . apparently . . . this is another important issue your father would like *me* to handle . . . so, Edgar . . . it
has come to our attention . . ." She looked at Remy again, as if to see if
this were the right way to start.

Remy nodded. He felt sick. What had come to their attention?
Drugs? A pregnant girl? Honestly, he'd prefer drugs. He wasn't ready to
be a grandfather, to be responsible for another person. Suddenly, he felt
guilty for not worrying more about the boy. Edgar had been only nine
when Remy realized that his son was smarter than he, and from that
moment they had started growing apart, as if Edgar had reached his father's height and had begun growing out, in directions that Remy

couldn't comprehend. And, honestly, Remy had simply stopped worrying about him then. There didn't seem to be anything more Remy could
do to help him. And now . . . whatever this was, he hoped it wasn't permanent. He hoped this problem was something manageable. An F. Or
a messy room.

But surely he wouldn't have been summoned to Jericho for a
messy room.

"It has come to our attention that . . . well . . ." Carla searched for
the words: "Brian, are you sure you don't want to do this? It really has
more to do with you."

"Uh . . . no. I think it'd be better coming from you."

Carla turned back to Edgar. She took a breath, looked once more at
Remy and then back at their son. "Edgar. Honey. Your physics teacher
called yesterday . . . and . . . said . . ." She seemed to hit a dead end, and
tried reshaping her point into a question. "Apparently you've been
telling everyone at school that your father died the other day, in the . . .
well . . . in the events of the other day?"

Edgar nodded as if his mother had just proposed a math problem.
"Mmm," he said. "Ri-i-ight. I had a feeling that's what this was about."

Remy slumped forward with a mixture of relief and something a
few miles south of relief.

"Well . . . you do realize . . . your father isn't dead. He's right here."

Edgar looked up at his dad, brushed the hair out of his eyes, and
nodded again. "Ri-i-ight."

Carla looked over at Remy for help. He offered none. But Steve
had come back into the room with another beer, and he leaned on the
arm of the couch and jumped in. "Edgar, why would you go around
telling people that your old man was dead?"

"Well." Edgar took a deep breath. "Let me start by saying that I appreciate your concern." He smiled warmly at Remy. "Obviously, I know
my father's not dead. I'm not delusional, and I certainly don't *wish* he

were dead." He cocked his head. "I haven't told anyone that he's dead. I simply haven't corrected that impression."

He shrugged as if that covered it, but when no one said anything, Edgar laughed impatiently. "Look. What if I'd written a story for a class about a boy who lost his father? We'd be talking about my A paper, instead of everyone looking at me like I'm sick." Edgar laughed again, as if this cleared it all up.

Remy couldn't think of a single word to say.

Carla spoke up. "But Edgar, honey. This isn't a story you wrote. This is something you're allowing your classmates to believe. Your homeroom teacher said that you sit at your desk crying. She said you got out of a physics test and that you've stopped going to PE altogether."

"Yeah . . ."

"Well, I guess I don't understand."

Edgar shrugged as if it were the simplest thing. "If I *had* lost my father, would you really expect me to take a test? Or to play Frisbee golf?"

"Well . . . no. I guess not."

"Okay," Edgar said, as if that solved it.

Carla shifted on the couch, so that she was facing their son. She broke out her gentle relationship voice, the one Remy recalled from the awful counseling sessions they tried before the split. "Honey, is it that you don't get to see your father enough? Is that what this is about?"

Edgar cocked his head.

"That he works too much, sweetie? That he's gone all the time."

"No."

"Is it his drinking? Are you trying to tell your father that his lifestyle is going to kill him? Is this a kind of metaphoric death you've created for him? Is that what you're trying to tell us, honey?"

Remy wondered how far this line of questioning would go. Maybe this was about the time he flirted with that waitress in front of Carla.

Or maybe it was about the fact that he didn't like her family. The way he used to drop his dirty clothes next to the bed?

Steve leaned forward helpfully. "Is it to impress chicks, Eddie? Is that what you're doing, ol' buddy? Trying to get a little sympathy ass?"

"No, Steve," Edgar said patiently. "I'm not trying to get . . . ass."

Remy wished he could infuse his own voice with as much flatness when he spoke to Carla's new husband, that he could speak so ironically with such an apparent lack of irony. Suddenly, his pride for his child overwhelmed him, and Remy flashed on the idea that if he actually *had* died, he might save Edgar this awkward questioning.

"Well, I think we deserve an explanation," Carla said. "That's all."

The boy looked around the room for help. When Edgar was little, Remy used to find solace in the shards of himself that he saw in the boy's in-trouble stare, in his shrugs and shifts, in the things he feared. But now Edgar was so self-assured that Remy could barely remember why his son had ever needed whatever shelter he'd once provided. Edgar was a stranger to him, an alien with long, blocky hair and sinewy arms and a clipped, hyper-intellectual way of speaking that made it seem as if he were reading.

"Okay," his son said. "First of all, by agreeing to talk about this, I want you to know that I'm not apologizing. This is entirely my business." Edgar took a deep breath and stared at the carpet. "Grieving is personal."

"That's fine, Edgar, honey. But *what* are you grieving? The divorce? Your father's inability to commit emotionally—"

Remy interrupted: "You know, I think we've covered that."

"I'm grieving my dead father!" Edgar was losing his patience. "I don't know why that's so hard to understand."

"But . . . your father isn't dead, honey."

"I *know* that." Edgar rubbed his temples, as if talking to these morons was more than he could bear. "Weren't there fathers who died that day?"

"Of course they did."

"And didn't they leave children behind?"

"Sure."

"And didn't I have a father?"

"Yes. Of course."

He put his arms out as if finishing a magic trick. "Then why is it so hard to believe that I could be grieving the same thing as those other children? I suppose you'd rather I behave like everyone else and grieve *generally*. Well, I'm sorry. I'm not built that way. General grief is a lie. What are people in Wyoming really grieving? A loss of safety? Some shattered illusion that a lifetime of purchases and television programs had meaning? The emptiness of their Palm Pilots and SUVs and baggy jeans? Look around, Mom. Generalized grief is a fleeting emotion, like lust. It's a trend, just some weak shared moment in the culture, like the final episode of some TV show everybody watches. It's weightless. You wake up the next day and wonder when the next disaster is scheduled.

"But *real* grief . . . oh, God." He cocked his head and stared at his mother. "Real grief weighs on you like you can't imagine. The death of a father . . . is the most profound thing I've ever experienced." Edgar's eyes seemed to be tearing up. "It's hard to get out of bed. And you want me to take a test? Play softball? Are you kidding? There are times when I can barely breathe. I can't . . . get over it. And I don't want to. The only way to comprehend something like this is to go through it. Otherwise, it's just a number. Three thousand? Four thousand? How do you grieve a number?"

His voice was a whisper. "So . . . yes . . . I have chosen to focus my grief on one individual. On the death of my father." He shrugged and looked down at the carpet. "And you know, frankly, I guess I expected a little more support from you."

"I . . ." Carla looked from Steve to Remy and back. "I . . ."

Remy squeezed his eyes as tight as they would go, and then opened them again. *Still here.* Except for Steve, who apparently sensed that the potential for humor had faded, and backed carefully out of the room.

Edgar wasn't finished. "Ask yourself this: what separates me from some kid whose father actually died that day?"

"The fact that I'm alive?" Remy asked. Even to him, his voice sounded like it was coming from another room.

"Fair enough," Edgar said, without meeting Remy's eyes. "Okay, now let's take *that* kid, the one who actually lost his father, but is some-how coping by getting consolation from his girlfriend or from drinking or from writing poems. Are you going to tell him he isn't grieving *enough*? Are you gonna tell some poor kid doing his best that he should feel *worse* about the death of his father?"

"No . . ." Carla shook her head. "No. Of course not."

"Then don't tell me I shouldn't be devastated by the death of *my* father just because he isn't dead! I mean . . . Goddamn it, Mom. All things considered, I think I'm doing pretty well. . . . Do you know there are kids out there getting high every day? Kids selling drugs. Is that what you want me to do?"

"No, of course not." Carla started crying; this had always been her deepest fear for her child, that he would use drugs. "We don't want that. Do we, Brian?"

Remy just stared straight ahead. Honestly, he'd rather have Edgar smoke a little weed and acknowledge that Remy was alive, but he knew better than to say so.

"I'm sorry, honey," Carla said. "I'm sorry we got divorced and I'm sorry about your father."

"Thank you." Edgar straightened the black armband. "Thank you. That means a lot to me. It really does."

They *all* stared at their shoes for a moment, and then Carla held out her hands. Edgar stood, walked over, and melted into his mother's arms. They cried together. Remy watched them from across the room and found he could imagine another life in which he'd never met either of them. Carla looked up at Remy then and wiped her eyes. "Well, Brian. I suppose this is as good a time as any to tell him *your* news."

"I suppose," Remy said.

Carla put her hands on Edgar's cheeks. "Honey, your father has got a new assignment at work. And he's going to be gone a lot. In fact, he's taking a trip very soon. I know this is a bad time, with you so upset over his death, but he'll be back. He promises. Don't you, Brian?"

"Yes," Remy said. "I promise."

Edgar looked up at his father, and Remy worked to place those eyes, and then it hit him. When Edgar was a little boy, you couldn't get him out of the tub. He'd spend hours in there, lying on his back, staring up at the ceiling, Carla always adding more hot water, his fingers and toes like raisins, and when you went in to ask if he were ready, he'd look up with those pleading, impatient eyes, as if you were too stupid to comprehend the seriousness of Edgar's work in the bath. Remy loved seeing those eyes again, staring at him from his mother's embrace, across the room. In fact, the moment was so nice he didn't have the heart to ask Carla where he was going.

AT NIGHT, The Zero was lit like a stage. Or a surgery. It was quiet— not exactly peaceful, but a person could think. The work seemed less showy to Remy, the loss more personal, less produced than during the day, when everyone posed for photographers and TV cameras, when grief and anger became competitive sports. At night people were left alone with their emptiness. The bucket brigades mostly gave up their symbolic place and the pails sat in huge piles, while a skeleton crew worked quietly, without the frantic edge of the daytime workers. Generators chugged and machines ground away and men hid in the long shadows behind the spotlights. Remy liked the night better. It felt . . .

appropriate. For another thing, in the darkness there were fewer streaks and floaters. The world behaved, stood still.

Near him, three firefighters sat on the edges of collapsed wall, eating their lunches from metal buckets, respirators hung around their necks, legs dangling, like kids fishing from a dock. Forty feet away, a masked construction worker sat on his yellow iron horse, its massive jaws pointed down, waiting for permission to nibble at the pile. Below them ran the soft grinding hum of idling trucks and heavy equipment and portable generators, the hushed conversations of engineers and welders. At Remy's feet, someone had made a pile of popped rivets; it looked like a marble collection. Was this an official pile with some purpose, Remy wondered, or the obsession of someone who didn't know what else to do down here? There were so many people standing around, *dying* to do something. Anything. Had he made this pile himself? He didn't think so, but the rivets made him uneasy and he felt the urge to leave. He drifted and found himself on a side street, staring at a line of scorched, mashed cars, picked up and stacked four deep, bumpers and side mirrors snapped off, bits of burned rubber clinging to the rims of the wheels.

Remy walked the bent edge of the city, everyday things suddenly as mysterious and suggestive as archaeological artifacts. Coffee cups. Parking meter heads. Edgar had written a paper once about Pompeii, and Remy kept thinking about the pictures he downloaded, the plaster casts of victims covering their faces, plates and tureens and sandals, the sudden artifacts of lives frozen by shit luck. Then something else in the street caught Remy's attention, gray and familiar, until it focused under his eyes: an airline seat belt. Debris from the planes went in specially marked bins, so Remy picked up the belt and carried it over, dropped it in with engine parts and seat cushions. Nearby, beneath a tarp, dog handlers were feeding two panting German shepherds, while a third curled up and napped against a twisted I beam. The dogs watched Remy, sniffed the air, decided he wasn't a corpse yet, and put their heads down together. Remy took a wide berth in case they changed their minds. Across West Street he found himself inside WF II, cold, dark, and empty, the face of the building scarred and scorched, the marble lobby coated with light gray soot and strewn with broken glass and paper, along with detritus from the firefighters—tables and foldout chairs, mattresses, water bottles, and ladders. His flashlight hit something in the middle of the room: a shoe. He walked over, bent to look at it, picked it up: Size eleven. Loafer. He tried to think of a scenario in which its owner was alive, but his imagination failed him. He flipped the tassel, turned it over, and set it back where he'd found it. Some things you just left where you found them; the fact that other people had walked past the same things somehow ritualized it.

Remy sauntered up the grand stairs, past banks of paper pushed to the sides like snow on a well-traveled stoop. Presumably, the Docs just hadn't cleared this paper yet, although Remy thought he remembered hearing something about hidden cameras positioned to try to catch rescue workers and equivocators looking through documents. On the second floor he made his way down a narrow hallway that looked out on The Zero. The hall was lined with grit and more paper, pushed into more snowbanks along either side so people could pass. A line of windows facing The Zero was blasted open; black fangs hung from the frames. Through the jagged opening Remy stared down on the well-lit pile. At the edges, the rubble was dark, a black tangle of shadowed forms, but the center was spotlighted bright; it was like coming across a high school football game in the middle of a bomb crater. American flags hung everywhere, from cranes and earthmovers, pinned to crumbling walls and across the hoods of crushed cars. On a tall section of iron lattice, a welder's spark dripped light onto the ground. A guy in all black inched slowly along an I beam, down into a burned black steel crevasse until only his shoulders and head were visible, and then nothing. Guys crouched everywhere, resting or thinking. Herds of construction workers and firefighters moved along the street, their hooded and masked heads pointed down. They sniffed the air, and one another, and kept moving.

Remy was tired. He wandered the hallway, wondering if there were someplace he might catch a nap. He came to a clothing store, a little boutique—the clothes so tiny, the little jeans like children's knickers, scraps of fabric with straps, all of it covered in that same dust, a circular rack of once-colorful sweaters, arms twice as long as the torsos, everything the same shade of gray now. He freed a price tag from a crust of sprinkler-pasted dust. Ninety-two dollars—not ninety or ninety-five, ninety-*two*. Remy tried to picture the store that morning: a woman considering the price tag, trying to decide whether she should pay that much for a sweater. Ninety-two. The number bothered him, its concrete arbitrariness. Did the woman let the tag fall, hurry out of the store? Or did she buy one of these sweaters, already anticipating winter? Normally, she would never have given a second thought to where she bought that sweater, but now it would always connect with that day; now that sweater was the most important piece of clothing in her life. Or maybe she bought one of these sweaters the day before and wore it to the office, thinking the guy in HR would finally notice her. And she was wearing a sweater just like this one as she huddled in the smoke-choked stairwell with a bunch of strangers and stragglers, the brave and unlucky in the same narrow space when it began, the thunder of the world clapping down to nothing.

Remy let the sweater fall and backed out of the store. He continued down the hall to the lobby of an accounting firm. He ran his hand along a dusty leather couch. A door off the lobby opened onto a small workout room: three universal gyms, a stair stepper and two exercise bikes, gray bottles of water abandoned in the cup holders. There was a TV up in the corner; Remy could imagine the accountants taking their lunches in here, eyes tracking the ticker on CNBC while secretaries moved past in tight skirts and cross trainers, clutching yoga mats . . .

He stepped out into the hall, where another jagged window over-looked The Zero. On the floor in front of him a mound of paper and debris was raked into a pile. Remy reached in and pulled out a day planner, about the size of a motel Bible. He dusted it off. Engraved on the cover in gold was a name—G. ADDICH—and a phone number and address. Remy flipped through the pages. Each page recorded a single day—appointments on the top of the page, notes from the meetings on the bottom. This Addich had meetings every day—so many meetings. There had to be a thousand of them. What could a person possibly do at these meetings? The notes on the bottoms of the pages were cryptic—mostly numbers. Most of the meetings seemed to be held in restaurants or coffee shops. Maybe he was a restaurant supplier, Remy thought. He flipped through the days, approaching the end nervously.

When he arrived at that day, he found only two meetings sched-uled, one at four o'clock in the afternoon and the other one in the morning, recorded in small block letters: "Remy: Windows—9 A.M. Early."

Remy shivered. He held the day planner at arm's length, blinked, and read it again. Of course it couldn't be him. Another Remy. He'd never heard of anyone named Addich. Of course Remy wasn't a com-mon name, but there were certainly others. It was just a coincidence, he thought—a strange one, but that's what coincidences were, *strange*. And yet, some voice in his head was dubious: *That day? My name?*

He looked back down at the planner. The word *Early* was under-lined. How early had G. Addich arrived? Too early and he or she would have been pulverized, this planner blasted out the window, across the street and into this building. And what about the other Remy? Maybe he could check the list of the missing, see if anyone with his name had died.

And then Remy heard raised voices. Someone yelling from the street below. At first he thought they were yelling at him, and he dropped the day planner guiltily. But then he realized the voices were coming from outside and he picked up the black book and stuffed it in his coat. He jogged back down the flotsam-lined hall toward the marble stairs, toward the yelling.

On West Street, a handful of cops in masks and riot gear were holding off three firefighters who had come down drunk from the Heights and gotten into it with one of the construction crews. A crowd had gathered. The young firefighters were wearing jeans and T-shirts, even though it was cold outside; their roped veins strained at the skin, ready to burst. They all had facial hair—various mustaches and wispy goatees—and opaque, boozy eyes. A red-faced construction supervisor, his ventilator pulled down around his neck, stood behind the cops, pointing with a blunt finger, demanding that the smokers be arrested, but the night commanding officer had interceded and was suggesting that they just be driven home.

"I'll take 'em." Remy stepped from the shadows.

It took the night boss a few seconds to see him. "What are you doing here?"

Remy paused a moment. "I could ask you the same thing," he finally said.

That seemed to work. Without another thought, the young firefighters started trudging along behind him, down the West toward his car. One of the firefighters went to sleep as soon as they got in. The other two sat staring out opposite windows. They were so young that for a moment Remy flashed on a night years earlier—driving Edgar and two of his friends home after a movie. Only . . . no, that wasn't right. He breathed into one of his hands, and was strangely comforted by The Zero smell. He skirted the lights and midtown, cutting west until he found an avenue that flowed beneath him, a black stream centered with gold lines, faster and faster, yellow cabs parting and then closing in his wake, and he flicked on the siren's false cheer—*whoop whoop whoop whoo*—and decided to ignore the traffic lights, his car nearly coming off its axles at the cross streets. He pushed the speedometer to ninety-two, same as the sweater—just to see—swerved to miss something that turned out to be a flasher inside his eye crossing against the glare of a streetlight, and finally eased off the gas. The tanked firefighters were nonplussed, their mouths half-open.

"Like the way you drive," one of them said.

"Thanks."

He volunteered to drive each of them home, but the smokers wanted to go back to their firehouse for breakfast, so Remy let them out there. He wanted to ask them something, anything, but they climbed out of his car without a word, stretched, and walked toward the red station house decorated with cards and bouquets, the steps littered with picnic baskets, the walls covered with the smiling dead. They looked so small. Remy watched them go inside and, for just a moment, he envied the smokers their brotherhood, their warm house.

WORD CAME sometime before lunch: The Boss wanted to see Remy tomorrow. He and Guterak were at Fresh Kills, taking two state senators on a tour of the massive salvage, recovery, and remains operation at the old landfill when Paul asked if Remy was nervous about the meeting.

"I don't know," Remy answered honestly.

"Well, you probably should be," Paul said through his paper mask. *Was* he nervous? Remy tried to remember. Sometimes the gaps were like this: He was unaware that any time was unaccounted for except some bit of information that he didn't recall getting—how he knew The Boss wanted to see him, how he inferred that it was serious business, whether he knew anything more about the meeting. There was a gap where that knowledge should have been. A phone call? That was the obvious answer, but Remy couldn't remember any call. He hadn't even replaced his phone. It was somewhere among all those window blinds and rebar. Had the message come over the pager he'd been wearing? Or maybe The Boss had called Paul to arrange the meeting. Paul certainly seemed more nervous about it than he was. But why would Paul be the go-between?

These were the most common gaps that Remy had been suffering, holes not so much in his memory but in the string of events, the causes of certain effects. He found himself wet but didn't remember rain. He felt full but couldn't recall eating. It wasn't important, he supposed, *how* he came to know that The Boss wanted to see him, except that he should be able to remember whether it was a phone call or someone telling him. Instead, it was as if he'd always known that he had a three o'clock meeting tomorrow afternoon, a one-on-one, and that Paul was nervous about it.

"Remember, wait for the questions, think hard about them, and then answer slowly." The paper surgical mask muffled Guterak's voice.

"Okay," Remy said through his own mask.

Paul turned back. They stood on the pavement at the edge of the rolling landfill, a moonscape of busted concrete and scorched steel. Pockets of methane gurgled and belched from beneath the debris—the city's history in garbage: Andy Warhol's coffee filters, Ethel Merman's dress shields, Mickey Mantle's chaw. Every gust out here seemed to stink in some new, groundbreaking way, and now there were these new hills of debris. Above the mounds seagulls broke and rolled and caught the wind, rising on waves of dust. The fine dust was everywhere, drifting and reddening the sun, which seemed higher out here, as if even the heavens were repelled by the smell.

Remy watched the senators in their work boots pause and shake hands with two space-suited techs who had been using rakes and pitchforks on eight-foot stacks of rubble in a corner of the debris field. Remy hated the way they'd imported the air out here on barges of concrete and rebar. It was not as sharp as at The Zero, and there was the underlying smell of methane to compete with, but the dust rose, and the smell found you, and Remy could imagine that one day everything in the world would be reduced to such a fine dust—replacing even the air, so that you not only smelled it but tasted it, and felt it too, on your skin, in your mouth, deep to your bones like a chill, that the whole world would swim in dust—finer and finer until there was nothing but an absence of substance and meaning.

At the waterfront, gulls rose on updrafts of methane and stink, and swooped down among the cranes unloading beams and bars from barges onto dump trucks overseen by thick guys in sweatsuits and gold bracelets, all the connected guys waiting for their piece. Crushed debris dripped from the cranes and barges, and trucks paraded endlessly up to the landfill and spread their loads out on rolling hills, where it looked like a fleet of plane crashes, all of it raked and sorted by crews of twelve, under close invisible supervision by rumored officials from the Office of Liberty and Recovery. The piles themselves were hard for Remy to comprehend: tangled steel and rebar and concrete dust, and no matter how long you searched the gray mass you never saw anything normal, a telephone or a computer or a floor lamp. These things were just . . . gone, he supposed, liquidized into dust and endless tons of bits, indistinguishable pieces of rubble to be sifted in big construction-site shakers. Every so often he saw a truck head off to a series of big temporary buildings nearby, carrying loads of hastily stacked paper and *organic material*, jigsawed bits of people.

"They found a chin yesterday," Paul said. "Some mismatched fingers, part of a foot . . . got a whole head the day before. That's the biggest piece so far, at least out here."

"Paul—"

"A head," Paul repeated. "Can you imagine, Bri? Look at my head. Can you imagine it just . . . showing up? Or your head. How did we miss that? Can you imagine your head bein' out here, buried under all this, fuggin' steel on top and shit on the bottom? What kind of look would you have on your face, do you think?"

Remy shifted uncomfortably.

One of the state senators, the fat one, his suit pants tucked into his work boots, was coming toward them. He had been struggling all morning, beet-faced and breathless. Twice he had started crying and his eyes and nose were lined with gray. He walked over to Paul and Remy and removed his surgical mask, red-eyed and nauseous. It was clear he'd been vomiting. "This is very difficult for me."

"Yeah," Guterak said. "We really feel for you."

"I didn't expect everything to be so . . ."

"Raw," Guterak said.

"Yes," the senator said.

"You see the chin?"

"No," the senator said.

"Got a head yesterday. Biggest single chunk I've seen."

"Really?" The senator looked around, uncomfortable.

"Still, there aren't enough pieces," Guterak said, "for how many are still missing. Not even close."

The senator nodded and looked back at the space-suited workers. "I feel like they want me to say something," he said. "Like I should know what to say. But I don't have any idea."

"Tell them they're doing a good job," Paul said.

The state senator nodded, took several breaths, wiped his brow, and said, "Thanks." He pulled his mask back up. Remy and Guterak watched him walk away, trip on a tangle of something, fall forward, and recoil when his hands hit the debris. He got back up and picked his way over the piles of steel and rubble.

"Go fugg yourself, fat boy," Guterak said quietly, almost gently, when the senator was gone.

Afterward, they drove back in silence. At the bridge Remy looked back, beyond the exhausted senators, the island receding behind them. At the toll plaza, Paul pressed his E-Z Pass against the window. Somewhere, accounts were tabulated, identities recorded, order inferred, and they passed easily over to the other side.

"These things can read your thoughts now, when you come over the bridge," Paul told the senators, although Remy had the feeling Paul was talking to him. "It's new. Top secret. Very hush-hush. They just started it."

The senators exchanged a glance.

"It doesn't work very well, yet. Staffing is tough, from what I hear . . . All those fuggin' thoughts of all those people crossing in and out of the city. You can't keep up with it, all the shitty things that people think. They got six big rooms with agents sitting on wires, watching what people think as they drive on and off the island. Got translators and psychiatrists and charts and espresso machines, but it's still too much. The burnout alone . . . they can't keep up. Every day they fall further behind."

"Paul," Remy said.

"Aw, I'm just fuggin' with the senators," Guterak said. "They know I'm screwin' around, right, fellas? Right?" He smiled at them in the rearview mirror so long that Remy had to fight the urge to grab the wheel. Finally, Paul looked back at the road. "Just fuggin' with 'em."

They dropped the senators off at their hotel in midtown. But Paul didn't drive right away. He turned in the driver's seat to face Remy. "Listen," he said. "This meeting with The Boss tomorrow. Be careful. Think of it like a session with IA, or with Psych on a shooting review. You with me? And Jesus, Bri, don't say anything about me. For God's sake. If he doesn't ask about me, don't volunteer a fuggin' word about it. And if he asks how I'm doin', you just say fine. Nothin' else. I don't want no problems. Tell 'em you haven't seen any weird behavior, no mention of nightmares, nothing like that." Paul took a moment to reconsider this, like chewing the last bite of sandwich. He raised a finger. "Unless . . . you know . . . they think it's weird that I'm not having nightmares. Then tell 'em I'm totally fugged up . . . can't sleep . . . cryin' all the time. And Jesus, that shit I was sayin' the other day?"

"About the Nextels?" Remy asked.

"The Nextels? No. Fugg the phones, Brian. I mean that shit about bein' happy. About this bein' a good time? The funerals and all that? You gotta forget that shit, okay?"

"Okay," Remy said.

"Okay?"

"Yeah. Okay."

"I mean . . . I was just talkin' out my asshole there. I just wanted a be funny. Don't mean shit, what I said. I don't even *know* what I was talkin' about." He squinted like he'd eaten something sour and waved his hand at the world.

"It's okay," Remy said. "I've already forgotten it."

"But it's not that I'm *un*happy. If they want to know that."

"Sure."

"I'm just fine. Fine. But not happy. At least not unreasonably." Paul chewed his thumbnail and looked over his shoulder, then started driving.

Traffic lurched and halted, the cabs pulsing like blood cells. Guterak was too distracted to blow the siren. A white passenger van pulled up beside them and the passengers pressed their faces against the windows, waving and giving them the thumbs-up, but Paul had lost his feel for even this and he drove in silence, without acknowledging the waves from the vehicle next door.

Remy closed his eyes and watched the wallpaper peeling down his lids, strips of fiber drifting down in the jelly. *Soup of his own . . .* Sometimes it was calming. He opened his eyes and saw Guterak chewing his thumbnail as he pushed the Excursion through muddy traffic.

"Relax," Remy said. "I'm sure this has nothing to do with you, Paul. There's nothing to worry about."

"Yeah." Guterak nodded uneasily and glanced out the window, at the people lining the street, desperately cheering the cars going into The Zero. He pulled the E-Z Pass clip off his visor and tossed it in back. "Still."

They pulled up to the entry point on the West and the same cop stepped forward.

"Hey, boss. How's it goin'?"

"Goddamn tough duty, you know?"

"Fuckin' raghead motherfuckers."

"Yeah. That's right. That's right."

Remy fell back in his seat and smelled—

SMOKE WAFTED across forests of dusted steel. "Hey. You okay?" The guy in front of Remy lowered his ventilator. His cheeks were pink beneath the mask; above it, his eyes were banded with soot. He was wearing heavy coveralls and thick gloves, the kind a welder might wear, and holding out a yellow five-gallon bucket for Brian to take.

"Oh. Sorry." Remy looked away from the cloud and took the bucket by the handle—light, this one, just a few twisted pieces of aluminum, maybe ductwork, gray and bent—and passed it back to the pair of hands behind him, connected to an ancient firefighter, struggling to keep up. The buckets kept coming, each one a game of *name that piece*. You watched the guy's shoulders in front of you to see if he strained with the bucket before you grabbed for it; the ridge of Remy's gloves were worn at the pads on his palms. He squeezed his blistered hands.

More heavy pails passed, and then the buckets stopped and Remy took a minute to look around. There were tents everywhere now; he wondered when they'd arrived, some new team every few minutes, search and rescue from Ohio, Missouri, Maine, new volunteers seemed to spring from the cracks and crevices, people asking if he wanted energy bars or bottled water or socks. There were so many socks. Had there been a call for socks? Did he need socks?

In line, the guys edged forward and peered around one another like kids waiting for recess, trying to see why the buckets had stopped. Their boots crackled on the surface of the debris, tiny shifts like the warm pack on a deep snowfall. Remy stepped around the snaking line of men to see what was ahead. And, as was happening to him more and more, even though he didn't exactly *remember*, he *knew:* the buckets only stopped for one reason. As if on cue, in place of a bucket, a question slowly made its way back.

"Cops? Any cops? Any cops on this line?"

Remy stepped out of line and raised his hand. He made his way carefully over the shards, each step tentative and sharp, bent steel and aluminum giving beneath his feet. As he passed the others on line, they nodded or touched him on the back. It was hot. Remy's breath buzzed in his mask. It was a strange feeling—humbling and horrifying—to be called forward. At the front, the line took a sharp turn upward and dropped into a steaming crevasse. Halfway down, a burly ironworker had made a ledge for himself on a blackened piece of steel. He removed his ventilator and held up a bucket for Remy to see. There was something gray in there, curled and flat, and at first Remy saw a snake in the process of swallowing a rat, but then he realized what he was looking at. It was a holster. A dust-covered belt and flashlight holster. A cop's belt and holster.

"We haven't found anything else yet," the ironworker said. "But we thought . . . someone should . . . I don't know . . . do you want to take it?"

Remy bent over the lip of the void and reached out for—

* * *

THE BOSS was wrapping up his daily meeting in a conference room at the Javits, getting everyone ready for the next round of press conferences. He was wearing slacks, a PD polo shirt, and a satin jacket, although he changed his outfit five or six times a day. Every morning the sub-bosses had their chiefs of staff check in with The Boss's chief of staff to see what the succession of outfits would be. They all kept at least one dust-covered jacket handy; it magically inoculated them from any second-guessing.

The Boss anchored a U-shaped table covered with odd blue bunting—as if there had been a retirement party or an anniversary—and lined with the other bosses, he at the point of the table like the star on a spur. Sub-bosses flanked him, falling away in importance: his *capo de capi*, the blackguard police boss, then the droopy-eyed fire boss, sanitation and housing and emergency services, tourism and legal services, and a couple of bosses Remy had never even seen. Remy remembered meetings he'd attended as the police liaison to the city counsel's office. Their role was to present numbers to The Boss every month, and for each meeting they made up the figures a few minutes beforehand, arbitrarily increasing the numbers The Boss liked to see bigger (attorney caseload) and subtracting from the ones he liked to see smaller (claims against the city). The Boss liked to have everyone in his field of vision in these meetings, so that he could look from one to another without moving his head.

Remy looked down. He was still covered in dust, wearing work boots and coveralls, and a few people wrinkled their noses and stared at him. He edged along the wall with the sub-bosses, the *capos de regime* and chiefs of staff, the outer ringlet of ringers, comers and clingers, made men, drivers and ass-sniffers who sat behind the commissioners and directors and handed them briefing sheets and hankies, took notes, covered for them, and occasionally turned away to talk on cell phones, to set up lunch with mistresses and cronies. Behind The Boss, at the head of the table, was a map of the city, covered with pins, and a more detailed map of The Zero. The ceiling was low and white and it flattened the room. TV lights were set up in the corners; the light coming from them seemed like a liquid, filling the squat room.

They were getting the daily roundup, the list of casualties, and the room was suitably quiet and tense as an aide read off, one by one, the names of those gone and those barely holding on: perishable retail down sixteen; nonperishable down forty-four; advance ticket sales down fifty-nine; door sales down eighty-one; restaurant and hotel down fifty-two. The Boss shook his head at the carnage: shops failing to make lease payments, some of his favorite restaurants threatened. He struck that look, concerned but resolute, and rubbed his temples throughout the recitation of numbers. "No," he said. "No, no, no." A film crew was capturing the meeting for posterity, or for something, and he was careful to give them time to set up the next shot before he continued.

"Listen," he finally said. "This is what it's about. *This*. These bastards hate our freedoms. Our way of life. They hate our tapas bars and our sashimi restaurants, our all-night pita joints. . . . They hate our very . . . economic well-being. This is a war we fight with wallets and purses, by making dinner reservations and going to MOMA, by having drinks at the Plaza. And we will fight back. We will fight back even if it means that every American sits through Tony and Tina's goddamn Wedding!"

Applause and nods and then The Boss sat back in his chair. Out came the briefing books with that day's message, schedules, and a chart that showed everyone where to stand during the next presser. Someone dumped a box of hats in the middle of the table, and they all reached in. When they were done, there were still four Port Authority hats on the table, and while The Boss read a briefing sheet his chief of staff threw up his arms at the lowered eyes around the room: "Come on, people. Someone needs to trade a police hat for a PA hat."

Hats were swapped and then someone mentioned that the Jets wanted to come down and The Boss snapped to attention. "All of them?"

"Yes, sir."

"What, twenty-two guys?"

"Actually, that's just the starters. There are, like, fifty on the team."

They debated why a football team needed fifty players and whether it was fair for teams to put healthy players on Injured Reserve and then the discussion turned to whether they could get Jets jerseys for their kids, and whether they couldn't just get the stars' jerseys or if they had to get the whole team and who the Jets' stars might be. Then a deputy assistant on the wall murmured that it might be logistically impossible to bring fifty players down to The Zero without disrupting the work.

"Impossible? Hell, if I decide I want to do it, I'll get the Jets *and* the Sharks down there!" The Boss slammed his fist on the table again and the camera crew became agitated. "I don't ever want to hear that word again. Do you understand me? What kind of message does that send? That it's impossible to get a little football team where we need them to go? That it's impossible to get a decent curry at two A.M.? The world is watching us and if someone tells me I can't get the Jets to the scene of a national tragedy . . . then goddamn it, that's all the justification I need."

Plans were made to get the Jets downtown, the meeting ended, the film crew's lights went out, looks of defiance faded, and the bosses and sub-bosses began drifting out of the room, complimenting one another for their courage and compassion. The Boss glanced over at Remy, raising a hand for him to stay behind. He turned away for a moment and talked under his breath to his advisers and to a couple of commissioners. And then The Boss sat back down, lowered his head, and waited for the room to clear.

When everyone was gone he looked up at Remy with a forced smile. They shook hands and sat down at one corner of the long conference table. The Boss stared. He crossed and uncrossed his legs, waiting for something. One of his aides—a waifish young man in round glasses—brought him a beige file folder, which had the word *SECURE* stamped on it. The Boss held the folder in his lap and waited for the aide to clear the room. Then he smiled like a guard dog showing his teeth. "How are you, Brian?"

Remy thought of Guterak's warnings. "I'm good, sir. Fine. Okay. Good. Fine."

"Excellent." More staring. And then The Boss opened the file folder he'd been given. Remy could clearly see there was only one page in the folder, and that it didn't appear to have anything on it, but The Boss pretended to flip through pages. He even licked his fingers at one point, to pry apart the one blank page.

Remy shifted in his chair, wondering what was on the page The Boss was pretending to read. The Boss ruffled the page and made popping noises with his lips. "Just a moment," he said, running his finger down it. "Yes, yes," he said. "Right. Et cetera."

"Sir?"

The Boss looked up. "First of all, I want to thank you for agreeing to this. When I heard what they were looking for, in my mind, there was only one choice. Your combination of expertise and willingness to sacrifice, to do what needs to be done. . . . But before we finalized things I wanted us to meet face to face, to make sure you haven't had any second thoughts."

Since he couldn't recall having *first* thoughts, Remy laughed. "Well . . ."

The Boss cocked his head.

"Honestly . . . I'm not sure what you're talking about."

"What do you mean?"

"I don't . . . really know what we're doing here."

The Boss's face flushed red. He leaned forward. "I hope you're not questioning the direction of the country?"

"The country? No," Remy said quickly. "I don't . . . I don't think so."

"Good." His lips were pursed. "Nothing pisses me off more than that. That's exactly what the other side wants, Brian. For us to start doubting our actions before we've even had a chance to take them. Every question we ask is a love letter to our enemies."

"No," Remy protested. "I'm not sending any love letters—"

The Boss snapped out of it, as if he'd just realized he was no longer delivering a speech to the cameras. "Of course you're not. You're with us. You, of all people." The Boss held up the one-page file and rolled his eyes. "I'm sorry. I just get so . . . emotional . . . when I think of people questioning our resolve, our commitment to reclaiming our place in the world, our heritage, to gathering everything that was lost, recapturing the record of our people, and our commerce . . . well, I don't have to tell you, Brian."

Remy sort of wished he would, but he shook his head. "No."

"I chose you for that very reason: your commitment to your country, and your unbending personal loyalty. You are in a unique position, Brian, a pioneer, a bridge between two worlds. Running interference between the police and the city attorney was difficult, but I'm sure it taught you how to live in two worlds—the suits and the shields. In a way, you'll be doing that again now—living in two worlds."

"Okay," Remy said.

The Boss smiled. "That's all I wanted to say, Brian, to make sure you knew my genuine . . . and complete . . ." His voice cracked and he stared at the folder in his lap. Then he assumed his campaign voice again and fell back into his usual patter. "By God, we will gather every receipt, every purchase order, every goddamned piece of paper . . . otherwise . . . well, I think you know."

"Sir?"

"They win," The Boss whispered.

"Win, sir?"

"They win, Brian. They . . ." The Boss opened the empty file again. "They win." He put on a pair of glasses and looked down at the blank page. "As a side note, your reports on Sergeant Guterak have been very informative."

"My reports?" Remy rubbed his temple, trying to recall if he'd said something about Guterak. He wondered how you undo what you don't remember doing. "Paul's a good man."

"Yes, we can't have that."

"No. Paul's just fine, sir."

"It's taken care of." The Boss rubbed his mouth. "I know this is also a personal favor to me, Brian. Your commitment and sacrifice—" He rubbed his mouth and launched into a version of his inspiring speech again, but after a while it seemed to devolve into random words. ". . . courage . . . liberty . . . reconstruction . . . resilience . . . faith . . . spending . . ." He shook his head. "And this thing you're doing . . . well . . . obviously." The Boss closed the file folder and focused again. "But we'll need a story. We'll work it through disability. What do you want? Back? Disability loves backs. Or would you rather do the thing with your eyes?"

"My eyes?" Reflexively, Remy squeezed his eyes shut to check on the strings and floaters and when he opened them he saw—

THE FACE, young and lineless, the face from the ghost bar, stared at him from atop the same thin neck, perched above the same body of a man in the same deep black suit. Remy looked again at this perfect little face, like a blank sheet beneath short brown hair. He'd never seen such a smooth surface. Just as he had in the ghost bar, the man wore a generic federal ID tag over his suit's breast pocket: "Markham."

He was speaking: ". . . your background, of course, on the street and in the office. This is a unique assignment, removed as it might first appear from the initial . . . mandate of Liberty and Recovery. There's an argument that this assignment encroaches somewhat on the activities of the bureau, or the agencies, which is one reason we wanted to go out of shop." Markham waved this off. "But we'll figure out jurisdiction issues after we blow up that bridge. This is neither the time nor the time to debate such things. Am I right? Huh?"

They were in a small conference room, nothing on the walls, in black executive chairs. The room had a high ceiling; Remy could hear mechanized sounds coming from beyond the door.

Markham was still talking. "Of course, your work must be treated with the utmost discretion. I will be your primary contact. I trust you haven't told anyone about your negotiations with us to this point."

"With—"

"With us," Markham said.

"Yeah." Remy laughed nervously. "Well, I don't think that's going to be a problem."

Half of Markham's young face smiled. "That's good."

"Hell, I don't even know who you are."

Markham seemed momentarily startled, then smiled. "Wow. Yeah. That's good. You could be in one of our training videos." Markham sat smiling at Remy a moment longer, then set his thin briefcase on the table and opened it. "Okay, then, why don't we talk about what we're here to talk about?"

Markham pulled an eight-by-ten photograph from the briefcase and slid it across the table. It showed a young woman with round cheeks, dark eyes, and long black hair, a beautiful girl. In the picture she was sitting in a restaurant patio wearing a spaghetti-strap evening dress and holding a martini up to the camera.

"Gibson," said Markham.

"What?"

"You said martini. It's not a martini. It's a Gibson. Onions instead of olives." His perfectly manicured index finger pointed to the tiny glass in the picture.

Had he said martini out loud?

"Yes, you did. But see, it's a Gibson." Markham pointed to the glass again. "You can just make out the cocktail onions. Here, you can see them better in this one." He thumbed through his briefcase until he came up with another photo, a blown-up detail of the drink showing fuzzily but unmistakably that there were, indeed, two tiny white onions in the glass. "I don't like onions. I prefer olives myself," Markham said. "Without pimientos. You have to request it that way or they'll just assume you want pimientos. I mean, honestly . . . what is a pimiento? A fruit? A vegetable? A legume? I mean, come on—" He was taking on the tone of a standup comic. "Does it even *occur* in nature?"

"I think it's a pepper," Remy said.

"I know. It was a . . ." said Markham, clearly disappointed that his joke had fallen flat. "Oh. Well, then . . ." He put the onion picture away and pointed again at the picture of the girl. "This is March Selios."

Remy looked at the picture. Marge?

"No, March. Like the month."

Remy bit his lip so no more words would sneak out. He looked at the picture again, taken from across the table of a restaurant, ferns everywhere.

"She worked for a firm that managed legal issues for importers of various goods through foreign contracts, international consortiums, that sort of thing. She was trained as a paralegal. That's two legals." Markham spit laughter, but became serious so quickly that Remy wondered if there had been another gap. "She specialized in shipping, trade law, tariffs, oil. Spoke fluent Greek, but also passable Arabic and a bit of Farsi. Did a lot of work with Middle Eastern and Mediterranean companies: Greek, Italian, Saudi, Syrian, Lebanese. Intelligent girl, single, moderate drinker, liberal politics: for a time in the 1990s, she raised money for Palestinian relief charities, protested Israeli aggression, that sort of thing. A bit of a wild child, a drinker, no drug use that we can find. She wasn't afraid of sex, but then, she was in her twenties. Worked for this firm, ADR, for approximately two years. The firm's offices were sprinkled throughout the top floors, so as you might guess, the company was hit hard—a third of its employees, everyone who was at work that morning, twenty-three people, all MPD. Although—"

Remy looked at the picture again.

"—the number of Missing Presumed Dead from that firm would be twenty-two . . . if one were to take Ms. Selios off the official list." Markham let this hang in the air.

"You think . . . she shouldn't be . . . on the official list?"

"We have reason to believe . . ." Markham paused again. "There are indications . . ." He stopped again. "There is some *evidence* that . . . Ms. Selios may not have died that day. She may, in fact, be alive."

Remy waited for more, but this Markham seemed to revel in dripping details one at a time. "How?" Remy finally asked.

Markham crossed his hands and put his index fingers across his lips. "Based on document re-creation and interviews, we are exploring the theory that she may have gotten advance warning and fled moments before . . ."

Again Markham was quiet. Remy made an effort to speak out loud. "I'm not sure I'm following you."

Markham pulled on a rubber glove, reached back in his briefcase and pulled out a zipped plastic bag with a small piece of paper inside.

He put the bag on the table, then pulled it back. "Obviously, this is classified." Then he slid it forward again, as if it contained some magical secret.

Remy reached for the baggie. Inside was a single index card. On the card was a recipe, handwritten with a blue pen, for something called pecan encrusted sole. Remy read through the last ingredient (*1 tsp sea salt*) and the preparation (*Drip with virgin olive oil*), all the way through the directions (*Let stand for five minutes, garnish with two twisted orange slices, and serve*). He stared at the recipe, then looked back up at Markham. For several seconds, there was no noise in the room.

"A recipe," Remy said.

"Ah! Somebody's got some college," Markham said. "And where do you think we found this recipe?"

"I . . . I don't have any idea."

"Do you know where Crystal Beach is?"

"I don't think so."

Markham looked suspicious, but he continued. "Crystal Beach is in southern Ontario, on Abino Bay, across Lake Erie, near Buffalo. Lovely place. Cold in the winter, though . . . cold as a sober lesbian at a frat party. As you might guess." He waited for a laugh again, and then became serious. "We found this recipe . . . in the possession of a forty-six-year-old homemaker, Mrs. Linda Vendron. Mrs. Vendron claims she was at Kennedy Airport *that day*, after a visit with her sister, and was waiting for a commuter flight to Buffalo when she heard about the attacks. Do you see what I'm getting at?"

"No."

"When the airport closed, this Mrs. Vendron wasn't able to get a flight to Buffalo, so she returned to her sister's house. Finally, two days later, she took a bus to Buffalo. A very crowded bus, as she says now." Markham leaned forward. "This Mrs. Vendron claims she found the recipe wedged in the seat of the bus. She says she picked it up because . . .

she thought it would taste good. She thought her husband would like it. He *likes pecans.*"

"But you . . . don't believe her?"

Markham looked stung. "Yes, we believe her. Of course, just to be sure, we polygraphed her." He shook his head. "But why would anyone lie about liking pecans? Who doesn't like pecans? Especially in a good fish recipe, a tender filet? No, the pecans give it some substance, some crunch. Some weight. They're soaked in honey. I think you could substitute corn syrup. But it specifically calls for honey. A hint of cayenne. Sea salt. You bake it for twenty minutes on low heat. Some chives. No, it's a good little fish for a summer meal. Tasty. Light. We had the lab make it, just to be sure it was, you know . . . good." Markham leaned back. "We'll probably make it again; I'll let you know."

He leaned forward again, his index finger at his mouth. "But the question is not what does this fish taste like, or even what wine should you serve with the fish—I suppose you could get away with a Gewurtzemeiner or even a buttery Chardonnay. The question, Brian, is this: Who left this recipe on that bus?"

"Her?" Remy picked up the photo.

"March Selios," Markham said, gesturing with his palms as if he'd performed a magic trick. "It's a Greek surname. Second-generation immigrant. Older sister lives here in the city, works in real estate. Younger brother lives back at home in Kansas City with the parents. Dad runs a Greek restaurant there."

Remy looked at the recipe again. "And what makes you think this recipe belonged to . . ." He looked at the girl again. ". . . to March?"

"We don't have the luxury of *thinking*, Brian." He reached in his briefcase for another photo. This one showed the same girl, March, sitting at her cubicle, smiling, holding some red Mylar balloons with *Happy 26th Birthday* written on them in silver. Markham reached in the briefcase, returned with another detail blowup, and handed Remy a jeweler's loupe. "Here," Markham said, and pushed the picture over to Remy. "Look closely. Over her shoulder."

It was hard to make out at first, but then . . . yes, there was no doubt. On the wall of March Selios's cubicle was the very same hand-written recipe for pecan encrusted sole that sat on the table between Remy and Markham.

"Jesus, that's amazing," Remy said.

"Thank you."

"I mean, how did you know to look for . . ." Remy was having trouble following all of this. "How did this . . . I mean . . . it's just one piece of paper. All this for . . ."

Markham got serious again. "What are you saying, Brian?"

"Nothing . . . I'm not saying anything. I'm just amazed. I just don't see how you knew to connect . . . and you did all this work for . . . a recipe?" Remy looked through the jeweler's loupe again. "You don't even know that it had anything to do with that day . . . I mean . . . maybe she took it off her wall months earlier."

Markham pointed to the birthday picture again. "Her twenty-sixth birthday was six days before the attack. That's when this photo was taken, her twenty-sixth birthday—six days before she supposedly died."

"Maybe someone else picked up the recipe after . . . I mean, the paper went *everywhere*, didn't it?"

Markham nodded as if he'd been expecting such an answer. "There is no dust on this recipe, Brian. None. We had it tested in the lab. Right after we made the fish. This sheet of paper had to be in a brief-case or in a purse. It was not blown out of the building. It was taken out beforehand."

Remy looked at the office picture again. She was even prettier in this one, shy and wide-eyed, and it occurred to Remy that she was in love with whoever took the picture.

"Yeah, that's what we think, too," Markham said.

Jesus. Was he still saying aloud what he was thinking? Remy looked up to see if he was speaking this thought too, but Markham didn't seem to notice if he was. He put the two pictures side by side: March smiling in a restaurant, March smiling at her desk.

"These pictures were taken with the same camera. Whoever took them is the key. A lover. Possibly illicit. We find the person who took these pictures, we're halfway there," Markham said. "I believe that if we find this camera, there's a good chance we'll find March Selios alive. And there's a good chance we'll find her with someone you might find interesting."

Remy felt slow, as if he were thinking in mud. "Who?"

Markham reached in his briefcase and emerged with another picture, of March sitting outside at a little table on a rooftop with a handsome young Middle Eastern man, his hair and beard both at stubble length, his deep-set eyes seeming to peer through the camera.

"This was taken on the roof of March's apartment building. March cooked the meal and a neighbor served them and took this picture. The man is Bishir Madain," Markham said. "Saudi ex-pat. In the United States for twelve years. Worked for an importing consortium. Romantically linked with Ms. Selios until about eighteen months ago. Mr. Madain hasn't been seen since the morning of the attacks. We have recovered documentation—telexes, e-mails, rustic catalog order forms—that could indicate that Mr. Madain is part of a sleeper cell here. We believe he may even have had advance knowledge of the attacks that morning, and that he may have decided to alert his old girlfriend."

"But I still don't see how—"

Markham slid a two-page interview report across the table. On top was stamped the word *Classified* and the initials *D.D.* "That morning, at 7:12 A.M., soon after arriving, Ms. Selios called in a repair order for the laser printer on her floor. At 7:48, the technician arrived, as you'll see by his interview. The technician had always found Ms. Selios to be—"

Markham looked at his notes. "—*smoking hot.* That morning, he flirted with Ms. Selios, who was, he claims, not entirely unaware of his intentions or unimpressed by his *mac-daddy game.* Dude was *workin' it,* when March suddenly received a telephone call. She appeared agitated by the call. The technician was removing a jammed sheet of paper from the laser printer when he looked up and saw March Selios walking toward the elevators, crying. The technician himself left a few minutes later, arriving on the main floor, and was, as far as we know, the last person to get off that floor before . . ." Markham mouthed the word *boom,* and shrugged, as if that explained it.

Remy was surprised to hear himself asking questions. "Did anyone see her leaving the building? Or afterward? Is there any other evidence that she's alive?"

Markham looked pleased. "These questions are why we brought you in."

Remy looked down at the interview transcript. "I don't know. I mean—couldn't that call have been anything?" he said. "An argument with a boyfriend? Maybe she wasn't going to the elevator. Maybe she went to the bathroom. What have you got here—a horny repairman and a recipe. And that's supposed to prove she got advance warning?"

Markham pointed at the close-up of March Selios's cubicle. "Imagine the walls of a young woman's cubicle. Covered in pictures and recipes, Cathy cartoons, and Buddhist koans. Now, let's say she has a fight with her boyfriend, as you say, and she runs off to the bathroom. Would she really stop to strip the walls of her cubicle on her way out? Would she grab recipes and pictures? Why would it occur to her that she was not coming back?"

Markham held out his palms again, then began collecting his papers. He glanced up at Remy. "Any questions before you get started?"

Remy didn't know where to start. "This all seems so . . . *sketchy.* Maybe it's just me, but . . ." He rubbed his eyes, trying for the millionth time to clear the streaks. "I'm having a lot of trouble . . . *connecting* things."

Markham stared at him for a long moment and then nodded and looked like he might cry. "I know. It's hard. I forget sometimes that you guys went through hell that day. I can't know what that was like. None of us can. This is tough. And it never gets easier. But that's precisely why we wanted you." Markham reached back into his briefcase for the index card in the baggie. "Read the last line of this 'recipe.'"

Remy read it: *Garnish with two twisted orange slices.*

Now Markham handed him another detail blowup, this one from the photo of March and Bishir Madain at dinner on her roof. On the platter between them he could clearly see what looked like a piece of fish garnished with two twisted orange slices. Then Markham cocked his eyebrows, as if he'd made another ironclad case, and took the picture back. "Look, this is going to be tough. I'm not going to kid you. But we've got to find March Selios. And if it turns out she is, in fact . . . *dead* . . . well, then everything is copacetic. Not for her, obviously . . ." He laughed uncomfortably. "But for the record. That's our federally mandated charge, after all—to have a pure record. All the columns adding up. But if, in fact, she's alive—well, then, we've got a problem. In fact, we've got a big problem." And he closed the briefcase.

"A FORMALITY," said a woman in her fifties, tall and professional, staring over the rims of stylish glasses up at Remy. She sat at a wide desk, next to a rooster-haired man roughing up his nose with a wet handkerchief.

"There are no right answers," the man said. "Relax."

The woman asked, "Chronic back pain?"

"What?" Remy asked.

"Just to get the paperwork flowing," the tall woman said. "A formality. We just have to check a box."

The man asked, "Chronic back pain?"

Remy looked around the room. There was a poster on the wall behind him showing a cartoon man with a push broom through his head like an arrow and the caption: *Industrial Accidents Are Nothing To Laugh At*. Remy leaned forward. "My back is fine," he said. "I mean, if I need anything, I guess it's some kind of counselor. See, I'm having some trouble . . . focusing. There are these gaps. I lose track of things."

They stared at him.

"And my eyes . . . my eyes are flaking apart. Macular degeneration and vitreous detachment. I see flashers and floaters."

A few seconds passed. Remy laughed nervously. "My son's been telling everyone that I'm dead."

They stared.

"And I . . . I drink a lot. Most days, I think. And . . . uh . . ." He rubbed his eyes. "I shot myself in the head. But I think that was an accident. Or . . . maybe a joke."

They stared.

"But . . . you know . . . I'm fine."

They stared.

"Well . . . except for the gaps, obviously."

After a moment, the man chewed his pen and looked down at the file, running his finger down a list of some kind. "Chronic back pain," he said.

"I WATCH a fair amount of television, Mr. Remy," said the nervous woman with a silver skunk streak in her black hair. She glanced over at a set in the corner of her small apartment. Remy looked from the woman to her TV. On the screen, a man in coveralls was holding a piece of wood against a lathe. The sound was turned down. The skunk woman continued: "I haven't turned off my TV since it happened. I was glued to the news coverage for the first few days. I even turned the TV so I could see it from the bathroom. I ordered out every meal and just went from channel to channel, watching it from different angles, listening to the newscasters and the public officials. Then, just like that, a few days ago I saw the first thing on TV that wasn't news coverage. It was four in the morning." The woman took a drag from her cigarette. "It was an infomercial. For a psychic. You know, that Jamaican woman with dreadlocks who tells people what's in their future? Everyone's either going to find a new job or fall in love, right? No one's going to get cancer or fall down a well shaft. No one's going to have a day just like the day before, lonely and sad, watching TV and ordering takeout. No one's going to be burned to death on the eightieth floor of a building. It's all new jobs and hunky new boyfriends. I suppose there was part of me that still hadn't given up on March coming back—but I'm watching this psychic and she's saying she'll read your future for fifty bucks and they're showing these people reconciling with their mothers or falling in love or getting promotions at work and it just hit me that I was never going to see March again. And I just lost it. I yelled at this TV psychic: *Okay motherfucker! Where the hell were you?*"

Remy shifted. He looked down at his palm-sized notebook. Written on the page in his handwriting was a series of fragmentary notes: the name *Ann Rogers,* an address on the Upper East Side, the words *neighbor* and *family money*. Remy looked around the apartment, a simple postwar studio. She was stick-thin, with long, black hair and that perfect gray stripe. She was wearing baggy pajamas. She had two cigarettes going, one pinched between her long, manicured fingers, another smoldering in the ashtray.

Below *Ann Rogers* and *neighbor* was a short list of abbreviated questions, also in Remy's handwriting. He looked at the first one: *That morning?* "That morning," he said.

"That morning?" Ann Rogers took a deep breath and sighed. "That morning, March and I went off to work. Like any other day. We walked to the subway station together. It was . . . six-thirty. We got a bagel at the World Coffee place on Lex. She had a cappuccino. I don't drink caffeine, myself." Ann Rogers set one cigarette down and picked up the other one.

Remy stared at the notebook before him. Should he be writing any of this down? That Ann Rogers doesn't like caffeine? That she has a streak in her hair? He had the sense that any detail would become important if he wrote it down, that its importance would be determined by the record he kept.

"March and I hit it off right away, right after she moved into the building . . . oh . . . I don't know, almost a year ago." Ann Rogers ran her hand over her hair. "We'd meet in the hallway every day on our way to work. Sometimes we shared a cab. Or we'd walk to the subway together. We both rode downtown, although she went twice as far as me. It was amazing, really. We never said, Hey, let's meet at this time or let's meet at that time. It just happened. I'd step outside my apartment to get something to eat and March would be there, and she'd be going out to eat at the exact same time. It was amazing, if you think about it."

Remy thought about it. "I guess so."

Ann Rogers shrugged. "Anyway, that particular day, we caught our train, sat next to each other. We talked about the weather, our weekends, and then we got to the Union Square station and I got off. And that was it. I imagine she kept going downtown."

The second question read: *Unusual?*

"Anything," Remy said, "unusual about that day?"

"Hmm. Let me see. Oh, you know what. There was this one thing. About three thousand people died. Yeah. Including my best friend. And I haven't been able to leave my fucking apartment or turn off my fucking TV since then. But otherwise, no, I'd say it was just like every other peachy fucking day."

"No, I'm sorry, I . . ." Remy looked down. "I guess what I mean is . . . that morning. There was nothing unusual about that morning? *Before?* She didn't say anything before . . ."

"Oh, sorry. Hmm. Let me think. Oh yeah, now that you mention it, she did say that she had a bad feeling she was going to burn to death in an inferno."

Remy shifted in his chair. "Look, I didn't mean to upset you, Ms. Rogers."

Ann Rogers stared at him. Flat.

Remy looked back at his notes. Question three: *Seeing anyone?* He took a breath. "Do you know if she was seeing anyone?"

"Seeing?"

"Romantically."

"Who did she fuck? Is that what you're asking me, Mr. Remy? Who did March fuck? Is that what you're asking?"

"Look, Ms. Rogers, I—"

"You want to know who banged my neighbor?"

"I guess . . ."

"Then why don't you just ask that, you fucking pervert?"

"I did."

"No, you didn't. You asked if she was seeing someone. I'm seeing you right now, but you're not fucking me. Or are you? Are you fucking me, Mr. Remy? Is this as good as it gets with you?"

"Look, I . . ."

"Do you want me to tell you who she *saw* or who she fucked?"

"The latter, I guess."

"The latter? What's the matter with you? Say it. Say it, you piece of shit. Say, *Excuse me Ms. Rogers, but who did your neighbor fuck?*"

"Who did your neighbor fuck?"

"Oh my God! None of your business, you fucking pervert."

Remy felt dizzy. "Look, I don't know how this has gotten so—"

"What makes you think I would even know that? We were neighbors. I can tell you she didn't fuck me. Does that help? You want a full list of all the people who haven't fucked me? Is that what you want? Because I'll get some paper and get started."

Remy cleared his throat. "Look, we got off on the wrong foot or something. There's no reason—"

"No reason to what? No reason to be upset? What . . . are you asleep? Are you out of your fucking mind? Have you seen what's happening out there?"

Remy tried to soldier on. He looked at the next question: *That night*. "That night . . . did you hear or see anything . . . anyone in her apartment?"

"Fuck fuck fuck! Screw hump dick lay! Fuck fuck fuck! There. Are you happy, Mr. Remy? Does that turn you on, you freak?"

Next question: *Bishir*.

"Did you know a man named Bishir Madain?"

She waved him off like an insect. "Fuck fuck fuck! She didn't come home! Fuck fuck fuck! Are you happy, pervert? Fuck fuck fuck!"

Remy closed his notebook. "Maybe we'll try this some other time, Ms. Rogers."

She stared at him for a few seconds, and then turned back to the TV. She reached for her remote control and the sound came up, the guy in coveralls: ". . . *abrasive substances will work, although traditional sandpaper is still* . . ."

Remy started for the door, but paused. "Why did she live all the way up here?"

Ann Rogers jerked her thumb across the remote control, barely able to contain her disgust. "What do you want from me? Are you trying to get me to confess or something?"

"No," Remy said, "I was just wondering . . ." *What was he wondering?* "March worked in the financial district—"

"Yes. You know she did. That's why she died, you fuckhead pervert scumbag."

Remy ignored her. "And she lived all the way up here? In this building? On a paralegal's salary? That doesn't make any sense. She could have found the same space over the river for a third the price. Where'd she get the money for this?"

Ann Rogers seemed calm, suddenly. Her eyes narrowed. "I don't think I like what you're implying," she said.

Remy held his hands out. "What am I implying?"

"Aren't you implying something?"

"Honestly," Remy said, "I have no idea."

Ann Rogers reached for the remote control, cocked her arm and threw it at—

THE GUY standing in the doorway was in his late thirties, the fat settling between knees and shoulders, a week's growth coming in gray. Expensive haircut. He wore black slacks and a black T-shirt. He was barefoot. "Yes?"

Remy removed his hand from the doorbell and looked around. It was a nice house, two stories, blue-gray, with a square patch of new sod in front and a kid's bike leaning against the Lexus in the driveway. He looked down the block. Every house was the same, as far as he could see, like dominoes, each one with an American flag tipped from the porch.

"Can I help you?" asked the guy.

". . . I don't know." Remy's badge was in the hand he'd used to ring the bell, so he showed it to the man, hoping one of them would know how to proceed. "Um, I'm sorry, but . . . do you . . . where am I?"

The guy just stared. "Englewood Cliffs."

"Oh. Right."

"What can I do for you?"

Remy looked down. In his other hand was the planner he'd found at The Zero. G. Addich's day planner. *Ah.* "What's your name?"

The guy pulled back just a bit. "Tony Addich. Why?"

"Oh. I found this." Remy held out the thick black book. "I'm glad you're all right. I didn't know if you—"

Addich stared at the planner as if it were a ghost.

"It looked like there were a lot of meetings in there," Remy said.

The man didn't say anything.

Remy tried to appear nonchalant, as if they were sharing a laugh waiting for the subway. "It's funny. When I found this, I thought to myself . . . what did we do at all those meetings? I used to have a lot of meetings, and now . . . I have no idea what we talked about." He tried to laugh this off, just two guys talking about how important things can suddenly become trivial, but the whole thing came out shallow and raw.

The man just stared at the planner. "That's my father's," he said. "Gerald Addich. How did you get it?"

"Oh, Jesus," said Remy. "Is your father—"

"No. He's not here right now."

"But he's . . ."

"He's fine. He's at a senior citizen function. I think they went to a casino." Tony Addich took the planner and looked through it. He shook his head. "He used to work for the city, in the sixties. He's retired now. Suffers from dementia."

"Yeah," Remy said. "But see, I found this at—"

"Yes, thank you," said Tony Addich, and he closed the door in Remy's face.

Remy stood on the porch for a minute. He looked around the neighborhood again. Should he knock on the door again? Ask who his father knew named Remy? All of a sudden he wished he'd kept the —

GRAY DUSK, smoke-tinged and heavy, crept up from the horizon. Remy was standing outside Famous Ray's on Sixth, trying to decide if he was hungry, when he noticed a picture of March Selios with a phone number below it. The window in front of this Ray's was being used as a makeshift bulletin board, covered with desperate flyers, the whole store-front papered with pictures of the missing, arranged in crude rows like a mockup of a high school yearbook. This was a different picture of March, one he'd never seen before, but it was definitely her, smiling po-litely in a living room somewhere, maybe when she was younger. Remy stood in front of the window and looked past the reflected glass into the flatness of all those photographs, March Selios among her people, like members of a lost tribe, their images trapped forever on the inside of this window. Each picture was glued or printed on a sheet of paper with a description of the missing person and phone numbers to call. Some of the notes were pleas for mercy, as if the missing had been kid-napped and might be released if the kidnappers found out they had two children, or had just overcome cancer; others were even more emphatic, punctuated with exclamation points and descriptions of the kindness of the person, their hardworking drive, their love of family, and punctuality—as if these things could somehow help in identifying them. The corners of the pages were beginning to curl. There were vic-tim walls like this every few miles in the city now. They sprouted up in parks and at hospitals, on schools and on subway platforms—anywhere people could think to tape up pictures. As soon as one photo went up, people rushed from their apartments and houses to fill the entire wall with pictures. There could be no single photograph of the missing; every wall had to be covered, every space filled. And as a survivor, you had to stop and look at the pictures because that was what was required of you. Of course, these weren't missing people anymore; they were dead people now. Everyone knew they were dead. There were no stories of people from these walls being found alive (and still: the dream of amnesiacs wandering suburban hospitals) and yet Remy stopped and looked anyway, and as the walls made this quiet shift from the missing to the dead, he looked at them differently, mentally riffling the faces and pausing on the familiar— a glimmer of recognition and hope— until he remembered that he'd just seen that face on the wall in Washington Square, or at St. Vincent's, and eventually Remy came to wonder if maybe he hadn't known them all, every one of these people, and when he stepped away from the walls, he sometimes saw those faces on the passing bodies, in the stares of strangers—such looks of sorrow and bewilderment, such gazes of disbelief and betrayal.

He noticed distinctions on the walls, too, that he couldn't help making. Remy had read once that America was a classless society, but the walls of missing and dead disproved this. These walls were testaments to class, and even though the pictures were all jumbled, Remy could mentally break them into three strata. The first: bankers, lawyers, brokers, executives and their assistants, mostly white, some transplanted browns, mostly in suits or tuxedos or dresses, or photos from their weddings or their college graduations or company Christmas parties. Some of the younger ones, like March, were in casual clothes: with family or, more often, outdoors, hiking or vacationing in some canyon or on a beach in the Caribbean. These people were always smiling in their death photos, not exactly as though they were happy, but as if they'd been told at some point that they had nothing to complain about.

The second class was comprised mostly of firefighters, a few cops, and these were nearly all men, or boys, most with mustaches, in old xeroxed pictures, in uniforms, in their official portraits, shaggy sideburns or military haircuts. They were rarely smiling, but had an eager severity. They were ready. If they were pictured in candid shots, their faces were invariably washed out, as if the photographers were always too close . . . too proud. These people all had a look that Remy had seen on the faces of people who died too young—as if they'd known—a look that said this was simply more than they bargained for, that they had only wanted a life in which they made a little bit of money and lived comfortably.

They seemed like good people: white, black, and Latino, all with that look of someone who had just arrived somewhere. Remy could imagine thought bubbles above their heads: *It will be easier for my kids.*

And finally there was the last stratum, the workers who had been mostly invisible before, faces on the subway or at a bus stop: black and Hispanic, or foreign-borns, so many names heavy in consonants or vowels, the grunts who staffed the restaurants and cafeterias, the mailrooms and custodial sheds. These pictures were grim, like mugshots: work IDs and grainy family portraits and Polaroid-framed moments of forced relaxation. These people all seemed exhausted, as if they'd known disaster before this day, too, like flood survivors clinging to trees. Often, the missing person wasn't even the focus of the photograph—you could see two other people had been cut away from the picture and all that was left was poor Jupaheen in a secondhand suit, standing in a building lobby, hands folded in front of his lap. Bleeding patience.

Remy was lost in the faces when he glanced over and saw a guy standing next to him, a Middle Eastern man in his sixties, about Remy's height, wearing a beautiful wool coat, with razor-short hair, round glasses, and several days' growth on his craggy face. "Do you want to know what I have always believed?" he asked, with a dentured whistle, and the faintest shadow of an accent.

"Okay," Remy said.

The man turned back to the wall. "I have always believed that there are two kinds of people: those whose every day is a battle to rise up, and those whose every day is a battle to fit in. There are no other kinds of people. No races or religions or professions—you are either trying to rise, or trying to fit. That is the only war, between the risers and the fitters. That's all."

Remy looked back at the pictures. What was this man saying, that it was *democratizing*, all these people dying together? Remy couldn't see it that way, didn't imagine them coming together in the end, grabbing hold of one another in burning corridors or comforting each other as the heat rose and the ground beckoned. He'd seen too many people fall alone and it was too easy to imagine the rest crying alone, huddling alone, and burning alone—generally being alone, which, no matter how we live, is always the way we go. Remy looked down at his own hands, calluses on the pads and palms, gray dust in the creases of his nails.

"We miss Communism," the man said. "Not as a form of government, or economics—obviously that was a failure, as rife with corruption and disincentives as any other system. But the ideal, the childlike optimism—without it the world grows into cynicism. Sometimes I think we need another way, a political or economic route to morality and generosity. When I was a young man I believed that my faith was a path through the violent thicket of modernity, but honestly, I just don't know anymore. Maybe we all have to be dragged through, huh?"

The man gestured toward the photos. "Did you know that Jesus is mentioned ninety-three times in the Koran?"

"No," Remy said, "I guess I didn't know that."

"Nobody knows that," the man said. Then he put a manila envelope in Remy's open hands. "I think this may be what you're looking for," the man said and turned to walk away.

DARK AT the edges, and in the center a blinding, narrow green light an indeterminate distance in front of him, sliding back and forth across a short horizon. "And tell me, Brian. What are you seeing now?"

Remy's chin and forehead were pressed into some kind of smooth, cool plastic. The green light moved back and forth. "Brian? Are you seeing the streaks right now? The floaters and strings?"

"Yes," Remy answered. "Streaks. And the ones that look like chains. Floating."

"Okay. Look up, please."

He looked up.

"Now down."

Down.

"Okay. That's fine. You can sit back now."

Remy sat back in the chair, which had a cushion for his head. The lights came up and Remy's eyes burned as the pieces scrambled for cover. His wild-eyed ophthamologist, Dr. Huld, wore a small light above his head, a tiny miner's helmet. "I wish I had better news for you. But it's definitely gotten worse. Much worse." The doctor turned and looked maniacally at Remy—his bulging round eyes framed by thick black lashes, Marty Feldman after corrective surgery—and then scratched some notes on a pad. "I definitely don't want you to fly. The change in air pressure would be bad for your retinas. Do you think driving would be too hard on your back?"

"No," Remy said. "My back is fine."

"Well then, if you must take this trip, I think it's best that you drive. At least for now . . . until we get the pressure stabilized."

"Okay," Remy said. Then he would just have to drive. "Uh . . . Dr. Huld. Did I . . . by chance . . . Did I happen to tell you where I was going?"

Dr. Huld didn't look up as he wrote on his pad. "Kansas City."

"Right, Kansas City," Remy repeated. He laughed, as if trying to pass this all off as a game, but the doctor ignored him and spoke without looking up from his pad.

"How's the medication working out for you? Do you need another prescription?"

"I don't know."

The doctor looked up again, his eyes bugging. "Are you taking the pills I prescribed, Brian?"

"Honestly, I'm kind of having trouble remembering some things.

There are these . . . gaps. They're coming faster now. . . . Could that be a side effect of the medication?"

Dr. Huld removed the miner's light. "What kind of gaps?"

"Well, sometimes—"

HIS OWN face stared back at him from the bathroom mirror: thinning brown hair, faint beard over a jutting jaw, seams of blood in his left eye, and on his lips a distant, wan smile. And of course, the whole picture was covered with flecks, like a crackling old movie. Remy looked down. He was naked. He was getting thinner, lean muscles popping at the skin. And he was half-aroused. "The good half," he said quietly, surprised by his own raspy voice. Jesus, was he drunk again? He breathed on his hand and smelled sweet booze. Brandy? Port? He didn't drink port. Did he drink port? He imagined the syrupy coolness and suddenly craved a glass of it. Maybe he did drink port. Or maybe he should start. Remy looked around. This wasn't his bathroom. Okay. The floor was tiled with small alternating tiles; there was a sink, a medicine chest, and a toilet. It was very clean. Okay. Okay. There were candles draped in ribbon on the back of the toilet. Candles. This was a woman's bathroom. Well, that was good, anyway. If he was going to be naked in a strange bathroom, better to have it be—

"Is everything okay in there?" A woman's voice . . . youngish, a little tentative, maybe, but . . . nice.

Remy stared at the door. "Yeah. I'll be right there." He tried to come up with the girl's name: *Amelia? Olga? Maria?* Jesus, it could be anything. *Betsy? Phil? Rotunda?*

He looked around wildly and then opened the medicine chest, looking for prescriptions. But there weren't any. He opened a drawer and there were two medicine bottles. He read the names on the bottles:

April Kraft. *April. Kraft. April. April Kraft.* Was he with this April Kraft? What if April Kraft was the girl's roommate, not her?

"Uh . . . you don't have a roommate, do you?"

She laughed on the other side of the door—a sad, distant sound that trailed off.

Remy reached to open the door when he was frozen by a troubling thought. Had they already had sex? Didn't he usually piss *after* sex? He looked down at his half-erection. Was it the *before* kind of half-on or the *after* kind? If they'd already done it, and he tried again, it might not work. He might look . . . how exactly would that look? Valiant, for giving it an effort? Or like a jackass who can't close the deal? And if they hadn't had sex yet . . . Suddenly, he thought of the prescription bottles again. He opened the drawer. The first was for Celexa, prescribed for "anxiety and depression." The second was for penicillin, the fourth refill of five. That's all it said. Shoot, people took penicillin for all kinds of things. No reason to assume the worst. Had he used a condom? Was he about to use a condom? Did he have a condom? His erection was totally gone now.

"Please hurry . . . before I change my mind," she said. Okay, *before*. Maybe he was looking for a condom. She laughed a little, but there was some quality in her voice that gave him pause and made him think this wasn't just something she said, that this was a tentative match, that the moment could slip the way so many moments slipped now—loosed of their context and meaning and floating gently to the ground.

"Okay," he said, and he reached for—

SCOTCH. REMY tasted it in his mouth and felt the heavy glass in his hand. He let the booze trickle down his throat. It was delicious. He closed his eyes and watched the floaters drift by, like leaves on a pond. When the taste had faded Remy opened his eyes. "Wow. That was good." He was sitting in an oak-lined room, on a leather sofa, across from a handsome guy in his forties. The guy was wearing a suit with a striking shirt: sky blue with a bright white collar and white cuffs pinched by gold links that just barely peeked out of his jacket. His hair was carefully combed and curled up at the collar. He was holding copies of the photographs of March Selios and he was glaring at Remy.

"Look, friend," the guy said—Remy caught a slight Texas accent—"I've been shaken down before. So go ahead and act tough. Take my drink. Try to intimidate me. Arrest me if you want. But I'm not answering any questions until you tell me how you found my name."

Remy had no clue. "I'm afraid I can't do that," he said.

The two men stared at one another for a long moment, before Remy held up his glass and asked: "I don't suppose I could get some more of this?"

The guy rubbed his jaw and then raised the index finger on his right hand.

Remy looked around. They were in a club somewhere, rich dark wainscoting on the wall behind them, and above that a thickly painted landscape and a plaque engraved with the club officers' names. Two guys in tennis clothes were sitting a couple of tables away, watching them carefully. Remy and this immaculately dressed guy were sitting across from each other on leather couches in the center of the room, an ornately carved mahogany table between them.

A waiter approached and spoke sotto voce. "Mr. Eller, shall I call security?"

"That's not necessary, Carlos. In fact, why don't you bring Mr. Remy here another scotch."

"And for you?"

"No. Thank you."

Eller looked around the butterscotch room. He hissed: "Okay. I knew March . . . Yes. Obviously." He carefully set one photo down between them: March drinking the Gibson. "And you're right. I did take this one." Then he set down the other picture, the one of March in her office. "But I didn't take this one. I don't know who took that one. I'd guess they were both taken with her camera. She always had that camera. She was always giving that camera to people to take pictures of her in different situations. She used to say she was recording her life in case she forgot anything."

The memory made this Eller lose his voice for a moment. He rubbed his jaw and continued. "We met about a year ago. I had just moved here from Houston. My company had some business in the Sudan, oil futures." He pronounced it *ol' futures*. "We were having some . . . difficulties with Khartoum, and we hired March's firm to help us. While the lawyers hammered everything out, March gave us some cultural advice—how to play certain families, which palms to grease . . ." He shifted on the couch. "When the first part of the deal was finalized, I asked her out to dinner to celebrate." He shrugged. "And yes, Mr. Remy, for a short time after that, we were . . ." He looked around. ". . . *fucking* . . . as you so bluntly put it.

"So, there, I've answered your question. Now I'd like an answer to mine. How did you find me?"

Remy thought about the Scotch that was coming. He wanted to extend the interview at least long enough to drink it. "You don't know?"

Eller cocked his head. "I don't think any of her friends knew. I don't even think she told her sister. She was embarrassed about seeing a married man. . . . Maybe someone at her office? Someone in her building?"

"You're getting warmer," Remy said, treading water. A few seconds later, his Scotch arrived and Remy reached out and accepted the caramel-colored glass. "This is really good," he said to the waiter. "What is it?"

"Oban. Twenty-two years old."

"God. It's really good."

"The lease on the apartment," Eller said, slapping his head. He looked from the waiter to Remy's glass and back. "Carlos. Do you think you could get Mr. Remy a bottle? Put it on my account."

"Of course, Mr. Eller." Carlos backed away from the table.

Remy held the drink in his mouth, savoring it.

"You'll excuse my earlier outburst, Mr. Remy. It occurs to me that it was actually thoughtful of you to contact me here at the club, rather than at my office or my home, where this might have been . . . misconstrued. Clearly, you're a reasonable man."

"Thank you," Remy said, draining the glass.

"I'll help in any way that I can. . . ." Eller tapped the photo of March in the spaghetti-strap dress. "You're right—this is the Olympic Four Seasons in Seattle. How did you know that?"

Remy shrugged.

"I understand." Eller nodded in a kind of admiration. "Well . . . I was at a conference there, last spring. I took March. I wanted to talk to her, outside the city. She was sensitive about my being married. She told me that's all she'd met since she got to the city, married men. Except this one boyfriend she had briefly . . . Basil, I think his name was, something like that. An Arab student, real womanizer. They'd just broken up. She was bitter—looking for something different, I guess.

"Anyway, I guess I may have . . . uh . . . led her to believe that I was separated. It was on that trip, when I took this picture, that I explained that I actually wasn't exactly separated, technically." He cleared his throat. "That my wife and I were still together."

Eller waited for a response, but Remy couldn't muster one. "Technically," he repeated.

"Yes." Eller bit his lip. "Anyway, March ran out. And I didn't see her for several hours. She was walking around Seattle. When she came back, I could see that she had been crying. But her face was set. Very determined. March could be that way. She was one of those people who lashed out when she was hurt. And, oh boy, was she hurt." Remy thought Eller seemed almost proud of this fact, and he had to look away. "She started by saying that she was tired of feeling like a victim in every relationship and then she just laid out everything she wanted from me: bang, bang, bang. An apartment. A cell phone. A car. Stipend. Clothes allowance. She said that if she was going to be a mistress, by God she wanted to be compensated like one." Eller stared at a spot over Remy's shoulder. "Honestly, Mr. Remy. That outburst was the best thing that could've happened. For both of us. This might sound . . . cold. But I'm a businessman. This is what I do. It's what I understand. Negotiations. Arrangements. I tend to gravitate toward those things I can control. And in that way, shoot, the arrangement was . . ." His eyes drifted down and for the first time, he looked like a man who'd lost someone. "Perfect."

Something stuck in Remy's mind, amid all these pointless details, one word: "Car? Did you say you bought her a car?"

"I *gave* her a car."

"But she took the train to work."

"I needed to be somewhat discreet about the car." Eller squirmed. "My firm . . . provided it, a company car. I tied it to the work she was doing for us. March parked it in the garage below her office. We used it on the weekends to go to Connecticut."

Just then the waiter returned with a tall, narrow box and set it on the table between them. The scotch. Eller stared at him, waiting for a question, but Remy just looked back at his scotch. Eller cleared his throat and filled the space. "About three weeks before . . ." he rubbed his mouth ". . . before she died, March suddenly said that it was over. I wasn't happy, as you might guess. I asked if there was someone else . . . and when she hesitated, I knew. I asked if it was her old boyfriend, but she just said it wasn't anyone. It was just . . . time, she said."

Remy nodded.

"I know what you're thinking." Eller picked up the photograph and stared at it again. "Was I in some way . . . *relieved* that March died that day? Because I didn't have to hold my breath every time the phone rang at home? Or look over my shoulder when I went to her apartment? I was bitter about the breakup; I won't lie. But I cared deeply for her, Mr. Remy. I did. There were days when I thought I loved her."

Remy didn't say anything.

"I'm sure you don't believe me."

"Why wouldn't I believe you?"

Eller straightened his neck. "I don't care, Mr. Remy. Go ahead and mock me. March knew how I felt about her. I sleep at night. I—"

He coughed and seemed about to break down, but quickly composed himself. "That day . . . I watched TV and I was sick. I tried her cell phone but I couldn't get through. I called the apartment and the hospitals. . . . That night I went to the apartment. I still had my key. I just sat there thinking about her, and—" He trailed off and rubbed his jaw, looking down at the ground as if the magnitude of his actions was just making its way to him. "I gathered everything that might get back to me." He looked up. "A magazine with my name on it. A razor and deodorant I kept in the bathroom. A bottle of wine from our cellar. I got those things . . . and I left." Eller stared at the spot over Remy's shoulder again, as if reading cue cards. Finally he looked back and met Remy's eyes, composed and icy. "You said you were going to see her family in Kansas City?"

"Did I?"

"I doubt she told them anything about me, but if she did . . . can you tell them how genuinely sorry I am—for everything?"

"Sure."

"Does any of this help?" Eller asked.

Remy looked at the scotch. "Yes."

They both stood. Eller straightened his coat and looked at a spot on the ground. "The last time I talked to her . . . was two weeks before. A

Sunday. She asked how I was doing. Miles . . . my son . . . had a soccer game. I told her about it, and she said, 'I hope he has a great game.' With no irony, either. March would've been a wonderful mother, if she'd ever gotten the chance." He sighed. "Mr. Remy, if you knew that a conversation would be the last one you were going to have with someone, what would you say?"

Remy reached for the bottle of—

"I JUST keep thinking we forgot something," Guterak was saying on the other end of the phone. He sounded drunk.

"What do you mean?" Remy adjusted the phone in his own ear. He sounded drunk, too. "What did we forget?"

"Not just us. Everyone. We just kept going on and . . . it's like we all forgot to do something important. Like when you leave the stove on and go on a big trip."

Remy didn't know what to say. He looked at his watch. It was three in the morning. He was alone, fully dressed, lying on the bed in a hotel room that he didn't recognize. He was wearing the suit he wore to funerals. He reached in the pocket and pulled out a funeral announcement. There was a picture of a forest and a verse from Luke: *Father, if thou art willing, remove this cup from me; nevertheless not my will, but thine, be done.* Below that was the name Donald Michael Morrone. Aw, Jesus. Not Donnie. They'd been at the academy together. Had he known about Donnie? Remy was drunk, but there was nothing around him to drink. His mouth felt velvety, warm. He edged with the phone over to the minibar and rifled through the browns.

"What did we forget, Paul?" Remy cracked a little dark rum and drained it.

"The people," Paul said, as if it were obvious. "We forgot the people. I mean . . . where are they? It's like they're in a giant room somewhere, sitting, crouched against walls, and . . . if we just find that door and open it, they'll all be in there, just staring at us. Thinking, *What the fugg took you so long?*"

"Jesus, Paul . . ."

"Sometimes I wish we'd just gone to a bar that morning and watched the whole thing on CNN. You know what I mean? I envy people who watched it on TV. They got to see the whole thing. People ask me what it was like and I honestly don't know. Sometimes, I think the people who watched it on TV saw more than we did. It's like, the further away you were from this thing, the more sense it made. Hell, I still feel like I have no idea what even happened. No matter how many times I tell the story, it still makes no sense to me. You know?"

There was something important Remy wanted to say, but he felt dopey with booze and the gaps seemed to be coming so fast now. Remy gripped the side of the bed, as if to keep himself from sliding out of the moment until he could remember what he wanted to say.

"People always ask the same question," Guterak said. "When everyone is around, it's all respect and bravery and what-a-fuggin'-hero and thanks for your sacrifice, but the minute someone gets me alone, or the minute they have a drink in 'em, they get this creepy look and they ask me what the bodies sounded like when they hit the sidewalk. They ever ask you that?"

Remy couldn't say. "What do you tell 'em?"

"I say to clap their hands as hard as they can, so hard that it really hurts. Then they clap, and I say: No. Harder than that. And they clap again, and I say, No, really fuggin' hard. And then they clap so hard their faces get all twisted up, and I say, No, *really* hard! And then, when their hands are red and sore, they say, 'So that's that what it sounded like?' And I say, 'No. It didn't sound like that at all.' "

"Paul, have you thought about getting help? Maybe take some time off?"

"What? Take disability for my back, like you?"

Remy couldn't tell if Guterak was mocking him. He knew there was nothing wrong with his back, didn't he? "I don't think I'm on disability, Paul," he said. "I think I'm working on something."

Guterak laughed. "Oh. Then I guess I can cancel your going-away party."

"I swear, Paul. I'm working. On some kind of case."

"Yeah? They put the blind guy with the bad back on some big, top-secret assignment, huh?"

"My back is fine."

Paul laughed again. "What do you do on this secret assignment?"

"I go places . . . Talk to people."

Guterak seemed to be tiring of the joke. "Yeah? Then what happens?"

Remy put the funeral announcement back in his pocket and unfolded another piece of paper he found there. It was the flyer from the wall at Famous Ray's, with the picture of March Selios and the phone number beneath it. Remy put it on the bedstand. "I don't know," he said into the phone. "I guess . . . the days just skip by."

"Yeah," Paul said. "Well. I know that feeling."

HIS PANT leg was caught on something sharp. It was dark and he had to feel with his hand along the wall of a narrow, paved tunnel, until he found the cuff of his jeans, snagged on a jagged section of pipe. He yanked it away, banging his elbow on the wall of the tunnel, and then continued crawling toward the light. He was wearing a respirator; the sound of his own breathing echoed in his ears. His hands were chalky with wet dust. There was a sound somewhere like a dentist's drill. Two other men were crawling down this narrow tunnel ahead of him, the soles of the closest man's hiking shoes twenty feet ahead. He followed the shoes toward a leaking yellow light, which bobbed ahead in a larger space, until, one by one, the two men ahead of him fell through an opening into a short white cave, or—no, he recognized it, even in its current state . . . a subterranean parking garage, the Orange level, apparently.

Remy pulled himself to the mouth of the tunnel and stared out. Along one wall the concrete pillars had been snapped and the roof had caved in, gunmetal Benzes and black BMWs crushed and blanketed in a fine coat of dust. Some of the car doors were open, as if people had gone through them and simply left the doors open. A CD wallet lay open on the floor next to one of the cars, and Remy imagined a rescue worker looking for something to listen to on the way down. The garage floor was wet, the dust piled where rivulets had run along construction seams and the newer cracks produced by the collapse above. Strings of utility lights had been laid like holiday garland along the remaining standing pillars, their bare bulbs illuminating the dank underground and lighting the dust particles like firebugs, dread shadows thrown in every direction.

Remy spilled out of the opening onto the concrete floor. The two men ahead of him were already standing and brushing themselves off, the beams from their flashlights creating plumes of dust and light. One of the men was Markham, the Documentation guy who had assigned him to find March Selios. The other man was someone Remy had never seen before, an older guy in coveralls and a utility jacket. This older man removed his respirator, and so Remy and Markham did the same. Markham's smooth face screwed up in a sneeze.

Remy's first breath was choked with dust. The Zero smell was even stronger down here, and he couldn't help wondering if, as they moved down, they weren't nearing some hot wet core of the thing—and he imagined a river of smell, perhaps guarded by a robed ferryman or a cabbie sitting on a beaded chair. Markham pulled blueprints from his back pocket and walked over to the hood of a Mercedes coupe, its front end pristine except for the dust, its trunk bashed by falling concrete. Markham spread the prints out, pulled a flashlight from his pocket, flicked it on, and put it in his mouth between his teeth.

When Remy didn't budge, Markham had to pull the flashlight out of his mouth and beckon him over. "Brian. Please. We don't have much time."

Remy edged over. Markham put the flashlight back in his mouth and pressed down on the creased blueprint. It showed the levels of this underground parking garage, both from above and in relief, its ducts and staircases and elevator shafts, its relation to the commuter train tubes. The other man, who wore gray coveralls, pointed with a drafting pencil at a long slender line on the page, and then at the collapsed parking structure in front of them. "Okay. We're here." He pointed to a spot on the blueprint. "On the northeast corner. There were six basement levels down here, filling up most of the entire sixteen acres— parking, shopping, public transportation, air condition, elevators and other machinery—like a honeycomb. About sixty percent of all that was destroyed."

He ran his pencil along a tunnel. "This part of the garage where you say this woman's car might have been parked is here. Like I told you . . . it's blocked, if not entirely collapsed. We might be able to follow this PVC cluster to the PATH tunnel, assuming the line is still there. And passable. But this is the way to the place you fellas want to go, and as you can see it's blocked off. If we go this way—" He dragged his pencil across the print. "We're going to hit the fire. This direction, we run into water. And all of this area is probably contaminated by Freon."

"Well, that's a hell of a choice," Markham said, as his flashlight fell to the ground, the light frantically testing the walls for escape before hiding beneath a crushed Lexus sedan. "Fire or flood or poison. Burn or drown or choke on your own vomit. I guess I'd take drowning, you know, if I had to pick. How about you, Brian? You seem like a burn guy . . . like you'd want to go out in as much glory as possible."

Remy picked the flashlight off the ground, extinguished its light, and handed it back to Markham.

The guy in coveralls talked to Remy as if he were in charge. "Like I told you up above, this is as far as we can go. Maybe after they get the fire down here controlled and pump out some of the lower levels. But even then, I doubt it." The guy gestured toward the crushed cars. "You could try the lowest level, B-6, and then try to move up, but like I say, that's seventy feet below the surface, and in this section it's either on fire or under water. We could go north, but then you got the potential of gas from them old Freon tanks."

Markham looked at Remy seriously. "What do you think?"

"What do *you* think?" Remy asked.

The guy in coveralls interrupted: "Look, I appreciate how important this is. I want you to know that if there was any way we could do this, I would . . . Because I think you fellas are the most important people down here, far as I'm concerned. I mean, I heard them talking about all them documents on TV. But this is a needle in a . . . haystack." He looked around. "A really scary haystack."

Remy looked around the garage. The collapsed corner troubled him. What was above that? How far up did the rubble go? To the pile? The Spires? Against another wall, a stream of black water minded its own business, flowing through the ruined garage into a fissure in the wall. Where did that water come from? Where was it going? And why was it black? These seemed like the real questions they should be asking.

Markham put his hands out. "Okay, Brian. You've gotta call the ball on this one. What do you want to do? Go back or follow the sewer line?"

"I don't . . ." Remy surprised himself by laughing. "I can't say."

The guy in coveralls glanced at Markham, who sighed with disapproval. He took Remy by the elbow and pulled him aside. His voice was low. "What's the matter with you today, Brian?"

Remy heard himself laugh again, maniacally. He said, under his breath, "I don't have the slightest clue what we're doing down here."

Markham stared at him for a moment. Then he nodded. "Yeah, you're probably right. Hell, even if we got to the floor where her firm kept their cars . . ." Markham walked over and folded up the blueprint.

"Were we looking for March's car?" Remy asked.

"Yeah, when you put it that way, it does seem crazy." Markham turned to their guide. "Brian thinks we should just turn back."

The guy in coveralls sighed. "Thank you." He looked over his shoulder, headlights of ruined cars peeking out from collapsed roof. "I don't like it down here."

Markham watched Remy for a moment, his face noncommittal. "Don't worry about it, Brian. It was a long shot anyway. You made the right call."

Markham and the guy in coveralls put on their respirators and moved back to the opening they'd crawled through. Remy looked around once more at the dusted windshields, which stared at him inscrutably. Then he put on his mask and followed the two men back into—

"MIDNIGHT SATURDAY I'm jacked up on some waitress, half-to bangin' the ass off her when my fuckin' pager goes off *nine-one-one* and I'm thinkin' *Oh shit, my wife found out I ain't workin' this weekend*, right, but when I check the page, who do you think it is? Brian fu-u-uckin' Remy, that's who." McIntyre gulped a breath as the guys barked laughter and Remy took the moment to glance around. About half the old detail was here, six of The Boss's guys and five guys from the PC's office—where Remy had been assigned for six months—twelve guys including Remy and Guterak, who sat at his right, laughing so hard he lacked the breath to say anything inappropriate.

"Right? Right? So Remy's got body that night—and I don't have to tell you which boss we were assigned to then, 'cept to say that poor Remy's sleepin' in one of the Town Cars outside some skank's apartment in Alphabet City while the boss drills for soil samples, right—" The guys all laughed knowingly. "And that's when the fuckin' boss comes down barefoot with his pants undone, in a T-shirt—remember that? Remember, Bri?—stupid fat fuck, too goddam furious to use the phone, he wants to get in someone's face because he's gone and picked another whore with a tool, right? He's out of his fuckin' mind, wants *every* transvestite hooker off the fuckin' street. That night! And this jackass is so in love with his own power and with his phony fuckin' statistical results, he really thinks this can be done, right? Like it's just a fuckin' number on a graph—eight hundred or something. 'So great,' I tell Remy, 'call patrol.' But genius here—" McIntyre pointed at Remy "—says the boss wants *us* to do it. And I'm like, 'He wants *us* to do this?' And Remy says, 'Yeah. He wants us to do this. Right now.' And I'm literally half in this fuckin' waitress, on the upstroke, right? And I'm on the phone and I'm like, 'Right now, Brian?' And he says, 'Right now, Billy.' And I'm like, 'All of 'em, Brian? All the whores?' and this unflappable motherfucker here, this asshole thinks for a second, then says, 'Well . . . I guess all of 'em with dicks, Billy.'"

The guys slapped the table and held their chests, doubled over, Carey's high, squeaky laugh rising above the din.

"And I'm like, 'How the fuck are we supposed to know which ones have dicks, Brian?' And this brilliant son-of-a-bitch—"

Another delighted squeal from Carey stopped McIntyre's story for a second, and the room dissolved into drunken laughter: deep, dissonant howls and hoots like a brass band warming up. Remy looked around at his friends and past them, through the filmy strands in his eyes to the banquet room of an Italian restaurant and then down at the checked table, covered with oval plates, gnawed scattered T-bones, surrendered piles of noodles and glimpses of garlic potatoes and green beans, spent shells of empty beer pitchers, wine bottles and highball glasses. For a moment he worried about their appetites, and wondered if they could ever be made full, these men, until this thought was replaced by a more important thought. Which glass was his?

"This! Cool! Mother! Fucker! Over he-yah!" McIntyre pointed to Remy again. "He says, 'Well, from what I hear, you can tell by the hands.' And I'm like, 'You can tell *what* by the fuckin' hands?' And you gotta remember, while I'm talkin' to Remy here I'm fuckin' doin' a pushup on this waitress, and that's when she and I stop what we're doin' for a minute and we both look at her hands. And Remy says, 'You can tell it's a woman by her hands.' And I'm lookin' at this waitress's big mannish hands and I say, 'Jesus Christ, Brian, if we're gonna get close enough to look at their hands we might as well reach up and see if we get a handful.'"

"Aaaagh!" Guterak made a noise that sounded as much scream as laugh, and clapped Remy on the back.

"So all night, fuckin' Remy and me are driving around lookin' at hookers' hands and I swear to God, they *all* look like dudes to us, right? And I got mixed feelings. First, I'm startin' to panic . . . if the fuckin' boss wants tranny whores, then goddamn we better fuckin' find some chicks with dicks, you know? But the other thing is this: I'm gettin' so fuckin' horny drivin' around lookin' at hookers that I'm half tempted to try one out just to see. And that's when Brian remembers this fuckin' Dominican scumbag up the Heights he's arrested, what, five, six times, Bri? This motherfucker used to run a bunch of tranny whores . . . what the fuck was his name . . . Kiko something?"

Someone called out: "Ramirez!"

McIntyre pointed. "Right! Right! This fuckin' mutt Kiko Ramirez, little fuckin' Dominican pimp lived up off a hunnert and fifty-third by Broadway, we go drag this motherfucker out of his cousin's bed and take him downstairs and I'm like, 'Listen up, fuckball, you're privy to some information we want, you know . . . very important investigation, top priority . . . you play along and you'll get a two-month pass, right?' Guy's like. 'Whatchu wan', mang,' and I say, 'I need you to find us five whores with optional equipment,' and this little shit looks at me like I'm fuckin' king-a-the perverts, you know? And Brian says, 'It's not for us, Kiko, it's for our boss.'" The laughter rose again. "And this little shitbag Kiko, he must know which boss we're talkin' about, because he just nods like we've just ordered five pizzas. Kiko, he got this thin little mustache, and he just shrugs, like, 'Hey mang, eet don' matter to me. Diff'rent strokes, mang.' Yeah? Like this fuckin' Scarface motherfucker he's seen it all, right? All the shit in the world." The laughter rises again.

"Now the three of us are drivin' around in the fuckin' Town Car, Brian and me in the front and Kiko in the back like we're his chauffeurs, and at one point old Kiko goes to light up a fuckin' cigarette and I turn and say, 'You can't be serious, Kiko? You smoke in my boss's car and you know I'm gonna have to clean you like a fuckin' fish, right?' And we're runnin' down Broadway, cruisin' the Deuce, and this shitbag Kiko is starin' out the window like a fuckin' four-year-old at a parade, checkin' out all these whores, sayin': 'No. Ees a woman. No. Ees a woman. Ees a woo-man too.' And finally, I turn around and I'm like, 'Kiko, I'm gonna shoot you in your fuckin' face you don't find me a whore with a goddamned cock.'"

Laughter cascaded and crashed and Remy became slightly worried that someone would have a heart attack.

"And Kiko . . . this fuckin' mutt Kiko, he's just starin' out the window, every few minutes, 'No, ees a woo-man. No, ees a woo-man.' And Remy and me are checkin' our fuckin' watches, thinkin' the boss is gonna fuckin' have us for breakfast, right? And then, finally, Kiko comes to the window, says, 'Maybe her. Yeah, I think she's a mang.' So we park and walk closer and he says, 'No. Ees a woo-man too.' And by this time I've had about enough of this shit, I'm like, 'Motherfuck Kiko! How the fuck do you know that one ain't a guy?' And this greasy fucker points to this whore and says, 'You can tell by the hands, mang.' "

The room broke in screams and groans, guttural and full, the aging men given over to a grinding death rattle and release, and even Remy found that he was smiling, not exactly remembering, but wanting to, and thinking there's not such a difference, that the best memories might be those you don't remember, and the gales smoothed and calmed and guys hummed and wiped their eyes, and someone yelled, "Speech! Speech!" and then the others joined in and Remy was yelling, "Speech," before he realized that it was him they wanted the speech from.

"Wait. Wait." Ass Chief Carey held up his left hand. "Before we let Remy say something the rest of us will regret, I got something for you cocksuckers." Carey bent over. "To mark the occasion. A taste." He came up with a backpack that he set on the table. "Compliments of the bosses." He unzipped the backpack and began removing watches, still in the bottom halves of their boxes, as if they'd been on display, like tiny open caskets. He handed around the table, to whistles and hoots. One by one, the guys slid watches ("Aw, boss." "No fuckin' way.") onto thick, hairy wrists.

"Goddamn, boss. This is too fuckin' much."

Carey waved them off. "Ain't half what you guys deserve. You're the best fuckin' crew in the city. I mean that. The other bosses mean it, too."

Remy looked down at the half-box in his hand. It was dark wood, and in the center was a pointed crown, the word Rolex engraved in gold.

"Come on. Put it on," Carey said. Remy stared down at the dark face of a gold watch, and caught the bursts of light in the face's jewels. He wiped a thin coat of fine dust off the glass.

"They're limited edition Gent Omegas," Carey said. "Fuckin' James

Bond watches. Remy's is gold-plated." The guys were all sloughing their sleeves and holding their wrists in the air. Guterak held his arm out to Remy. "Look at this shit, Bri. How's it look on me? Jesus, you ever think I'd wear a fuggin' Rolex?"

There was a folded envelope under Remy's watch. He removed it and opened it. Inside was a small note signed by The Boss: "To New Opportunities. And Old Loyalties." The word *Loyalties* was underlined.

"Speech!" the guys began yelling again, and Guterak pushed Remy up.

He was still holding the watch loosely in his hand. He looked down at it, and then rubbed his mouth again. "I . . . I don't really know what to say. Honestly, I'm not entirely sure what's happening to me. Or why."

Some of the guys laughed. Others nodded as if he'd struck a chord, the infinite emptiness of the last weeks.

He rubbed his short hair. "I mean . . . I can see that I'm leaving. Am I retiring? I'm supposed to be taking disability, right?"

The laughter built.

"I mean . . . I'm not dying or anything, am I? Is it my eyes?"

Ass Chief Carey made that high-pitched squeal again. Guys were hugging and laughing and holding each other up.

Remy looked down at the table. "Can anyone tell me which glass is mine?"

This seemed to be the perfect end to his speech. Waves of laughter rolled through the room and Guterak stood and hugged Remy. "That was great. Classic Remy. I love you, man." The guys came by one at a time, paying their respects, hugging him and telling him to relax or to have good luck or not to worry, and after a while Remy couldn't imagine what difference it made, what was happening to him. This was the important thing, these guys who had risked their lives, these guys who loved him so much, and whatever it had taken to accommodate this occasion . . . well, it was going to happen whether he knew about it or not. "I hope you realize what a lucky motherfucker you are," McIntyre said.

"We're goin' down to Copley's girlfriend's strip club, you wanna come," Carey added.

"No, I don't think so," Remy said.

McIntyre hugged him again. "I'm gonna miss you, asshole."

Finally, Remy was alone, watching as the guys moved in packs of two or three to the door. Guterak gave a quick wave as he went with the guys. When they were all gone, Remy carefully put the watch back in its case.

Sometimes the gaps came like cuts in a movie, one on top of the other, with Remy struggling for breath; at other times he seemed to drift, or even to linger in moments that had ended for everyone else. Was there something he was supposed to take from such moments? Remy pulled the watch from its box bottom again and looked at its face, half expecting to see the second hand standing still, jittery and frozen, waiting for Remy to be jolted into the next moment. But the needle slid gracefully around the numbered face, scratching away moment after moment after . . . Remy put the watch back in the box bottom and walked out of the banquet room, down a paneled hallway past the kitchen. He peered in the round window on the swinging doors and saw an old Puerto Rican guy in a paper apron working on a tall stack of dishes, pots, and pans. Remy opened the door and slid the watch box along the floor, then let the door close. He looked through the window again. The old dishwasher was bending over to pick up the watch.

Remy walked down the hallway, through an empty restaurant and outside. He recognized the skyline across the river. Behind him, the huge four-faced clock tower loomed like a dragon. He thought of the watch face. No zero on a clock. Around and around. No rest. No balance. No starting place. Just on to the next number. The sky was clearing, cold, the clouds opening between the brownstones. He stood on the sidewalk and looked back at the city, the burnt tip of the island and the bright hole in the sky.

THE AIR was cool and dry and huge fans whirred above his head. Remy was standing in a vast airplane hangar, holding a memo, apparently from the information technologies consultant Lara Kane to Travis Fanning in the personnel department of Anderson Dugan Rippet, March Selios's firm:

> Re: status report: Firewall, Acrobat, Monitoring.
> CC: Duncan, Wallace, *Selios.*
>
> UTMI up and running as per meeting of 8-4 and inventory under way for separate worksheets regarding hardware, software, tools, Mac and PC, upgrades, printers. For access rights for MGT group, see confirmation e-mails and logs . . .

Remy looked up from the page. The airplane hangar was full of people, filing cabinets, and tables of burned and dirty paper. Temporary fluorescent lights were strung about ten feet off the ground, along the length of the hangar, which was otherwise completely filled with these long tables and filing cabinets in long rows that seemed to stretch forever. As far as Remy could see, these tables were covered with paper— notes, forms, resignations, and retributions, as if the whole world could be conjured up out of the paper it had produced. Next to each table was a filing cabinet. There were big posters hanging from the ceiling with letters written on them. Remy looked up. The sign above him read: **AM–AZ**. There appeared to be a sign every hundred feet or so, perhaps ten tables and ten filing cabinets per sign. At the far end of the hangar he strained to make out another set of letters: CO–CY. So how many other hangars did that mean, he wondered. Five? Eight? At each of these stations several attendants were working away, some of them combing over the paper mountains on each table, others filing. Each of them wore a white paper suit, a mask, and white gloves.

"Obviously, you're interested in the partials, too," said a young woman at the table in front of Remy. Her mask was pulled down around her neck.

"Partials," Remy repeated. Their voices seemed both distant and loud in the cavernous hangar, which hummed with the low throttle of so many other voices.

She handed him another dusty sheet of paper, this one rounded and burned along the edges like a perfectly roasted marshmallow. It was a ledger sheet with several columns of numbers, although the top row had been burned off, so he couldn't see what the numbers referred to.

Compensation	71	26	44	6
Employee benefits	11	11	12	11
Travel & Entmnt.	9	92	14	71
Subtotal employees	**91**	**129**	**70**	**88**
IT (see Selios attachment)	463	903	138	314
Communication	21	34	42	12

He held the paper to his face. It smelled like The Zero. That same fine dust coated everything, almost a liquid form of grit. Remy looked down at the woman sitting at the table. She was tall and thin and wore glasses. Her hair was tied back. She seemed tired. She leaned in and confided, "I try to explain the smell to people, and I can't."

She smiled warmly and handed him another sheet of paper. It was an interoffice memo, its subject *Portfolio Market capitalization statistics as of 7–01.* There were about forty names in the cc: line, among them *Selios.* A note at the top said, *All Market Cap Stats in millions.* Then there were some mutual funds listed:

	# securities	weighted median	percentage
AF Small Cap	107	2,009	49.4
AM Mid Cap	65	6,795	6.7
Cap. Apprec.	62	67,698	.9

Remy looked up from the memo. He handed it back to the nice woman. Attractive—

"This one is intriguing," she said, and quickly handed him another sheet of paper, a cargo receipt from a Venezuelan ship called the *Sea Cancer.* Listed under the consignee were two companies, including Anderson Dugan Rippet. Remy couldn't understand most of the document. At the bottom was the ship's gross weight, *136.153,320 KG,* and:

Number and kind of Packages, said to contain 06 containers of 40',
said to contain rack with: RH side rail, 5087.117.334 LH side rail,
5087.117.235 (signatore: Selios, March for Anderson Dugan Rippet)

Remy handed the memo back. "You know, that's probably enough."

"Sure, we'll send these over, and anything else we find," she said. "Shawn said you just wanted to have a look at the process."

"Oh, okay." Remy looked around and then bent over to speak quietly to the woman. "Am I supposed to do something with these?"

She nodded. "I know. It's a lot of information to process."

Remy looked around the hangar and cleared his throat at the low buzz of working conversations. He rubbed his mouth. "How many hangars are there like this?"

One corner of the woman's mouth went up in a kind of wry smile. "Is that some kind of test, Mr. Remy?"

"No," he said.

The woman stood. "I understand you spent the morning in Résumés and Cover Letters?"

"Did I?"

"I know what you mean," she said. "It does tend to run together down here. There's one other place." She pulled up her mask and began walking, and, after a pause, Remy followed her down one of the rows of tables. Each table was stacked with mounds of burned and dusty paper: business cards and charts and index cards and company stationery. The workers all wore white paper jumpsuits and gloves. Most of them also wore surgical masks. A few met Remy's eyes, but most concentrated on the paper. Remy and the woman approached the closest end of the hangar.

Above the door was a billboard-sized sign that quoted The Boss: "Imagine the look on our enemies' faces when they realize that we have gathered up every piece of paper and put it back!" There were such inspirational posters and signs all over the place, quoting The Boss and The President. Below this one was a smaller warning sign from the Office of Liberty and Recovery: "Removing unauthorized documents may result in prosecution for treason under the War Powers Act."

The woman paused at a camera above the doorway, in some kind of metal detector, or the kind of merchandise scanners used in clothing stores. She held her hands at her sides. The door buzzed and she passed through. Remy did the same thing, holding his hands out, and was buzzed through the door.

They were in a long dark aluminum tunnel, as if several Quonset huts had been laid end to end. The tunnel made a ninety-degree right turn and ended at a door marked "M.P.D." There was a buzzer and a small white intercom box next to the door. A smaller sign quoted The

President: "Our enemy are haters who hate our way of life and our abil-
ities of organization! We will confound them!" The woman stood in
front of the door, staring at it, but didn't touch the buzzer. She turned
to Remy, who stared back at her.

"Mr. Remy?" she asked, finally.

"Yes."

"You know I don't have clearance beyond this point, right?"

"Oh," he said, and looked at the door again. "Do *I*?"

She laughed, reached out and touched his arm. "You're funny."

"Thanks," he said.

She turned and began walking the other way down the dark tunnel.

Remy watched to see if she'd look back over her shoulder, but she
didn't. Finally, he turned back to the door and pressed the buzzer.

After a moment, the door buzzed and the lock clicked. Remy
waited for just . . . a second and then reached for it. He opened the
door and passed through—

"A DREAM. That's what it seems like to me, like a kind of fever
dream." It was the same voice he remembered hearing when he was in
that bathroom, the tentative woman's voice. She was lying across his
chest, facing away from him, so that all he could see was the whorl of
her dark hair in a warm nest of blankets and sheets on a bed Remy
didn't recognize—hers, apparently. His legs felt tired. He was staring
down at the crest of her dark hair and he could feel the vibration on his
abdomen as she spoke, but he couldn't see her face.

"You know what I mean?" she asked. "The dreams you have when
you're sick . . . or drifting in and out of consciousness, not quite asleep
and not quite awake . . . ?"

Remy leaned sideways, hoping to see around the back of her head
to her face, but all he could see was that tangle of dark hair. Her voice

was low and he could feel it as much as he could hear it. "You're not sure what's real and what isn't . . . the real world intrudes on your dreams, but you can't quite find your way into either world . . . not completely. The phone rings and you stare at it, wondering if you should answer it, or if it's a dream and if you shouldn't bother, if the phone is just going to turn into a cat anyway."

Remy looked around the bedroom. There were two dressers. Hers was a vanity with a mirror on top; on the other side of the bed was a more masculine dresser, a *His* dresser, upright, with a watch tree on top, and some bottles of cologne. Not Remy's watch tree. Not his cologne. There was also a picture in a frame, facedown on the dresser. *The man who's facedown on that dresser probably owns it,* he thought.

"Voices come in and out. People hover above your bed. You open your eyes and real people are silhouetted and this becomes your dream, too—these halos, ghostly figures. You don't know: Are the things they're saying real? Or part of the dream?

"You can't wake up and you can't go back to sleep. Physically, you're in that . . . middle place, moving in the real world while your mind is in a dream."

Remy felt her hand on his thigh and he closed his eyes. "April?" he tried, quietly, a kind of plea.

She made no noise for a moment and he worried that he'd gotten it wrong. "Yes?" she said finally. "What is it, Brian?"

He was just so relieved that this woman's name was April, and that she knew his name, that he could think of nothing to say. Finally: "Do you know what time it is?"

"Eight thirty," she said. "Why? Do you have to be somewhere?"

"I don't know." In fact, he had no clue why he'd asked the time, maybe just to have some real detail to cling to. It was eight-thirty. He looked down at her then, sprawled across his chest. He wished he could see her face. He put his hand on the narrow small of her back and traced the steps of her spine. Her skin was cool and damp. He felt dizzy . . . and he realized he was in love with her, even though he couldn't recall ever seeing her face, and really had no idea who she was.

"Did you ever read the science stories in the *Times*?" she continued. "They always made me feel so lonely. That's what the feeling reminds me of. They're always running stories about some new experiment done in the supercollider, or some new particle of light that's been bouncing around space since the beginning of the universe, without really explaining how they know this. They discover new stars, galaxies exert some effect on some other body, effects they can only determine mathematically, and none of it means anything. It's like that now—like we've all become theoretical, bending light or exerting gravity, but never really touching."

Remy wanted badly to agree with her, but he had no idea what she was talking about. His eyes burned, the flecks rising like ash from a fire. "April . . . I'm losing track of everything," he whispered.

She patted his stomach. "I know."

"It's getting worse."

"I know. You told me."

"Oh," he said. "Good." At least someone knew. He reached out and felt the warmth of her back. "Good."

"Maybe we're *all* like people in dreams now," she said, "aware that something isn't right, but unable to shake the illusion. And maybe we could save each other, but we just drift pass, bending each other, moving through our own dreams like loosed worries."

Remy reached out and stroked—

THE MAN was in his fifties, tall, thin, and aristocratic, with an expensive haircut and braces on his teeth. He wore a golf shirt and khaki pants, the way a man does when he's trying too hard to be casual.

"Well?" the man asked. He was sitting across from Remy. They were at a table in a Starbucks. Remy could hear the steaming of milk behind them.

"Dave? Double caramel macchiato for Dave?" said the barista. Apparently this man's name was Dave because he stood and got his drink. He took a sip as he returned to the table. "Macchiato means mark. They're just supposed to *mark* the latte with espresso. They never do it right." Foam coated the man's braces. He put his hands out, as if he'd been waiting for Remy to say something. "So?"

"So," Remy said.

"What do you want?"

"What do *you* want?"

Dave cocked his head and looked like an expectant professor who's just called on a sleeping student. "What . . . can I do for you, Remy?"

"I guess that depends," Remy said, "on what you can do for me."

Dave looked both confused and intrigued. "I guess," he said, "what I can do for you . . . depends on what you have to offer."

"And what if I don't have anything to offer?"

His face reddened. "Then you're a complete idiot, because you're the one who called this meeting."

Remy was afraid of that. He took a drink of the latte in front of him. Cinnamon. "Okay." Remy looked around for his notebook. "Maybe you could start by telling me what you know about March Selios."

"What *I* know?" The man laughed through his nose and then his eyes narrowed again, became formidable, and it occurred to Remy that this might not be one of his standard interviews. "You really are something, Remy. You want me to tell you what I know about March Selios? Okay. I'll tell you. I know that I requested any documents that related to this Selios woman, and I know your sleazeball handlers over at the DD saw this as an opportunity to fuck us. So, instead of cooperating with the agency—with a real intelligence gathering organization—they rejected our request and decided to launch their own investigation. And I know that since they're all just a bunch of paper pushers, they had to bring in a mercenary—you—to do the actual work."

Remy took another sip of foamy cinnamon as the thin man in braces continued talking.

"I know that they're using this *investigation* to justify their outrageous encroachment on agency turf. And I know they're hanging it all on the notion that this—what, some trampy *import paralegal*—might still be alive, which is laughable."

"Is it?" Remy asked, more suspiciously than he intended.

Dave's eyes narrowed. "Isn't it?"

"I don't know," Remy said.

Dave stared at him. "What do you know, Remy? Do you know something?"

"Probably not."

Dave cocked his head again. "What are you offering, Remy?"

"What makes you think I'm offering something?"

The man sat back in his chair and stroked his solid chin. Remy thought he must have had a beard at one time, because he ran his fingers over his face like a man with a beard.

Finally, Dave smiled. "You'd better not be messing with me, Remy."

"I'm not," Remy assured him.

Dave looked around. "Okay, so you and I stay in touch, outside the official channels? Show a little . . . professional courtesy? Is that what you're saying?"

"I don't know what I'm saying."

The man considered Remy again. Finally, he took another drink of his latte. "Okay. I'm going to give you a little bit of rope. But if you amateurs get in our way on this investigation, I will hang you." He stood up and grabbed his drink. "Do we understand each other?"

Remy took another drink. As the man walked away, he said, "Not so much."

"GONE BUT . . . : A night of one-act, student-written and student-performed plays and monologues," according to the playbill, which was photocopied on folded green paper and had a single firefighter's helmet below the words. Remy arrived late, and sat by himself in a corner fold-out seat in the back row, watching the streaks in his eyes swarm over the low stage lights. He could see Carla and Steve down near the front, Steve's arm around her shoulder. A woman bent and said something to Carla, who nodded and covered her mouth proudly.

The curtain came up with a jerk and the grind of ropes on pulleys and then the stage was bare except for a single light shining on a standup microphone. The first student was a mousy girl in dark jeans who shifted her weight every few seconds and delivered a monologue in which she described being at school that day, having her mother come get her, watching the whole thing on television, and then hearing, later that night, that her uncle hadn't come home from work and was presumed dead. She liked her uncle, although he was really a step-uncle. She explained that he was a bond trader and that he was gay, and that he was the only gay person in her family and that she thought he was the coolest person in the family. She finished by describing a meal that her step-uncle had cooked for the family once, pasta with shiitake mushrooms and sun-dried tomatoes. She vowed that every year on that date, she would eat pasta with shiitake mushrooms and sun-dried tomatoes. The last words of her monologue were, "And the thing is: I hate mushrooms."

The applause was rich and full, and then two thin white boys came out and performed a rap tribute to a dead firefighter who had graduated from the school ten years earlier (". . . y'all seen it on television/them boys packin' some heroism . . .")

And then it was Edgar's turn. There was a thunderous applause that caught Remy off guard, people sitting up in their seats. The woman next to Remy whispered to her husband, "His father," and he nodded sadly. And then Remy's son came out in tousled black hair, in an untucked white dress shirt, apparently having given up the armband. He looked good, if a little thin, but it was odd seeing him down there, in that harsh light. He seemed both smaller and older, and so far away. He sat at a small table on the left side of the stage, where he set up the chessboard and pieces that Remy had bought him when he was a kid. He walked over to the stand, removed the microphone, and returned to the chess table. He was quiet for a long moment, staring at that chessboard.

"My dad taught me to play," Edgar said, and he moved a pawn out. Remy felt a chill, seeing him at the table, playing chess alone. "My dad showed me how all the pieces moved." Edgar moved his knight out to protect the pawn, even though he was playing by himself. "I had trouble with the knight at first. I used to ask, 'Is it two up and one over or one up and two over?'

"'It doesn't matter,' my dad said. 'You end up at the same place.'" There was a low murmur of laughter. Edgar spoke his father's parts in a mock deep voice, and between each line of dialogue he pretended to wait for his opponent to move, then hunched over the board again. But no pieces ever moved on the father's side of the board. "You end up in the same place," Edgar repeated.

"My dad always let me win," he said, and he moved another pawn. "'Boy, you got me again,' he'd say. But one time when I was nine, the weirdest thing happened; it was like the board opened up for me and I could see in all of these directions at once. And I looked up and I knew he couldn't see the board like that. That he'd never be able to see like that. And I beat him. I mean, I really beat him. I beat him fair and square. I think he'd been drinking that day. He drank some, my dad.

After that, he won a game, and then he went back to letting me win. But that one night, I saw fear in his face, fear because he knew that I'd beaten him fair and square. That he had lost to his nine-year-old son."

Edgar brought out his other knight. "My father was a police officer, but he always wanted to be more, so he went to law school at night. But he dropped out before he could finish. He worked for a while as a liaison between the police and city. I asked him once what a liaison was and he said it was the person who was halfway between things. That's how I thought of my dad. As someone who only got halfway to the places he wanted to go. He told me once that he'd always wanted to see the West Coast, but the farthest he'd ever made it was Chicago. I remember thinking, if that's your dream, how hard could that be, to go to the West Coast? It's not like he wanted to go to Tibet, right?"

There was another low murmur of laughter and Remy had to fight the urge to stand up and defend his life. You think there's always going to be time for things like travel, and then, it just gets away from you. But he didn't stand.

"So that was my father," Edgar continued. "And after I beat him at chess, when I looked at him, that's all I could see for a long time—the unfinished half of his life. Maybe that's the life of an adult: You reach a certain age and your life is defined more by the things you don't do than by the things you do."

Edgar stared at the chessboard, one side still unmoved. Finally he stood. "The night my father didn't come home I stood at my bedroom window and wondered what becomes of all the conversations we have with each other, and all the feelings we have, the ones we talk about and the ones we don't. Does everything just . . . evaporate? If one end of a conversation is still there, does the conversation still exist? Or is the whole thing gone the moment it hits the air?"

"People talk about the unconditional love of a parent for a child, but that's not really it. It's really the other way. Parents *choose* to have their kids. No kid ever chose to have his parents. They're just there when you wake up one day. And you can't just keep having sex and have more parents if those two don't work out."

There was a bigger laugh this time. Edgar was killing. He laughed, too, tossing off all the navel-gazing, as if these were the thoughts of a boy. "It always seemed like my dad had something important on the tip of his tongue, something he was just getting around to saying. The night he didn't come home I thought about that. About how we always think of things we wished we'd said.

"I don't know what I'd say to my father. But I know what I *wouldn't* say. This is what I *wouldn't* say: Dad, even when I didn't love you . . . I never wanted you to stop loving *me*."

Edgar put his hands in his pockets for a moment, then removed them and returned to the chess table.

"I never told my dad this, but after I turned nine, I could've beaten him at chess any time I wanted. I let him let me win."

Edgar reached out to take a chess piece and the single light went dark.

HE SAT in the passenger seat of an unmarked, watching the alleyway entrance of a restaurant through small binoculars. The back door was painted black, the window covered with iron bars, empty boxes and garbage cans piled on either side of it. Remy peeked away from the binoculars to the driver's seat, where Markham sat reading a *National Geographic*.

"Anything?" Markham asked. He was wearing a trim beige suit.

Remy glanced down. He was wearing a suit, too, a new one—dark blue. He looked back through the binoculars again. "I don't think so."

Markham turned the page of his magazine. "Hey, Brian, do you know how much time deer spend with their mates?"

"No."

"Try to guess."

"I don't know."

"I know you don't know. That's why I want you to guess. If you knew, you wouldn't be guessing, you'd be telling me, and what would be the point of that?"

"Uh . . . their whole lives?"

"Nope. One day. You believe it? One day. An entire species of animal capable of nothing but one-night stands. Isn't that perfect? I mean, if you're a deer?"

Remy let the binoculars fall to his lap. "I don't know."

"Don't you think deer are kind of sexy? For an animal?"

"I . . . I couldn't say," Remy said.

"I do. Not . . . you know, for me, specifically. I'm not saying I'd necessarily want to have sex with a deer. But just the way they're put together, big asses and long legs, they're kind of like people. And those cute little faces. Shoot, I'd do a deer. I mean, if I was a deer. You know? I can't say that about every animal. If I was a hippo? Nope. Or a raccoon or something? I'd just be celibate. Or a cat? No way. You'd think we'd be more attracted to gorillas or other primates, but other than those little spider monkeys, I just don't see it. But deer . . . I don't know, I find it kind of evocative, the idea of all these bucks nailing those leggy does once a year and then just running off into the woods."

Remy put the binoculars to his eyes again. A man was moving down the alley away from the back door, his back to Remy, carrying a plastic grocery bag, walking toward a car parked in the alley. "Are we looking for someone?"

"Is it him?" Markham said. He grabbed the glasses from Remy. "Yeah. That's him. That's our friend. Let's go."

Markham tossed the magazine in the back. "Don't forget your

briefcase." Remy grabbed the briefcase at his feet and he and Markham hopped out of the car and began run-walking down the alley.

"You want me to do the talking?" Markham asked.

"I think you'd better."

Markham stepped up his pace. "Excuse me. Mahoud?"

Twenty steps away Mahoud turned and stepped away from an Audi convertible. He was thick and bald, vaguely Middle Eastern. He wore a tunic under a black windbreaker.

"Mahoud. I'm Mr. Markham and this is Mr. Remy." Markham offered a badge, which he took, studied, and then handed back.

"How are you, Mahoud?" Markham said.

"I am not good, as you can imagine," he said. "I have reported hours ago this vandalism upon my restaurant and all day I have waited for you to come."

"Yeah," Markham said. "They passed the report along to us. I'm sorry. There are a lot of cases like this, as you might guess. Some of them are pretty serious. We have to concentrate on the ones with violence. Families, children . . . that kind of thing . . . we're up to our assholes in this stuff."

"Families? Oh. Oh my God." Mahoud looked at Remy, his eyes dark and inscrutable. "I had no idea there was violence. Well, look here. Do you want to see the letter? I have it. I was taking it to the police department now." Mahoud opened the bag and showed them a note. In red block letters it read: "Go home, camel-fucker. We know where you live." Paper-clipped to the note was a wrinkled pink triangle of skin.

"Is that a pig's ear?" asked Markham.

"Some jerk's idea of a big joke, yes?" Mahoud said. "Give a Muslim the ear of a pig." He frowned bitterly at the two men. "I can't even look at it, I get so mad. My son is in the American army. My son!" Mahoud's eyes teared up.

Remy stared at the note. He felt sick. Those block letters, that *G*. Jesus . . . he knew that handwriting.

"Yeah." Markham had pulled a notebook from his back pocket. "And I understand they threw a rock through your window?"

"Yes. This note and the ear of the swine were duct-taped to the rock. That window is going to cost me four hundred dollars. Four hundred dollars! And I can't turn it over to my insurance."

"Yeah, that's tough."

"I put up a sign today that said, 'I am Pakistani not Arab!' but do you know what I think? I think I should not have to do that. I think in this country I should not have to explain that I am not a terrorist. I think these things are not anyone's business but my own." He was worked up. He wiped his mouth.

"Yeah, that's tough, Mahoud. I wish there was something I could do, but there are a lot of these harassment cases and . . . frankly, between you and me . . . it's hard to get one to float to the top . . . over just a rock." Markham put his notebook in his back pocket. "In fact, we have to concentrate on the ones where there has been actual violence. As you might expect. I know it's not a lot of consolation." Markham looked over at Remy. "After they hurt someone, we'll come back."

"This is outrageous," Mahoud said. "I am a citizen of this country too."

"No," Markham said. "No, you're right. I mean . . . all I can do is write up the report and put a good word in for you. And after that . . . shit, I'm sorry." He turned to Remy. "Unless you have any other ideas, partner?"

Remy was still staring at the note, trying to figure out how . . .

Markham turned to leave, but hadn't even taken a step when he turned back. "You know what, Mahoud. There is one thing. Maybe I could go in and plead your case to my superiors. See if I can't get some special attention on this."

"You could do that?"

"Yeah, maybe if you were . . . helpful to us in some other area of our investigation, we could take an extra look at this harassment you're getting." He looked at Remy. "What do you think, Brian? Do you think it could work?"

Remy just stared at him.

"Yeah," Markham acted as if Remy had agreed with him. "You still got those pictures, right, Brian? Maybe Mahoud can help with our pictures."

Remy looked down at the briefcase in his hand. He opened it. There were three sheets with six mug shots on each sheet, all of them Middle Eastern men. Remy handed them to Markham and wiped the sweat from his face.

"These are some undocumented aliens that we're trying to find," Markham said nonchalantly. "Some fellas we suspect of not being very good guests in this country. We're . . . showing these pictures to restaurant owners, cab companies, you know . . . see if anyone remembers employing any of these guys. Maybe if you've seen one of them, Mahoud, we can try to get some attention to your situation here. Some peace of mind for your family."

Mahoud looked from Markham to Remy and back again. "I don't understand . . ."

Markham shrugged. "Just look at these. It's probably nothing."

Mahoud looked at the first sheet. "No," he said. "No one." Then he began looking at the second. He looked up, his face red. "This is my brother-in-law, Bishir. The younger brother of my sister-in-law."

"What?" Markham looked up at Remy, then at Mahoud. "Really? Which one? This guy? This attractive fella here?"

But Mahoud didn't show him which one. He looked from Markham to Remy and back again. "I told the other agents who came to my restaurant that I have not seen him in more than a year and my wife has told them the same thing. Four times we have told agents this. Why do you continue to ask if I know where Bishir is?"

"Do you?"

"Do I—"

Markham got serious. "Do you . . . know where Bishir is?"

"No! No. I have told you!"

Markham smiled. "Look, this is just a little mixup. That's all. It's no big deal. We had no idea they'd already shown you this, Mahoud, or we wouldn't have wasted your time. It's not like we're trying to *harass people*." He laughed, strained and high-pitched.

Mahoud took a small step back from the pictures. "Why did you contact me in this alley, instead of coming in the front of my restaurant? Did you not want anyone to see you come here?"

". . . What?" Markham put his hands in his pockets. "Come on, Mahoud . . . don't go all paranoid on us, now. I know you're a good citizen."

"Yes," Mahoud said.

"And that you'd do anything you could to help your country."

"Of course."

"Well, look at it this way. Now you've got your chance."

Mahoud covered his mouth. "Who are you?"

"Listen, there's no reason to get upset. All you have to do is help us find Bishir," Markham looked over at Remy, and then back. He said, in a voice so flat it was barely audible: "Then maybe we can protect your family."

"My God. I don't . . ." Mahoud's voice skipped. "Please!" He took a step back. "Maybe in Miami . . . there were two brothers he . . . knew. Assan and . . . Kamal. The last I heard, one of them was in Miami."

"Okay," Markham said. "Okay." He handed Mahoud the notebook. "Write the brothers' names down. I won't even mention that you gave it to me. Sound good, Mahoud?"

Mahoud scribbled a name on the pad without saying anything.

"I need you to look at one more picture," Markham said. He reached his hand out to Remy, who looked down in the valise and saw another print that had escaped him, up against the side of the case. He pulled it out. It was the picture of March Selios with Bishir. Remy handed it to Markham, who flicked it in front of Mahoud's face. "Remember her, Mahoud? Bishir's girlfriend, March. Do you remember her?"

Mahoud studied the face. "Yes. I think so. About two years ago. Bishir had . . . a lot of girlfriends. They run together."

"Do you know why they broke up?"

Mahoud looked uncomfortable. "I don't listen to wives' chatter. . . ."

"Do you know if he was still in touch with her?"

"No. I have no idea. Look, I have told you . . . Bishir has not contacted my family in more than a year. I am sorry." He said this to Remy, who had to look away. "I cannot help you find him. Or her. I am sorry."

Markham took the picture of March Selios back. "Okay. We're going to check this out. I really appreciate your help. And you won't mind if we contact you to help us out again, right Mahoud? I mean . . . if it means we can protect your family."

"Who are you?" Mahoud asked again.

"Oh . . . one more question," Markham said. "I couldn't help noticing that you have a peculiar dish on your menu. Pecan encrusted sole. Is that a common Mediterranean dish?"

"We have a diverse menu. We also have Thai noodles and pizzas."

"Sure." Markham stared holes in the restaurant owner. "Diverse. Well, we'll have to come in and try your food some time."

Mahoud backed up and then turned and hurried away. Remy and Markham watched him go and then retreated to their car.

"Damn, you're good," Markham said, chuckling to himself. "When you turn on that silent thing . . . it's really chilling. Mute cop, bad cop, huh?"

Remy opened the car door and sat down, trying to catch his breath, trying to remember . . . He felt sick. "Look, I don't think I can do this anymore."

Markham stared at him a moment longer. The alley was quiet, the hum of the city seeming to be blocks away. "Okay," Markham said finally. "Next time I'll throw the rock and you can do the talking."

REMY STOOD on the curb outside his apartment and watched flakes come down from the sky, each one appearing lit from inside, each one like a cold secret. It occurred to him that maybe this snowfall was occurring in his eyes, and even as he quickly dismissed the idea, it seemed eerily plausible, that it could be snowing in his vitreous. He closed his eyes but the flakes were different, the familiar floating of tissue, up and down, flouting gravity; he opened his eyes and it was snowing down again. He felt for the stitches on his head, buried in his stubbled hair. He was about to go back inside when a stretch Town Car pulled up and double-parked in front of his building. The car sat there idling until finally the back passenger window lowered with a whir. Remy stepped closer, edging between two parked cars, to see The Boss's oval face floating in the dark. Remy bent down to look inside and his eyes quickly adjusted. The Boss was wearing a tuxedo, and across from him sat the thick Police Boss, his own tuxedo tight around his neck as if it were a snake and he was a boar it was in the process of swallowing. He was telling some story but stopped grumbling when The Boss held up his hand. There were two other men in the car, one on each side, young guys with little round glasses, each holding a tape recorder.

"Hi, Brian," The Boss said. "I'm sorry I couldn't get here earlier."

The window went up and Remy stepped back as the door opened. The Boss climbed out of the car, followed by one of the young guys with the round glasses. "Let's take a walk," The Boss said, and pushed the door closed behind him. They moved down the sidewalk, shadowed by the stretch, which followed at their heels like an old dog, and the young guy, who walked a few steps behind them, holding out his microcassette recorder.

When Remy looked back at the young guy, The Boss looked over his shoulder at him, too, then he shrugged. "Ghostwriter," The Boss said. The ghostwriter didn't acknowledge the acknowledgment.

The Boss looked back at Remy. "So why don't you tell me what this is all about, Brian?"

He hated when this happened. "I . . . called you?"

The Boss laughed. "Touché. Look . . . I'm sorry it took me so long to get back to you. The first time you called, I thought I should talk to the counsel's office, to find out what . . . we could do for each other while I'm still technically on the public dime. But I'm here now. What's on your mind?"

"I don't know," Remy looked at the ghostwriter again, who didn't meet his eyes. Then he said to The Boss, "I'm not sure . . . this thing I'm supposed to be working on—"

"Wait." The Boss grabbed Remy by the arm and raised his hand as if he didn't want to hear the rest. He nodded at the ghostwriter, who turned off the tape recorder and drifted back a few steps. Then he said to Remy: "Go ahead."

"It's just . . ." Remy struggled. "I'm having a hard time keeping . . . *track* of things. And I may have . . ." Remy looked back over his shoulder at the ghostwriter, who had his hands in his pockets. Remy leaned in close to The Boss. "I may have done some . . . really bad things, sir."

The Boss pointed his finger at Remy's face. "Look, don't you for a minute doubt yourself, Brian. I know for a fact you haven't done anything that wasn't necessary. In fact, I've heard"—he paused— "*unofficially* . . . very good things . . . from the top. Do you understand?"

He mouthed a word that might have been *Pentagon*. "Your resourceful-
ness and commitment, Brian; you are striking a blow for . . . really taking some heroic . . . true leadership . . . showing that we won't . . . I
can't begin to . . ."

Remy rubbed his temples.

"Wait a minute. I think I know what's bothering you," The Boss said.

"You do?"

"Sure. You feel like you're alone."

"Yes."

"You think I don't feel the same thing?" He waved his arm out at
the city. "We took on their fear. And now they think they can do without us? Without us? They think anyone can just step in? After all I did
for those frightened little *fuckers*?" He spat this last word, and then The
Boss coughed. "No." He glanced at Remy and seemed to realize that
he'd shifted the discussion to himself. "They owe us, Brian. This thing
we discovered that day . . . it has real value. It can make fortunes. Win
elections. Wars. This thing . . . it could remake the world. And they
owe us for that."

The Boss looked around, at the quiet buildings. "Meantime, what
does this all mean? That is what you're asking, isn't it?"

Remy wasn't sure. "Maybe," he said.

The Boss veered between parking meters to the limo, which came
to a stop alongside him. The long car seemed to be a living thing,
slithering, a long sleek black lizard guarding The Boss. He opened
the car door and gestured to his ghost, who slid into the backseat in
time to catch the end of an anecdote the police boss was relating
about ". . . three Thai hookers and a bottle of rice wine." The Boss listened for a moment, then walked back onto the sidewalk, until he was
just a few feet from Remy.

"Look," The Boss said quietly. "You need to have faith in what
you're doing. I'm going to give you two simple words to keep you going.

Two words that will give you some sense of where this leads, of what will save you and me, what will save the entire country. And it ain't plastics."

Remy waited for the two words.

"Close your eyes," The Boss said.

"What?"

"Close your fucking eyes, Brian."

Remy hesitated, and then closed his eyes and when he did he saw a kind of captured reality: a black screen with snowflakes falling and streaking, like crawling beasts beneath a microscope lens. Paper falling against blooming darkness.

The Boss said the two words: "Private. Sector."

For a moment, Remy stood with his eyes closed, waiting for something else. He heard a car door close, and when he opened his eyes the limo was pulling away slowly, brake lights blinking once from the corner, their red eyes taking him in one last time before the big car turned a corner and he was gone—

SITTING ALONE alongside a freeway, on the outskirts of a city, in the new FEMA Excursion, staring at a huge sign along the roadside. The Excursion was turned off. Cars were flying past him. He looked all around. There must have been a storm. The roadside was soaked, leaves pasted to the pavement. The sky was dark and seemed porous, like pumice, and Remy could still smell the rain. He looked all around his vehicle but didn't recognize the stretch of freeway where he sat. He appeared to be in the suburbs of some town or city, a row of windbreak trees separating him from a development of homes and a mini-mall. He looked at his watch. Two o'clock. It was light outside. Two in the afternoon. He looked back at the sign, advertising one of the businesses in this mall. The top part was written in script letters: "Pure

Interiors." The bottom half of the sign was a reader board with movable block letters. It read: "God Bless America. New Furniture Arriving Every Day."

In Remy's lap was an open pint of Irish whiskey. His hands were shaking. He took a drink and looked back up at the sign: *God Bless . . . New Furniture.* He stared at the sign until the words threatened to make some sense, then started the Excursion and began driving. He passed two more exits that he didn't recognize, and after a time it was no longer important where he was, and he just drove.

"DO YOU need to hear it again?" The man's voice broke and then steadied, then quavered again. He cleared his throat. "I'm sorry." He wore navy blue pants and a white T-shirt, his clothes dusted with flour, exposing thick, working arms and wrists. He was probably fifty, with a simple, good face, olive-skinned and framed by curly black hair, eyes rimmed with red and pearled with tears. Remy was sitting on a worn, slipcovered loveseat while the man stood above him in this small family room. They were surrounded by family pictures: young adults and children, senior pictures and vacations. Remy recognized March Selios in some of the pictures. The man in front of him, who appeared to be March's father, held a telephone answering machine as if it were a holy relic.

Remy looked down at his notebook. He'd written the words: *I just wanted you to know that.* He'd underlined the words. After that he'd written, *Twenty minutes before.* And *Saying Goodbye?*

"I'm sorry," Remy said. "Maybe play it just once more."

March's father nodded, braced himself, and shuddered as he hit the big black button on the answering machine. A young woman's voice filled the room. "Hi, Mom. Hi, Pop." In a room behind Remy a woman sobbed. "It's March. You must be on your way to work already. Um . . .

I guess . . . I just wanted to talk. I had kind of a . . ." On the machine, March Selios sighed. She sounded troubled. "Okay, well, that's it. I just wanted you to know that I love you both and I . . . I just wanted you to know that. Well . . . bye for now." A hint of sadness at the end, and then a mechanized voice: "Tuesday. Six fifty-eight A.M."

"Thanks," Remy said.

Mr. Selios's face was tracked with tears. He wiped at them like they were mosquitoes he could kill. "She always went to work early, because she was working on things in Europe and the Middle East, other time zones. She called when she knew we had left for the restaurant. I think sometimes that she wanted to talk to us, but she didn't want us to talk to her. We weren't allowed to ask questions about her personal life."

"The phone call was at six fifty-eight—?"

"Yes," he said, "seven, *that* morning . . ." He covered his mouth.

Six fifty-eight in the city that morning. Forty minutes before. Just minutes after the technician said she got the call that agitated her. Minutes before she left her desk.

March Selios's mother, tall and pretty, with a broad face and silver-streaked black hair, came into the room with a cup of coffee. The woman Remy had heard crying in the kitchen. She'd tried to compose herself but her eyes were red and swollen. "Here you are." She set the coffee down on the table in front of him, which was covered with photo albums, school yearbooks, and letters.

"Thank you," Remy said.

He picked up the coffee, and just then the wife fell into her husband's arms.

They held each other, and the woman's shoulders shuddered as she cried. Her husband cried too, but forced himself to do it silently. Remy was caught in the room because they were in the doorway and he was on the loveseat.

"Excuse us a moment," Mr. Selios managed to say.

"Of course," Remy said. "Take your time."

They left the room and Remy rubbed his eyes. He put the note-book back in his pocket and looked around the room. Then he picked up one of the photo albums. There was a family picture: the parents, March, a young boy and another girl, an older sister who looked like a thinner, lighter version of March, pretty and dark-haired and familiar. Had he interviewed the sister and forgotten her? Or was it just that she looked like March? He flipped through the pages and came to the older sister's wedding pictures. March was the maid of honor; the young brother, who shared their dark hair and eyebrows, was a groomsman. He looked at the young bride again.

March . . .

Remy's throat went dry. *April?*

He stared at the picture. It could be, although he couldn't recall her face just now, only the back of her head, the girl he had—April? April Kraft.

He stood and looked around the room. There were pictures of the two sisters everywhere, but none of the back of her head . . . senior pic-tures in front of fanned chairs and phony grottos, candid photos of the two girls in footed pajamas at Christmas. March. April. Was that when they were born? Some new immigrant's trick to make them sound American? And what was the brother's name—June? Remy sat back down and rubbed his temples. Had he slept with March Selios's sister because he'd wanted to, or because he'd wanted information? Was he genuinely interested in her, or . . . he didn't want to consider the alter-native. His throat felt salty and dry.

Mr. Selios came back into the room. "You must excuse my wife. This has aged her twenty years, Mr. Remy. A horrible time for our family."

"Yes." Remy pretended to concentrate on his notebook. "Your other daughter . . ."

"April . . . this has been hardest on her, I would assume, losing both of them."

Remy's head fell back against the couch.

"Unfortunately, April and I . . ." Mr. Selios frowned. "We don't really talk. We haven't for years. She was the first to leave and I said some things . . . I thought this might make her realize . . . but she still won't talk to me. She didn't even come home for March's funeral." Mr. Selios shrugged. "Maybe it was just too much, losing March and Derek the same day."

"Derek . . . her husband?"

"Yes," he said. "They were separated when it happened. He worked in the same building as March. He was a contract lawyer for another firm."

"Derek . . . Kraft?"

"That's right."

"How did they meet?"

Mr. Selios didn't seem to find it odd that Remy had changed the subject to his other daughter. "March introduced them. Her company used Derek's firm for some contracts and she thought he and April would hit it off, I guess." Mr. Selios sighed. "I was furious. I believed Derek was a pushy man with women. Frankly, I did not approve when they married. He was older and too . . . fast. Everything was so fast with him. You have to understand, I did not want my daughters moving to the city, especially April. I was not as worried about March. Even though she was the younger, she always seemed more . . . solid. But I have always worried about April. I didn't like her selling real estate. She is not a salesperson. She has the mind of a poet, too sensitive and . . . aware. Too trusting."

Remy's teeth felt like sandpaper.

"I wanted April to have a man with his feet on the ground, not this slick lawyer, this man who was so fast. So I refused to pay for the wedding and—" Mr. Selios cleared his throat. "April was angry and said that she had never expected me to pay for the wedding. I told her she was disgracing my family." He covered his mouth, but composed himself. "Are you married, Mr. Remy?"

"Divorced."

"Do you have daughters?"

"A son." . . . *who believes I'm dead,* he almost added.

Mr. Selios nodded and looked up at the picture of his own son. "Sons are the devil's payback, yes?"

"Your son . . ."

"Augustus. Gus."

"Yes," Remy said. "Where is he now?"

"He's in . . ." He paused, as if it were too difficult to admit.

Prison? Remy wondered. A cult?

"Entertainment," Mr. Selios said. "He lives in Los Angeles."

"Oh. I'm sorry."

Mr. Selios shrugged. "Yes," he said. "But girls. Ah, girls." The old man's eyes reddened beneath black lashes. "I suppose I was a rash and difficult father to them, Mr. Remy. Even though March still talked to me, she would never think of telling me about her life. Both girls believed that I was . . . disapproving. Old fashioned. And I suppose that I was. I wanted for them . . . what women have wanted for centuries. That's all. Marriage and children . . . I wanted for them to work in the family restaurant, to stay here in Kansas City. Where I could protect them." His head bowed forward. "When March was eight, she used to have nightmares. Every night . . . a dream that she was falling. She would brace and scream and I would run to her bed and hold her and tell her it was okay. Does that sound like a bad father, Mr. Remy? Does that sound like a hard man, a disapproving man?"

"No."

Mr. Selios looked up and wiped at his mouth. "I am desperate to know what happened to her that day. I watch on the TV as long as I can but I always have to turn away. I imagine her curled up beneath a desk, crying . . . or tumbling . . . like when she was little. Every time they show one of those poor people falling . . ." Tears rose and migrated into the stubble on his round cheeks and his voice caught. "I just want to *know* what happened. Maybe it would be too hard to know, but maybe there would be some . . . peace." His voice shattered and he spoke with wavering force, as if pushing each word through a mask. "As it is . . . Mr. Remy, I can't forgive myself for not being there."

"There was nothing you could have done," Remy said gently.

"I could have caught her," he cried. "I would have."

Remy let Mr. Selios compose himself and then he stood. "Thank you for your time, sir." He looked down at the wedding picture in the open album. As he put his coat on, he looked down at a mug shot he'd paper-clipped to his notebook: Bishir Madain. "Do you know this man?"

Mr. Selios looked at the photo. "No. What is his name?"

Remy shrugged. "Bishir Madain. He knew your daughter."

Mr. Selios stared at the picture. "I never heard of him." He sighed. "But as I say, she did not share such details with me."

"Okay." Remy started to put the picture back but Mr. Selios reached out and stopped his hand. He stared at the picture and tears pearled in his eyes again.

Finally he let go of the picture and wiped at his eyes.

"Can I ask one more question," Remy said. "You said April was estranged from her husband when he—"

"Yes," Mr. Selios said. "For a few months, I think."

"Do you know what happened between them?"

"All I know is what March told me . . . that Derek wasn't right for her."

"Was she . . . was April sad?"

"Please." The man's face drained of color. "He was her husband, Mr. Remy."

"Of course. I'm sorry." Remy handed the cup to Mr. Selios and backed out of the room.

*   *   *

THE SOUND of whiskey was what he craved sometimes. Tip a half-full bottle, like this twelve-year-old Jameson, and the bubbles made a tinny gurgle as they ran up the neck into the bigger part of the bottle. And the gurgle got deeper with each tip. He made the sound over and over and the warmth ran through his chest and into his armpits.

It was a shitty little hotel room: two double beds across from a TV on a swivel. The HBO movies for the month were on a card on the nightstand. Someone was watching porn in a room next door, or below; he could hear thumping and synthesized music and metronomic grunting. Remy made the whiskey sound again, got a little less warmth this time, and made his way to the door. It opened outside onto the second floor of a motor hotel, horseshoed around a parking lot with trucks and motor homes and a couple of square sedans. The streaks and floaters were mild out here. It was night but there was a full moon, and Remy could see across the parking lot to a long fallow field that seemed to stretch forever.

Still carrying the bottle he walked along the second-floor railing, down carpeted steps and into the parking lot. The freeway ran behind the motel, and this horseshoe faced away from it, into the flattened field. Remy crossed the parking lot and stood on the edge of the field. Behind him, the hotel was alone against the sky, like a ship run aground. A few trucks rumbled by on the freeway, but before him there was only the lavender sky and the burning hole made by a full moon. A bank of gray-white clouds was on the horizon, a perfect straight line at eye level, like the floor of a stage. The colors ran from black through purple to a bruised red to this gray-white line. Remy had never seen anything like it, and yet there was nothing to it. It was just a set of parallel lines: the line of the prairie and the line of the horizon and the line of the clouds, nothing but lines and the hot pit of a moon, nothing but lines and the flecks in his eyes and the sound of bubbles gurgling through the neck of a bottle.

When he opened his eyes, a man was standing next to him in the parking lot. He was someone Remy thought he recognized, although he couldn't be sure. The man was in his sixties, Middle Eastern, with small, round glasses and a beautiful gray wool coat. He had short gray hair and several days of whiskers on his cheeks. The whiskers and the coat were so mismatched that Remy had trouble imagining them on the same man. They stood at the edge of the field, side by side, staring at the sunset.

"So many countries in this one country," the man said, "nations spilling out into nations, bordered by mountain ranges and great rivers. I sometimes think that people here used to believe that when one country disappointed them, they could simply move west and find another one. But then you ran out of room."

Remy considered the man again. He wore jeans, dirty at the knees, and a black T-shirt, and over it, bizarrely, that beautiful wool coat. He looked so familiar. "I know you," Remy said.

"Do you?" The man looked full at Remy.

"Don't I know you?" Remy asked.

"How could I possibly answer that? I suppose I could answer whether *I* know *you*, but it would be presumptuous of me to say who you know."

Remy couldn't think of anything to say. And even that seemed familiar. "Maybe you can just tell me if I'm east or west of Kansas City."

The man nodded. "Yes. You are."

Remy took another drink and considered the man again. And then it hit him. "No. Wait. I remember. In the city. In front of Ray's. You handed me an envelope."

"No," the man said. "I did not."

"Yes, you did."

"What was in the envelope?" the man asked.

"I . . . I don't know."

"So you're telling me that I handed you an envelope. But you can't tell me what was in this envelope? This is not a very convincing story."

"No, I guess not." Remy stared out at the horizon again.

"You seem troubled."

"Yeah. I am." Remy laughed. "I can't keep track of anything anymore. I slip in and out of my own life."

"Sure," the man said.

"I find myself in these situations. I don't know how I got there, or what I'm doing. I don't know what's going to happen until after it happens. I do things that I don't understand and I wish I hadn't done them."

"Maybe that's what life is like for everyone," the man said.

Remy took a long swig of whiskey. "Is it?"

"I don't know. But what makes you think you're so special?"

Remy considered the man again. "And you're sure I didn't see you in the city?"

"How can I possibly know what you have seen or not seen? How can I know what exists in the frames of your eyes? There are millions of people in that city. Am I to tell you that I have never been one of them? That I have never passed before your eyes? How can I possibly say what you've seen? No man has access to another man's vision."

"I'm going crazy," Remy said.

The man looked at the horizon again. He tapped the bottle in Remy's hand. "They say *this* makes a man crazy."

"Who says that?"

"I don't know. The wise. The sober. People who say things."

Remy handed the man the bottle. "I almost killed myself once." He was surprised to hear himself confiding in the man.

The old man took a swig. "When?"

"Recently." Remy touched the stubble on the side of his head.

"How?" The man took another drink, then handed the bottle back.

"Shot myself in the head." After a moment, Remy laughed. "Isn't it odd that I just told you I tried to kill myself and you asked *when* and *how,* but not *why?*"

"Why?"

"Well." Remy stared at the ground, cast purple by the dye of the fading sun. "I don't really know. At first I thought it was an accident. Or a joke. But I'm starting to think—" He looked at the man, then back down at the bottle in his hand. "—that I was afraid of what I might do if I didn't."

"Yes," the man said quietly. They watched the sunset together. Then, after a moment, the man reached in his coat and handed Remy another manila envelope. And then he walked away, across the parking lot, to a four-door sedan, which he climbed in without looking back.

Remy knew that if he waited long enough, he wouldn't have to open the envelope, that whatever was going to happen would happen. This thought should have been freeing. It probably didn't even matter if he threw the envelope away. But he found himself curious and so he opened it. There was a name, *Assan al-Hafar*—he knew that name, too, *Assan*—and an address for an apartment in a building on something called Treasure Island. Remy looked up, but the man's car was gone, and the next thought he had was—

SLIDING, CLUTCHING, hands and toes clenched, hail streaking behind his eyelids, Remy woke in a gasp of stale air, claustrophobic, strapped in, his face pressed against a cold round window.

He looked around. He was on a dark jet, everyone around him sleeping. He was in a window seat, alone in his row, sitting in coach toward the front of the plane. He sat up and looked around. It was a light load, but all of the passengers seemed to be asleep, curled up on tiny white pillows or holding small gray airline blankets like toddlers with stuffed animals. No one stirred. Remy had heard stories of flights in which the ventilation system failed and everyone passed out and the plane crashed. Honestly, he wouldn't mind; just going back to sleep. He checked his watch. 2:12. Dark outside, so 2:12 A.M. What time zone? Did it matter? Had he set his watch in Kansas City? Or was it on East Coast time?

He frisked himself and finally found a boarding pass, folded and stuffed in his pants pocket. *Miami*. He was going to Miami. On the back of the boarding pass he'd written "Markham" and a cell phone number. He stared at the number for a while, then wadded the paper and stuffed it in the pocket in front of his seat.

A pretty Korean-American flight attendant came by with a cup of coffee and sat in the aisle seat in his row. "I didn't know if I was supposed to wake you . . . if you guys are supposed to sleep or not," she whispered. "But you looked so tired, I didn't have the heart to disturb you."

Remy took the coffee. He wondered: what guys?

The flight attendant squeezed his arm.

"Thanks," Remy said. "You know . . . I don't think I'm supposed to fly. My eyes."

She laughed politely, as if this had been a misfired joke. Then she stood up and walked away, bent over as if walking beneath a helicopter. When the flight attendant was gone, he patted himself and found a plastic case inside his breast pocket. He pulled it out and wasn't entirely shocked to find a badge with his picture, and beneath it, the letters *NTSA*, and the words *Air Marshal*. He put his badge back in his jacket, leaned back in his seat and looked out the window.

REMY HATED the ocean's smell, and the way it burrowed, not only into your nose, but your mouth and your ears, in your whole head. It was like the smell at The Zero in that way, overpowering and everywhere. You took it home with you, and once you smelled it again, it seemed to never have left you. Remy closed his eyes and felt the lurch of the boat as they churned through a rough patch of chop, the shore a narrowing band behind them. The sun was setting back there, too, and he felt a cool blast of sea wind that told him they were chugging toward night. He had the sense of the heat pouring off his skin, as if he'd been warm all day and now was about to get cold. He was in the open-air cabin of a cruiser about thirty feet long, sitting across from Markham, who wore a ridiculous nautical windbreaker and a jaunty cap, both with a gold anchor stitched onto them. He was sniffing at the air like an old captain who'd been away from the sea for years. The only other person on this boat was the man piloting it, a thin Hispanic man, pinch-shouldered, in black jacket and jeans, the smoke from a thick cigar drifting off him like morning fog. Next to the wheel a computerized screen showed their position on a topographical map, and the pilot kept checking it, until finally he turned and gave a toothy smile. "That's it! International waters, my friends!" he yelled. "*Tres Cubanos, por favor!*" He reached beneath his seat and came up with three fat cigars, two of which he offered his passengers.

Remy waved his cigar off, but Markham happily took one. "Can I have yours?" he yelled over the rumble of the motor and the blasts of wind.

Remy nodded, and then closed his eyes and let the wind buffet his face. He imagined that he deserved this, whatever this punishment was. Cigar smoke wafted in the salt air. "Hey!" He yelled to Markham. "Am I an air marshal?"

Markham and the pilot both burst into laughter. "See what I mean?" Markham asked the pilot, who nodded furiously. "Guy's a pro. Every once in a while he just pops off with that deadpan material."

The boat's pilot shook his head in appreciation. "So what do you guys do, back in the world, before all this?"

"Remy here used to be a cop," Markham said. Then he glanced

over, to see if Remy was listening and said, quietly. "And actually, I was an executive chef at a resort in Idaho."

"No shit?" the pilot asked.

Remy closed his eyes again and held them shut for a long time, and when he opened them it was noticeably darker; the sun had fallen behind the thin, faint line of shore. He wondered if a normal amount of time had passed or . . .

Ahead of the cabin cruiser, a larger ship, a small freighter, bobbed on the water. It may have been an old fishing boat, or maybe a ship used for canning, the hull rusted and lightly pocked with barnacles, its profile growing as they approached it, a ketchup-red stripe just at the waterline.

They came abreast of the bigger ship, and in the dusky light Remy could see a rope ladder hanging off its inky black side. The pilot of the cruiser cut his motor and they drifted up against the freighter, their boat maybe an eighth its height, the hulls slapping together like someone smacking his lips. "Thanks, Chuck," Markham said. "We should be right back. Wait here." Markham hoisted a small pack on his shoulder, then grabbed the rope ladder and started up. Remy followed him, hands gripping the wet ladder, and swung over the railing onto the abandoned deck of the larger ship, which was about eighty feet in length, with a two-story cabin and stairs leading below. There was no one up top, although Remy could see in the bridge where a coffee cup sat next to the wheel.

The deck lilted back and forth on the light swells as they made their way toward the stairs. Remy peered below into the narrow staircase leading to a hallway, lit by bare bulbs strung along the wall. At the top of the stairs, Markham turned. "Okay. We all set?" He didn't wait for an answer, but grabbed the railings and began lowering himself down the stairs. After a moment, Remy followed.

The hallway was too narrow for both of them to fit, so Remy followed Markham's back as he made his way the length of the ship, past the closed, rounded doors of cabins. Remy couldn't place the smell down here, or rather he couldn't separate the blend of smells: sweat and salt and cigarette smoke and strong coffee. Finally, Markham paused in front of a white metal door, turned the handle, and stepped inside. Remy followed and they entered a long, narrow compartment, with chipped paint on the walls and a low, flaking ceiling, all of it illuminated by a bright, bare bulb in the center. There was no furniture, just a metal pole parallel to the ground, like a banister, or a high ballet bar, stretching the width of the room, about five feet off the ground. Remy gasped.

There, on the bar, a man was perched like a trophy, hanging forward, his arms tied behind his back and slung on the bar so that it held him by the armpits, his feet against the wall dangling a few inches from the floor. The man was wearing nothing but a pair of tight red briefs and one white sock. It was cold and clammy in the room and his thick chest hair was wet and matted. A bucket of water sat below his feet. His shoulders and clavicles rose to points well above his head, which hung limply, bushy black hair dripping wet. Two other men were leaning against the opposite wall, bored-looking young men in jeans and plain sweatshirts, with short haircuts, standing guard, laughing at a private joke.

"Hey, fellas. You takin' a break?"

"We thought we should save you some. Guy's an hour from being jerky." One of the big guys walked over, got a tin cup out of the bucket, and threw water on the man's face. His head rose slowly. Remy could see cuts on his cheeks and forehead and his lips, and guessed it was salt water they'd thrown on him. The man looked around wildly, his eyes finally settling on Remy, who had to look down at the ground. Markham nodded to the two men in the room and they backed out, leaving just Remy, Markham, and the young Middle Eastern man hanging by his arms. Remy could hear steps in the hallway, then on the stairs leading back up top.

Markham stepped up to the man. "Hey there, Assan. My name's Doolittle." He pointed at Remy. "And this is Poppins. Do you know why we're here?"

Assan just stared.

"Because your name showed up on some checks, Assan. Some big checks."

"My brother asked me to write those checks. Years ago. I told the other guys—" Assan began.

"The *other guys?* Those other guys are pansies, Assan. They can't close the deal. Have you been in America long enough to know what happens when a used car dealer goes to get the manager to close the deal? Well, that's us. We're the closers. So what's it gonna take to get you to drive off the lot today, huh?"

"What?" Assan looked around wildly.

"What's it gonna take for me to get you down and pitch you overboard?"

Assan shook his head no.

"See, those other guys, Assan? They're just interns. We're the partners at the firm. They're the JV. We're the varsity."

"P-please . . ." Assan's lips were caked with white scum. He spoke with a faint accent, falling a bit heavily on the consonants. "Please . . . I have done nothing wrong." He struggled against the bar and fell back.

"You hear that?" Markham turned to Remy. "Assan's done nothing wrong." He turned back to the man. "So what. You always tip fifteen percent, never cheat on your taxes, always pick up your litter? Is that what you mean, Assan?"

Assan's bottom lip quivered as he looked from one man to the other.

"Are you some kind of police?"

"No. We're no kind of police."

Assan's voice cracked. "This is wrong. I was taken . . . from my home. At night. I have not been charged. This is . . . not right. It is illegal. I demand to speak to a lawyer."

"I'm a lawyer," Markham said. "He's a lawyer. The guys you were playin' with before? Lawyers. Captain of the ship is a lawyer. Hell, everyone in America is a lawyer, Assan. I'd have thought you'd know that by now."

He struggled on the bar.

"I'll tell you what, Assan. The next civil rights lawyer I see on this boat I'm going to send in here. Okay? Now . . . why don't you tell me why your name shows up on checks to Bishir Madain?"

"I have . . ." Assan's cracked lips slid back over bright teeth, his head fell forward and he began crying, like a child. ". . . explained . . . my brother is in Saudi Arabia. He used to raise money for Islamic studies. He worked with Bishir on a program with exchange students."

"I don't care about that, Assan." Markham got closer, until his voice was hardly more than a whisper. "I care about one question. Answer one question and it gets better. Where is Bishir?"

"I told them . . . I do not know where Bishir is."

"You haven't told *me*, Assan."

He looked up, took short, shallow breaths, and said: "I have no idea where Bishir is. I promise you! He is my brother's friend. I have not seen him in more than a year. I swear it. Now, *please!*"

Markham turned to Remy. "Wow. That's pretty convincing. What do you think, pardner? Is Assan telling the truth?"

Remy felt the boat lurch and then fall back. His mouth tasted like salt and bile. He tried to say something, but there was nothing.

Suddenly Assan struggled against the bar, his feet running in place, his head swinging back and forth. After this burst, he roared at the ceiling: "There are laws!"

"True enough." Markham nodded to the stern of the ship. "Two hundred yards west of here, anyway. But out here—"

Assan's head fell again.

There was a knock on the door. Markham stepped away from the prisoner and listened as one of the guys whispered something in his ear. Then Markham approached Remy, walking like John Wayne. "What do you think, pardner?"

"I don't believe this," Remy said. "We can't do this . . ."

"Yeah, yeah. I know. It's sloppy. My apologies. I'm gonna go up deck and find out if this asshole said anything useful before. I'll be right back. You watch him."

Remy watched Markham open the white metal door and listened to his footfalls in the hallway outside and on the steps leading back above deck. The walls seemed to leach salt. Finally, Remy moved.

Assan's skin was cold and clammy. "Come on," Remy whispered. He lifted the man off the bar and lowered him to the ground, removed his own jacket and put it around Assan's shoulders. "You're going to be okay." The man stunk like urine and sweat.

Assan lay in a pile on the floor, his back shuddering as he cried. His hands were bound with a zip-tie. Remy found a pocketknife in his front pants pocket and cut the plastic off his wrists. Assan opened and closed his fists.

"Thank you—" Assan began.

"We have to go fast," Remy said. "Come on."

He draped Assan's arm over his shoulder and pulled the smaller man through the door, edging sideways down the hallway. When they reached the stairs Remy peered up, but he didn't see Markham or the other two. He wasn't sure what he was going to do once they got above deck. He didn't think he had a weapon. He patted himself down—nothing but the pocketknife. "Wait here," he whispered to Assan.

It was dark now, the night sky lit with stars and a three-quarter moon. Remy emerged from below deck and looked around. He counted four silhouetted heads in the pilothouse, and guessed they wouldn't be able to see out into the dark. He reached back and grabbed Assan by the armpits. He winced again as Remy lifted him through the opening. The air was cool and briny. They crept along the deck, with the creak of the tight, wet planks beneath them and the smack of small waves against the side, until they reached the rope ladder, still slung over the stern of the ship. Remy looked down. Chuck, the pilot of the cabin cruiser, was sitting on the back of his chair, working another cigar. "Follow me!" Remy whispered to Assan, and began lowering himself over the edge of the freighter.

"Where's Shawn?" the pilot of the cabin cruiser asked Remy when he'd dropped down into the smaller boat.

"He's gonna stay a while. He wants us to take this guy back to shore."

"Doesn't the guy have any clothes?"

"He fell overboard," Remy said. "They're all wet."

If the pilot registered the strangeness of this he didn't show it. "Am I supposed to come back for Markham?" he asked.

"First thing tomorrow morning," Remy said. "They're having a party."

The pilot stared at Remy for a long time before shrugging. "Okay."

Remy helped Assan down the last steps of the rope ladder and then pushed him down onto the floor of the boat and covered him with the jacket.

He pushed off and they drifted away. The smaller boat started with a lurch, and soon they were speeding off. Remy looked over his shoulder. He could see the men still in the wheelhouse of the bigger ship, apparently looking the other way. Only now did Remy notice how quickly his heart was beating, how short were his breaths.

Remy crouched down on the floor of boat Assan was sobbing. He rearranged his jacket on the shaking man.

"It's okay," Remy said. "You're gonna be okay."

Assan grabbed his wrist. "Listen to me. I don't know where Bishir is. I swear. You've got to tell them. I barely knew him . . . in his dress and speech, he is very . . . American." Assan shrugged. "I hadn't heard from Bishir until maybe two years ago, when he suddenly contacted me."

Remy's voice was hoarse over the churn of the boat motor. "What did he want?"

"He had gotten my name from Kamal. He was raising money for charity from American Muslims. He wanted me to donate."

"Did you?"

"Yes. A little. I told the men on the boat this. But I have not spoken to Bishir since that day. I swear it." The boat jumped against the edge of some bigger swells and the pilot turned to angle across the chop. Remy stood and looked back over his shoulder, but he could see nothing in the dark. Not even the lights from the larger ship. He lowered himself to the deck to talk to Assan again. He caught the man's imploring black eyes.

"The thing about Bishir—" Assan chewed his bottom lip.

"What?" Remy asked.

"I don't want to get my brother in trouble . . . he and Bishir shared a fondness . . . for American women. Especially Bishir. More than his family, more than anything, I think sometimes, he liked these women. Kamal said he had a name for them . . ."

"What?" Remy asked.

"Vines."

"Vines?"

Assan looked embarrassed. "Tarzan, yes? You know the movies? Bishir said that a man in America could swing from vine to vine here without ever touching earth."

"Is that where you think he is . . . with one of these vines?"

Assan rubbed his temple. "I remember my brother once stayed with one of Bishir's women. In Virginia. Near Charlottesville. A divorced woman. Very wealthy. Bishir considered marrying her at one point. He would stray with other women and then come back to her. He was see-ing a young woman in New York—"

"March Selios," Remy muttered.

"Maybe," he said. "Kamal told me that Bishir genuinely cared for this woman, but that the woman in Virginia had a great deal of money, and when he got bored he would always return to her."

"Do you know her name?"

"Herote." Assan spelled it. "I don't know her first name." Remy put his hand in his coat pocket. There was a pen right next to the pock-etknife; he tried not to dwell on the significance. He pulled out the pen and wrote on his hand: "Herote. Virginia."

The air was cold now and Assan was shaking harder. Remy put his hand on the smaller man's shoulder. "It's okay. You're going to be okay." He lifted his head to look forward through the windshield of the cabin cruiser, to see if he could spot the shoreline. Instead, bobbing three hundred feet away, he saw the cabin lights of a ship.

As the cabin cruiser slowed, Assan lifted his head and cried out when he saw what Remy was staring at: the ship they had just left. Markham was standing halfway down the rope ladder, his arm hooked in it, smiling. The other two men were leaning over the side of the boat, holding bottles of beer.

Assan slumped back to the floor and began crying.

The cabin cruiser slowed and pulled up next to the ship. Markham lowered himself the rest of the way and plopped down on the floor of the smaller boat. "How was your ride, Assan? Did you get some fresh air?"

Markham fastened another pair of plastic zip-ties on Assan's wrists, pulling them tight and cuffing the man's hands in front of him-self. A rope was lowered from the ship and Markham looped it around the cuffs, tied it, and then tugged on the rope. Assan was jerked from the boat, his arms above him, dangling like he was being hanged.

Remy rubbed his eyes. He would have liked to be more surprised. He watched as Assan was pulled up, banging against the ship, and then finally slipped over its side onto the deck like a huge fish.

"You're right," the driver said to Markham. "This guy is good." He looked at Remy with something between respect and fear. "Scary good. He had me convinced."

"So . . . you get anything?" Markham asked.

Remy felt sick. He showed Markham the writing on his hand: *Herote. Virginia.*

"So Assan *was* holding out on us." Markham bowed in front of him in worship. "I was dubious, but damn if that didn't go just like you said it would."

"Is he gonna be okay?" Remy asked.

"Oh, sure," Markham said.

"I'm serious. You need to let him go."

"Of course," said Markham. Then he smiled and turned back for the rope ladder. Remy slumped down in the seat on the cabin cruiser. The pilot offered him another Cuban cigar, and this time Remy took it. He leaned back, closed his eyes and listened to the waves lapping against the side of the boat, and even though he wished as hard as he could, for once, time was still.

PART TWO

Everything Fades

APRIL STARED DOWN AT HIM, eyes flitting over his forehead, and then drifting down to his chin, back up to his eyes and down again, as if she were measuring each feature of his face, comparing it to some face in her memory. But there was an expectant look in her eyes, too, and he saw that she was waiting for the answer to a question. This happened sometimes now—people waited for answers to questions he didn't recall them asking—and he struck his contemplative pose. "Hmm," Remy said.

She waited. He was lying on his back and she was crouched over him, breathing softly, naked from the waist up. He glanced down at her lovely jutting collarbones, at her cupped breasts and the flat plain of her lovely stomach. Before this moment he could only recall brief glimpses of her—strobe flashes of her face, an arm, a thigh—and so it amazed him to see her so fully, to trace the narrow, lovely terrain of her body. She wore plaid pajama bottoms and nothing else, and he kept thinking that word: lovely. She stared at him inquisitively, as if trying to read him in a poker game. "Hmm," he said again.

"It's not a test." She laughed at him. "It's a simple question."

"Right. What was it again?"

"I said . . . do you want to know what I hate?"

"Oh. Yes."

April rose and flopped across his lap, so that she was facing the other way. She slapped at the newspaper, which was at that end of the bed. "This." After a second, Remy sat up. She had the Sunday *Times* spread out at his feet. He was shocked by the date—could so much time have passed? Could he account for all of those days?

"You hate the newspaper?" he asked.

"No, not the paper. I hate this page." She held up the *Portraits in Grief* page, where the *Times* ran little cross-section obits of the people who'd died that day—four or five every day, presumably until their inventory ran out. "I hate the way I read this page now," she said. "It's the same way I used to read the wedding announcements. When I first moved to the city I didn't know anyone and I'd read the weddings like someone trying to learn a language. I'd look for people I knew—maybe someone I went to school with, or someone I met at a party, someone I sold an apartment to. Then I'd look for attractive people. Where they went to school, where they vacationed, where their parents lived, where they went to college. Like an entire life could be captured in a paragraph. I'd imagine my life in a paragraph: grand ceremony, two sophisticated families coming together, a romantic honeymoon, the couple going back to their fascinating jobs. *The bride plans to keep her name.* It filled me with such jealousy and self-loathing." She swallowed. "That's how I read these portraits now. Don't you think that's crazy?"

"I might not be the best judge," Remy said.

"Of . . ."

"Crazy."

"I don't mean crazy, I guess. I mean shallow."

"You're not shallow."

"How do you know that?"

Remy had no answer.

April turned back to the newspaper. "Reporters still call me all the time." She folded the paper. "They come across so caring and compassionate; 'It must have been horrible to lose two people in one day.' I say, 'Oh. Do you think?' I put them off . . . say I don't want to talk about it yet. 'Maybe later.'"

"Why don't you want to talk about it?"

"You don't talk about it," she said, "what happened that day."

"I don't really remember it."

"Oh," she said. "I remember it." She looked away, at the place where the floor met the wall. "Lawyers call, too. They're even more persistent."

"What do *they* want?"

"A third." She looked back down at the newspaper again. "It just surprises me, I guess. Afterward, I really thought that everything would change . . . I don't know . . . that we would be different. Stores would never open again . . . businesses shut down . . . lawyers quit their practices and run into the woods." She smiled wistfully. "I just assumed the newspaper would stop coming out. Instead . . ." She chewed a thumbnail. "This whole thing . . . it just became another section in the paper. Like movie reviews. Or the bridge column."

Remy looked up at the dresser in April's bedroom, to see if the picture she'd kept up there was still facedown. Her husband. Derek. But his picture was gone.

April was staring at the newspaper, and seemed to be choosing her words with great care. "I just don't know how we all got so . . ." And then she stared off again, as if the rest of the sentence were somewhere out the window.

"So . . . what?" Remy asked.

"Used to it," she said.

April looked back, one breast peeling off the comforter so that he could see a dark nipple. His eyes traced her neck and her face: dark, serious eyebrows arched over candy brown eyes. She watched him staring at her. "What?" she asked.

"You're beautiful."

"You always say that like it's the first time you've ever seen me."

"It is," he said.

She turned back to the paper again and read for a few seconds.

"Here. Look at this woman." April slapped the paper. "Allowed herself to be cut in half by a magician for her twin granddaughters' birthday party. I mean . . . that's so . . . what? Funny and ironic and sad and wonderful. Everything. I don't know what to feel about that. How are we supposed to feel about that?"

"Alive?" Remy asked.

"Well, I'm tired of feeling like that."

She reached back with her hand and rubbed his thigh and Remy thought that maybe he could take this skidding life, as long as he landed here sometimes, in this nest of bedding in April's apartment, glancing down at her body, at her slender back and notched waist. He wondered if this could be enough, if this could tether him, the pressure of another person against his skin. Remy wanted to say something, about *them*, or *her*, but he found it impossible because he had no idea what had already been said. Maybe that was normal, too. Maybe every couple lived in the gaps between conversations, unable to say the important things for fear they had already been said, or couldn't be said; maybe every relationship started over every time two people came together.

She hit the newspaper again. "Or this guy. Bought a vintage motorcycle for himself when he turned twenty-two. Rode it across the country and camped in the Canadian Rockies for a month to shoot photos of migrating geese. Jesus. Who does that?"

April turned to face him again and her long dark hair pooled in his lap. Remy recalled the pictures of March. Her face was wider than April's, and darker. Their father was right: even though she was older, April seemed younger and frailer than her younger sister had been.

April's eyes narrowed then as if she were thinking the same thing. "So . . . do you ever think about what yours would say?"

"My—" Remy opened his eyes.

"Your portrait in grief. They're not like obits—see. They're not résumés or tributes. They're more like crosscuts, a strobe flash on one part of your life. One moment. One theme. So what would yours say?"

"I don't know," Remy said.

"I know what mine would say."

"What?"

"She saw death as just another wedding she wasn't invited to."

"AND DO you see them now?" The voice was calm, almost to the point of being alarming.

"See what?" Remy asked. His eyes were closed and he was sitting on a soft couch somewhere. He felt with his hands. A leather couch.

"These . . . what did you call them . . . floaters? Flashers?" the calm voice asked. "Can you see them now, with your eyes closed? Yes? Are they here? Are they with us?"

The calm voice made Remy increasingly anxious and he crossed and uncrossed his legs. "Sure. They're always here. I get used to 'em, but they're always here."

"Describe them. What do they look like?"

"Strings. They look like strings."

"Strings."

"Right. Little segmented strings."

"Strings?" The man sounded intrigued.

"Yeah. I said. Strings."

"And do these strings tie you to the world, Brian? Is that what they do? Are these ropes binding you, or holding you down? Are they keeping you from being who you long to be?"

"No. Not ropes. Strings." Remy opened his eyes. The man across from him was in his late forties and balding, wore narrow blue-rimmed glasses and had pursed lips like someone sucking a milk shake through a straw. He had a yellow pad of paper open on his crossed leg. The nameplate on his desk read: Dr. Rieux. They were in a small office in an old building, an office with nothing but a desk, a chair, and the couch where Remy sat, his arms at his sides. The rest of the room was taken up with bookshelves, a framed diploma, and a cartoon poster of a boy fighting a huge dragon, the dragon huddling in fear as flames burst from the little boy's nose.

"Isn't this what your strings are?" Dr. Rieux asked. "Aren't these the tethers that keep you from floating away?"

Remy looked back at the psychiatrist. "No. They're little pieces of tissue floating in my eyes. My ophthamologist says they're floating in the gel inside there, the vitreous humor. The tissue surrounding it is shredding. He's worried it could eventually lead to the retinas detaching."

"Oh. Retinas." The psychiatrist was noticeably deflated. "Huh." He frowned and flipped through his notes. His voice lost its smoothness. "Okay, what else have we got?"

"Well," Remy said, "there are the gaps."

"The what?" Dr. Rieux didn't look up from his notes.

"I'm having gaps."

"You're having what?"

"Gaps," Remy said. "I'll be doing one thing and suddenly—"

"EVERYTHING FADES after a while," Guterak was saying. "Maybe that's all it is." His pool table was heavier than it looked. Remy waited at the top of the stairs to see which direction they were going—in or out. Paul pushed. Okay. They were taking the table out. Remy strained under the weight as he backed it down the wide staircase.

"I mean, it couldn't last forever, right?"

"I don't know," Remy said. Even though it was a small one, and even though the legs were taken off, the slate top was massive and unwieldy, like moving a slab of concrete, like moving a driveway.

"At first, the whole thing felt like a break from the world, like a fuggin' snow day," Paul said. "Remember? You know, when you were a kid and it snowed so much they closed the school? Remember those days?"

"Yeah," Remy said, struggling against the pool tabletop. "Kind of."

In the kitchen, they turned the tabletop sideways, grunting and huffing. Paul kicked away a plastic football, but it hit the counter and rolled right back in his way. "Just a sec. Hold up." Paul set his end down to move the ball. Remy looked over at the Guteraks' refrigerator, which was littered with paper: school lunch menus, report cards, pictures of friends' kids, even a picture of Edgar. The kitchen had a vague, stale smell, and Remy imagined a crust of bread wedged beneath the dishwasher, or an orange rind behind the fridge. Finally, they got the pool table through the back sliding door and loaded it onto the bed of Paul's black pickup truck, next to boxes of tools, a television, a dresser, and an ice chest. Paul went back in for the legs of the pool table as Remy stood outside, watching a checkmark of birds dissolve into an ashen sky.

"I really appreciate you helping me," Paul said when he came back out with the last two legs. "I know I keep saying that."

"It's okay," Remy said.

"I just feel bad. Here you are, your back and eyes too fugged up for you to work anymore, and I make you carry all this heavy shit."

"My back's fine, Paul. And my eyes—" Remy closed his eyes and saw paramecia swimming in the diffuse light. He opened them and the world became faded and flat again, filled with static as in an old movie.

They went back in and Remy followed Guterak upstairs, to the bedroom, which was littered with Paul's jeans and wrinkled button shirts. He piled hangered shirts, jackets, and pants on Remy's arms and they started back down the stairs.

"I tell you what happened last week?" Paul spoke over an armful of jackets.

"I don't know."

"I got a call from an agent," Paul said. "Out of the blue. A talent agent. The Boss's guy. Big sloppy bug-eyed fugger who helped him get his movie deal. Guy specializes in stories about that day, right? He says The Boss wants me taken care of, so I take him on a tour a The Zero and tell him my whole story and he says I got one of the best he's heard. Says I pitch it good, too. Money in the bank. He says there's gonna be all kinds of entertainment possibilities. TV shows are starting to . . . what did he call it . . . *stockpile material.* It's going to be a while before anyone writes directly at it, but there's lots of what he called *subtext.* And he said I could get gigs in the meantime."

"Gigs?"

"Sure. Appearances and shit. Malls. Boat shows. Parades. They're looking for cops and smokers to cut ribbons and salute flags and throw out pitches and read poems and shit. The agent says I'll do gigs until the movie market matures for my kind of story. He says everything goes through this cycle of opportunity: first inspirational stories, kids and animals, shit like that; then the backdrop stories, he called it the home-front . . . and then the big money—thrillers."

"Thrillers," was all Remy could think to say.

"Oh yeah. Guy says it's all about thrillers now, says history has be-come a thriller plot." Paul shrugged. "After thrillers come anniversaries: five years, ten, and the real money—" Paul dragged it out, took a long drink of coffee. "Nostalgia."

"Nostalgia?"

"He said a story like mine is like owning a good stock. And that nostalgia is like the moment my little company goes public. So, after he goes through this whole explanation of everything, guy asks, do I wanna sell my stock? Do I wanna sell him my experiences?"

"What'd you tell him?"

"I said, 'Bet your ass I'll sell my experiences. I sure as hell don't want 'em anymore.'" Guterak threw the clothes into the back of the truck. "You want me to see if they want yours, too?"

"My . . ."

"Your experiences."

"No. That's okay. I'll hold onto mine."

"Hey, if you change your mind . . ." Guterak said.

They finished loading Paul's pickup truck and climbed into the cab. It smelled like cigarette smoke, but otherwise it felt nice, sitting in a truck with Paul. It was like being a kid, Remy thought, riding in a car with no idea where he was going, no expectation of how long the trip would take, just the sun fluttering between buildings.

They turned a corner and Remy looked back to make sure the tarp was tied down and that's when he noticed a beat-up silver Lincoln behind them, probably fifteen years old. It looked like a gypsy cab, but it had two guys in front. That seemed strange to Remy. Gypsy cabs never had two guys in front. Paul turned the truck twice more and the car stayed with them. At a stoplight, Remy adjusted the side mirror and got a good look at the two men in the car. The driver was a white guy with a mustache, wearing a ball cap, staring straight ahead. The passenger was a heavyset black guy, also staring straight ahead. He looked over at Paul, who didn't seem to notice the car behind them.

Paul was rambling about women. "And do you know why? Because they don't really want what they say they want. Look at Stacy. Spends twenty-two years riding my ass: *Why don't you tell me what you're thinking? Why don't you talk?* Then when I finally decide to start talking, she says I won't shut up."

Remy looked behind them. The gypsy cab was still there.

Paul stopped at a diner. As he got out, Remy watched the car tool slowly past, the driver—the thick guy with the mustache—glancing in Remy's direction and nodding. Remy followed Paul inside and they took a booth in the corner. They got a couple of coffees. Paul ordered hash. Remy ordered huevos rancheros. He watched the door.

Paul lit a cigarette. "I tell you they divided The Zero into quadrants?"

"No."

"Yeah, each quadrant is under a different bucket company. The fuggin' hard hats are pushing us out. They wanna work faster. Snow days are over, man. Even the smokers—they want those poor shits out, too. But they're havin' trouble there. The smokers are in no fuggin' mood. Some of those guys are total pricks, showboats, like the fuggin' Yankees of grief, you know? But . . . I hate to admit it . . . I know how they feel. I mean, after a while . . . you start to feel like it's *yours*. Like you own it."

Remy drank his coffee.

"You remember that night, Bri? When we went back down there, afterward? You remember that? How quiet and spooky it was?"

"Not really. No."

"All of those black smoking shapes . . . and the searchlights and the glow from the fuggin' fires . . . and you couldn't see the end of it. It was like goin' someplace where people had never been, like some dark jungle. Remember? You'd be on a street, but all of a sudden it wasn't a street any more . . . you take five steps and you're in some place you can't imagine, like some hole in a kid's nightmare. I couldn't believe the next morning, how gray it all was. That night it really seemed black to me." Guterak rubbed his scalp.

"Here's what gets me," he went on. "Remember, the first morning, the flatbed trucks were already there? They took a hundred-some trucks to Fresh Kills. *On the second fuggin' day, Bri!* From the beginning they were already cleaning up the mess . . . before they even knew for sure what it was. I mean . . . what is that? Is that right?"

"I don't know," Remy said.

"You wanna know what I think?" He looked over his shoulder, and then leaned in closer to Remy. "I think the bosses knew all along that we weren't gonna find anyone. I don't think they cared. They wanted to clean it up fast, but they had to pretend that they expected us to find people. Right? All along they're saying, *We will not rest until blah-fuggin'-blah* and *There is still fuggin' hope,* and all the time what they're really thinking is *we gotta move a million tons of shit before we can rent this fugger out.* I mean, how do you move a million tons? You should see it. It's like a strip mine down there. Like we're digging for something."

The words sounded familiar and disturbing, and Remy badly wanted to end this line of conversation. He excused himself to go to the bathroom. He walked past the counter and into the men's room. He stared at himself in the scratched mirror, through his scratched eyes. Behind him, one of the urinals was overflowing, with the insistent sound of running water. Remy went into a stall, closed the door, undid his pants and sat, his head in his hands.

A few seconds later, the door to his stall flew open.

"Hey! Do you mind?" Remy looked up and saw one of the men from the gypsy cab, a heavy guy with a crooked mustache, teardrop sunglasses, and a baseball cap that bore a single word in block letters: BUFF.

"Have you had time to consider our offer?" the man said.

"I just sat down," Remy said.

"We're not going to interfere in your work, if that's your concern," the man said. "All we're asking is that you show us a little . . . professional courtesy. Keep us in the loop. And, in return, the Bureau keeps you informed about what we find. Cooperation. That's the key, am I right?"

Remy felt strangely compliant, hunched over in a stall with his pants at his ankles, and this thick man blocking the door to the stall. "Yes," he said. "Sure."

"Outstanding," said the man in the BUFF hat. "See? We're cooperating. Easy as that." He put two fingers to his temple and then tipped the fingers toward Remy. "I'll be in touch."

The man was gone before Remy managed to say, "That's not necessary."

Remy finished his business and came out of the stall gingerly, looked around, washed his hands, had to dry them on his pants because there were no towels, and returned to the restaurant edgily, looking around for the man from the gypsy cab. He didn't see anyone. When he got back to the table, Paul was chewing his hash. He pointed his fork at Remy, as if he'd been waiting to finish his sentence.

"Look, Paul," Remy said, "I'm not sure we should be talking about this stuff."

But Guterak couldn't stop. "We don't do many tours anymore. Too many people. They're building a goddamn observation platform. Like it's the Grand Fuggin' Canyon. They got these apartments overlooking The Zero donated for the rescue workers, and the bosses are using 'em for parties, to bang their girlfriends and hand out drinks to celebrities. Billionaires and soap actresses. The whole thing looks different now. Every day, they take shit away and it just never comes back. Take it to Fresh Kills and squeeze it like orange juice until all the paper and blood comes out and then they go back for another truckload." He spoke in a low groan. "They're gonna take it all away, Bri. All of it. The paper gets filed, bits of flesh buried, and you know who gets the steel? The mob. Goddamn bosses give all the steel to the mob. Everyone gets a piece a this thing."

"Listen to me, Paul. You shouldn't talk like this. Okay?" Remy scanned the restaurant for the man from the gypsy cab. "You have to be careful. You need to be quiet."

"Yeah," Paul said, "that's what this agent of mine says. He says every time I open my fuggin' mouth I give away what we could be getting paid for. *You only got one story,* he says, *you have to protect it.* So I promised him I'd shut up." Paul shook his head. "But sometimes I think it's crazy we don't talk about this shit. Sometimes I think it's crazy that we aren't standing up and yelling about it."

"Paul—" Remy began.

"I just wanna tell 'em, *'Leave it!'* You know? Leave the shit. Everything. The piles and mounds. What's the fuggin' rush? Let me and the smokers spend the rest of our lives going through it one piece at a time if we want."

The waitress filled their coffees.

"Maybe you should see someone," Remy said quietly. "A therapist."

"A what?"

"A therapist. A psychiatrist. I think I might be seeing one."

Paul shrugged. "They got counselors and priests down there all the time, always trying to strike up conversations, staring at me like I'm a fuggin' mental. One day I'm pissing and this guy with a ponytail comes up to me and asks me how I'm doing. I say, 'My stream's all right, but it looks like I could use a little more water in my dict.'

"And this humorless fugger says, 'No, how are *you* doing, friend?' So I turn to him and say, 'You really wanna know how I'm doing, friend?' and he thinks he's got a live one and he perks up. 'Yes,' he says. I say, 'Not so fuggin' good, you really wanna know.'

"This jerkoff says: 'Well, don't worry. It's gonna get better.' That's it. It's gonna get better. That's my fuggin' counseling. Right? So you know what I said? I said, 'Fugg you. I don't want it to get better.'"

They ate in silence. Remy watched the door but he didn't see the guy from the gypsy cab. "What happened with Stacy?" he asked.

"Come on, Brian."

"Indulge me," Remy said.

"Indulge you." Paul drank his coffee, then shrugged and stared at his fork. "Well . . . pretty much the same thing. She said maybe it would get better and I said, 'Fugg you, Stacy. I don't want it to get better.'" He took a bite of his hash, and stared out the window into the parking lot as he chewed. Remy looked outside, too. The silver gypsy cab tooled past once more, the two men staring straight ahead at—

THE DESK in front of him was smooth, whorls of blond wood like a satellite image of oak storms. He ran his fingers along its mostly empty surface, over a monthly planner with nothing on it, to a nameplate that was turned away from him. He spun it around. The nameplate read

REMY. Next to his name was a phone, with buttons for five lines, none of them marked. He picked up the receiver, listened to the buzz of the office dial tone, and set it back. There was a computer, turned off. Remy pushed the button beneath the screen, but nothing happened. He looked around his windowless office. It seemed to be brand new: very little on the walls. It was a good-sized room, with dark-wood walls, two chairs on the other side of the desk, and a lawyer's glass-fronted bookcase. Remy walked over and crouched to look at the books in the case, hoping they would provide some clue about what he did in this office. But the only thing in the case was a *World Book Encyclopedia* set from 1974 and two rows of faded old *Reader's Digest* condensed books that looked like they'd been picked up at a yard sale. There was also a photo on the wall, of him at The Zero in the days after—The Boss on one side, The President on the other. Remy stared at the picture. He didn't remember meeting The President. There was nothing else in the office—no file cabinets, no photos of April or Edgar. He went back to the desk and began opening drawers. In the top drawer was a stack of blank paper with the word *SECURE* written across the top in a bold font. He tried the big bottom drawer next, but it was locked. The middle drawer was empty, except for a manila envelope with *REMY* written on it in black block letters.

Remy hefted the slender envelope, turned it over, set it on the desk, and stared at it. Was he supposed to open it? Was it some kind of report *on* him, not *for* him? Was it a test?

Remy took the report, walked to his office door, and opened it, looking for someone to ask about the report. He stuck his head out and looked both ways, down a wainscoted corridor that stretched about forty feet in either direction. A half-dozen closed office doors lined the corridor, all of them with unlabeled windows of frosted glass. Remy turned right and followed the corridor to its end, where it came to a T with another hallway. Remy turned left this time and walked about fifteen feet, until he came to a pair of swinging doors that opened on a vast room, a maze of soft-walled cubicles bathed in fluorescent light. Again, there were no windows. He could hear the tapping of computer keys, like rainfall, and the low hum of people talking. The cubicles spread out before him like a huge field of crops, broken only by pillars every thirty feet or so. Inside the first cubicle a woman was hammering away at her computer keyboard, a telephone headset perched on her head, a plastic sealed document in front of her. "Hell he did," she said into her headset. "Bullshit. Come on now!"

Perhaps sensing Remy behind her, the woman turned. "Oh, hello, sir."

Remy held up the envelope with his name on it. "Do you know—" he began.

The woman gestured to the phone headset, and Remy nodded and backed away. Leaving the room, he followed the T-shaped corridor in the other direction. It ended at another, more impressive pair of doors, the word *SECURE* lettered on the frosted glass. Remy opened the door and peeked inside. A woman sat behind a round desk reading a furniture catalog; behind her a big dark-wood door led to another office. Remy backed out, eased the door shut, turned left, and followed this hallway until he found himself back at another entrance to the huge maze of cubicles. He looked back over his shoulder. On the wall above the doorway he'd just come through was another sign like the ones he'd seen in the airplane hangar and the Quonset huts: "Our enemies should know this about the American people, which will not rest until Evil is defeated."

Finally, Remy backtracked again down the T and down the corridor toward his office. Inside, the phone was ringing. He walked in and picked it up. "Hello?"

"Oh, good, you're still there." It was a woman's voice.

"I'm still here," Remy said.

"Did you get the envelope Shawn sent over?"

Remy set it on the desk. "Yes."

"What do you think? Any of it helpful?"

"Uh . . . Probably too early to tell," Remy said.

"Sure," she said. "I tried to tell them it could wait until he got back from Washington, but you know those assholes in Partials."

"Do I," Remy said, surprised that it didn't come out like a question.

"I know it. They're all so mystical. I swear they could find significance in a used scrap of toilet paper. I guess it's the training they get."

"I guess," Remy said

"Have you noticed how everyone in Partials eventually stops speaking in full sentences?"

"I hadn't noticed that," Remy said.

"Anyway, they're ready for you now."

"Right. Who's that again?"

"Isn't that the truth?" She laughed and hung up.

Remy hung up and opened the envelope. Inside were two sheets of paper sealed in Ziploc bags. The first was a crumpled empty letter-sized envelope addressed to Lisa Herote—the name Assan had offered him at the interrogation—at an address in Virginia. There was a coffee cup stain on the envelope and a stain that might have been yogurt, as if it had been found in a garbage can. There was no return address on the envelope, but someone had affixed a yellow flag: "CKed w/Bishir's hw sample—positive."

Remy heard footsteps in the hallway. He looked up from the letter and saw the silhouette of a man standing behind the frosted glass.

Remy waited for a moment, then said "Hello."

The silhouette moved on.

Remy looked back at the documents on his desk. The second plastic bag contained a half sheet of burned paper, its corners like burned toast. Remy carefully picked up the document and read it through the plastic, his fingers instinctively avoiding the blackened edges to keep from

crushing them. It was a printout of an e-mail from MSelios@ADR to a
BFenton at the same company. The right-hand corner of the paper was
burned, leaving only the left side readable.

> *So guess who calls last ni*
> *asleep. What am I suppose*
> *around makes me fee*
> *sex is good, though and I*
> *part of the attraction*
> *worried about t*
> *scared to*
> *March*

Remy turned the page over, but there was nothing on the other
side. The yellow flag indicated that a copy of the e-mail had been "For-
warded by Markham, Investig. Unit. Doc. Dept., reconstruction under
way from Partials." It was initialed three times; he didn't recognize any
of the initials.

Remy put the two baggies back in the envelope, walked back to the
door, and looked once more down the long, empty corridor. The last
time, he had ventured right; this time he turned left, following the corridor to another T and another right turn. He walked a short distance
and knew, even before he went through the swinging doors, that he
would find himself again in—

THE SKY, impossibly close, shimmered like the surface of a lake, giving Remy the perverse impression that if he stepped off this fire escape
he wouldn't fall, but float up instead into that perfect autumn blue.
Every summer when he was a kid Remy took swimming lessons at a
camp upstate; the instructor had always told him that he would float if

he'd just lie back and trust the water to hold up his body. Finally, one summer at a family reunion for his mother's side in West Virginia, Remy tried it. And he floated. Not the way he expected: He didn't float on top of the water, but rather seemed to *become* the water, to float *within* it. Maybe that was the answer. To float in this life, like paper on a current. Just lie back and let himself be.

Remy looked down at the barbecue tool in his hand and he knew to lift the cover on the little charcoal grill. There were three thick steaks and a veggie burger, all sizzling above ash-white coals. He didn't question it, just flipped them. Perfect: black lines like prison bars across the steaks. The smell was so precise, so *not-Zero* that he simply stood there, inhaling. *Right. This is what cooking steaks are supposed to smell like.* Maybe this was not some condition he had, but a life, and maybe every life is lived moment to moment. Doesn't everyone react to the world as it presents itself? Who really knows more than the moment he's in? What do you trust? Memory? History? No, these are just stories, and whichever ones we choose to tell ourselves—the one about our marriage, the one about the Berlin Wall—there are always gaps. There must be countless men all over the country crouched in front of barbecues, just like him, wondering how their lives got to that point.

Remy glanced around—he was kneeling on April's fire escape. Looking down the block, he saw a couple walking below him on the sidewalk, holding hands, leaves cartwheeling before them. Their low voices rose on the air to the fire escape, the man saying ". . . and the lucky bastard found the last beater in Park Slope."

There was a glass of red wine next to the little charcoal grill. Remy grabbed it and took a drink, relieved that it tasted just like wine. Cause met effect. Good wine. Shiraz? Yes, this felt better. There were places—in bed with April, here on her fire escape—where he felt grounded. Real. The steaks, as steaks tended to do, needed a few more minutes.

He crawled through the window into April's living room. A man in his late forties, with thick brown hair, black glasses, and a sports coat, was sitting on one of April's dining room chairs in the cramped living room, sipping a glass of wine. He straightened up a bit when Remy appeared. April sat on one end of the couch, and at the opposite end sat a sharp-featured woman with short, spiky blond hair. The woman was attractive in the way that women of a certain age could be, with the post-foreplay directness of someone who was finished wasting time. She engineered a smile for Remy. A red scarf was tied at her neck in a real-estate ascot, blooming as if someone had cut her carotid. There was nowhere to sit but between the two women. Remy sat.

"The meat will be just a few more minutes," Remy said.

"I can't wait," said the woman.

"Smells great," said the man.

"You get to taste Brian's secret marinade, Nicole," April told the woman.

"Oh! What's in it?" asked Nicole with mock interest, turning her unblinking blue eyes on Remy like prison spotlights.

"You know," Remy said, "I couldn't tell you."

"I told you it was secret," April said.

They all laughed, like real people. They stared at their drinks.

Nicole cleared her throat and spoke as if reading from a script. "Well, April, we are just so excited to have you back."

"Thank you."

"It must have been such a difficult time for you."

"Yes," April said.

"I suppose we can't imagine what it was like," Nicole said.

"No," April said.

"So awful, losing two people like that."

"Mm," April said.

"Must have been harrowing."

"Mm."

"Yes." Nicole seemed to finally understand that the subject was closed. "Well, it's great to have you back. Our group is hanging onto fourth in gross commissions right now, and with you back in the mix we really believe we'll be third by the end of the quarter."

"I hope so," April said unconvincingly.

"Associates like April are playing a bigger role all the time," Nicole confided in Remy. "The growth is all under forty right now."

"Oh," Remy said.

"I'm just sorry it took this long for me to come back," April said, and she reached for Remy's hand.

"Oh. My God! No." Nicole leaned forward, her round eyes big with concern. "No, no, no! I told you to take as much time as you needed. We got along fine. And with what you've been through . . . no, it's good that you didn't rush back." She sipped her wine. "Honestly, April, for those first couple of months, there was very little movement anyway. But now . . . we're almost back to the number of listings we had before. In fact—" She leaned forward as if spreading rank gossip. "Everything points to an upsurge. An explosion. It's taking off again, April. It's about to get white hot."

"White hot," the man in the dark glasses repeated, staring directly at Remy.

"The downtime is looking like nothing more than a blip," Nicole said.

"A blip," said the man in dark glasses.

"It's a very exciting time for you to be coming back," Nicole continued. "There are going to be innovations . . . partnerships with developers . . . buying our own stock . . . options and hedges. Louis says the whole country is about to leverage its best asset." She paused for dramatic effect. "Our optimism." Then she sipped her wine and shook her head. "You watch. There will be a feeding frenzy. People will be buying product based on nothing more than models. People will be buying artists' sketches. Ideas."

"Ideas," April said weakly.

Remy took this opportunity to rise. "I'll bet the steaks are done." He smiled at Nicole. "And your soy burger."

April had kept his hand in hers when he stood, and now she squeezed it. And only then did he realize how nervous she'd been, about her performance tonight in front of this woman who must be her boss. He let go of her hand and walked toward the window, thinking again that perhaps life *had returned to normal*, and that normal was a string of single moments disconnected from one another. No reason to think that anything had ever been different. You worked in an office all week. Your girlfriend's real estate broker boss came over with her husband and you cooked them dinner. And when it came time to eat, it wouldn't matter whether you remembered *planning* the dinner. A meal doesn't care about the cook's intention; it just gets eaten. All over the city, all over the country, people rose from bed and scurried and fought and returned at night to sleep, independent of any meaning except the rising, scurrying, fighting, and sleeping. They drove cars made in places they'd never been, used cell phones and computers and a thousand pieces of technology with tiny pieces collected from factories all over the world, in places whose existence they could never be sure of, technology they couldn't begin to understand. The news played whether they watched it or not. And none of them ever stopped to say: *Wait! I don't understand how this car got here! Why this telephone takes pictures!* They answered their phones. Ate their steaks. And if they woke up one morning divorced or with cancer, or if they found themselves at war, they assumed the reality of irreconcilable differences, malignant tumors, premonitions of evil.

This is a life, he thought, smooth skipping stones bounding across the surfaces of time, with brief moments of deepened consciousness as you hit the water before going airborne again, flying across the carpool lane, over weeks at a desk, enjoying yourself when the skipping stopped, and spending the rest of your life in a kind of drifting contentment, slipped consciousness, lost weekends, the glow from televi sion sets warming placid faces, smile lines growing in the glare of the screen. He drained his wine.

It was cool on the balcony. Remy drank in deep breaths of city air. The steaks smelled so good he could barely stand it, and his eyes watered as he reached for the cover of the grill as—

HE SAT in his car, disoriented, wondering if the gaps were somehow widening. Maybe it had to with the car, because the worst skips often occurred like this, when he was on the road, or waiting in traffic, only to look up and find himself in a tunnel or on the turnpike, with no clue where he was going or where he'd been (one time he found himself wet to his waist, reeking of sewage) or when he'd suddenly find himself in an unfamiliar neighborhood, parked outside a building, a notebook open in his lap and binoculars around his neck.

This time, he immediately looked around the car for his binoculars, figuring that he was on some kind of assignment he'd have to piece together later, or simply abandon. But he quickly realized that he had no binoculars and no notebook. He was in the suburbs somewhere. And that's when he became reoriented and recognized the neighborhood, and Carla and Steve's big house, in a herd of similar big houses grazing in a cul-de-sac on a gradual hillside, this neighborhood that couldn't be more than two years old, where, Steve had once confided, there were four basic models, and his—the one with brick façades and pillared front porches—was the most expensive, *an extra hundy thou.*

Remy checked his watch. Quarter past three. Okay, so what was he doing here at three fifteen in the afternoon? He was wearing khaki slacks and a zippered jacket. He wasn't in front of Edgar's house, but four houses down the block. He looked around the neighborhood. For the most part, the lawns were obscenely green, like wet moss; in some of them you could still see the seams where new sod had been rolled out—perfect little patches like felt on a pool table. How many turns of a lawn mower? Four? Five? And yet, in front of some of the houses, this little patch of grass was already beginning to die in places, brown circles like age spots where the roots hadn't been able to take hold. And there were sickly trees, too, in most of the yards, still young, lashed to stakes and bundled in burlap turtlenecks. Little yellow ribbons were tied around the thin trunks, like scarves above sweaters.

Remy heard the squeak of hydraulic brakes, and watched in his rearview mirror as a school bus stopped at the corner behind him; then came the sigh of the bus door, and Edgar and another boy stepped off the bus, trudging off in different directions, without saying a word to one another, like duelers who forgot to turn and fight. The stop sign came in, the lights blinked off, and the bus rumbled on, Edgar bouncing to the beat in his tiny headphones as he walked on the sidewalk toward Carla's house on the other side of the street. He looked good, though it was hard to tell in his baggy clothes, the hooded sweatshirt and pants bunched up at the ankles of his floppy tennis shoes. Remy thought he saw Edgar steal a glance toward his car, but the boy just kept walking toward his house as if he hadn't noticed his dad. He paused at the mailbox, took out some catalogs, and continued to the house, up the steps to the pillared porch, fished in his pocket for a key, put it in the door, and disappeared inside. Remy thought he saw the boy's face appear briefly in one of the windows, but it was gone too quickly to be sure. A few minutes later the boy came out, wearing the same clothes, and loped off again, without a glance in the direction of his father's car.

Remy sat there a moment, trying to imagine what he'd wanted to say to the boy, but he couldn't come up with anything. Hell, that didn't seem so strange either, now that he thought about it—a father unsure what to say to his boy, haunting his kid's adolescence. After a minute he started his car and drove away.

* * *

SOMETHING FAMILIAR in the flow of people past him, something he recalled from that day, moving against the current, a barely
civilized rush on tight stairs, but reversed, like a photographic negative:
They were climbing the stairs he descended. "Excuse me. Excuse me,"
Remy said, his shoulders turned, hands and arms and knees grazing
him as he passed, although no one paid him any attention, either before
or after he begged their pardon. They looked past him with pleading
eyes, their hands high, as if ready at any moment to begin pushing to
escape this subway station. They were intimately familiar, these faces,
with their constrained lust for escape, barely held panic, an underground face, an elevator face, a train station face. He'd seen people hold
their breath in crowds; now he saw it again, as they came up, clutching
their handbags and briefcases and shopping bags like they were babies,
pulling at their actual kids' arms like luggage on the way to a late flight,
muttering *Come on come on come on*, and craning their necks to see what
was taking so long at the top of the stairs, where others emerged onto
the rain-spackled street and . . . Air! Did any city value air more than
this one now? Near the bottom the faces were more frantic; tears
streamed down a woman's face as she held her little pigtailed girl high
against her chest. "Please," was all she could manage. "I have a child.
Please."

As Remy neared the bottom of the stairs, on the dark final landing,
the crowd thinned until it was only stragglers, subway workers and a
homeless woman playing a saxophone that looked like it had been in a
hailstorm. She held her hand open for money, even as she was evacu-
ated, and Remy managed to slip her a dollar as they brushed past one
another. Her hand was rough and calloused. "Bless you," she whispered,
and when she had the money, "ass munch."

There were smells he associated with newsstands and subway maps, although Remy wondered how these things in themselves could stink. As he descended, though, for just a moment the atmosphere of the subway replaced the acrid flour of The Zero, and he breathed in the burning brakes, roasted chestnuts, and spilled coffee as if it were a beautiful garden.

The subway cages were empty; Remy had no tokens, but found an open gate. A nervous transit officer, a fat cave cop, was standing on the platform, shifting his considerable weight on black shoes, breathing through a paper surgical mask. He removed the mask and spoke without inhaling. "You the expert?"

"Why not," Remy said.

"Over 'dere," the cave cop said, replacing the mask. Remy looked down the line to a small staging area, where two other cave cops were putting up police tape while two space-suited agents stood nearby, taking photographs of a backpack leaned against a pillar. White powder appeared to have spilled out from the backpack. "Civilian spotted it. Twelve minutes ago." The cave cop quickly replaced his mask again. He reached in his pocket and held out a paper mask for Remy, who ignored it, looking back toward the white powder.

"Maybe this is what it feels like to be a soldier," Remy said. "That you just move forward because if you stop to think about the context, what it all means, you'll just go crazy."

"What are you talking about?" the subway cop asked through his mask.

"Nothing." Remy walked toward the backpack.

As he got closer, the guys in the space suits approached him. There was a click and a voice came from somewhere in the left suit. "You must be the guy Documentation sent."

"I must be," Remy said.

The space suit nodded. "Stupid question. Sorry." He winked. "We found some papers in the bag, near the USUM."

"USUM?" Remy asked.

"Unidentified suspicious materials," said the other space suit. "There was some cryptic writing in the papers; we think it might be a manifesto of some kind, so they said we had to call you guys in."

"Manifesto," the other agent agreed.

Remy stepped between the agents and toward the backpack.

"Hey! What are you doing? Shouldn't you wait for . . . someone?" one of the space suits called after him.

Remy said, "I am someone."

As he got closer, he could see the white powder piled on the ground next to the backpack. He bent down, dipped his finger in the powder, and put it on his tongue.

"Jesus! What are you doing?" the space suit asked.

"Creamer," Remy said, surprised at the disappointment in his own voice. He could hear sirens on the street above. "French vanilla." He hoisted the backpack and dumped it out on the platform. He poked through the remains: a spiral binder, a bagel in cellophane, a circular birth control pill dispenser, a pack of cigarettes, some matches, and a report on a book: *In the Labyrinth*. Remy read the report. She didn't like the book very much. She said it was too diffuse, too hard to follow. He opened the binder. The girl's name, Ailea Mendez, was in the upper right-hand corner, along with a phone number. He carefully put Ailea Mendez's manifesto back in the backpack, then straightened and walked over to—

THE MAN was a lawyer, a good one, if Remy had to guess. He wore a dark suit and tassled loafers, and there was something in the way he leaned his big-assed slacks across the conference table—like a kid showing off a new car to buddies—using a pointer to gesture at the PowerPoint presentation on the wall, a blue screen with red letters that promised to lay out the basic facts of "Applying for Federal Victims Compensation."

April was sitting in the chair next to Remy, holding his hand and practically crushing his knuckles in her sweaty fist. She was wearing a white lace sweater buttoned once over a plain shirt and Remy imagined that perhaps that one button was the only thing keeping her from coming apart. She breathed in fits and starts.

The PowerPoint screen: *1. Survivor/victim agrees to drop any claim against airline, city, federal government, etc. . . .*

"And you're sure about this part—" the lawyer began.

"Yes," April said quickly. "I think so."

"Good," said the lawyer, "because that's the first step. It's probably going to be close to ninety-eight percent of victims by the end. So . . . you're in good company." The lawyer smiled with his big picket teeth and clicked to the next screen: *2. Pain and Mental Anguish: a quantifying formula.*

A noise escaped April that was like something between a grunt and a sigh, as if the air had been knocked out of her. She tried to pretend she was clearing her throat. Remy took her hand.

"Everyone starts with a base of two-fifty," said the lawyer. He stuck his jaw out and rubbed the right side of his neck, which was covered with a purplish shaving rash the size of a tangerine. "For pain and mental anguish. That's what the guidelines have determined each life is worth, essentially, at a base level of grieving. Now if we get to the appeal process, we could always plead some special circumstance, but in your case, given the recent estrangement between you and the decedent, we're probably better off taking the two hundred fifty thousand and not opening up that can of worms." He stroked the rash on his neck tenderly.

"There is one issue we need to discuss," the lawyer said. "And it's going to be difficult, but it's necessary. And understand: I have to ask. Is there any chance . . . someone else . . . might step forward to make a claim?"

"Oh." April's hand began shaking a little. "Do Derek's parents want the money? Because I wanted to—"

"No. No. Not his parents. That's not what I mean. They *could* challenge, of course, but since Derek left no will, this falls under the state's intestacy laws, which reward the entire estate to the spouse, and therefore the entire settlement is yours."

"Even though we weren't together?"

"Estrangement is not the same as divorce. You could have gotten back together."

"We wouldn't have," April said quickly.

"I understand your feelings, but if I may . . . you don't know that. Mr. Kraft's mother and stepfather certainly don't know that. And the hearing examiner and special master can only follow the Compensation Fund rules, which clearly stipulate that the spouse is entitled to full compensation for pain and suffering. Now, the parents can appeal some aspects of pecuniary loss, especially if the decedent was supporting them or contributing to their income. But no, when I asked if someone else might make a claim what I was talking about was a . . . woman, a girlfriend . . ."

"Oh." April looked down at her shoes. "There was someone," she said quietly. She glanced up at Remy, and then looked back down.

"A woman," the lawyer said, not a question.

"Yes."

The lawyer turned his body a bit and stopped stroking his rash. Remy thought he seemed . . . titillated. "Do you think she'll make a claim?"

"No," April said.

"I understand this is difficult, but I need you to tell me about their relationship just in case some children miraculously appear, or some document in which he agreed to—"

April seemed to be straining with every word. "There were no children. And she won't make a claim."

The lawyer glanced at Remy. "Nevertheless, I should have the information—"

"She worked in his office," April said. "She died, too."

"Oh," said the lawyer, and Remy could tell that the lawyer was somewhat pleased to have this wrinkle out of the way. "Office romance. Sure. Oldest story." Then he remembered his client. "I'm sorry."

"But I do want Derek's parents to have some of the money," April said, trying to change the subject.

The lawyer looked back at April disapprovingly through his bifocals. "I wouldn't advise that." Then he looked at Remy, as if hoping he might talk some sense into her. "If you give them money, it doesn't preclude them from taking action to get more . . . and in fact, it sends a message that you believe they are deserving."

"They are deserving."

The lawyer was becoming frustrated. "It is my responsibility to tell you . . . that you are entitled . . . to his entire estate. All of it. What you do beyond that, well . . ." Then, as an afterthought, "But you should know that even if you give his family some money, my fee comes out of the full settlement, and not simply the portion you choose to keep, so you should—"

He clicked to the next screen. "Remember that." The screen read: *3. Factoring in Dependents*. He swung his head back to the wall.

"Now. Dependents. You would also be entitled to one hundred fifty thousand for each dependent . . . but you and your husband had no children, is that correct?"

"Yes," April said meekly. "That's correct."

"But at one time you were planning to have children."

"No. We weren't."

"I just mean, at one point, there was certainly talk of children," he said, as if dropping a hint. "Young couple . . . that kind of thing."

"No. I told you. We were separated."

"Right. I understand. We've established that. But surely at some point you *talked* about having children."

"No. It never came up."

He turned his body again, wearily, as if it were a strain to look away from his PowerPoint presentation, and his hand went quickly back to the rash on his neck. "Look. Mrs. Kraft. I don't mean to tell you what to say, but what couple doesn't at least *talk* about having children? See? These are the kinds of details that can influence the examiner and the special master and have an impact on compensation—"

"We had no plans for kids."

"—a young, attractive couple, their lives ahead of them, who had once planned for a family but were going through a difficult period, a temporary trial separation—"

"I can't have children," April said quietly. "I had a hysterectomy when I was nineteen."

"Oh," Remy and the lawyer said at the same time. April looked over at Remy.

The lawyer stuck his jaw out. "Okay. Right." He opened his mouth, and Remy thought he was going to find some angle to exploit, but perhaps he sensed that he shouldn't because he simply nodded and flipped to the next PowerPoint screen: *4. Computing Future Earnings.*

The lawyer took out a pair of glasses, put them on, and looked through the bifocals at the chart on the wall. "This is going to be woefully less than the decedent actually could have earned . . . that's just the way these settlements are being paid out . . . but you should know that in your case, we're going to try for more because, frankly, this is one of the few areas where we can make up some ground. Now, the tables, based on age and income put . . ." He looked down at his legal pad to find the name. ". . . Derek's total future earnings at two-point-two million, but we're going to ask for three based on the high-risk high-reward nature of business law, and his potential for making partner based on evaluations from his personnel records. They won't give you that much, but we need to ask. Now, if you could bring pay stubs, W-2s, copies of your income tax, any bonus letters he might have gotten . . . that will help us greatly."

April nodded without looking up from her shoes.

"As far as other supporting documents: any medical bills, funeral expenses, counseling you may have undergone, any after-tax income that your husband might've received. And we're going to make the argument that as a contracts lawyer with a degree in finance Derek had virtually no risk of unemployment." He smiled at April. "This is when you get paid back for him spending all that time at work."

Remy coughed and they both looked at him as if it had meant something. He looked away from them to his shoes and eventually the lawyer turned back to the wall and then thought of something else. The lawyer spun back around to face April and Remy. "Can you bring photos to the hearing?"

"Photos?"

"Yes. Wedding photos, vacation photos, holidays, that kind of thing. Pictures are tremendously effective . . . you can have the best sob story in the world, but what really sells it are photographs." The lawyer began to turn back to his presentation, but then thought of something else. "Oh. And bring pictures of your sister, too. You're not entitled to any compensation for her, obviously, but it doesn't hurt to have the pictures handy."

"Excuse me." April jumped up and left the room, covering her mouth.

The lawyer stuck out his jaw again, stroked his neck again, and sighed. "That happens a lot. It's . . . difficult."

They waited quietly for a few minutes and then the lawyer checked his watch. "I have a noon, so I'm going to go over the rest of this with you and you can explain it to Ms. Kraft afterward, okay?" He began flipping through PowerPoint pages, pausing on the important ones.

Remy looked down the hall to see where April had gone.

"Now these are the breakdowns of deductions that the compensation board will factor from the total: for life insurance, pension plans, social security, and workers' compensation, the sum of which we've calculated to be about one-point-six million, which we subtract from the two-point-seven we arrived at to get . . ."

"I don't remember things too well," Remy said, his voice a low croak.

"Don't worry. It will all be included in the report that Mrs. Kraft gets." He spun through several more pages before the lawyer arrived at a page with smaller writing than any of the others. It was a breakdown of the fees the law firm would take. He said that they were taking a reduced rate, but the lawyer pointed to two columns on the bottom of the page, deductions for "Vicarious Trauma" and "Compassion Fatigue."

Remy leaned forward. Compassion fatigue? "Are those for . . . you?"

"Yes. For the lawyers working on the case. As you might imagine, these are difficult cases . . . emotionally." He removed his glasses and wiped his dry eyes. Then he seemed to think of something else and put the glasses back on. He looked hard at Remy. "Oh, in case you are wondering, April can remarry without affecting her settlement in any way. You wouldn't have to wait, in other words." He smiled as if he and Remy were in the same profession. "So that's good. For you. Obviously." He smiled and reached in his pocket, pulled out a tin of mints, and offered Remy—

A BIG truck, the biggest he'd ever seen, sat on risers in front of him. It was a pickup as high as a two-story building, on tires taller than a man.

At first Remy thought his sense of scale had been thrown off, that his eyes were playing some kind of trick, but this was, in fact, a giant truck. Remy looked around. He was in an arena of some kind—empty and dark—except here in the center, where spotlights shone down on the dirt floor and on this giant truck. He looked closer at the pickup. It was painted red and blue, airbrushed with American flags fluttering in an unseen wind, with an angry-looking eagle perched on the hood and, on the doors, a long list of familiar names, cops and firefighters, Italian, Irish, and Latin, like the roster of a Catholic school football league.

"So what do you think?" Guterak came around the truck and stood next to Remy, gaping at it. He was wearing a suit without the tie and his hair was forcefully parted to the side. He seemed nervous. His voice seemed to disappear in the empty arena.

"Big truck," Remy said.

"Yeah," Paul said. "It's pretty cool. Hey, thanks again for coming down."

"Sure."

"Impressive up close, isn't it?" A woman was speaking behind them. Remy turned and saw her approach from an open door on the floor of the arena. She had curly brown hair, blonded at the tips, and wore a tight denim skirt, like a country music singer. A cell phone earpiece sat perched on her head as if she'd just walked away from a fast-food drive-through window.

When she was closer, the woman handed Guterak some papers. "Here you go, Paul. Countersigned contracts, as Michael promised. And the schedule for next week. Tractor pulls at seven each night, followed by the demos, and then before the finale we're going to have a moment of silence. That's where you come in." The woman was in her thirties and her thin legs disappeared in elaborate cowboy boots. She smiled. "We'll announce the *Eagle Truck, Hero-One,* and that's when you come out with the firefighter—" She looked down at her notes.

"—Davie Ryan, both of you in uniform. The two of you walk out, wave to the people, look . . . you know . . . serious or whatever. Then you climb that staircase over there and stand on that platform in the dark. Take off your hats. We have a moment of silence and then Bam! The lights come up and we play 'America the Beautiful' and then Hero-One comes out. People go ape-shit and the truck runs over a bunch of shit and everyone goes home. Easy, right? I'll bet it's much easier than chasing bad guys." The woman handed Paul a brochure, which he read and handed to Remy.

WE'RE TURNING VETERANS ARENA
INTO A GIANT MUD PIT
TO HONOR OUR DEAD HEROES!*

Tractor pulls, monster trucks, demolition derby!
And for the first time anywhere: The Eagle Truck, Hero-One
With its *haunting display of airbrush artistry* featuring America's lost heroes.

*Ten percent of all proceeds to go to the widows and orphans fund.

"When do I talk?" Paul asked as he leafed through the program.

"Talk?" the woman asked. "About what?"

"Well." Paul looked around the arena. "I don't know. Maybe I misunderstood. I thought I was going to get to talk."

"No, no." The woman smiled. "We don't need you to talk."

"Oh. Yeah. See, I was under the impression that I would get to talk."

"No. There's no talking."

Paul took a couple of steps and looked at the truck. "No. See that's what I do . . . I talk. You know . . . about what I saw?"

"No," she said. "No talking." She leaned forward. "Honestly, I don't think people want any more talking. For a while they did. But I think they've had enough of that kind of thing. I think we get it. No, all we need you to do is . . . look appropriate." The woman shrugged, opened her handbag, and handed Paul an envelope. He held it for a moment before opening it.

While Guterak stared at his paycheck, Remy walked toward the truck and read the names, and indeed they were airbrushed with such artistry that the shadows seemed real and the letters had a disquieting depth. The names—all that was left of good people—rose like bruises from the metal-flake paint.

THE DOCUMENT looked just like Australia; in fact, in a way it was Australia, its edges burned into a perfect representation of the coastline, in that distinctive, thick oblong shape of the continent, bent in the middle, with a hole at the top corresponding perfectly with the Gulf of Carpentaria. Helpfully, someone had paper-clipped an actual map of Australia to the file; he glanced from the burned page to the map and then back again, and at the yellow flag on the plastic baggy in which the paper was placed: "Forward to SECURE. Isn't this uncanny? Doesn't it look like Australia?—SM."

Remy looked around. He was back behind his desk. There was still nothing on the walls except the photo of him between The Boss and The President, nothing to make this office look like anyone actually worked here. He opened the top drawer, found a pen, and wrote, "Yes," on the flag. Then, after a moment, he initialed it. Before that day, when it became Australia, the page had been a simple expense report from a lunch meeting between March Selios and a man named Bobby al-Zamil, identified as "vice pre—" (the rest burned away down near the Great Sandy Desert) of a business called "Feynman-Mid-Ea—" something (burned away down in the populous regions near Melbourne and Sydney).

Remy glanced around his office. He turned the nameplate around again, just to be sure. It said REMY. Good. He'd begun to feel he could manage the skips with nonchalance, and he thought it best to treat this burned piece of paper with the same knowing shrug. He picked up the phone and hit zero, and a few seconds later an operator's voice came on line.

"This is Diane."

"Uh. Hi. Diane. This is Brian Remy." He looked around again. "I've got this piece of burned paper that looks like Australia. Am I supposed to do something with—"

"Let me see if I can get him on his car phone."

A few minutes later, Remy heard the buzzing of a phone and Markham picked up, apparently in traffic. "Markham."

"It's Remy."

"Hey, buddy. We're just on our way back. So . . . did you get the Australia document I sent over? Isn't that wild?"

"Yeah," Remy said, holding it up again.

"I wanted you to see the original before the probability companies started fighting over it."

"The probability companies?"

"Yeah. We're getting bids already."

"Bids?"

"You know, to study the burn patterns?" Markham just kept going, as if all Remy needed was a little more information and then the whole thing would click. "Applying models of randomness and linear motion probability to the patterns in paper burns?"

"I don't—"

"You didn't see the story in the *Times*? The whole booming randomness industry . . . partial documentation recovery and interpretation . . . the old thought experiment about the drunkard's walk? . . . Inevitability and random patterns, assuming unreversed trajectories and nonpreferred directionality? Applying that to burn patterns? You know."

"No, I guess . . . I don't— "

"The whole partials pedagogy . . . Jesus on a Fish Stick?"

Remy was afraid this would go on forever, and so he said, "Oh. Jesus on a Fish Stick. Sure. Look, do you need me to do anything with this?"

"No, I just wanted you to see it, that's all. We got everything else handled. We're on al Zamil right now—should be ready to work him tonight."

Something in Markham's voice made Remy uneasy. "Work him?"

Markham laughed. "Would you relax. We're following the protocols you wrote. We adopted 'em. No more sloppiness, I promise."

"Wait. What protocols?"

Markham laughed again. "Come on, don't test me. I swear: no more screwups." Over the phone, Remy could hear a man saying something in Markham's car, perhaps *He's moving*. "Hey, I gotta go," Markham said. "I'll call you when we're ready."

"Wait!" Remy said, but Markham was gone. He dialed the operator again, but after a moment she came back on the phone and said that Markham was unavailable.

Remy hung up and looked down at his desk again. Had he written protocols? He tried the desk drawers but they were empty except for some blank paper, a letter opener, and a few pens. The big bottom file drawer was still locked. Remy yanked on it, then looked around the office for something to pry it open with. He tried the letter opener, but it just bent the metal blade. Wait—this was *his* office. Remy pulled his keys from his pocket, and separated a small one he didn't remember having. The key turned the lock and he pulled the drawer back.

The files were alphabetized and primary color-coded under different titles, which were typed on the tabs. Some of the tabs (*AGENCY*,

BUREAU, FLORIDA, ICEMAN) were intriguing to Remy, but he was worried about losing the moment, so he skipped ahead to the file called *PROTOCOLS*, and was about to open it when he saw the titles of the next two files, *RECIPES*, and the one that really intrigued him, near the end of the drawer, a tab marked *SUBJECT A*.

It could be anything.

He pulled out the file. It was thin, just two dated reports four months apart, each no more than a few short sentences. The first read, simply: "Made contact with Subject A. Continuing deep cover." It was signed with his initials—BR. Remy read the second report, which was slightly longer:

> Subject A remains reticent, possibly suspicious, could be deep grief . . . too early to determine if subject is concealing informa-tion . . . Recommendation: continued recon, deep cover and intel gathering.

Again, the document was initialed by Remy. He swallowed. This wasn't necessarily April. Subject A could be anything.

Or anyone. He turned the report over. There was a handwritten note on the back, dated what he thought was just a few days earlier.

> Took Subject A to attorney to file claim on dec. husband. Continuing to gain trust—recomm. extend cover . . .

Remy's head slumped. He opened the top drawer and found a pen. He scribbled across the top of this second short report: *Cancel.* Then he thought better of it, balled up the two reports, and threw them in the garbage. He tossed the empty folder away, for good measure. He felt breathless. He had convinced himself that that if he just abandoned himself to this skidding, lurching life, without questioning it, things would turn out okay. Once you started down a road, what good did it do to question the road? But maybe that only worked, he thought now, if you can trust yourself in the moments between bouts of consciousness. *What am I doing in those moments I don't remember?* He fell back in his chair, closed his eyes, and felt the moment leak away.

HE FOUND notes like this sometimes, notes written to himself, pointed questions on index cards that he'd unearth in his briefcase or his pocket: "What did you do today?" and "Where did you go?" But he never seemed to answer the notes, or if he did, it was such a cryptic response—a partial number or an acronym or some other obscure piece of work product—that it almost seemed like a taunt. He stared at this particular note, written in his normal block letters on the back of a business card that he found in his wallet behind his credit card. It said, simply: "Don't Hurt Anyone." He looked up.

A bartender was staring at him.

"Did you say something?" Remy asked.

"I just asked if you want the usual, Brian?"

"Oh. Okay."

Don't hurt anyone. Remy slid the card back in his wallet and looked around. It was late afternoon and he was sitting in another downtown hotel lounge. He often found himself like this in the afternoons, sitting in some hotel lounge or restaurant bar. He tried to differentiate in his mind between these lounges but they all seemed vaguely similar, like this one, and it was only when he saw their odd, one-word names on his credit card bill later—Affair and Hedge and Nine and Chain, as if the words had been chosen at random in a dictionary—that the places became different in his mind. And even though the names were all different, he couldn't help imagining them as one lounge that changed its name and its décor every few days. All of the bartenders in these places seemed to know him intimately, and he seemed to have a *usual* in each place—generous pours of scotch or bourbon or gin that arrived magically on paper coasters before he even had time to take off his suit coat. He could usually get in two or three drinks before April showed up, and then they had dinner. They ate quietly, without feeling the need to chatter. He appreciated this. Sometimes she'd ask about his day and he'd say it was good, or that he couldn't remember, or that it had simply flown by. When he asked about the real estate business, she rolled her eyes and took so long to chew the food in her mouth that he often forgot the question. At dinner, he found himself ordering the same thing whenever it appeared on the menu, duck marinated in a red wine sauce and spiced with wasabi, and since he seemed to find it at so many restaurants, he thought it must be the recipe of the moment. He'd find himself wondering how the duck tasted, and so he'd order, forgetting each time what it had tasted like the last time.

How's the wasabi duck? April would always ask.

He'd shift the bite to the other side of his mouth. *Mm.* But he seemed to forget after each bite what it had tasted like.

Remy thought about April as he looked around tonight's version of the lounge, with its high ceilings and spinning fans, its smoke-mirrored walls. He picked up the restaurant's menu; *wasabi duck marinated in red wine,* never failed. Twenty-eight bucks. The hostess smiled at him as she walked past. "Hi, Brian. Meeting April tonight?"

"I sure hope so."

The bartender reappeared. "Looks like you're ready for another, Bri."

"You know me," Remy said, and set the empty glass on the bar.

April came in two drinks later, wearing black pants and a short green jacket that stopped at her ribcage, like something a bullfighter might wear. It made her look long and exotic, and Remy felt that exhilarating embarrassment that he imagined was experienced by middle-aged guys with beautiful, younger girlfriends. "You look great," he said. He stood and kissed her.

She smiled nervously. "Thanks for doing this."

"Oh." He reached for his fourth whiskey sour. "Sure." Remy took her hand and followed her into the restaurant, listing a bit from the booze, and taking in the open stares from the tables, shadowed faces peering up in the harsh light of tabletop candles. They all seemed to be trying too hard to have a good time, to be casual, and it crossed Remy's mind that they might be spirits of some kind, the ghosts of people who used to go out to dinner, before it became a form of patriotism. The candles agitated the flashers and floaters behind Remy's eyes, but he couldn't look away, the bits swarming like summer insects around flickering candlelight. Finally he closed his eyes and let April pull him through the maze of tables.

When he opened his eyes, Remy saw why April had thanked him for coming. The sharp, older real estate broker who'd been at April's apartment, Nicole, was sitting at a corner booth, waiting for them. Nicole wore a smart pink suit that made her seem like a design on a sketchpad. The first time she blinked, her long lashes snapped like castanets.

"Troy couldn't make it?" April asked.

"Uh . . . no," said Nicole, and she sized up Remy as if considering a purchase. "I didn't ask him. I thought it was just going to be the two of us, April."

"Oh, really?" she said. "I must've misunderstood."

Remy had already taken his jacket off and draped it over the chair back. "Oh," he said. "Should I—" April grabbed his hand.

"No." Nicole sighed. "That's okay. You may as well join us . . . as long as you don't mind a little shop talk."

"I don't mind," he said.

He sat and they all sipped at their waters, Remy momentarily startled by the taste of liquid that wasn't distilled. "I trust you saw this?"

Nicole asked April, and slid across a real estate listing from another company showing a photo of the balcony of a high-rise apartment. Remy read the words *concierge* and *glass conversion* before April took the slick sheet of paper and read it. "Six to eight rooms," Nicole was saying. "Both fulls and halves. This would have been perfect for Morgan. But the assholes at Klinerman Davis used the long weekend to hide the listing; they were at forty-eight hours before anyone had any idea the building was open. And then on Monday they didn't answer their phones until four. Look, we can't whiff on a building like this, April. This is exactly the kind of thing we need our associates to bird-dog for us."

"I'm sorry," she said.

"We can't sit around waiting for these sharks to share their listings, because their goddamn clients will be unpacking boxes before we've even heard about it. We have to have a heads-up when something like this is about to come on line, whether it means paying secretaries or blowing someone at the real estate board. But whatever we need to do, we need to do it now. Do you understand? There is no more honor out there," Nicole said. "It's a war, now, honey. This is about defending our values. Because they will beat you to death for a dime on the sidewalk. And the only way to deal with that kind of aggression is to beat *them* to death for a nickel."

There was more of this talk, and Remy found himself drifting as Nicole ranted. April held her menu to her chest like a shield, but she couldn't look away from Nicole, whose menu remained folded in front of her while she criticized April's work, while pretending at the same time to be concerned ("The partners all agree: it's just not like you to let things get away from you like this"). Drinks came and Nicole turned to the inspirational part of her speech, rambling on about the great opportunities and the new listings that April should be getting. More drinks came and Nicole's voice rose to cover the restaurant din—higher and faster, speaking with a frenzy that seemed to make April even edgier: competing brokers were snakes, clients idiots, developers thieves, "and April, honey, we need to know that you can handle every one of them," April nodding slightly and reaching for her empty water glass as Nicole warned about partners who would cheat her out of commissions, a broker at the firm who was known for hoarding the 'burbs and a seemingly cooperative agent uptown who wouldn't think twice about spreading rumors to potential clients that April had AIDS.

April coughed in her hand and looked around the room, as if trying to find an escape route.

"Listen, dear," Nicole said, "the bottom line is that we're going to look back at this period as the dawn of a new age, an unprecedented period of growth in real estate wealth, and I don't want you to miss it. I won't allow any of my brokers to miss it. I won't allow my group to miss it. And I won't allow the firm to miss it."

April said she understood, thanked Nicole, and changed the subject, twice, but even when Nicole talked about other things—she told a long story about her son Milo getting into a prestigious preschool—Remy realized that she talked about her son the way she talked about real estate, as if there were a thriving market somewhere in which Milo's development could be tracked and profited from, and getting him into the right school was just another function of waiting for market forces and gentrification and favorable interest rates. At one point April tried to speak, but she made the mistake of referring to the market as a bubble and Nicole came out of her seat, arguing that this was "the triumph of the concentrated work of generations."

They ordered wine and appetizers and Nicole talked about real estate, about her secret hope to partner with a developer looking to "furb and flip fifteen boxes in the Heights." They ordered entrées (Remy ordered the wasabi marinated duck) and a wine bottle came and went and its brother came and went, and this seemed to mellow Nicole a bit, because she shifted to an easier subject—real estate fables, stories about people who got the last great deal, who chanced upon the next Williamsburg or got a foothold on an undiscovered street, or the last unrehabbed building in the Bowery, or the only quiet block in the meatpacking district. And maybe it was the booze, or maybe it was the stories coming out of Nicole's pinched little mouth, but it seemed to Remy that she was describing a world in which everyone was in the process of moving, and he had the image of a colony of disturbed ants scurrying back to their hills. Everyone was in the market to buy apartments and condos and houses, whether they knew it or not. Everyone was the agent of his own destiny, shifting from one place to another, and he imagined an historic migration, Okies closing up dusty family farms and cashing out 401ks, climbing in their Benzes and driving sixty blocks uptown to five-room walk-ups with river views. Remy took a long pull of wine and looked up at April and smiled—didn't it all sound . . . sort of . . . nice? Food came and went, and still Nicole talked, her voice rising in a kind of poetic incantation as she recited wondrous new listings from memory, or produced them out of the air, and Remy thought she must know every apartment in the city by heart, or perhaps all she had to do was imagine them and they became real: a three-bedroom with a wrap terrace in the West Nineties, a northern exposure with a doorman in the East Twenties, the Village building about to go co-op with the little Montessori school across the street. And Remy understood that every conversation now was really about real estate, and that a conversation about real estate was really a conversation about progress—the blossoming of civilization, the spread of democracy. This neighborhood had turned or was turning or was on the verge of turning. No neighborhood ever went down in Nicole's estimation. In police work, there had only been decline; in real estate, there was only ascension. He found himself drifting happily as Nicole described a world in which the wealthy selflessly tried to save the city, maybe the whole country, maybe the whole world, one neighborhood at a time, cleansing blocks and doubling property values. If the city before had seemed to him always on the verge of decay, strips of lawless, decrepit neighborhoods in danger of being overrun by criminals, now it was being transformed through a million tiny regime changes—nice professional couples cleansing blocks with shutters and window flower boxes, with curbside Saabs and Lexuses.

Remy listened to Nicole as if he were listening to music, drifting in and out and not always catching the lyrics, but entranced by the melody. Another wine bottle came and went and he closed his eyes, the images washing over him: a two-bedroom prewar, lofts with cook-kit, Hudson River alcoves and meat-pack rehabs with ten-foot ceilings and restored box beams, six rooms with a library and city views and frontage and pet friendly—Nicole's voice settled over him like fog, until it seemed to him that she was describing a different city, an infinite city, each block a solar system in neighborhoods of galaxies in universes of boroughs: a big bang of five-room walk-ups and remo'd townhouses and partial park views, elegant, sumptuous, grand. And when April, pale and shaking, stood up to take a cell phone call, Remy found himself drunk and unable to look away from Nicole, who just kept talking ("luxe lofts" in Hell's Kitchen, a Bryant Park "shut-and-gut") and even when Remy was too drunk to understand the words, he found he could still intuit the world Nicole described, a world of glittering wealth and endless beauty, where there was no longer a need for cops or firefighters, only pink real estate agents, floating above the city on gusts of possibility.

THIN LIPS against his, and then teeth biting his bottom lip, and maybe it was the tug of those teeth that caused Remy to open his eyes and see Nicole, kissing him, her right hand frisking the front of his pants like someone looking for her car keys. They were sitting in his idling car in front of her apartment. "No, no," he said. "Wait." The leather scoffed as he settled back into the driver's seat. "This is not a good idea," he said, his voice thick from too many drinks. "I shouldn't be doing this."

"Hey, *you* kissed *me*," Nicole said.

"Oh." Remy rubbed his head. "Well, I'm sorry," he said. "I shouldn't have done that. I haven't been myself lately."

"Okay," Nicole said. "The cake wasn't exactly rising anyway," Remy looked down and saw that she was right. Nicole flipped the visor down and checked her face in the mirror. "I suppose it's for the best," she said. "I've got a crazy morning tomorrow." She flicked at the corner of her mouth with her pinky fingernail. "And I'm sure I'll appreciate the six extra minutes of sleep." Nicole smacked her lips together and closed the visor. Then she looked over at Remy, as if seeing him for the first time. "Tell April I hope she feels better. And I'll see her on Monday." Then Nicole climbed out of the car, tugged at her tight skirt, centering its seam. She reached for her jacket and then walked away without looking back.

No, no, *no*, Remy thought as he drove fast down the black avenue, cabs swirling around him, back toward April's building. He tried to piece together what had just happened. At least he had stopped himself. Maybe he always stopped himself before he went too far. Yes, he was in control; this is just what happened to men. They did things they regretted. That's all. Remy found a parking spot on the street near April's building and jogged the rest of the way, abandoning the sidewalk for two couples walking abreast, holding hands.

He could see April's window from the street. The light was out. He went to the door, wondering if he should ring her, and was surprised to find the door propped open with a menu from the restaurant where they'd eaten that night. Remy picked up the menu and slipped through the door, which locked behind him. He climbed the stairs and eased down the hall. Her door was unlocked. Remy came in and walked into the bedroom. He stood above her bed. She was asleep, curled up on one side of the bed, hair spilled out on the pillow, mouth open a little, as if some tiny thought—some plaintive fragment of a dream—had pried open her lips and crawled out. He began to undress and then turned again to watch her sleep. Finally, he turned back and hung his suit coat on the closet doorknob and began unbuttoning his pants.

"Thanks for driving Nicole home," April said without opening her eyes.

"Sure," Remy said.

"I'm sorry you had to sit through my evaluation."

"It's okay."

"And I'm sorry you had to deal with Nicole."

Remy turned. Her head was nestled deep into the pillow. He opened his mouth to say that it was okay, that he'd enjoyed himself, but thought he might be able to find a better choice of words.

"Did I tell you who was on the phone?" she asked.

"The phone?"

"At dinner?"

Remy tried to remember her phone ringing at dinner. "No," Remy said. "You didn't tell me."

"Gus."

"Oh."

"He's coming through town and he wants to see me."

"Really? Huh," Remy said, as he finished undressing. He was relieved when April's breathing became heavy again, so they wouldn't have to talk about Nicole anymore, although he wouldn't have minded asking who Gus was.

THERE WAS a mark, a stain of some kind, on one of his shoes. Remy stood in the entryway of his apartment, looking down at the stain. His shoes were next to the door, right where he always slid out of them when he came home.

Remy picked up one shoe. The stain was reddish brown, kind of glossy. He touched it and it flaked off in his hand. There was more of the reddish brown stain on the sole and on the heel. He turned the other shoe over and found more of the dried red stuff on the sole. Remy put the shoes back on the floor and backed away from them, rubbing his jaw. Okay. He looked outside. It was still dark. Must be three or four in the morning. *Okay.*

There were any number of explanations, he thought; it would do no good to go crazy imagining things again, trying to find some meaning. He went to get a dish towel from the kitchen. No, he thought, there were no good explanations. Remy looked over, to where his jacket was hanging on a kitchen chair. He pulled it off the chair and fumbled through the breast pocket until he found his wallet. He slid out the card, on which he'd written: "Don't Hurt Anyone." Below that, in his own handwriting, was written: "Grow Up."

Brian Remy stood in the entryway, holding the card in one hand, the dish towel in the other, thinking that this couldn't go on, but the moment and the thought slipped before he had a chance to wipe the blood off his shoes.

THE CAR was familiar, a silver Lincoln, pocked and key-scratched, a shit bucket of a gypsy cab (a bit *too* ragged, Remy thought on seeing it again) driven by one of the men Remy had seen following him and Guterak, the man who had barged in on him in the restroom of the restaurant, a fat white guy in mirrored sunglasses, thick-necked, with a bushy mustache longer on one side than on the other, as if the thing had been trimmed by a blind man. Remy stared at the car again and understood why it hadn't seemed quite right: It was a shitty old car, but

the tires were brand new. The back door of the car was thrown open.
"Get in," the man said.

Remy looked around. He was standing in front of an old six-
story brownstone, not his building or April's. The façade was covered
with scaffolding, which was topped with razor wire and sided with
plywood, which in turn had been tagged with graffiti. A tunnel beneath the scaffolding led to a doorway. He was the only person on
the sidewalk. He crouched and looked inside the car. The driver was
definitely staring at *him*, even though his black sunglasses hid his
eyes. He wore a flannel shirt and old jeans—not so much what a
gypsy cabdriver looked like, Remy thought again, but what someone
thought a gypsy cabdriver might look like. He also wore the baseball
cap that read BUFF. And, whether or not it was his name, it seemed
to fit.

"Get in," grumbled the buff man again.

"What?"

"Get your ass in the goddamn car, Remy," said Buff. "What the
hell's the matter with you?"

Fair question, Remy thought. He looked around and finally sank in.
He had just settled into the worn vinyl backseat when the car bolted
like a spooked horse. The back door swung closed and Remy lost his
balance, falling sideways, and then righting himself as they swerved
through traffic.

"So," Buff said. "So . . . you wanna tell me what the fuck you're doing?" He veered in and out of traffic like a particularly bad cabbie.

"What . . . I'm doing?"

"You're making side deals with the agency, aren't you?"

"What agency?"

"Don't play stupid with me, Remy."

"I'm not."

The man stopped at a traffic light. He had a manila envelope and he reached in and removed a photo. He tossed it into the backseat. Remy picked up the picture; in it, he was in a parked car with a thin, aristocratic man that he recognized at once: Braces. Caramel macchiato. Khakis.

"Dave," Remy said.

"Yeah. I know his name, asshole," said Buff. "What I want to know is what you're doing meeting with him."

Remy had no idea. "Why don't you tell me?"

Buff glanced up at Remy in the rearview mirror, and with his mirrored sunglasses, Remy saw the man reflected in his own eyes. "You arrogant fuck." Buff suddenly cranked the wheel without slowing and Remy slid all the way across the seat as the car squealed onto a side street without slowing. The car cut around a double-parked truck and seized to a stop, Remy's hand curled white on the door handle.

The driver removed his sunglasses and slapped at the rearview mirror so that he was staring Remy in the eye; the man's left eye was slightly crossed, on the same side his mustache was crooked. "Come on. What do I look like, a fuckin' moron?"

"Well . . ." Remy said, and looked away from the man's reflection.

"We had a deal, Remy. The bureau provides you with information . . . and you keep us apprised of what your gay little secretarial outfit is up to. I went to bat for you, Remy. How does it look when my director comes to me with these pictures of you meeting with this agency queer? How do you think that makes me look?"

"I . . . I don't know."

"What did you possibly think this would accomplish?"

"I don't know . . . maybe help me find this girl, March—"

"Come on," Buff said. "We both know that's not what you're doing."

"What am I doing?"

"You're trying to get a fuckin' foothold. You're playing the bureau against the agency, figuring that Dave would never find out you're working with me and that I'd never find out you're working with him. Well, that, my friend, is a dangerous fuckin' game. Do I need to show you the other picture I got in here?"

"I . . . I don't know."

"Come on. You can't guess what's in here?"

"No."

The man tossed Remy the manila envelope.

Remy stared at him in the rearview mirror before opening the envelope. The photo showed a man crumpled up on a sidewalk, a Middle Eastern man with a thick beard and short hair, wearing tan slacks and a white shirt. The man was facing sideways, his legs cocked as if he'd just fallen off a bike. A slick of blood spilled out from his neck and head.

"Remember him?"

"No," Remy said. But he did remember the blood on his shoes and he swallowed.

"Oh, so you've never seen this guy before, is that it?"

"No," Remy said again. "Never."

"And I suppose the name Bobby al-Zamil doesn't ring a bell?"

Remy covered his mouth. The lunch reimbursement report, the man who'd had lunch with March before she died, the man Markham was going to *work*. Remy looked back at the photo again. "Is that him?"

"Fuck you, Remy." Buff sped off again and Remy fell back in his seat. "I told you *we* were working al-Zamil. So what? Then you happen to meet with an agency field supervisor, and the next thing we know al-Zamil gets depressed and takes a walk out his apartment window?" He caught Remy's eyes in the rearview. "You tell your little friend at the agency that if he thinks this gets us off the case, he's fucked in the head."

"I swear, I don't know anything about this," Remy said. "I saw his name on a piece of burned paper that looked like Australia. That's all."

Buff spit laughter. "Australia. You're a fuckin' piece of work, Remy. You know that?" He stomped on the gas again and the car took off.

Remy stared at the photograph and covered his mouth. "I swear—"

"Look," Buff said. "I'm gonna give you another chance—you've been getting us solid stuff, and we might need you." He shrugged. "And we hadn't turned al-Zamil yet anyway. . . . But you made me look like a horse's ass. You gotta give me something to take back to the director."

"I don't know what I can give you."

"Gimme your source."

"My source for . . ."

"You've been one step ahead of us on this cell, Remy, and I need to know how. Give me the goddamn name of your source."

"What name?"

"Yeah, and who's on first, you smug son-of-a-bitch," the man said. He put his sunglasses back on. "Okay, tough guy. Fine."

The car's tires chirped again as they skidded around another corner, and then the brakes jammed and the car came to a shuddering stop against the same curb where they'd started. "Get out," Buff said.

Remy opened the car door.

The man turned and faced Remy for the first time, his face wide and uneven. He spun his cap around so that it faced forward, so that Remy could see the word *BUFF* again. The man held up his right index finger, which bent sideways at a thirty-degree angle. "You go ahead, play your little games. But if I was you, you calm, cool motherfucker, I would keep this one thing in mind—"

"HALLUCINATORY IMAGES," Remy's psychiatrist, Dr. Rieux was saying. "What you're describing is textbook PTSD. Visions. Stress-induced delusions. Dissociative episodes. Maybe even Briquet's syndrome. Look—" He laughed. "I'm pretty sure you're not working for some top-secret department, investigating whether or not your girl-friend's sister faked her death."

"I'm not?"

"I don't think so, Bri. Secret agents interrupting you on the toilet? Yelling at you in gypsy cabs, buying you lattes? Mysterious Arab men in wool coats?"

"That's all . . . hallucinations?"

"Sure. Why not. It's very common, Brian. I see it all the time."

"You do?"

"Well . . . no, I haven't *personally* seen it. But it's all right there in the literature. Survivors can expect to experience delusions, persecution, paranoia. Delirium. Hell, after what some of you guys went through that day . . . I'm surprised you don't have flying monkeys drive you to work."

"So . . . the paper? The blood on my shoes?"

"You got a better idea?"

"I don't know. It just . . . doesn't feel like that. Are you sure?"

"Am I sure?" He spun in his chair and pointed at the diploma hung on the wall. "Do you think they give these out for masturbating? Well . . ." He laughed again and then assumed a serious face. "Listen. I don't mean to be condescending, but some of the real issues you're describing—not this fantasy stuff, but your son growing away from you, your inability to commit to a monogamous relationship, concerns about the ethics of your profession, alcohol abuse . . . this is pretty standard stuff for a man your age."

"Are you saying," Remy asked, "this is some kind of midlife crisis?"

"I don't mean to minimize it. But you are a certain age. You've been through this severe trauma. Lost friends. Coworkers. And then, when you should be coming out of it, you had to suddenly abandon a successful career with the city because of back problems—"

"No, it's not my back," Remy protested weakly. "It's my eyes."

"No. I don't think so." The psychiatrist spun in his chair, opened a drawer, flipped through his files, and came up with a short report. "See, it's right here." He handed over the report, which read clearly *Disability due to chronic back pain.*

"No, this is a cover story," Remy said. "For the work I'm doing."

But Dr. Rieux pulled a prescription pad from his desk and scribbled something on it. He tore the sheet out and held it up for Remy. "Here."

Remy read the prescription. "What's this?"

"This will help," he said.

Remy held up the medical report on him. "How come there's nothing in here about the gaps?" he said.

"Gaps?" Dr. Rieux held out the prescription. "What gaps?"

"The *gaps*," Remy said, as he reached for the prescription sheet and—

A MIST hung in the air, fine droplets suspended as if on strings from the sky, distorting distance so that the grand house seemed miles away, across rollers of wet mounds and wild grasses. The house sat between two massive oaks; at three stories it was half their full height, with shutters and a wraparound front porch—a beautiful colonial country house with a fenced horse corral and barn beyond it. Remy stared at the house through the mist, which flattened everything and made the world appear sluggish and slow. Two hundred yards beyond the house Remy could see cars crawling along a narrow highway, slowing to make the switchback like mourners pausing over a coffin. It was dawn and he was sitting alone in this field two hundred yards from the house. He looked down. There were binoculars in his hands. He held them up and zeroed in on the top floor of the house. An attractive woman in her thirties was eating a cup of yogurt. Remy had a headset on—a small earpiece and mike—but he couldn't hear anything. He watched the woman walk around the top floor, from window to window. She was wearing workout clothes, bicycle tights maybe, with a collared shirt.

At one corner of the house he could see her turn from side to side, as if checking herself in a mirror, the cup of yogurt in her hand.

Remy dropped the binoculars and looked down at himself. He was wearing camouflage pants and a black jacket. He pulled a black stocking cap off his head and stared at it. Did he own a black stocking cap? A green camo backpack was spread out in the grass. Remy opened the backpack and began flipping through it. He found a notebook and pen, gloves, a semiautomatic handgun, and a box of Dolly Madison Zingers, like Twinkies with yellow frosting. Remy opened the box, took one out, and had a bite. It was good: spongy yellow cake with filling and frosting. Then he cracked the notebook. There were two listings written in the notebook, in his handwriting: *0645—light on. Subject Herote awake. Alone. 0724—Subject out of shower, dressing in workout clothes.* He glanced over at the backpack and saw, at the bottom . . . a full prescription bottle. Remy set the Zinger down, looked around the field, and then pulled out the bottle. He opened it and swallowed two of the capsules. He closed his eyes and curled up on the ground, hoping his psychiatrist knew what he was talking about and that this hallucination would dissolve. But with his eyes closed Remy could only see streaks and floaters, and when he opened his eyes he was still in the field. He fell back in the grass, discouraged.

"Fresca Two. This is Fanta One. Do you copy?"

Remy wedged himself into the deep grass, hoping the medication would kick in and this would all go away.

"I'm gonna make the call now." It was Markham's voice. "Wish me luck."

Remy raised his head and looked all around the field. It was all still there, the house, the oak trees, the barn and corral, the highway behind, a creek bed to the right, lined with bushes, and on his left, a ridge, its base ringed by shade trees whose branches moved in the soft wind like fingers on a piano.

A few seconds later, Remy could hear a telephone ringing in his earpiece. He held the binoculars to his eyes and saw the woman in the big house skip across a room and pick up the phone on the second ring.

"Helloo," her voice chirped in his ear.

"I'm looking for Lisa Herote," he heard Markham say.

"This is she." He watched her through the binoculars, her lips moving just slightly ahead of the words.

"Hi, this is Mike Brady, with Brady Florists here in town," Markham continued. "We have an arrangement we're trying to deliver for you from a . . ." Papers shuffled. ". . . Bishir Madain."

"Oh," she said, and through the binoculars Remy could see the woman put a hand against her chest, as if she'd just received a compliment. "Bishir? Really?" Her head cocked and she said, "Oh," again.

"Yeah, sorry to ruin the surprise," Markham said. "Unfortunately, our computer was down when he called and my kid wrote the information on a piece of paper and then spilled Dr Pepper on it . . . so we don't have Mr. Madain's credit card number or any contact information for him. We can't deliver without—"

"Oh, I'll pay for it," she offered quickly, as if she were used to paying for Bishir.

Clearly, this hadn't occurred to Markham, who coughed and cleared his throat. "Yeah, that's against our policy. But if you just could give us Mr. Madain's phone number, we can clear this all up."

"I don't have it," she said. "I haven't talked to Bishir in months. I have no idea where he is. That's why it's such a pleasant surprise that he'd send me flowers."

"Oh. No idea where he is?"

"No. None. We had a difficult breakup," she said. "He wasn't exactly . . . committed to the relationship."

"Yeah, I'm sorry," Markham said over the earpiece. "And you have no idea—"

"No, none. I'm sorry."

"That's too bad."

"I mean . . . I assume he's still in San Francisco. Is that where the call came from?"

"San Francisco," Markham said, perking up. "Yes."

"That's where he said he was moving."

"Okay, well—"

"Do I get my flowers?"

In his earpiece, Remy heard the line go dead and then:

"Fresca Two, this is Fanta One. How was that? Pretty good, huh?"

Remy ignored him.

"Come on, Brian. I did okay, right? Come on. I know you're down there. I'm staring right at you."

Remy wedged himself down in the grass again.

"Hey, did you open those Zingers yet? I'm starving up here, man. I ate all my corn nuts already. You were right. I shouldn't have gotten corn nuts. Can I have a Zinger?"

Finally, Remy said, "They're all gone."

"No they're not," Markham said. "No way you eat a whole box of Zingers before eight in the morning. It's physically impossible. Come on, man."

"Leave me alone," Remy said again. "This isn't even real." He took off the headset and threw it down in the grass.

It was quiet in the field, but for the rustle of deep grass. Remy looked at the prescription bottle again; then ate another bite of Zinger instead. He couldn't believe how good it was. He grabbed the box to see the ingredients. There was no mention of the things he could taste: cake, cream, and frosting . . . it was as if those things didn't really exist, as if what he believed was a piece of frosted yellow cake was really nothing more than this list of sugars, acids, preservatives, sulfates, and yellow dyes.

"I saw that, you stingy jerk." Markham's voice was a tiny whine from the headset lying in the wet grass. "I know you're—"

LYING NAKED on the queen-size bed, on top of the covers, Remy looked around the hotel room. It was a big room, with a window over-looking a park. He wasn't sure where—it didn't look like anyplace in the city he'd ever been. A grove of willows stood guard outside the window, above a meandering river. Remy's clothes were piled on a chair and a wine bottle sat on the nightstand, half-full, next to a glass with nothing but the dark red rim around the stem. He sat up and poured himself another glass of wine.

Then he heard the toilet flush. He looked at the bathroom door, which was closed. Behind the door, the water ran.

Remy pulled the cover across his lap. A few minutes later, she came out of the bathroom. It was Nicole, April's boss.

"Oh, Jesus," Remy said.

"That's better," she said. She was wearing a short, red silk robe, tied at the waist. She was holding a glass of wine, the same color as her painted finger and toenails.

"Whew boy," she said. "I'm not used to the sex taking that long. With Troy it's more like getting a flu shot." She took a slug of wine.

"Oh, God," Remy said. "I didn't . . . did I?"

"Oh, I think you did." She smiled, and then cocked her head. "Oh, no. Are we having second thoughts, hon? I was afraid of that."

"No. I can't do this," Remy said.

"Well, probably not for a few hours, no."

"Look, I'm sorry but this was wrong . . . I shouldn't be here."

Nicole stood staring at him, and finally took a sip of wine. "Look, if it's any consolation, no one wants to have done it right *after* they've done it." She shrugged. "Except maybe teenagers." She winked. "And women of a certain age." She set her wine down on the nightstand. "I'll tell you what . . . I'm going to go now . . . I'm not really into the whole . . . regret part."

She returned to the bathroom and began getting dressed. Remy caught flashes of her in the mirror, as she wrestled her way back into a pair of unlikely string underwear, and thrust her legs into a pair of black pants. She came out buttoning a pink suit jacket.

Remy was trying to figure out how to explain himself. "Listen, I'm not myself these days. I shouldn't have . . . I'm not . . . entirely in control."

"Right," she said, and swilled her wine. "Isn't that . . . kind of the point?"

"No," he said. "I don't want to hurt April. So . . . if I try to . . . sleep with you again . . . I would really appreciate it if you just ignored me."

She flinched. "Sure. Will do." Then she smiled wistfully, slid her feet back into a pair of high heels, and looked back at him, her face red. "You fly me here, feel me up like goddamned airport security, and then, the minute the gun goes off, fall back in love with your girlfriend. I'll tell you what—it'll be a huge relief when everything down there finally dries up. Then maybe I *can* ignore assholes like you."

Remy put his head in his hands.

She'd regained herself. "You can go back to being a good boyfriend now. I'll see myself out." She slipped out into the hall and the door eased closed behind her. After a minute, Remy got to his feet. He fumbled in his pants for the pills his psychiatrist had given him, wondering how long they took to kick in. He opened the bottle and took two more pills. Then he put the "Do Not Disturb" sign on the hotel room doorknob, slid the deadbolt shut, and his head fell against the door.

* * *

REMY DRIFTED down the jetway. He fell in behind a couple in matching cargo shorts and backpacks and a woman with a huge baby balanced on her hip, and they all spilled out into the clean terminal, which was mostly empty, a couple dozen travelers waiting at gates, furtive behind newspapers or hunched over cell phones and cups of coffee, as two soldiers moved like shepherds among them, M-16s aimed at the ground. Remy made eye contact with one of the soldiers, who looked him up and down, glanced once more at his eyes, and finally moved on.

Remy stood beneath the sign announcing forks for ground transportation, baggage claim, and ticketing. He chose a direction at random, walked down the stairs and out the door, and was relieved to see Guterak, leaning against his car, talking to a traffic cop. The sun was setting, the sky behind him a smear of humiliation.

"You have a good time?" Paul asked, as the cop moved on.

"I don't know."

"You come back from vacation and you don't know if you had a good time? What's the matter with you? You got luggage?"

Remy looked back at the airport. "I don't think so."

"Doesn't look like you got any sun to speak of," Paul said. "Probably wore sunscreen. That's the hardest thing for me now—putting on sunscreen. Or fastening my fuggin' seat belt. All these things that used to seem like common sense . . . now . . . I mean . . . come on? I gotta slather on SP-fuggin'-80? I gotta stop for red fuggin' lights? I gotta put on oven mitts to take out a hot pan? I mean, come on . . . oven mitts?" He showed Remy burns on the sides of his thumbs.

They climbed into Paul's unmarked. He swerved into the crowd of waiting taxis and gypsy cabs and curbside loaders and began angling away from the airport.

"So how you doing?" Paul asked.

"Not so good," Remy said.

"Back bothering you?"

"My back? No. My back is—"

"Did I tell you the agent sold my story?" Paul asked.

"No," Remy said. "That's great."

"I suppose. I'm not gonna get rich anytime soon, but it's still a good deal," Guterak said. "They optioned my story, but it could really pay off if we actually go into production."

"So . . . a movie?" Remy asked.

"Well, no . . . not exactly," Paul said. He put on his blinker and looked over his shoulder, drifting across lanes. "This company makes all sorts of products. DVDs. Cigarettes. Food. Cereal." He glanced over.

"Cereal?"

"Yeah. That's what they want me for. This new cereal called . . ." Paul hesitated, then just spit it out. "First Responder."

"First Responder?"

"Yeah," Guterak said. "They needed one smoker and one cop for ads and PR and shit. They were gonna go with actors, but they decided they wanted true stories and real guys on the boxes. The smoker's a guy named Brad. I like him. He's a solid guy. He's on the flakes and I'm on the one with marshmallows. My agent says I was real lucky to get the marshmallows."

"Yeah, I could see that."

"Yeah." Paul shrugged, a moment of unusual circumspection.

Remy looked over at his old partner and friend. He thought about confiding in Paul that he'd cheated on April, but he wasn't sure he wanted to admit it to himself. Paul's hair covered the peak of his head like spring snow, cut high above the ears and melting on his forehead. He turned the steering wheel gently with one hand and the car listed that way, and Remy felt as if he were on the ocean again.

He grabbed the armrest and held onto it, trying to fix himself in the moment.

Remy closed his eyes and the streaks did a slow waltz for him, bits gently circling one another in the dark, like a choreographed fight. He opened his eyes and looked out the windows at the flattened landscape slowly dragging alongside the turnpike—brush-lined riverbanks and ledges of condos, freight cars stacked and lined like old shoeboxes, river-flat refineries, and, across the gray slick of water, the brick, steel and glass anthill of the city. April was there, in one of those buildings. And that's when Remy had an idea.

He fell back against the headrest. "Paul. Can you do something for me?"

"Anything, buddy. You know that. I'd do anything for you. I mean . . . within reason. You know, obviously I wouldn't eat garbage off a sidewalk, or sleep with a man . . . well, I mean, if it meant your life or something . . . you know, depending on how much shit. And I guess what the dude looked like."

"I need you to follow me."

"Follow you."

"Right."

"Follow you?"

"Yes."

Guterak scratched his head. "You mean . . . like keep track of what you're talking about? That kind of follow?"

"No. I want you to physically tail me. Follow me around and see where I go. What I do. Keep track of it. Don't let me see you."

"You don't want to see me."

"Yeah. I don't want to know you're doing it. And then write down everything I do and tell me about it afterward. Make up a report."

"Who do I give the report to?"

"Me."

"And why am I doing this?"

"So I can figure out what I'm doing."

"Uh-huh. You want me to follow you so you can figure out what you're doing."

"Yeah. I need to see if I'm hallucinating or if I'm really involved in something . . . something bad."

"Oh," Paul said. "Okay then."

"You'll do it?"

"Of course I'll do it," he said. "I'll use my black helicopter. I'll shove one of them fuggin' GPS transmitters in your ass, put a wire in your teeth. Get one of them Air Force drones to track you. Or . . . remember that movie where they shrunk those guys and put 'em in the president's body? I'll do that." Guterak shook his head and laughed as he steered the car through traffic. "You fuggin' kill me, man." He looked over at Remy and shook his head. "You know, you get funnier every day."

"WAIT. WAIT." A stout woman wearing jeans and a bulging fanny pack came into April's living room. "Look, that was great, but we didn't quite get it. Do you think you could repeat that exchange?" Remy was sitting on the couch with April, across from a young man sitting on a chair in front of them, leaning across his knees as if he were breaking something to them. The young man had olive skin and thick eyebrows that ended just inches from his bushy hairline. But it was in this boy's eyes that Remy saw April and especially March and old Mr. Selios, eyes that made him realize right away that he was staring at Gus—April's brother Augustus Selios.

Behind Gus, a man with a television camera on his shoulder and a utility belt around his waist was scurrying to change positions as the woman with the fanny pack moved the power cords and a bundle of audio equipment. The lights in the room were blinding.

"We need to get this again in a two-shot," said the fanny-pack woman cheerily. She and the cameraman both wore windbreakers reading *From the Ashes.* "That was amazing, Gus. Really powerful."

Gus smiled in spite of himself and then worked to clear his face.

"Okay," said the producer in the fanny pack. "When I say go, I want you two to repeat what you just said. Just like you did it before. Natural."

"Sure, Tina," said Gus. Remy searched Gus's face for connections to April, but they seemed to have less in common the longer you looked at their faces. Behind him the cameraman moved into position in the dining room.

"Mike pack," said the cameraman, and Tina the producer adjusted the microphone pack strapped to the back of Gus's belt so that it wouldn't be visible in the shot. "I wish we could use a boom."

"Well, we can't use a goddamn boom," the producer snapped, and then smiled, and asked, "Ready?" She pointed to Gus, who nodded and took April's hands in his.

"Look, Sis." Gus stared into her eyes. "I'm sorry I wasn't here for you, then. Afterward, I mean. I just . . . couldn't face it. I guess I was . . ." He stared out the window, and took a practiced pause. ". . . angry. Angry at myself for not being here."

April glanced at the camera through the corner of her eye and then looked at Tina the producer. "Don't look at me," she said in a stage whisper.

"What am I supposed to say?" April asked.

"Say something like, 'That's okay, nothing you could've done would've brought March and Derek back, anyway,'" Tina said helpfully.

"I don't think I can say that," April said. She looked at Remy, who tried to look supportive, even though he felt like he'd been banished to the farthest corner of the room.

Tina the producer and her cameraman huddled for a moment near him but Remy could only make out a few words: *first unit* and *truck* and *boom* and *editing bay*.

Then Tina turned and smiled. "You know what? Okay. That's okay," she said. "Pete says we have the audio and we can cut away. No . . . we're good. Why don't you just do your goodbyes and we'll take care of it in editing." She chewed a thumbnail and shrugged to the cameraman as if that were all she could do.

April and Gus stood awkwardly, like actors in a scene that's just broken. Gus drank water from a plastic bottle and rolled his shoulders while April looked around the room, as if looking for some place to hide. Tina grabbed April's arm. "Look, April, I totally get your discomfort. Totally. And I respect it. In fact, I don't want you to do anything that makes you feel phony. That would be creepy. Do you know why we call it 'reality'? Do you? Because it's best when it's . . . *real*. The realer the better. That's what our show is about. Taking these stories of tragedy and letting people inside."

April looked at Remy again.

"So . . . you just forget we're here. Just say *goodbye* . . . to your brother," Tina said. "Just say goodbye, whatever you feel like saying . . . that you love him, whatever . . . that it's just the two of you now, you know . . . talk about your grief . . . and pretend we aren't here."

"It's kind of hard," April said.

"Sure. I understand. Just try to be as natural as possible. You know, give him a hug. Cry if you want to. The most important thing is that you act as if we're not here. Just do exactly what a normal person would normally do . . . when seeing your last living sibling for the first time since your sister . . . died such a horrible, unbearable death. This is reality; what we want is real emotions."

Gus shifted his weight and looked around the apartment. "Maybe we could just, like, hug at the door . . . and I could say something like—" His face melted in sorrow. "You look so much like her." When he was done his face returned to normal.

"Yeah, that's good." Tina pulled a piece of thumbnail off her tongue and stared at it. "Or . . . I have an idea." She walked to the window and looked down. "Pete." The cameraman came over, holding the camera by its handle like a suitcase, as Tina pointed out the window to the street below and they spoke in hushed voices. Pete shrugged as if it would be okay.

"Listen," she said. "Let's do this downstairs. We'll shoot it two ways. First, I want you two to go down there and say goodbye and we'll shoot it from up here. You can have some privacy right there on the sidewalk below us. We'll get audio from the mike packs and you two just . . . be yourselves. Just make sure you stand just to the right of the stoop down there. You know . . . just talk for a second and then hug . . . maybe grab her head, Gus, like you're consoling and convincing at the same time. And then, Gus, you walk away. Don't look back. Then we'll come down and get it again close in a two-shot. Okay? Everyone ready?"

April looked once more at Remy but he didn't know what to say, and finally she and Gus walked out the apartment door and started for the stairs. Remy was left with Pete the cameraman, who seemed infinitely bored, and who began setting up by the window while Tina the producer looked him over. "Your girlfriend seems a little uncomfortable."

Remy didn't say anything.

Tina shrugged. "Well, this is going to be a great segment. Her brother is . . . really . . . really something. We're gonna run it over the holidays."

"Ready," said Pete, and Tina moved over to the window. Remy walked over too, and looked down on the street as Gus took his sister in his arms and they hugged on the sidewalk below. She looked so tiny down there. She started to glance up at the camera, at Remy, but Gus took her face in his hands. Then he said something to her and walked away without looking back, the camera tracking him every step.

* * *

THE HANGAR didn't appear to be emptying at all. Remy stared out at the alphabetized signs—above him, AM-AZ—hanging over tables covered with paper, stacks and stacks of white paper. The white space-suited technicians were going over each piece, giving them out one by one to other people who filed them in the rows of filing cabinets beneath the strings of fluorescent lights. At the end of the hangar, two forklifts were moving palettes of filing cabinets.

Something was different about the paper, though, and it took Remy a moment to realize what it was. He walked over to the nearest table and saw what it was: These pages weren't scorched or bent or wrinkled. In fact, they were neatly stacked. Remy took a page from one of the stacks and was surprised to see that it didn't smell at all like The Zero. It was an electric bill from a house in San Leandro, California, dated months after the attacks.

Almost out of habit, Remy patted himself down for his medication.

"You shouldn't be handling that without gloves," came a woman's voice from behind him.

Remy put the power bill back in the stack. "These aren't even from that day." He walked over to the woman, who was standing between two signs, one reading PARTIALS, the other PERSONAL/MISC.

The woman's head tilted slightly; her voice took on a rote quality. "The Liberty and Recovery Act mandates the recovery and filing of documents. It doesn't specifically limit us to those documents recovered that day."

"So . . . you go through garbage cans . . . or what?"

The woman's face flushed. "Perhaps you should have this discussion with someone higher than me, Mr. Remy. I'm following my job description. I understand why you're in a bad mood, but taking it out on me is not going to make the mistake go away."

Remy felt awful. "I didn't—"

She shook her head. She was tall and thin, with adult acne scars. "Trust me. This is embarrassing enough without you mocking me," the woman said.

She handed Remy a piece of burned paper in a plastic baggie. "The reason the note was misfiled was that we mistook the signatory for the beginning of the date it was written." She winced. "I know. It's a bonehead mistake and there's no way, after all this time, that we should still be making mistakes like this."

Remy looked down. He was holding a note written on the letterhead of March Selios's law firm, scribbled in felt-tip pen. Most of the right side of the note was burned away, and he could see why someone might've thought it was the beginning of a date.

> *Hey—*
> *We need to talk. I changed my mi*
> *I can't to go through wi*
> *you understand.*
> *March*

Remy turned the note over. There was nothing on the other side. "I'm sorry," he said. "I wasn't implying that you'd done something wrong." He laughed. "I couldn't do that. I don't even know what you're supposed to do."

Her eyes welled with tears. "Now you're belittling me."

"No." Remy reached out and touched her arm. "No. I promise I'm not. I didn't mean anything. Look, can I just . . . ask you something?"

The woman shrugged.

"Do you think . . ." He laughed. "Is it at all possible . . . that this is . . . all an illusion, that this is all in our heads?"

The woman looked around the vast airplane hangar, crews of

workers filing millions of pages of documents. Her face flushed again and her eyes welled with tears. "Oh, go to hell," she said.

EDGAR WORE clothes so similar to the ones he'd been wearing the last time Remy had seen him—baggy pants, hooded sweatshirt, tiny earphones—that Remy wondered if they actually were the same. And yet, there was something different about him; he seemed . . . bigger. Had Remy been away so much lately that he'd missed a kind of growth spurt? He was parked a block behind Edgar, and on the other side of the road, watching him through binoculars as he moved down the suburban street, with that hip-hop bounce.

When he got out of sight, Remy started his car and drove a few blocks, until he was in front of the boy again. He parked at the crest of a hill, in a dentist's office parking lot, across from the back entrance to a mini-mall. He trained the binoculars on the sidewalk across the street.

Edgar came loping up the hill. Then he suddenly stopped, climbed over a retaining wall, and dropped out of sight into the mini-mall parking lot. Remy turned the key, pulled out, and drove around the block, finally turning into the back of the lot. The sky was low and overcast, as if a gray tarp had been thrown over the local suburbs.

Remy tooled through the parking lot, trying to find his son. The mall was shaped like a U, with a courtyard in the center and small stores clinging like barnacles to both the inside and outside of the U. As he drove, Remy ran his eyes over the storefronts—cell phone services and guitar sales and Army recruiting and bagels and ice cream and tanning beds and golf supplies and rattan imports and Remy could feel his blood pressure rising. Where was Edgar? Chiropractic and party supplies and maternity clothes. And Remy could feel something snap inside of him: I've had enough of this strobe-life, he thought. Fuck this! Why am I doing these things? Car stereos and tacos and espresso and computer repair. Why am I sleeping with April's boss? Why am I haunting my own son? Tax preparation and futons and insurance.

"Goddamn it, Edgar. Where are you?" If there was something he wanted to tell the boy, then goddamn it, he was going to tell him. He could feel his face flushing. And just then he felt powerful enough to simply decide to throw off this strange jerking life, whatever it was— hallucinations or an illness or just the way life was lived now. A life is made up of actions, and if he wanted the world to be different, then he only needed to *act* differently. Every minute of every day was an opportunity to do the right things, to make something of this mess. He didn't need to be unfaithful to his girlfriend. He didn't need to be involved in some shady investigation that may have hurt innocent people. And he certainly didn't have to drive around wondering what he wanted to say to his own son. When he found the boy, he would just open this car door and climb out, grab the boy by the shoulders, and say . . . something. Windshield glass and physical therapy and copies and—

THIS TIME, Remy didn't bother protesting, or asking what had happened, or taking his medication, or even pleading with her to leave him alone. His skin was covered with a slick sheen of sweat, not all of it his own, and even though he couldn't quite remember exactly what had preceded this moment, as he watched Nicole climb out of the big king-size bed and pad off to the bathroom, he knew it was too late. "Whew," Nicole said. "You do understand that the root of *quickie* is supposed to be *quick*, right?"

The sheets were twisted around his ankles. He looked around the room, apparently Nicole's bedroom: in each corner was a four-foot-tall Asian pot with a burst of dead sticks and flowers coming from it. On the wall in front of him was a triptych of abstract paintings, all with smears of pink on them. Next to that was a family photo of Nicole, her husband, and their son. When he heard the shower come on, Remy rose and slid into his pants, put on his shirt and his socks and his shoes, pulled his jacket off a chair, and slinked out of Nicole's apartment. He took the elevator with a woman holding a terrier. The dog sniffed at him and then looked up at the woman as if to confirm her suspicions. On the first floor, the doorman was reading the *Daily News,* but he looked up in time to wink. Remy hurried past him, out the door.

On the street he saw a car that looked like Guterak's, but it sped away from the curb. Remy watched cabs slide down the avenue toward midtown, and wondered if he had enough cash for one. He pulled his wallet out to see how much money he had, and he saw the edge of his "Don't Hurt Anyone/Grow Up" card. He slid the card out, read it, and slid it back into his wallet. And that was the first time it crossed his mind that there might be another way to consider this problem, that there might, in some way, be two Remys, one he knew and the other he didn't, and that these two men might be as different as—

HE WAITED as the old man was helped off the bus, which bore lettering on its side reading *Englewood Senior Services.* The driver, who had a shelf of long hair in back, nodded and spoke to the man in his loud senior citizen voice. "How'd you do today, Mr. Addich? You win all that money?"

"I always win all the money," the old man said. He was small and impeccably dressed, in a suit without a tie. He clung to a black day planner as big as a motel room Bible. "I'm a winner!"

"What about them old ladies? You hittin' any of those ladies, Mr. Addich?"

"I would never hit a lady. Unless she hit me first." The old man winked.

This made the driver laugh as he got back on the bus. The doors closed, the bus began to pull away, and Mr. Addich made his way toward his son's suburban house.

"Mr. Addich?" Remy climbed out of his car and hurried across the street. "Excuse me. Are you Gerald Addich?"

The old man turned slowly and looked at Remy without recognition. "Yes. Who are you?" The old man was all ears, two big handles divided by a spit of gray curly hair that lapped onto his forehead. His mouth was a pinched hole. He spoke with a gravelly third-generation Irish borough accent. "What can I do for you?"

Remy walked up to the man. "Do you know me?"

He took a moment. "I don't believe so, no. But if I had to guess I'd say you look like a cop."

"I'm the guy who found your planner downtown," Remy said.

"Oh, thank you," he said. "That was nice of you to return it. I'd be lost without this thing." He turned back toward his house.

"Your son said you weren't downtown that day . . ."

The old man turned back and cocked his head, as if he didn't understand.

"So I was wondering how it got down there."

The old man said nothing.

"See," Remy said and he tried to laugh nonchalantly, "the funny thing is that your day planner had a meeting listed on that day . . . with me, or a meeting with someone with my name."

Addich looked down at the planner in his hands. "What's your name?"

"Remy. Brian Remy."

"I've never heard of you," the man said. "So I don't know how I could have had a meeting with you—"

"Could I just look in there?" Remy asked, pointing to the planner.

"In here?" Mr. Addich held up his day planner.

Just then, the door opened and Tony Addich came out, in suit pants, a white tank top and socks. "Come on, Dad. It's almost dinner-time. We're having salmon."

"I'm sorry, I have to go," Gerald Addich said to Remy. "We're having fish." He stared at Remy for a moment before moving toward the house.

Tony Addich came out and helped the old man up the sidewalk. "Leave him alone," he said over his shoulder, through gritted teeth. "He can't help you."

REMY STOOD on the second floor of what appeared to be an old warehouse, in front of a heavy door, a kind of roughed metal, brushed and polished until it gleamed like a rocket. He looked around, then opened the door and stepped in the entryway of a huge loft apartment, unfurnished and mostly unfinished: exposed bricks and beams, joists and pipes hanging above stained wood floors, the whole thing feeling cold and exposed, lacking the civility and cover provided by basic dry-wall and carpet. "Hello?" he called out. "Anyone here?"

"In here," came a man's voice. Remy made his way through a long narrow living room, rough brick on the opposite wall and two big win-dows at the far end of the room. A small kitchen was on the right, with an angled slate counter lined with corrugated aluminum and a metal hood resting above a gas stove and oven. A young couple was standing next to the stairs, the man in faded jeans and a ski cap, the woman in form-fitting black pants. They both had the kind of windswept blond hair that made Remy think of places in Colorado he'd never actually seen.

"—not that I think holding out for a six-burner is worth losing this place," the woman was saying. Then she and her husband both looked up at Remy.

"Oh, hey," the windswept man said. "She's up there."

"Up there?" Remy asked, looking at the open staircase.

"Yeah, man," he said, "she was showing us this apartment and she got a phone call about something and she just lost it, man."

"She didn't seem right even before that," the woman said to her husband.

"She was fine," the man snapped, as if they'd been arguing the point. "But after the phone call she seemed really . . . spooked."

"She locked herself in the bathroom and wouldn't come out," the woman said.

"We didn't know what to do," said the husband. "We told her through the door that we were going to call the agency, and that's when she said she was going to call someone else instead. I'm assuming that was you?"

"I assume so," Remy said. He started up the staircase, which was lined with cast iron poles topped with what looked like bowling pins. Remy stepped closer and looked upstairs, where he saw a mural painted on the ceiling, a kind of sunspot, dark in the center with yellow drips of flame leading away.

"Excuse me," said the man. Remy turned and looked down at him, leaning on the railing in the kitchen. "Listen, we're kind of . . . we're worried about losing this place. If she's okay, do you think you could tell her that we want to move on it before someone else gets it?"

"Okay," Remy said.

He walked up the stairs and found her in the bathroom, sitting in the dark against the counter, still holding her cell phone. "April?" Remy turned on the light. He stared at the phone in her hand, wondering if Nicole had called her and said something. His stomach felt tight, as if it were folding up on itself.

"You think, at first," she said, distantly, "that it's a kind of penance you're being forced to pay. You think that after you've suffered long enough, that the people you've lost can just . . . come back." April's eyes drifted down. "But they don't. They never come back. That's the trick. They die all over again for you, every few months."

Remy removed his coat and tried to put it over her shoulders but she held up her hand.

"I dream about them . . . sometimes. I keep expecting them to say something profound or comforting. But they're too busy to talk. They're running around, late for things, and they won't even meet my eyes. And I think . . . what's the rush? You're dead. Where could you possibly have to be?"

She looked up and met his eyes. "There's something I probably should have told you. The reason I don't like to talk about Derek. Do you remember the night we met at the bar and I told you all about him?"

Remy nodded, even though he didn't.

"I said that when he died, I hadn't spoken to him in four months . . ." she trailed off. "Well . . . that wasn't entirely true. I don't know why I lied about it . . . I guess I wanted you—or maybe me—to believe that I totally was over him."

April rubbed her mouth and stared at a fixed point above Remy's head. "Right at the end of summer, he called . . . he said he missed me. He wanted to get back together. So we talked about it . . . all through August and the first week of September. And then, one night . . ." She trailed off.

"You slept together," Remy said.

She nodded.

"You were still married," Remy said and he shrugged as if it were no big deal, which it shouldn't have been, and yet he could feel a tug in his chest, like he was snagged on a fishing line. He thought of Nicole again and stared at the floor.

"A couple of nights later he spent the night again." She cleared her throat. "And it was . . . nice. The next morning . . . The next morning was *that* morning . . ."

She looked at him pleadingly, hoping he wouldn't need any more information, and he didn't. It seemed to him sometimes that that was the *last* morning; every day now started at noon.

"He left for work. I was lying in bed, thinking about him, and about us getting back together, and I saw that he'd left his cell phone on the bedstand. The light was blinking. There was a message. I wasn't going to listen, but I was curious about whether he'd changed the password on his phone. Of course . . . he didn't, the big idiot." She smiled. "So I listened."

Remy remembered the meeting with the lawyer. "It was the other woman," he said. "The one from his office?"

"Yes." April nodded.

Outside the room, Remy could hear someone climbing the stairs. Then he heard the Colorado guy's voice: "Excuse me?"

"Just a second," Remy said to April. He went out into the hallway and saw the man's head, just peaking at the midpoint of the stairs.

"Sorry," the guy said, "but my wife is really freaked that we're going to lose this place. Do you think you could tell your girlfriend that we're going to call someone else from her office about it?"

"Sure," Remy said. "Go ahead."

When he returned to the bathroom, April was staring out the window. After a moment, the cell phone slipped from her hand and clattered to the floor. April stared at it as if she'd never seen one before.

She took a deep breath. "The lawyer called," she said quietly. "While I was showing this place. He got my settlement. Six hundred twenty thousand." Her body seemed to hang from her spine like a robe on a hook. "I guess that's what you get for a slightly used, cheating husband these days. Six-twenty. I guess that's fair." She looked down. "I should've asked, just for comparison, what a sister was worth." But the joke was flat, and she covered her mouth with her fist and spit a kind of self-loathing laughter.

He began to move toward her, but bent and picked up her phone instead.

"I'm sorry, Brian," she said. "But the worst part has always been how much I miss him. I don't want to . . . but I do."

"I know," Remy said, and he handed her the—

BAR IN an Upper West Side restaurant, where he sat alone, staring through a full glass of whiskey, caramel colored and distorting everything in the room. Behind him, couples sat in red-tucked booths beneath beaded floor lamps; it was a jointy and comfortable place and Remy felt at ease here. He looked out the window. It was dark outside, that surprising early winter darkness that descended like a drawn blind. He looked back at the small glass of amber liquid on the bar in front of him, lifted it, hesitated, then brought it to his lips and downed it. So warm. He wondered if April was meeting him tonight. He pulled out his phone and thought about calling her and realized that he couldn't come up with her number.

"That's a fane whiskey, boyo." The bartender spoke with an affected Irish accent, but Remy didn't mind because it was, indeed, a fane whiskey. "D'ya know what you want to ate, than?"

Remy put his phone away and picked up the menu. Sure enough, there it was. He could take comfort in that, at least. "I'll have the wasabi duck marinated in red wine."

"Have way goat that?" The bartender took the menu and opened it. "Aye, thar 'tis. Moost be new, eh?" The bartender took the menu and snapped it against his leg. He winked, and slid another whiskey in front of Remy, who drained it.

"Excuse me. Mr. Remy?" There was a man at his shoulder, wearing the white shirt of a chef, buttoned at his shoulder.

"Yes?" He looked up, wondering for a moment how the chef knew his name.

"Brian Remy?"

"Yes. That's me."

"I have been instructed to tell you—" the man looked around the restaurant before bowing even closer. "This is reather embarrassing." He stared hard into Remy's eyes: "There is no wasabi marinated duck." When Remy didn't answer, he said, "Do you understand?"

"I think so," Remy said, pulling away from him. "Can I get something else?"

"You do understand what I'm saying?" the chef asked.

"There's no duck."

"Actually—" The man shuffled his feet nervously. "It's beginning to look like there never was any wasabi marinated duck." He tried to laugh this off, as if it had all been a funny misunderstanding, but his laugh was edgy and raw.

"O-o-okay," Remy said. "Can I get . . . a steak, maybe?"

"Of course," the man said, relieved. "Is that the course you'd like us to take?"

"I . . . I guess so. Yeah."

"Excellent," the chef said. "What kind?"

"I don't know," Remy said. "A ribeye?"

The man's eyebrows shot up. "A ribeye!"

"Yeah . . . I think so."

"I'll tell them," the chef said. He slipped Remy a matchbook and spun to walk away. Remy looked at the matchbook. He opened it. Written on the lip of the matchbook was one word: WALK.

Remy reached in his pocket, found the bottle of pills from his psychiatrist, and fumbled with the lid. Finally he got two out and swallowed them with a long drink of lemon water as he read the matchbook again.

"How did you want that?" The man was at his shoulder again.

Remy jumped. "What?"

"The ribeye, sir? How do you want it?"

"I don't know." Remy looked around for help. "Medium . . ." he said, but when the waiter looked concerned, he added, ". . . rare? Medium rare?"

"Excellent." The chef bowed. "I will let them know."

His steak arrived one whiskey later, steaming on a plate of potatoes, with a quiver of asparagus. The meat was lightly marbled and his steak knife glided through it. He jabbed it with his fork and it bled profusely, and he put it in his mouth. It was incredible, the best thing he'd ever eaten. The meat had a blue cheese glaze and the blood and cheese gave his plate a purplish tint. There were garlic mashed potatoes, too, and they turned purple from the blood, and the asparagus spears, too, the whole plate swimming in dark blood. Remy couldn't believe how much this steak bled and how good it was, and his eyes rolled back in his head as he ate. Another whiskey came, and it, too, was better than he could ever recall a whiskey being.

And when he was done, Remy put on his overcoat and began walking, across glaring traffic, down blocks with empty stoops, bags of garbage out for collection, across another street and into the park. It was a pleasant surprise, finding himself in the park, cutting across its northwest corner, and he was well into the park when he suddenly stopped and wondered why he didn't have his car, or why he didn't take a cab. What was he going to do, walk home forty blocks? Still, it was nice: a great steak, some whiskey and a walk through the park, especially this corner, his favorite part of the park—less traffic here, buildings that lurked over the tree line. He turned and began walking again, and had the warm feeling of being at the end of something, of being cradled by these warm buildings, by civilization. As the sidewalk curled past a dark stand of trees, Remy noticed that two streetlights here were burned out. He slowed. There was someone waiting in the shadows.

"Do you want to know what I find interesting?" asked a familiar voice.

Remy came closer and saw that it was the old Middle Eastern man in the long wool coat. He was leaning against a shadowed tree. Remy couldn't quite make out his face, but it was him, he was sure. "The way people here mock a religion that promises virgins waiting for martyrs in the world after this one. Your own culture would seem to indicate that there is nothing more profound than sex, nothing more humbling or graceful or suggestive of the mystery of creation. And yet the idea of virgins in paradise somehow seems to draw your greatest scorn. Do you honestly imagine yours is a sexless heaven? What kind of paradise is it that has harps and angels but no orgasms?"

Remy took a step back.

"What's the matter? You seem disappointed to see me."

"I was kind of hoping you were a hallucination." Remy reached in his pocket and emerged with the bottle of pills again. He popped the cap and two capsules spilled into his hand. He swallowed them. "My psychiatrist told me you didn't exist."

"That's not surprising." The man smiled warmly and spoke in a soft, mellifluous voice, like a professor giving a lecture. "You're always convincing yourselves that the world isn't what it is, that no one's reality matters except your own. That's why you make such poor victims. You can't truly know suffering if you know nothing about rage. And you can't feel genuine rage if you won't acknowledge loss.

"That's what happens when a nation becomes a public relations firm. You forget the truth. Everything is the Alamo. You claim victory in every loss, life in every death. Declare war when there is no war, and when you are at war, pretend you aren't. The rest of the world wails and vows revenge and buries its dead and you turn on the television. Go to the cinema."

The man moved away from the tree, so that his legs—and the bottom of that heavy wool coat—were bathed in light from the nearest street lamp. "Entertainment is the singular thing you produce now. And it is just another propaganda, the most insidious, greatest propaganda ever devised, and this is your only export now—your coffee and tobacco, your gunpowder and your wheat. And while people elsewhere die questioning the propaganda of tyrants and royals, you crave yours. You demand the propaganda of distraction and triviality, and it has become your religion, your national faith. In this faith you are grave and backward fundamentalists, not so different from the grave and backward fundamentalists you presume to battle. If they are barbarians knocking at the gates with stories of beautiful virgins in the afterlife, then aren't you barbarians too, wrapping the world in cables full of happy-everafter stories of fleshy blondes and animated fish and talking cars?"

Remy closed his eyes. Streaks and floaters swam against the current behind his lids, tiny birds rising endlessly against the stream. "You're going to give me something again, aren't you?" Remy asked. "A manila envelope or something?" He opened his eyes.

"No. I'm not," the man said.

And then he took a manila envelope from his coat and handed it to Remy. "And I think you have something for me?"

"I do?" Remy shifted the manila envelope to his other hand and felt in his pocket. Behind the bottle of pills he felt a thick envelope, half as big as a brick. How had he not noticed it before? Did someone in the restaurant give it to him? He pulled them both out. He handed the thick envelope to the man, who opened it and began counting bills.

"Can I see those?" The man nodded to the pills, without looking up from the money he was counting.

Remy looked down at the bottle of pills in his hand. He held it out.

The man stopped counting. He stepped out of the shadows, took the bottle, and read the label through the bifocals of his glasses. "For back pain." He looked up. "So do these help?"

Remy took the pills back and read them for the first time. He felt deflated. "I don't know," he muttered. "My back doesn't hurt."

"Then they *must* work," the man said, and he resumed counting.

Remy opened the manila envelope he'd been given. There was nothing in it but a phone number. Remy didn't recognize the area code. He felt exhausted. "What is this?"

"It's the number you asked for."

"But whose is it?"

The man didn't look up from his counting. "Don't be so suspicious."

"I'm not suspicious. I don't know whose number this is." Remy had always felt a strange urge to confide in this man. "Look . . . I'm not kidding here. I'm a mess. I'm drunk half the time. I cheat on my girlfriend when I don't even want to. In fact, I'm not even aware that I'm doing it until it's over. I apparently have this job where I file paper and chase down dead people, but I don't have the first idea what it means. I do these things that make no sense, and people get hurt. I come home with blood on my shoes and . . ." Remy laughed bitterly. ". . . my son won't even acknowledge that I'm alive."

"Morning in America," the man muttered, without looking up.

Remy felt himself slipping. "Look. Can you please tell me what I'm doing?"

The man was almost done counting.

"Please," Remy said. "Can't you tell me anything?"

The man held up one finger and stuffed the bills back in the envelope. "Did I tell you that Jesus is mentioned ninety-three times in the Koran?"

"Yeah." Remy slumped against a tree. "I think you said that."

"Oh," the man said. He slid the envelope into his coat pocket. "Well . . . it bears repeating now."

MAHOUD SHOOK. He licked his lips, holding the cell phone weakly in one hand while, in the other, he held a piece of paper. Remy looked around. He and Markham and Mahoud were sitting in a shiny red booth in Mahoud's restaurant, which was empty, lights out except in the kitchen, chairs stacked on the center tables.

"Calm down," Markham said. "Nice and easy. You're almost done."

Mahoud nodded as he pressed the buttons on the phone, looking back and forth from the sheet to the phone. He cleared his throat. "Hello," he said. "Do you know who this is? Yes. I am ready. I want in." He listened. "I know what I said, but I've changed my mind." He looked up at Markham. "Because someone has to do something."

The other person said something and Mahoud began writing.

Remy's head snapped, as if he'd awakened from a dream. "What is this?" he asked. "What are we doing?"

Markham looked and put his finger to his lips.

"No. No, I'm not going to do this anymore," Remy said. "I quit." He stood and walked to the door of the restaurant. It was locked, so he turned the deadbolt, burst out into the street, and began running. He ran down the sidewalk until—

REMY RODE the elevator up alone. There was no music. He looked down at the bank of buttons—two rows as long as his forearm. This elevator was apparently going to the twenty-first floor; he'd gotten used to elevators telling him where to go. So he waited until the 21 light flashed overhead, and when the doors opened he stepped out into the lobby of Shannon Phelps Breen, April's real estate company. Behind a curved desk, the receptionist was standing and facing away, tethered to her desk by the curling cord from her telephone headset. She was staring at a bank of glass offices, where some kind of argument appeared to be taking place. Other people were standing in the lobby, men and women in business suits, leaning against walls and staring into the same glass office, like kids in the playground gathering to watch a fight.

And that's when Remy heard April's raised voice, coming from the glass office. "I don't need to settle down!" she shouted. "Leave me alone!"

And then he saw her, through the glass, standing behind a desk. Two men approached her from opposite sides of the desk, their hands up, as if they were trying to disarm a suicidal person.

"Thanks for coming." Her voice.

Remy turned and saw Nicole, arms crossed, wearing a dusty pink suit that appeared to be made of fabric from a vintage couch. She had a spot of blood under her nose; Remy must have stared at it a moment too long, for she touched her middle finger to the blood, pulled it away, and looked at it. "I'm afraid she needs some help," Nicole said.

"Oh, God. This isn't about—"

Nicole dropped her chin and stared at him as if he were accusing her of being an idiot. "Come on," she said in a stage whisper. "Give me some credit. Do you think I would tell an emotionally disturbed subordinate that I fucked her boyfriend? Please. To my knowledge she is still unaware of that little fact. And a word of advice: If you're thinking of coming clean, I think this might not be . . . the best time."

Remy turned back to watch April through the glass. She was crying and waving something around; at first Remy worried it was a gun, but it was a stapler.

"She snapped," Nicole said. "I called her in for a conference call with an unhappy client, who said she wouldn't sell him an option on a hedge he wanted to buy. She just lost it, started yelling at him and throwing things. She broke a twelve hundred dollar vase. I hung up and got out of there, but she just kept screaming." Her voice settled into a dull monotone. "I suppose I should blame myself. She wasn't ready to come back to work. I thought it would help her, but I guess—"

There was no need to finish the thought as the men moved closer and April yowled and threw the stapler at one of them. The man ducked; the other one reached her and caught her in a bear hug. She tried to slip out of his grasp, but he had her. Only then did Remy move across the room, toward the offices. The other agents in the office, with their assistants and secretaries, stood along the walls staring, many of them with their hands over their mouths, as if they'd just witnessed a hit-and-run accident. Remy stepped between desks and arrived at the glass door of Nicole's office. A tall Japanese-American man in a navy blue suit was restraining April, standing behind her, his arms wrapped around her so that her arms were pinned. "Come on. Settle down, April."

She struggled against the man. "Goddamn it, let go of me! I'm fine."

"I'll let go when you settle down," the man said patiently.

April made a guttural noise and threw her head back but missed the man's face by inches.

"April?" Remy said from the doorway.

She looked up then, met Remy's eyes, and went slack.

"It's okay," Remy said. "You can let her go now."

The man stared at Remy like he was crazy, but something in his tone, or his stare, convinced him and the man let her go. April pulled away and looked around, saw everyone outside staring at her, and slumped to the floor, crying in little huffs of breath. Remy looked around the office. Photos and paintings were strewn everywhere, and broken glass. The desk was cleared of books and plants and family pictures, as if a bad magician had tried pulling a tablecloth out from under the whole room.

The two men backed away slowly. "I've never seen anyone go off like that," said one of them. He straightened his perfectly straight tie. "We were afraid she was going to hurt herself. Is she on something?"

"I don't know," Remy said. He stepped around the desk, to where April was sitting, hugging her knees to her chest. He crouched down. "Are you okay?"

She looked up and met his eyes. She swallowed. "Apparently not."

"What happened?"

Her head fell to one side and her face scrunched up as if she were going to cry. But she didn't. "I'm not sure. I just . . . I guess I had enough. I couldn't walk around pretending any of this made sense anymore.

Everyone is acting crazy, Brian. Here and . . ." She looked up at him. "Everywhere. Is everything okay with us, Brian?"

And suddenly, Remy thought he could see the world clearly. He had tried to go along, waiting for the fog to clear, for the terrain to make sense. But what if it never cleared? Then a word spoke itself in his head, as if not from him, but from outside.

Act, it said. Act. "Yes, everything's okay," Remy whispered. And then he said, quietly, so that maybe he wouldn't hear, "Let's go somewhere," and he was pleased at the way the thought seemed to catch its thinker, him, off guard.

She cocked her head. "What?"

"You and me. Let's . . . go somewhere. Just drop everything and leave the city. Why not?" He felt thrilled, in a way; that he could surprise himself seemed like an option he hadn't even considered.

"When?" she asked.

Don't think. "Right now," he said. "Tonight."

"Tonight?" She looked up, eyes rimmed with tears. "Really?"

"Sure. Let's just go."

"Where?"

"You pick," Remy said.

She stared at him, saw that he was serious, and wiped her wet eyes. "We can do that?"

"I think so," Remy said. "I think we can do anything. Can't we?"

She covered her mouth. "I don't know. I can't remember."

"Look, I'll be right back," Remy said. "Don't move."

He left her crouched behind the desk, obscured from the people in the lobby, and came back out of the office. "I'm gonna get her out of here," he told Nicole, the last onlooker left waiting for them outside. "But do you think you could clear everyone out? This is hard enough."

"Of course," Nicole said.

"We'll pay for any damage that was done," he said.

"You think?" Nicole smiled. "That's certainly a fatalistic way to look at it. If that's the case, maybe we should do some more damage." She ran her index finger along the waistband of his pants.

Remy pulled back. "I mean the damage April did to your office."

"Oh, that." Nicole shrugged. "Don't worry about it."

Remy started to turn back, then stopped. "What set her off?"

"Honestly, I have no idea." Nicole looked around him to her trashed office. "This young stock analyst wanted us to make an option offer on a hedge for a potential studio in a proposed rehab on some re-grade land possibly slated for rezoning down in BPC. And for some reason April just . . . refused to do it. She just kept saying it was crazy. That it made no sense. That it was too much money and that we were selling air. She said someone had to put a stop to it. She was crying and screaming, *This makes no sense. We're all pretending it does, but it doesn't.* As you might guess, this is not the best position for a real estate broker."

"I'm sorry," Remy said. And he had a thought. "How much was the apartment?"

"It wasn't an apartment. It was an option. Actually, it was more like an option on an option." She paused. "On an option."

"How much was it?"

"That's the crazy thing. It was only six twenty. A steal."

Remy closed his eyes. Six hundred twenty thousand dollars. Right. "Okay. Thanks." He turned to walk away.

"Will you call me?" she asked.

"I hope not," he said, without turning. He returned to Nicole's office, the broken glass crunching beneath his feet. He knelt down and took April in his arms again. When he looked over the desk, he saw that Nicole had cleared the lobby. Remy helped April to her feet and led her out of the office, his arm around her, her head against his shoulder.

"We can go anywhere?" she asked.

"Anywhere."

"How about—"

"Shhh," Remy interrupted. "Don't tell me. I'd rather be—"

WEDGED INTO the round window at the back of the plane, Remy saw what looked like toy ships on the bay below, their wakes like chalk scratches on a blackboard. The jet banked and Remy felt himself pressed against the door, and in a glance he could see where the water ended and then the rough line of shore and the city lay suddenly before him like a grid of transistors, gray and white rectangles and reflected bits of sun, rising in the center of the peninsula like a mound of sifted sand. San Francisco. He'd never been to San Francisco. At least, not that he knew. He'd always wanted to go to California.

The jet leveled. "Excuse me, sir." A flight attendant took Remy's arm and smiled at him. "The captain has turned on the fasten seat belt sign. You'll need to return to your seat. We're about to land."

Remy looked ahead at the full rows, a hundred heads bobbing above the cloth seats. He could hear low conversations but he couldn't see a single pair of lips moving, and for a moment the roar of the jet and the murmur of people seemed like the same noise, as if this plane ran on empty talk. Should he just walk forward until he found an empty seat? Remy felt his back pants pockets hopefully, and was relieved to come up with a folded ticket. Seat 2A. First class. Well, that was good. But something seemed wrong. If he was in first class, why was he in the back of the plane?

As he walked forward, Remy's shoulders slumped. Ten rows from the back, Markham was reclining in the aisle seat, wearing a Hawaiian shirt and sunglasses, and reading an airline magazine. How did he find out? As Remy approached, Markham stood and pretended to be looking in his overhead bin for something. Remy edged past and Markham turned and bumped him, pressing a cell phone into Remy's hand.

Remy put the phone in his pocket and walked toward the front of the plane. He looked over his shoulder once, but Markham was hidden behind his magazine. At the bulkhead Remy stepped through the open curtains into first class, relieved to see April in 2B. She had a glass of red wine. Another mini-bottle of Syrah was waiting its turn on her seat tray. Remy eased in, latched his seat belt, and looked out the window. They were south of San Francisco, circling back toward the airport.

"You're right," she said, toasting him with the wine. "This does help. This helps a lot." She filled her glass. "To more help."

Remy looked back over his shoulder.

"So why'd you go to the back of the plane?" she asked.

"I guess to meet someone."

"Really?" She laughed. "You a member of the mile-high club now?"

"No," he said. "It was a guy I know. He gave me a phone." He held up the flip phone for her to see.

"Someone gave you a phone?" She took his arm and nestled in. She laughed. "That makes absolutely no sense." She laughed again. "I like being drunk."

The new cell phone rang.

"Hey!" she said, delighted.

Remy stared at it before opening it. "Hello."

"Hey, so here's something funny," Markham said. "You know how people are always describing the exciting part of a movie as *a race against time*? Like, say at the end, they've got to discover a vaccine before the virus wipes out everyone, or they've got to cut the wires on the bomb before it blows up, or find the ruthless killer before he strikes. But think about how stupid that is: a race against time. You can't race time. It's like trying to swim faster than water. No matter how fast you go, time is the thing you're moving in; it's the thing against which your speed is measured. How can you race time? I guess Einstein showed how time bends at certain speeds, or that it slows down or speeds up, but that still isn't like *racing* time, and anyway, the truth is, we can't go those Einstein speeds anyway . . . they're science fiction, right? I mean . . . you can't go faster than time. It doesn't even make sense. It's like being taller than faith, you know? Or smarter than hope. Anyway, I just knew that's the kind of thing you'd get a kick out of, you know, given the situation."

Remy looked over at April, who was nestled into her first-class seat, holding her wine and smiling at him.

"Who is it?" she mouthed.

Remy didn't know what to say.

"Sir," said a male flight attendant. "You are not allowed to use your cell phone while we're in flight."

"I gotta go," Remy said into the phone.

"Oh yeah," Markham said. "Sure. I just wanted to tell you how that thing about racing against time occurred to me. It just cracked me up, that's all. And I knew you'd see the insanity in a phrase like that. Although, honestly, I don't know what you'd substitute: *A wrestling match against fate?*" Markham laughed. *"A game of cribbage against lethargy?"*

"Sir," the flight attendant said again.

Remy snapped the phone shut and the flight attendant moved on.

"Who was it?" April asked again.

Before he could answer, the plane shuddered against a wave of turbulence and April grabbed his hand and closed her eyes. "Oh, I hate this," she said. She drained the last of her wine and the flight attendant cleared the glasses.

"It's okay," Remy said.

Sometimes Remy knew things without specifically remembering how he knew them, and in this way he knew that this was the first time that April had flown anywhere since that day. He looked back at the faces on the plane, sets of wide eyes glancing around, one woman holding a string of beads and mouthing prayers. The couple across the row from him rocked with shared anxiety.

anywhere." And indeed, there was a syrupy languor in this hotel room in the late afternoon that caused him to believe her, and they fell into a rhythm that seemed to go on all afternoon, until Remy found himself experiencing a kind of overwhelming sentience that was disconnected from what they were doing, his body moving on its own while he found himself thinking pleasurably about the sounds of car horns and trucks on the street outside, and the *San Fran!* tourist magazine on the nightstand (with a photo of that famous, stupid crooked street on the cover) and tracking the drops of sweat on his own face, and listening to someone watching television in the room next door and, finally, with the sun setting through the open curtains and casting a fevered glow across their bodies, he fixated on the inside of her ear, a pink curling seashell of cartilage that amazed him with its delicacy and its utter efficiency— skin stretched over it like a drum, and somehow, all the sound in the room (*Oh yes mmm yes*) flowed into it, to be sorted, defined, and acted upon instantaneously. And this made him wonder about the other human miracles he took for granted: speech and smell and his own shattered vision, and at that very moment, such thoughts were vanquished by the sheer tyranny of nerve endings, those in his fingertips and, of course, those in the suddenly intense *elsewhere*, which was the only *feeling* right then, a wet hot friction that caused a low groan to rise in his throat and finally . . .

"Well," she gasped when he fell off her. "That was certainly . . . *a lot* of sex." She rubbed his belly and pulled a sheet across her own midsection as they lay on the big king-size bed, breathing deeply. She put her head on Remy's chest. "What's the opposite of premature?" she asked. "Postmature?"

"Sorry," he said, and he remembered Nicole, and squeezed his eyes shut to make her go away, lost in the swirl of failing tissue.

"Were you going for some kind of endurance record? Or just seeing if you could make me taller?"

Remy turned back. "Really. It's going to be okay," he said again a
the plane banked and lurched.

"I just hate it," she said. "I close my eyes and I see—"

"I know," Remy said, and he patted her hand and looked back agai
at the rows of imploring eyes. "We all see it."

The jet bore down, grinding and moaning, toward the runway, the
seemed to hover a few feet above it, before it lurched and skipped, fe
several feet, and leveled, the hydraulic landing gear spitting, spinnin
and catching and then the frantic clutch of elevators, strain of thou
sands of rivets, and the seize of brakes, and a thousand technologic
miracles later, Remy and April were walking down a jetway, Rem
looking nervously over his shoulder. Act, he thought. Just do what yo
have to do. This is your life. She paused to switch her carry-on bag t
the other shoulder, but Remy hurried her along, weaving in and out o
the crowds.

"Ooh," she said, "we're in a hurry."

They made their way downstream and were outside baggage clai
when Remy saw a flash of Hawaiian shirt behind him and sudden
pulled her toward the door and outside. "Come on."

"What about our bags?" April asked.

"Leave them," he said.

They stepped into the giant horseshoe of the airport turnaroun
the air buzzing in the late afternoon with cars and vans like insects on
carcass. Remy could hear his new cell phone chirping as he hustle
April toward a cab. He opened the door for her and she told the cabbi
the address of their Union Square hotel. "Just a sec," Remy said.

He ran back and pitched the ringing cell phone into a garbage car

THEY UNDRESSED quietly, and began making love, and at firs
Remy found himself hurrying, afraid that he would lose track befor
they finished. "Hey, hey," she whispered. "Slow down. I'm not goin

"I was distracted," he said. "Sorry."

"No, it was nice," she said. "I always wondered what it would be like to have sex with an oil derrick."

Remy stood next to the bed.

"Go get me a wheelchair and we'll go to dinner."

He walked to the window and looked outside. The sidewalks were full of people with briefcases, making their way down the city's hills, leaning back as they walked, as if they were being sucked down into the creases of the city, as if they were winding down a drain.

"Every man has the same ass," April said, leaning up in bed. "When you're young they're all different, but by the time you get to a certain age . . . same ass. So why is that? There are a thousand varieties of women's asses, but you all have the same one."

Remy came back to bed. April had gotten a little bottle of wine from the minibar, and she drank from it with one hand while she held the remote in the other, running through the channels faster than Remy could register the programs.

"I can't see anything," he said. "What are you watching?"

"Electrons," she said.

So he watched electrons with her, the screen flickering with transient images, and every once in a while he caught one, but they all seemed like pictures from an older America: a woman drove a farm truck; someone ran on a soccer field; a house burned; a couple was married; and then there were the faces, thousands of faces that failed to register anything but the idea of a single shifting face. Aside from the speed, there was something hypnotic and familiar, something intoxicating in this view of life, something that he recalled knowing. But finally the fluttering television was too much like the disorder in his eyes and Remy had to turn away. He reached for the room service menu. "Want to get a real bottle of wine?"

"That," she said, patting him on the thigh, "is exactly what I want."

Remy was flipping past the dinner menu toward the wine list when he suddenly turned back. The menu was contained in a three-ring binder, and a separate page had been slipped in, handwritten, and showing that day's specials.

"We have to leave." Remy got up and began dressing, the menu open on the bed below him to the dinner special: wasabi marinated duck.

AT NIGHT the homeless in San Francisco operate like cabbies, she explained to him as they hurried down the block. "Trust me, I know this city. If you make eye contact, they'll offer to give you directions or walk with you to where you're going. There's a whole underground city of the homeless and they come up at night to get money for wine and slices of pizza. And there is always one willing to show you to your hotel for a buck or two, or take you to the best club or restaurant. They all know each other and they wave at each other when they pass, and sometimes roll their eyes, just like cabbies with bad fares. I think there's even a union," April said, "like the Five-One-Six or something, the international brotherhood of the homeless and indigent."

She talked as they hustled down the street with only their carry-on bags, Remy occasionally looking back over his shoulder. He saw what looked like a flash of Markham's Hawaiian shirt a block back, in a crush of people waiting to cross Geary. Remy and April walked two blocks to Sutter, doubled back, and ducked into a dark corner hotel, the lobby bustling with a Japanese tour group waiting to go to dinner.

"We should go with them," April said. "Pretend we don't speak English. Take pictures of everything. Buy postcards and snow globes."

Remy pulled her through the lobby and out a side door, where they were met by a black man in torn jeans and an engineer's cap. His teeth were gray and placed at random, a handful on top, fewer on bottom.

"You folks need directions?" the man asked. "I know this city better'n you know your wife's poodum."

"We'll need to see your union card," April laughed.

The man ignored her as Remy fumbled in his pocket for cash. He handed the man a five-dollar bill. "There's a white guy in a Hawaiian shirt. Brown hair, really young looking. If he comes this way, I need you to stall him. Ask him for money, knock him down, anything."

They kept moving, zigging up streets and down their crosses as April turned and read the marquees of theaters and the names of stores and bars. Finally, Remy pulled her into a hotel lounge and they sank low into a table in the corner. "We'll just sit here for a while and then I'll go check in," Remy said.

"That sounds nice," said April sweetly, drunkenly. "We can wear wigs and grow mustaches so no one recognizes us. And I'll learn to sew. I'll sew all our food. We'll live off the grid, in a cabin built from empty wine bottles." When the waitress came he ordered whiskey for himself and a glass of red wine for April. Remy looked back over his shoulder to the street outside. Faces moved past like the flickering images on the TV.

April rubbed her foot against his leg. "We could take off all our clothes and crawl under the table," April said. "They'll never think to look for us there."

The waitress brought their drinks and Remy drained his whiskey and gestured for another.

April raised her wineglass. "Just for the record, Mr. Remy, I am having the time of my life."

Remy smiled. "Good." But then he had a troubling thought. He picked up his menu and leafed through it quickly, running his index finger down the rows of appetizers and entrées. When he saw that it wasn't there, he sighed, set the menu down and fell back in his chair.

"Relax," April said. "You're doing a great job, whatever it is you're doing."

"Have you decided?" The waitress was standing over them.

"Yeah. I have," he said, and with a relief that bordered on joy, Brian Remy ordered the yellow pepper, black bean, and artichoke quesadilla.

THEY MADE love in the new hotel room, too, and when they were done Remy took a long shower. He closed his eyes and let the hot water cascade over his face, pelting his eyelids and his forehead. He opened his mouth and it filled with water and he spat it out, over and over. When he came out April was sleeping and he watched her for a moment, the slow rise and fall of her breasts.

Finally, Remy dropped his towel and climbed into bed, nestling in behind her and staring into the tangle of her dark hair. He kissed the top of her head and she stirred slightly. She looked back over her shoulder at him, smiled, and faced the other way again.

"How was your shower?" she whispered.

"It was good."

"Good. I like showers. I like to let the water run right over my face like I'm standing in a waterfall."

They lay there quietly for a while, until her breathing caught up to his and for a moment they were inhaling and exhaling together, and then her breathing began to pull away again, with those cute little puffs of air. It occurred then to Remy that they had no clothes except the ones they'd arrived in, which were now lying on the floor. They'd either have to go back to the airport to get their luggage or go shopping.

"Listen, tomorrow—" Remy began.

"Shh," she said. "No tomorrow."

HE WOKE at ten to the sound of a light knocking at the door. April was still asleep. He looked up. The walls in the room were off-white, and the room had a light oak armoire that contained the television, re-frigerator, and stereo. The door was still deadbolted shut. "Yes?" he said.

"Housekeeping," said a voice on the other side.

"Can you come back?" Remy said.

"Chure. I comb back."

Remy sat up and looked around the room. It was smaller than the other hotel room, nothing in this room but a bed and a small desk with a business phone. He called downstairs for coffee, fruit, and bagels.

"We could stay here forever," she said from the bed.

"You think so?" Remy asked.

"Just run from hotel to hotel, screwing and pretending someone's after us."

Remy didn't say anything.

"We'll change our names every day. Today . . . I'll be Monique. Who are you?"

"What?"

"Who are you going to be?"

"Uh . . . Steve," Remy said.

"Steve and Monique. Good. Okay, who are we? What do we do?"

"I don't know," Remy said.

"Monique is a jewel thief. She's fifty-two. A former actress and fig-ure skater from the old Soviet Union who defected as a teenager, but after the Cold War ended she missed the old intrigue, so she works for an international cartel stealing jewels from wealthy industrialists and other assholes who capitalize on poor workers."

Remy looked back at her. "Monique doesn't look fifty-two."

"She's had a lot of surgery."

"So who's Steve?" he asked.

"A dentist. From Akron, Ohio."

"Yeah . . . I don't think I want to be Steve."

"Okay," she said. "Then I'll be Steve. You be Monique. Come here, Monique, lie on your back and show me your mouth."

And then a thought bobbed to the surface and he had to ask it. "April," Remy said. "If Derek hadn't died . . . is there any chance you and he—"

She looked stung and her eyes moved almost imperceptibly to a point just beyond him. "No."

"But you still loved him. You said so."

"Yes," she said. "I did."

"Was it the other woman?"

"No . . . I don't think there was really anything between them," she said quietly. "In some ways it was . . . incidental."

"So what . . . you just couldn't forgive him for doing that?"

"Something like that," she said. "Look, I don't—" She sat up and reached for her shirt, tugged it on without a bra and pulled the sheet up around her waist. "We were having so much fun, Brian. Why'd you have to—" But she didn't finish. She picked up the remote control and started running through the channels again. Remy watched the TV go from one reality to another and again—it was mesmerizing—and he thought about how familiar this was, the way the television skipped from news to sports to music videos, the way these imperceptible gaps led from sorrow to humor and pathos, from a game show to televised real estate listings to a panel talking about books. But this time, the pictures moved too slowly for April and after a minute of trolling inanity she turned off the TV and hurled the remote across the room. It hit the wall and fell in pieces of plastic and double-A batteries.

THEY BOUGHT new clothes in a store called Fugue. She got tight leather pants and a little spaghetti strap tank top, and Remy bought faded jeans and a powder blue dress shirt. Remy carried their old clothes in a shopping bag. They went to a boutique shoe store and picked out a pair for each other: hers had straps that wrapped around the backs of her ankles and he got low-cut boots with square toes.

"Wow. We look hot," she said when he came out in his new shoes. "I kind of want to screw us."

They hopped in a cab and April told the cabbie to take them to a romantic restaurant, so he dropped them off at a little place in North Beach, where they had lunch and a bottle of Chianti in a sidewalk café. The wine was gone before their entrées arrived, and they had another carafe and lingered over a split bowl of spumoni.

"What's your names?" asked the walnut-eyed Italian waiter.

"I'm Steve," April said. "And his name is Monique."

"Steve," the waiter said, looking at Remy. "Monique. Can I tell you something?"

"You can tell us anything," she said.

The waiter proceeded to tell them how he'd been raised in a vineyard and hotel on the western coast of Italy and how he'd gone into debt over some gambling expenses and escaped to the United States to work for an uncle, who had kept him in a kind of indentured servitude at the restaurant ever since. Remy didn't know if he believed the story, but he liked it very much.

"How old you think I am, Steve?" He put his face close to Remy's. He looked to be about fifty, Remy thought.

"I don't know . . . forty?"

"Come on," the man said. "I look sixty easy, yes? Well what I am, I tell you, is thirty-eight, Steve. That's all. Thirty-eight. An' you know why I look so old, Monique?"

She was resting her chin in her hand, smiling. "Why?"

"Because I never fall so much in love like you two." The waiter held his hands out between Remy and April, as if he were performing a wedding. "I never find no one make me so happy."

"You'll find someone," April said.

"No. Not me. No more."

"Sure you will."

"No. It's okay." He seemed to be looking for words. "In America," he said, "everyone thinks every story have a happy end, yeah? You're not happy about one thing, what do you do? Sue each other. It's so stupid. How can every story be a happy end? Someone got to be sad."

A SIGN on a light pole advertised an *End of the World Party* at a club near the Haight, and April wanted to go somewhere in their new clothes, so they took a cab and waited on line with people at least a decade younger, overgrown boys in sideburns and girls with lower back tattoos rising from their pants like bursts of hair, all of them bouncing on the balls of their feet and yelling into their cell phones. Remy and April stared at the door and listened to the thumping for about thirty minutes until a thick bouncer took twenty bucks and waved them past and they walked through an awning, around an iron gate and down a staircase into a cavernous basement with pillars, floor lighting, and a low ceiling. A disc jockey was playing punkish electronic music on a simple turntable set up on milk crates, the sound a slush of guitars, synthesizers, and sibilant voices, punctuated by that same thud of drums, merely suggestive from the outside, insistent now that they were on the pulsing dance floor.

It was so crowded that all they could do, all anyone could do, was bounce up and down, jerking their heads, everyone occupying his own airspace—and for such a writhing, wriggling mass of people, Remy was surprised how little they touched each other. He tried to place the music, but his points of reference seemed more than dated, possibly anachronistic—David Bowie covers played by robots? Inside, the crowd wasn't as young as it seemed on line, but it felt to Remy as if these people had all been given some sort of manual before they arrived explaining how to act in such a club. They all danced the same, heads jerking, bodies coiled, no partner in sight, and they raised their hands at the same time, but most of all they knew how to communicate with each other, bobbing in to the left ear of the listener so that, from a distance, every conversation looked like a mother bird feeding her chick.

There were no tables, and everyone along the walls was dancing, and yet people seemed to have drinks, so Remy began to search for the bar, and that's when he saw a staircase to the left of the stage, lined with people trying to get a drink.

April was dancing with her eyes closed, her body snapping like a stiff whip, her head nodding as if she were being forced, over and over, to agree with something she found distasteful. When did I forget how to dance? Remy thought. When did I lose track of music and what you're supposed to do with it? "Let's get a drink!" he yelled, but her eyes didn't open, so he did the mother bird and yelled in her ear. "Drink!" and she opened her eyes and grabbed his arm, shaking her head no.

"I'm going to get one," he said and pointed to the stairs.

He read her lips. "No. Stay here. Dance. Unless your back's bothering you?"

"My back is fine," he yelled. And so they danced for more than an hour, until Remy's back did ache, and his head swam with the unceasing drums, and finally he couldn't dance anymore and he just stood in the middle of all those swirling young bodies, watching as April—eyes closed—snapped her body over and over, from her tight leather pants to the tendrils of black hair that lashed her face unmercifully.

MORNING AND Remy sat up cold and naked in the hotel bed, all the covers wrapped around April, who slept peacefully facing away from him. He looked around the bright room. Two empty wine bottles sat on the table with two red-rimmed wineglasses and their new clothes were strewn around the floor in front of the bed.

There was a light knock at the door. "Housekeeping."

Remy looked at the clock. It was 9:45. "Can you come back later?"

"Chure," the man said. "I comb back."

Remy padded off to the shower and after a minute she joined him and soaped him into making love, and when they were done they went back to bed.

It was two in the afternoon before they made it out of the hotel room. They had gyros at a little Greek stand that April said reminded her of her father's cooking. They bought more new clothes—April got a tiny denim skirt and high boots, and she even talked Remy into loosening up and he got a shirt with wild cuffs and jeans with manufactured rips in the thighs, and when he said he felt stupid in them, she took him to a bar and made him down three whiskeys in quick succession and, he was forced to admit, he didn't feel stupid any longer.

"Where you folks from?" asked the female bartender.

"British Columbia," answered April. "A little town in the Rockies at the foot of this glacier. We hike up and carry buckets of ice down for our drinking water. There's no electricity or phone service and Dustin here has to cut logs for us to burn in our woodstove to cook and keep us warm."

"Maggie makes all our clothes," Remy said. "We eat only roots. In the summer we're always naked. I have a pet moose."

"Wow," the bartender said. "How'd you end up there?"

"Dustin was a draft dodger," April said. "Conscientious objector. He moved up to Canada and I went and joined him. Fucking government, you know? We just got so sick of America we couldn't take it any more. At some point, a place loses enough of itself that you have no choice but to abandon it." She leaned in as if sharing a secret. "And frankly, I think it's gotten worse."

"Ain't that the truth," the bartender said as she loaded glasses in the dishwasher. But then she looked up at the couple and Remy could see that she was calculating their ages.

"You went up there to avoid serving in *Vietnam*?" the bartender asked.

"No," April said. "Panama."

"Oh," she said. "Sure."

On the advice of the bartender, they took the train to the baseball stadium and walked to a nearby pier, where they found a man with striking gray beard renting kayaks and wetsuits from a huge shipping container. The man asked if they had experience with sea kayaks.

"Not specifically," April said, "but I was a river guide in the Grand Canyon the summer after I got out of the Peace Corps, and Toody here rowed crew at Princeton."

"JV," he said.

"Still," the kayak guy said, "you should have no trouble."

They set out awkwardly from the pier, where the water was still, and quickly figured out the balance required. Remy loved the way the edge of his paddle disappeared in the dark water and the way he could thrust the boat forward, the muscles in his arms and shoulders burning from the work. They developed a quick rhythm, April in front, digging with her paddle, her little shoulders beginning to quake with the effort, and when Remy tried to slow down, for her sake, she just pushed harder, and so he did too, their leans and pushes working together until they got going so fast that it felt as if they were carving the water, as if their wake might go for miles, across the bay to the rest of the world. And only then did April stop and look around, at the diffuse clouds battered by light blue sky.

"Why did you ask me about Derek?" she said without turning.

"I don't know," he said.

"He was from here," she said. "From San Francisco. Did you know that?"

"I don't know," he said.

"I'm sorry," she said. "Maybe it was wrong to come here. But I haven't been thinking about him . . . if that's what you're wondering."

"I'm not. It's fine."

She didn't say anything else. They drifted around the point and out into the heart of the bay, into heavier chop, the spray stinging their eyes as the wind pushed them toward deeper water and the shadows of sailboats glided past, bending on the waves like shimmering apparitions.

"Goddamn it," she said.

IN DREAMS, at least in this dream, Remy's eyesight was perfect, the world clear and crisp and devoid of the static that he'd grown accustomed to. And even asleep, he noted to himself that he hadn't been dreaming very much since . . .

He looked around, amazed by the clarity and the quiet of everything he saw. He was standing outside Edgar's old primary school, waiting for the boy to get out of school, watching the stream of familiar faces as they came out of the building: Edgar's old babysitter, followed by Guterak, and then Billy Joel, who became the gyro guy who used to set up outside Midtown and then the gyro guy from San Francisco and finally April's father, who stood shaking his head disapprovingly. But while the buildings and trees and everything within his vision was clear, when he looked up Remy could see flashers and floaters in the sky, which was a gray slate, clouds of ash and dust flowing overhead like a river of debris, and when Remy looked down, the flecks came down to the world, too. Edgar's school had become 1 Police Plaza—police headquarters—and Remy was standing outside the barricade as cops ran out of 1PP in a panic, and now Remy was terrified for Edgar, who must still be inside. He could hear someone crying and then Remy was jerked awake, sat up and opened his eyes. April was sitting at the end of the bed, still wearing the little denim skirt, but nothing else. She was sobbing, her eyes dark, wet swaths worn along her cheeks. Remy stirred to come toward her but she held up her hand to keep him from coming any closer.

"I went along with everything, didn't I?" she asked. "We were having a good time, right? And even when you acted all crazy and paranoid, I just pretended it was normal."

"April—"

"But then you had to ask about Derek."

"I'm sorry," he said.

She turned. "If I tell you . . . everything, will you promise you'll never ask about it again? Promise that we'll never have to talk about it."

"Okay," Remy said. "I'll try."

She stood and walked to the window, opened the curtain and looked out on the dark street. He could see the glow from the streetlights on her pale skin like a halo.

"We talked all that weekend and we went to dinner that Monday night," she said to the window, "and I let him spend the night . . . and he even went to work Tuesday in the same clothes. He thought that was so funny . . . and it felt so natural, like before he left. I kissed him goodbye at the door of our apartment. And I think that's the first time I really allowed myself to realize how much I missed him, and to think that we might be back where we were." She turned back to face Remy and it reminded him of the way she'd kept paddling the kayak, her shoulders straining with the effort. "It was after Derek walked out the door that I saw his cell phone on the bookshelf, with the message light blinking. So I listened—"

"The woman from his office," Remy said.

"March." She spit the name as if it had been caught in her throat, her voice cracking. April turned away again and seemed to realize for the first time that she was naked above the waist. She pulled a towel off the floor and wrapped it around her shoulders. "March was the woman he—"

"Ah Jesus," Remy said.

April smiled sickly. "I had talked to her on Monday . . . and I told her that Derek was coming over . . . that we were thinking of reconciling. She was so quiet. And I thought—" She laughed bitterly. "I thought she was just worried about me, worried that I would get hurt. So I told her not to worry about it, that Derek was a different man. And that I knew what I was doing."

April seemed unaware that tears were streaking her cheeks. "She and Derek had always had this . . . flirtation. I always thought it was aimed at me . . . you know, the way sisters try to make each other feel off balance? Jealous? But as soon as I heard her voice on his phone I knew. I knew. I wanted to throw the phone across the room. I wanted to hang up. But I couldn't. I just listened."

Remy asked what the message had said.

"She was rambling, freaking out. She wanted to know if it was true that Derek was thinking of getting back together with me . . . she said that he'd lied to her. And she felt awful. She never would have slept with him if she'd known he still had feelings for me. She said she'd been vulnerable because of her breakup with the married guy and Derek had taken advantage of that, and I don't know—" April laughed again. "She said that if Derek hurt me, she would kill him. If *he* hurt me . . . do you believe that? Goddamn her."

"What did you do?"

"I called her at work. I yelled at her."

"That morning?" It was as if the ground gave way beneath Remy's feet. "*You* called her? *That* morning?"

—March taking the phone call, crying at her desk—

"I told her she was a whore and that she wasn't my sister and I never wanted to talk to her again. I told her that I was going to tell Dad she was a whore." April shook her head. "March said I had it wrong, that it only happened once, that they were drunk, whatever . . . She kept trying to whisper, I guess because she was at work." April slumped back into her chair. "And that pissed me off, that she could still be thinking about what people thought of her. I hung up the phone . . . listened to the message again and then I called her desk. But she was gone. So I called Derek's office and . . ." April twitched. ". . . March was *there*. In his office. That was the worst part: that she was there with him. I was all alone in my apartment and they were twenty blocks away, in another room. Together. Forever, as it turned out."

"Was Derek's office on the same floor?" Remy asked quietly.

"No. Four floors above."

—March, agitated, hanging up the phone, running to the elevator—

"I knew she was there. He was talking, telling me to settle down, but there was . . . nothing. I just felt totally empty. Like I'd been hollowed out."

She stared past him for a long time and then laughed bitterly. "So . . . I hung up. I wanted to say something clever. Or mean. But I just took the phone off the hook and went back to bed. I didn't go to work. And it was an hour later . . . I heard people screaming in my building and . . . I turned on the TV and saw—" April began to buckle but caught herself. "I think of them . . . up there at the end . . . together . . . and I hate them most of all for that . . . that at the end, they had each other."

She was right, Remy thought.

They could've just lived in this hotel room forever.

Everything a person needed was in a hotel room.

It was the peak of civilization, a culmination of fire and the wheel and digital cable radio. It was all here.

If he'd just never mentioned Derek they could've just kept at this for years, making love and buying new clothes, eating in restaurants and kayaking around the bay, changing their names every few days.

"I'm sorry," Remy whispered.

She covered her face with her hands and the towel fell away and she shook with sobs again. Remy stood up, brought her back to bed and curled up around her tiny back until the shuddering stopped and she was breathing easily.

"Do you know . . ." She caught her breath. "What I kept thinking?" She looked back over her shoulder and met his eyes. She smiled. "For months afterward, I kept thinking: Wouldn't this make a fucking great portrait in grief?"

"HOUSEKEEPING."

Remy started. He looked back at the door of the hotel room and then at the clock on the nightstand. It was seven-thirty and April was sleeping more heavily than he'd ever seen. He kissed her lightly on the crown of her head, rose and got dressed, and walked to the door.

Markham's smooth smiling face filled the doorway. "Hi, Brian."

Remy edged out and closed the door behind him.

"You ready to go?" Markham was wearing a sportcoat and blue oxford shirt and carrying his thin brown briefcase. He did an exaggerated double take on Remy's new shoes.

"Wow! Look at the kicks!" Markham said. "Are those new? They have to be new. Look at you, Mr. Hipster. You know, I can't wear sweet kicks like that, those big square-toe clunkers. And I'm a shoe guy. But my feet are so long I'd look like Frankenstein in those." Markham took on his standup comic voice. "In fact, I'd look like a gay Frankenstein, like Frankenstein on his way to get a pedicure and meet his boyfriend the Wolfman for a caramel half-caff at Starbucks. Metrostein or something. Right, right?"

Remy felt beaten. "How'd you find me?"

"Housekeeping," Markham said again. " 'Chure, I comb back.' Hey, I'm sorry about the cell phone. You were right to pitch it and lose me for a few days. I could've blown your cover. I get impatient. It was stupid of me. Especially with us being so close."

Remy looked back at the door to the hotel room.

"So . . . did the change of scenery work? You get anything new?"

"Look, I don't want to do this anymore," Remy said. "Whatever . . . this is—I'm done. I'm just going to go back into this hotel room and . . ."

"Oh, I know what you mean. I've been jet-lagging since we got here." He leaned in closer. "Have you taken a dump? Because I haven't. Goddamn airplane food. Like eating paste."

"Look," Remy said. "For what it's worth, I don't even think March is alive."

Markham nodded. "Yeah . . . the whole March thing looks like a dead end. Excuse the pun. But no, you were right all along. March probably is dead. Unless old Bishir is a tougher cut of steak than he looks."

Remy couldn't help his curiosity. "You found Bishir?"

"Well . . . yeah. What do you think we've been doing here? Sightseeing?"

"And you talked to him?"

"Yeah, while you worked the girl, I thought we'd pick Bishir up and spend a couple of days softening him up before—"

"No . . . please." Remy put a hand out. He thought of the blood on his shoes, and of Assan, and of the photo of March's dead lunch date, al-Zamir. "Don't . . . soften anyone else up."

Markham smiled like a kid who has gotten into his parents' booze. "Oops," he smiled. "My bad."

"Jesus, what did you do?" Remy asked.

"Actually," Markham began, "that's kind of a funny story."

* * *

A HEALTHY chunk of pecan encrusted sole rested on the tines of a fork inches from Bishir Madain's open mouth. "Unbelievable," he said, and slid the fork into his mouth. "Mmmph," he said, and when he could talk again, "You were absolutely right. This is great. You wouldn't think it would be so flaky and moist. And the pecans!"

"What'd I say? Huh? What did I tell you?" asked Markham, who wore a blue cloth apron with salt-and-pepper shakers stitched on the pocket. "Nutty but light. So often you incorporate walnuts or pecans and you have to use something to bind it that makes it sweet or syrupy and it ruins the fish. But this is perfectly balanced. That's what I like about it. You can see why we went this direction." Markham held his spatula like a wand. "It's really a nice recipe."

They were in a huge hotel suite, with motorized curtains and colonial furniture, Bishir sitting in a fluffy white robe in a high-backed chair, over a plate of pecan encrusted sole, buttery green beans, and what looked to Remy liked mashed sweet potatoes. In the small kitchen Markham had two stainless frying pans sizzling and the oven door hanging open, wafting sweet fish.

"You sure you don't want some, Brian?" Bishir asked.

"No," Remy said. He was done, unable to make sense of anything anymore. He looked around the room for the bar.

"You want to know the secret to the whole thing?" Markham asked Bishir.

"Mmm," Bishir said through a mouthful.

"Tell him, Brian," Markham said.

No matter what he did, it seemed to Remy, this insanity was going to grind along and take him with it. He wandered around the room, looking on every flat surface for a key to the honor bar. "Honey," he said. "The secret is honey."

"Bullshit. Honey?" Bishir asked and took another bite. He had a precise, cultured manner that Remy found surprising. He nodded, as if . . . yes, now that Markham mentioned it . . . honey. He finished chewing, his fork near his temple. "I wonder . . ."

"What?" Markham asked.

"Nothing."

"No," said Markham. "What?"

"I was just wondering if a person could substitute corn syrup."

"Fair question." Markham pointed at Bishir with his spatula. "Bri?"

Remy had gotten the honor bar open and was crouched in front of it, rifling through the small bottles. He looked back over his shoulder. "Too syrupy. The honey cooks off better. Leaves a glaze without gumming it up."

"Sure," Bishir said, "I can see that."

A knock came at the door and they all looked up, except Remy.

"That's probably our friend," Markham said, a bit nervously. "Okay. Are we ready for this, Brian?" Markham walked to the door and opened it. "Come in," he said. "Thanks for coming down."

In came a tall, regal-looking man with braces and brushed hair, wearing a pressed golf shirt that hardly moved as he walked into the room. Remy wasn't terribly surprised that it was Dave, the caramel macchiato agent.

"Hello, Bishir," Dave said.

Bishir nodded.

"Shawn Markham," said Markham, offering his hand to the agent.

"Dave," said Dave.

"That's my partner, Brian Remy," said Markham.

"Good to meet you, Brian," said Dave carefully, as if they'd never met. "So, what are we serving this morning?"

"Pecan encrusted sole," Markham said.

"Of course," Dave said to Markham. "I've heard some good things about this recipe. Heard you used it to justify sticking your noses where they don't belong. You're not eating . . . Brian, was it?"

Remy ignored him. He cracked a tiny bottle of gin and downed it.

"Yeah, Brian Remy," Markham said. "He's doing some contract work for us."

Dave settled in at the table. He unwrapped his cloth napkin with a snap of the wrist. "So how is it going, Bishir? Are these minor league spooks treating you okay?"

"Can't complain," Bishir said, his mouth full of sole.

Markham slid a plateful of fish in front of Dave, who took a bite and nodded his approval. "So would you mind telling me what this is all about, Brian?" Dave asked. "Why two rogues from the paper department are holding my CI hostage?"

Remy ignored the question. He felt oddly at ease, nonplussed. He would just drink until this all went away. This seemed like a good strategy, although he noticed that the big flake was in front of his left eye again.

Dave waited, and then became agitated. He shot a glare at Markham, who looked away. "I don't even get an answer?"

"I just want to be left alone," Remy said.

"Oh, really. You want *us* to stay out of *your* way. Is that it?"

Markham chewed nervously on his thumbnail.

"So you really want to endanger this investigation, the security of the nation, over what . . . turf?" Dave stared at Remy.

Remy was getting dizzy crouched like this, so he dropped to his knees. Turning back to the drawer of tiny booze bottles, he was momentarily dazed by scale: Gulliver on a bender. He decided on Crown Royal and it went down like an easy compliment.

Bishir broke the icy quiet. "These guys thought I was holed up with an old girlfriend—this chick, March." He pointed his fork at Markham. "It was a crazy-ass theory, but you know what, if I could've warned one person, it might've been her. She was a sweet girl. Good lay, too."

Markham shrugged. "Yeah, we kind of whiffed on that one."

Dave set his fork down and spun in his chair. "All right," he said. "Let's cut to the proverbial chase."

"You know, I don't think that's an actual proverb," Markham said.

"What?" Dave asked.

"You said proverbial chase. No such proverb."

Dave stared at Markham with disbelief before turning to Remy. "What is it you guys want . . . was it, Brian?"

"Yes," Markham said. "His name is Brian."

"I told you," Remy said. "I don't want anything."

Dave leaned his head back and his Adam's apple moved up and down like a freight elevator. "Come on. We both know you didn't pick up Bishir accidentally. So what do you want?"

"All I want is for this to go away," Remy said. "All of this. All of you."

"Oh, that would be nice, wouldn't it?" Dave sputtered, his angular face reddening. "Look. We have been piecing together the members of this cell for more than a year. If you think for one second the agency is going to step aside so you can hijack our investigation . . ." His lips formed a thin scowl. "We need this! You want to screw the bureau, fine. But I don't think you fully appreciate the pressure we're under."

Vodka, Remy thought, and the pattern appealed on some basic level: clear, brown, clear, brown, clear. He cracked the seal, tossed the little cap, and drank it, like rolling a tiny red carpet down his throat. "Leave me alone."

"Leave you alone?" Dave crossed his arms defiantly and the anger seemed to be percolating in his red ears. "Fuck you, Brian. You want to go over my head, fine. I suppose you think that you're going to find some people on the Hill or some holdover in the media eager to hear that the agency might be operating slightly—" He looked for the words.

"Out of bounds," Markham contributed.

Dave winced as if those weren't the words he wanted.

The room was quiet for a moment. When Dave turned back to Remy he was smiling solicitously. "So we're at an impasse. Okay. But I have to believe we can come to an agreement. Right? That we can work together? Otherwise, you wouldn't have called us. I mean—we have a common enemy, right? The bureau? So, just tell me. What do you want?"

Remy wanted brown. He opened a bottle of Glenlivet.

"We want our piece," Markham said from the kitchen, looking at Remy for approval. "We want credit. We don't want our work to go to waste."

"And that means—" Dave said.

"Joint task force," Markham said, still looking at Remy, as if for approval. "Operational, tactical, command . . . we want our half of the pie."

"Your *half*? You're out of your mind," Dave said to Markham and then turned back to Remy as if he were the reasonable one. "Come on, Brian. You hassle my informant, stumble across a cell we've been investigating for months, endanger a deep intel project, and now you expect to get—"

"Joint. Task force," Markham repeated. "Or we go to Congress. Maybe even the press."

"Press?" Dave laughed. "Who you gonna call? Morley Safer? Edward R. Murrow? Come on. There is no press anymore."

"Joint task force," Markham said. "Final answer." He untied his apron.

"Wait. I know what this is."

"Yeah?" Markham said. "What is this?"

Remy drank.

"This is a shakedown," Dave said. He leaned back in his chair and crossed his legs. "That's all, a half-assed, political stab at creating a permanent seat at the table. You've finished your mandate and your funding is going away so you're pulling paper out of garbage cans while you try to get a foothold . . . turn yourselves into some kind of an actual investigative operation. You're like the bureau eighty years ago, under that swish Hoover. Well, I'm sorry, but I'm not going to write your funding for next decade. No way. Key investigative assistance," Dave said. "*My* final offer."

"Are you serious?" Markham laughed from the kitchen. "'Key investigative assistance?' Why not just say we answered the phones? Got coffee for you guys? Come on. You're offering us a handjob, Dave. You come in here on your knees offering us a handjob? What is that?"

"He's the one on his knees," Dave said, pointing to Remy, who was indeed genuflected before the most holy drawer of plastic booze bottles. But then Dave's mouth twitched and he smiled at Remy, and stepped toward him. He spoke under his voice. "Come on, Brian. Be reasonable here. Take a minute and think about what you're asking."

"I am not asking for anything," Remy said, and he took a plastic bottle of Gilbey's and drained it. His head felt like it was moving in tiny figure eights. The fleck in his left eye seemed to be growing.

"So, it's screw-with-the-agency day, is it? Fine. You want to screw with me? *Screw with me?*" Dave's voice screeched. Then he laughed bitterly and stepped in close, so that he was standing directly over Remy. "I know things, Brian. And I won't hesitate to start talking about what I know." When Remy said nothing, he spat, "Do you think I'm bluffing?"

Remy looked up through the flashers and floaters into the flared nostrils of the older man. "I have no idea what you're doing."

Dave hissed, "Goddamn you." But then he stepped away, rubbed his mouth, and looked up at Markham for a long moment, and then back down at Remy. "Okay," Dave said finally. "I can't give you Joint Task Force. I just can't. But here's what I *can* give you: Cooperating Agency. Solid second chair. You get one suit standing in the back at the presser and you can print up your own release about your involvement. But that's it. That's all you get."

Markham shot a what-do-you-think glance to Remy, who couldn't seem to get drunk enough fast enough.

"Cooperating agency," Markham said, pointing with his spatula, "*two* suits at the presser, joint release, *and* our logo on the dais."

"Your logo!" Dave boomed. "Your fu—!" His jaw fell. "Your . . ."

Markham continued. "*And* we make it clear that we developed our intelligence on this cell independently, through the Loose Materials section of the Liberty and Recovery Act," Markham said. "If you think about it, it's a good deal for you. There might be some information you gathered that might make some people uncomfortable, which we could provide some cover on. Some information that might even be seen as . . . illegal under the old rules."

Dave's eyes narrowed, as if he were considering this.

Markham could see this was his move. "Sure. You can attribute anything . . . uncomfortable . . . to us. Take advantage of the temporary latitude we've been granted for domestic intelligence gathering.

"And," Markham continued, "we all still get to fuck the Bureau."

Remy couldn't remember if he was on clear or brown, so he went with a tiny bottle of designer raspberry vodka. But it was too sweet. He looked over at Bishir, who was ignoring all of this, concentrating on the pecan fish on his plate.

"But . . . and this is important . . ." Markham said. "We get second mike at the press conference."

"Second mike!" Dave screeched again. "Come on! Be reasonable. Do you want our cars, too? Our sat-phones? Our chopper? You want my office?" He rose out of his chair and bent down so that he could see into Remy's eyes. "Come on, Remy," Dave said, all spotty and streaky. "Be reasonable. You got us over a barrel. We both know that. But for the good of the country—"

Markham and Bishir both laughed at this, Bishir choking for a second on his sole.

It was quiet. Dave straightened up, stared off into space, and finally sighed. "Fine. Cooperating agency, but there's no question that we're lead, right?"

"No question," Markham said. "Of course."

"We maintain operational and tactical control . . . we'll provide daily briefings to you on everything. And you can have a guy there when it goes down," Dave continued. "We make a joint release and you get your"—he choked on the word—"*logo* on the dais. But all I can guarantee is third shot at the mike during the presser. Third mike. That's all I got, fellas. I'm not giving you our spot no matter what you say."

Markham glanced over at Remy, who looked away and reached for another bottle. He was dizzy, and his hand missed. He stumbled and fell sideways . . . and in that moment it was as if something popped behind his left eye: a piercing pain shot through his skull and he leaned forward and clenched his eyes tight. He fell forward, against the minibar, then curled up in a ball, and rolled on the floor, moaning.

"Brian?" Markham asked.

He cried out in pain, his hands covering his face as he crawled across the carpeted floor toward the other wall.

"Fine!" he heard Dave snap above him. "You can talk second at the press conference."

Remy reached the wall, leaned against it, and opened his eyes. This wasn't right. There was a big problem with his left eye, a dark shadowy band across the middle of his field of vision. He squeezed his eyes shut and opened only the left one, but the black band was still there, as if the center of the room had been torn away, like a page in a magazine. And then the pain seemed to gather at the base of his skull and make another advance, until it was nearly unbearable and it doubled him over, the anguish blossoming outward and from within, like black water bubbling up from the earth. Like blooms of smoke roiling into a clear day.

PART THREE

The Zero

"MR. REMY, ARE YOU AWAKE?" Interesting question. Technically he *had* to be awake, since he'd heard her ask it. And yet, if he really were awake, would she have to ask? Wouldn't it be obvious? Maybe he'd dreamed the question. How had April described her grief—as a fever dream? A dream—that would help explain the gaps, and the general incongruity of life now—the cyclic repetition of events on cable news, waves of natural disasters, scientists announcing the same discoveries over and over (Planet X, dinosaur birds, cloning, certain genetic codes), the random daily shift of national allegiances, wildly famous people who no one could recall becoming famous, the sudden emergence and disappearance of epidemics, the declaration and dissolution of governments, cycles of scandal, confession, and rehabilitation, heated elections in which losers claimed victory and races were rerun in the same sequence, events that catapulted wildly out of control, like plagues of illogic . . . as if some faulty math had been introduced to all the equations, corrupting computer programs and causing specious arguments to build upon themselves, and sequential skips—snippets of songs sampled before their original release, movies remade before they came out the first time, victories claimed before wars were fought, drastic fluctuations in the security markets (panic giving way to calm giving way to panic giving way to calm giving way to panic), all of it narrated by fragments of speeches over staged photo ops accompanied by color-coded warnings and yellow ribbons on trees.

"Mr. Remy? Can you squeeze my hand?"

Another tough question. Was he supposed to answer or squeeze? Would a squeeze be an answer? What was it that April said? *I couldn't walk around pretending any of this made sense anymore.* Perhaps nothing made sense anymore *(the gaps are affecting everyone)* and this was some kind of cultural illness they all shared. But just as Remy was getting his mind around the question, he felt a woman's hand in his and he became aware of the pain behind his eyes; it roared and squealed into his head like a train pulling up to a platform, lights flashing, brakes screaming, and then it changed, became more specific, like someone nailing his left eye to his skull, hammer blows, cracks against a three-penny, and a pitched agony sought out the vacuum behind his eyes, wiping away the epiphany he was trying to have, just as Remy was putting words to it: *What if I'm the only one aware of this?* A lonely, chilling thought, and he wasn't sorry to see it slipping away, too—leaving only a momentary impression, like a print in sand, before it blew away. He squeezed the hand.

"Hurts," he rasped. He saw the usual streaks against the black, squirreling away when he tried to focus on them, but only half as many now, and only on the right side; the left was nothing but this sucking agony, a string of razor wire run through his left eye and into his brain, being tugged from the outside so that it strained everything on the way through. He tried to open his good eye but it was bandaged shut along with the bad one. He was grateful for the remaining flashers and floaters on the right side, so that there was at least something to see.

"I'll get you something for the pain," the voice whispered.

"Thank you," Remy said. He reached up and touched the heavy bandages over his eyes. The tape covered most of his forehead and cheeks.

"And I'll tell the surgeon you're awake. He wants to talk to you."

"What day is this?"

"It's Wednesday."

"Oh." Then he heard her footsteps on the hard floor and Remy wished he'd asked a different question, a question about April. Wednesday meant nothing to him. For a few minutes there was only the pain and then more footsteps and the smell of briny cologne.

"How are you today, Mr. Remy?" The doctor mispronounced it, with a long *E*, but Remy didn't correct him. "I'm Dr. Destouches. Orb cutter." The cologne doctor's voice was smooth and cool, like a disc jockey on a Sunday night jazz radio show.

"It really hurts," Remy said.

"I should hope so. That's the only way I know I've done my job." The doctor adopted the voice of a lecturing professor. "Post-surgical eye trauma presents a truly unique sort of pain, Mr. Remy. It's not localized, like a broken leg or a burn on your arm. You can't touch it; it's a generalized pain—but it's not an ache. It is, at the same time, both sharp and diffuse."

Remy just wished the man would stop talking about his pain.

"The body views eye surgery as such a severe violation," Dr. Destouches continued, "a unique shock on every level. The eye is not designed to be cut into, like the skin; the central nervous system doesn't know what to make of it when someone goes poking around on the top floors."

"What was the surgery for?" Remy asked.

"You don't remember?"

"No."

The doctor laughed. "Well, since I see your signature right here on the release, I'm assuming that's the anesthesia speaking and that we didn't randomly crack open your head and try reattaching your retina without your permission."

"No," Remy said. "I'm having trouble keeping track of things. Everything skips."

"That's the anesthesia," the doctor said. "You'll start to get your bearings back in the next few hours."

"No," Remy said again. "It's been that way for a long time. There are these gaps."

"Yes, it can seem like that," the doctor said, "but don't worry. Once the anesthesia wears off, and the pain medication kicks in, you'll be clear as a bell." He shuffled pages again. "As for the surgery, I'm sorry to report that we were unable to reattach the retina. It was too far gone. So the vision in that eye . . . is severely compromised, Mr. Remy. After we take off the bandages you may still see some blurry images, especially on the edges, but in essence that eye is . . . gone. Black. Kaput." He trailed off, but gave Remy little time before speaking again.

"I don't know that I've ever seen eyes like yours. It's like reading a textbook. The degeneration and detachment, the thinness of the retinas: remarkable. I've never seen such thin, tattered tissue on a human being that wasn't a cadaver. It's like mobile home curtains in there, Mr. Remy. It's like the sheets in an old whorehouse. It's like—"

"Okay," Remy said.

"Is there a history of eye disease in your family?"

"I don't think so," Remy said.

"Because you have the eyes of a man in his nineties," said Dr. Destouches. "And I have to ask—did you fly here?"

"Am I still in San Francisco?"

"Yes."

"Then I flew here."

"And did your ophthalmologist in New York approve that?"

"No. In fact, I think he told me *not* to fly."

"Well, so much for your malpractice suit." Remy could hear papers being shuffled again. "The good news, such as it is, is that you can still see out of your right eye—for the time being. You have a lot of debris in your field of vision . . . flashers, floaters, that kind of thing."

"Yes."

"Well, if you're one of those people who looks for silver linings in mushroom clouds, we did manage to cut those in half." The doctor laughed at his own joke and cleared his throat. "But please, do yourself a favor and take a train or a bus back to New York. Your eyes are as fragile as origami, Mr. Remy. As fragile as a fat girl's confidence on prom night. As fragile as—"

"I got it," Remy said. The word *fragile* made Remy think of April; he wondered if she was waiting to see him.

"The change in pressure from flying would be very bad for you," Dr. Destouches continued. "Do you understand?"

"Yes," Remy said, chasing the flecks around his good eye.

"I'm going to put that right here. No flying." Remy could hear the doctor scratching on a pad. "And a word of advice: You might want to cut back on the liquor. At least while you're on medication. You had a blood alcohol level of .039. That's four times the legal limit, Mr. Remy. Do you understand what I'm saying?"

"No drinking and no flying—"

THE PLANE shuddered and jerked with the rattle of molded and fitted plastic and the grind of jet engines, strained against the ground's pull, and when it felt as if it were on the verge of shaking loose its aluminum shell, finally broke with the ground and became still. They were in the air. Remy opened his eyes, but only the right one opened, the left still trapped beneath the gauze. He had a small airplane whiskey bottle in his hand. He looked over to the seat on his left, hoping to see April, but it was Markham, chewing a pencil, his face screwed up over a mostly open crossword puzzle. Markham leaned in. "Okay. Six letters. *Rift*. Last letter m. Third letter might be an h."

Remy closed his eye and leaned back. He opened his mouth to say *schism* but what came out was—

* * *

"THE CELL," the agent Dave said slowly, lingering on each word, "from what we have been able to gather over the last few months, is constructed thusly."

Remy looked around the simple conference room. He and Markham sat behind an oval table in swivel chairs. Dave, the tall, thin agent with the braces, stood in the glow of a big computer screen mounted on the wall in front of them. On the screen were the words *CELL 93* and a chart connecting six silhouetted heads in a small pyramid. Beneath each silhouette was a number: one, two, and three on the bottom row of the pyramid, four and five in the middle, and six at the top. One of the silhouettes, number five, had a red line through it; another, number two, had a question mark over it.

"Thusly?" Markham said to Remy, under his breath.

Dave spun to face them. "What's wrong with thusly?"

"Nothing. It's just . . . nothing."

Dave faced the wall, and then turned back to Markham again. "Look. You are guests in this operation. The agency does not typically cooperate like this. I'm out on a limb here. So I would appreciate some support. And professionalism."

"You're right. I'm sorry," Markham said. "My bad."

"Ninety-three is a classic, small, leaderless cell, *sui generis*," Dave continued, shooting a quick, defensive glance at Markham before going on. "Each of its members is connected to one or two other members, but no one member is aware of more than two others, so that if one person goes down, two or three can escape and the cell can theoretically regrow—like a snake losing a tail. This is why it's important for us to get to as many members as possible."

"Why's it called Ninety-three?" Markham asked.

"We're not sure. Maybe the group formed in 1993, although most of the relationships date from much earlier. Another theory, from our analysts, was that the name refers to the ninety-nine names for Allah, and that by subtracting the six members you get ninety-three. Of course, we are also monitoring FM radio stations with that frequency, listening to call letters, dedications, play lists, that sort of thing." Dave pressed his thumb to the clicker. "Now let's take a look at the cell members."

Onto the screen came a black-and-white surveillance photo of a thin Arab man in shiny sweats, talking on a cell phone outside an apartment building. The man's jaw stuck out in a severe underbite, making it seem as if he were working to keep his teeth from jutting out. "Subject Number One: Kamal al-Hassan, Saudi-born and educated, passionate and intelligent, speaks perfect English . . . Japanese sports car buff. May have become disillusioned with America as a twelve-year-old after his Taif team was eliminated in the first round of the Little League World Series."

Markham didn't look up from his notes. "Position?"

"Second base," Dave said. "All glove, no bat. Decent range but had an arm that would embarrass a six-year-old girl. As an adult, he moved to Syria and worked as an agent, raising money for jihadist sports clubs under the umbrella of refugee services." Dave clicked his thumb again and the next slide appeared, another photo of Kamal, this time in a business suit, stepping out of a limousine. "We have reason to believe he has recently made his way into the country, possibly through Canada."

A photo came up showing a familiar-looking young Arab man in a business suit. Dave said, "Subject Number Two—Kamal's brother Assan, lives in Miami—"

Remy gasped, but no one seemed to notice. It was the man they'd tortured on the ship outside Miami. Remy looked up at Markham, who shot a quick glance at Remy, scribbled something in a notebook on his lap, and then turned his eyes back to the screen.

"At least Assan *lived* in Miami," Dave said. "Honestly, we don't know where he is now. He's been missing for months. We had believed he was opposed to his brother's growing radicalism, but he may have gone underground in preparation for something."

"You said you were going to let him go," Remy hissed to Markham, who simply stared straight ahead.

"The next member," Dave said, and Bishir's picture appeared on the wall, "as . . . you well know, is the agency's CI, Tarzan—Bishir. We've designated him Subject Number Three, even though obviously he's providing us with intelligence. Of course, his cooperation gives us a huge advantage over our enemy—the bureau." He glanced quickly at Markham and Remy. "I don't mean to brag, but we believe this to be the deepest actual penetration of a terror cell by any U.S. agency."

Markham gave a polite golf clap.

Dave clicked his thumb again and it took Remy a moment to recognize the next face. "We've identified Number Four as the weakest member of the group, Bishir's brother-in-law—" It was Mahoud, the restaurant owner.

"Oh, come on," Remy said, incredulous. "He's not—"

But Markham reached over, grabbed his arm, and shook his head slightly.

"Mahoud Tasneem is a Pakistani restaurant owner here in the city," Dave said. "We're not entirely sure of his involvement or his motivation . . . all we know is that he recently contacted Bishir and volunteered to be involved, possibly in a support role, providing transportation, or a safe house."

Dave hit the button again and on the wall was an image that Remy recognized: a man lying in a smear of blood on the sidewalk. It was the photo Buff had shown him in the gypsy cab.

"As you know, Subject Number Five, Bobby al-Zamil, is dead." Dave cleared his throat. "Al-Zamil was a former associate of Bishir's.

The reason we initially approached you about March Selios was that Bishir brought her up under interrogation. He said he'd met her through al-Zamil, who had business dealings with her. We're not sure why al-Zamil was eliminated; perhaps the group wanted him out of the way because he was under surveillance, or it could be that he was having second thoughts, or maybe it's a kind of reality show thing and they just voted off a member. Whatever, it seems clear they killed him to avoid endangering the operation."

Markham nodded earnestly.

"But rather than dissuade the group, al-Zamil's death seems to have galvanized the others and, if anything, convinced them to step up the timetable. Which brings us to Subject Number Six," Dave said, "the cell's most mysterious member. Even Bishir isn't sure of his real name. The others call him *Ibn 'Arabi*, which appears to be a reference to a pacifist Sufi teacher. We've given him the code name Jaguar."

"Why not call him Iceman?" Markham offered.

"What?" Dave asked.

"Yeah," Markham said. "You know . . . if it was me, I'd call him Iceman."

Dave looked incredulous. "Iceman?"

"Yeah. Iceman."

"You want us to call him Iceman? But his code name is Jaguar."

"Isn't that kind of . . . predictable?"

Dave put his hand across his chest, chagrined. "No, it's not predictable . . . we chose Jaguar because of Tarzan. You know. It's an animal."

"Yeah. I guess. But isn't it a bit melodramatic?"

Dave seemed stung by the criticism. "And Iceman isn't?"

"It's a literary reference. It's more sophisticated."

"*Top Gun* is a literary reference?"

"No . . . Iceman from the Eugene O'Neill play."

Dave scrunched up his face. "It isn't that play with the obnoxious kids trying to make a chorus line?"

"No, that's *A Chorus Line*."

"Because that was awful."

"I'm not suggesting you name someone from *A Chorus Line*. I'm saying that you consider naming the cell leader Iceman."

Dave shrugged. "Well, we can't. It's too late. And we already have an Iceman in Riyadh. It would be too confusing."

"But *Jaguar*?"

"Yes," Dave said. "Jaguar. Now, as I was saying, Bishir believes—"

"Jaguar?" Markham mumbled.

Dave cleared his throat. "Bishir believes the cell is being funded by . . . *Jaguar*. Unfortunately, we have no idea where Jaguar is getting his money. We're following the usual charities, Swiss accounts, drug sales, energy markets, alt-country music royalties, et cetera . . . but so far we've come up blank. All we have is Bishir's post office box. A week ago, a blank postcard arrived there—no prints—with a rendezvous point."

The card appeared on the screen. It read WM PARK 0800. This time Remy wasn't terribly surprised to recognize the handwriting as his own.

"At this meeting, we believe, targets will be assigned. Once this happens, we have two choices. We could take them down at the meeting, but we cannot move until we can account for all of the members, especially Jaguar. If we move . . . too quickly, we risk allowing some of them to escape. Move too slowly and—"

"It's a race against time," Markham said. Then he snorted into his hand like a high school kid trying to suppress a laugh in class.

"What?" asked Dave.

"Nothing," Markham said, straightening up. But he closed his eyes and snorted again.

"What's so funny?" Dave asked again.

Markham straightened his face. "Nothing. Just . . . nothing."

Dave clicked his thumb and the next picture came up, Dave keeping his eyes on Markham disapprovingly. "This is the only photo we have of the man we believe to be Jaguar." It was a grainy photo of two men leaning on the railing of a ferry. At first Remy tried to make out the man on the left, who may have been smoking a cigarette. "The man on the left is Assan," Dave said, clicking the plunger again.

An enlargement of Jaguar appeared, even blurrier than the picture from which it was taken. His face was impossible to make out. But it was clear to Remy that the man was older, perhaps in his late fifties or early sixties, and that he was Middle Eastern, with short gray hair. And he was wearing a long, gray wool coat.

"Oh, no," Remy muttered.

Dave ignored him. "This is Jaguar, the man they refer to as *Ibn 'Arabi,* an ironic reference to the teaching of Islam as a religion of love. We think Jaguar may have been a professor at one time, and may have taught one or more of the members. We think he may have become radicalized when he lost a family member, perhaps a son, during the first Gulf War, although we don't know how, or to which side. We also believe he is Americanized, highly educated, with a knowledge of explosives—"

"No, I know that guy," Remy said.

"Yeah." Dave sighed and turned to face the fuzzy image of Jaguar. "That's how I feel." He walked to the wall and stared into the fuzzy image of the man in the wool coat. "When you finally see the enemy's face, it's like you've known him your whole life."

"No—" Remy began.

"Oh, there is . . . one other consideration," Dave said slowly, as if searching for the right words. "And it comes from the highest levels, and is not to be repeated outside this room." He took a breath. "There is some . . . concern—as I said, at the highest levels—that the perception of danger has . . ."

"Waned?" Markham said.

"Yes. And we think it's counterproductive for the public to view our enemies as a bunch of harmless nuts, lunatics with shoe bombs, ineffectual zealots. In other words, we can't afford to capture a band of unarmed cabdrivers and motel operators."

Markham looked over and raised his eyebrows, as if this were good news.

"We're not looking for anything fancy," Dave said. "It wouldn't even have to be necessarily operational. But an enemy without weapons is a dog without teeth. So we are not to move until the enemy has an incendiary device." Dave waited for this to sink in. "And then . . . we need to move fast."

And just as Remy was about to stand up and say this was all crazy, Markham burst into nervous, staccato laughter. "It's a spelling bee with death," he said. "A hockey game against evil—"

APRIL ANSWERED the door of her apartment and stared coldly at him across the tightened chain. She was wearing jeans and an oxford shirt buttoned over a tank top. Her hair was pulled back in a ponytail. Her face seemed thinner. Pale.

Remy was pleasantly surprised to be there. "Hi," he said.

She refused to meet his good eye. "What do you want, Brian?"

"What's the matter?"

"What do you want?"

"What do I want? I . . . want to see you."

"Why?"

"To talk."

"About what?"

Remy was surprised by her iciness. "I miss you."

"Tell me what you want, Brian."

"Well . . ." He wasn't sure where to start. "I seem to be involved in something and . . . I don't know. I need to see you."

Finally she looked up and seemed to notice the eye patch for the first time. But she didn't say anything about it. "I'm sure you'll figure it out," she said.

"What's the matter?" he asked again. "Can't I come in?" He looked past her, into her apartment. The living room was filled with cardboard boxes. Sweaters were stacked on the box closest to the door. "Are you going somewhere, April?"

"Yes," she said. It felt to Remy that they were speaking too quietly and too quickly, like actors working over a familiar scene. "I'm moving."

"What? Where?"

"I can't do this now, Brian."

"I can't come in?"

"No," she said. "You can't come in."

"Why?"

"I'm with someone."

Remy looked past her. "I don't see anyone."

"You can't see ghosts," she said.

"Ghosts? What are you talking about, April?"

"Please don't do this," she said again, staring at the ground.

"Do what?"

"Act like you don't remember."

"I *don't* remember. I never remember. There are these gaps."

"Yes," she said, easing the door shut. "So you've said—"

EDGAR LOOKED different—older, more self-assured—although it might have been his haircut. His mop of hair was much shorter, stubble on the sides and a small tuft in front; his old baggy clothes had been replaced by sweatpants and a rain jacket. And physically, he was definitely thicker, as Remy had noticed before, like he'd been lifting weights, his bony neck replaced by a kind of pedestal. Remy was parked along the street again, at dusk, at the top of the hill across from the same mall parking lot. He watched through one lens of the binoculars, traffic cresting the hill, and between the cars he caught glimpses of Edgar walking along the sidewalk. He stopped in the same place as before, hopped over the retaining wall, and dropped again down into the lot. Determined not to lose Edgar this time, Remy took off the binoculars, dropped them on the bench seat, jumped out of the car, and made his way across traffic. He ran down the sidewalk and climbed over the same retaining wall, his patched eye aching as he ran. It was drizzling as Remy dropped over the wall and into the parking lot, twisting his ankle on the five-foot fall. By the time he got back up, he'd lost the boy again.

"Edgar!" The parking lot was landscaped with little tree boxes at the end of every row, and Remy limped his way around cars and sickly trees, rising up on his tiptoes every few minutes to scan the mall for him. "Edgar!"

Groups of people moved along the sidewalks and into the courtyard at the center of the mall. A car honked and Remy got out of its way. He stepped up onto the sidewalk. "Edgar!"

He walked gingerly down the business storefronts, peering in each one: A futon store. A tax preparation business. Maternity clothes. Party supplies. A chiropractor. Rattan imports, golf supplies, tanning beds. He didn't see his son anywhere, and honestly couldn't imagine him in any of the stores. "Edgar! Where are you?" Stone ice cream and bagels, Army recruiting and guitar sales and cell phones and . . .

Remy stopped and stared at the stores he'd passed. He thought about Edgar's haircut. He walked carefully toward the narrow Army recruiting office. It was a shallow storefront, and it looked as if most of the space was behind a single door. A sergeant with disquieting blue eyes, a thin mustache, and a fading chin was sitting at a desk, talking on the phone. Remy went inside. The sergeant looked up and ended the call.

"Good day, sir," he said. "What can I do for you?"

Remy looked around. This part of the office was like a false front, a small space with a door leading deeper inside, or maybe to a back exit. "Did my kid come in here?"

"I'm sorry . . . ?" the sergeant said.

"Edgar Remy." Remy pointed to the door leading to the back of the office. A poster on the door showed the face of a rugged young man wearing fatigues, with smears of black eye paint as if he were simply going to play football. The poster read, ARE YOU READY? "Is Edgar back there?"

The man spoke calmly, reassuringly. "Sir, I'm not at liberty to say who is or isn't here, except to immediate family."

"I am immediate family," Remy said. He moved for the door, but the soldier moved quickly in front of him. They were a few feet apart. "Look, you don't want him," Remy said. "He's just a kid."

The soldier smiled warmly. "That's a common reaction when a young man volunteers. It's hard to acknowledge when a child becomes a man."

"He's only sixteen," Remy said.

The sergeant seemed genuinely amused. "You can rest assured, sir, we're not going to let a sixteen-year-old enlist."

This didn't make Remy feel better. Could Edgar be eighteen? He knew that time had passed, but Edgar wasn't old enough to join the Army. Was he? "This is a mistake. He's not supposed to be here. He hasn't signed anything, has he?"

The soldier took Remy's arm. "Listen. As I said, I can't say who's here and who isn't. But when a young man makes a decision like this, there is no turning back. And if that young man happens to be someone who lost his father, and wants to do something to avenge that good man, I find it hard to see how anyone who really cares for him could possibly call it a mistake."

"I'm his father," Remy said weakly.

"His stepfather?" the sergeant said.

"No. His father."

The sergeant smiled patiently. "Look, call yourself whatever you want. I'm sure it's not easy to raise another man's child. A selfless job. I can see that—"

"Listen to me—"

"No." He spoke so quietly that Remy had to lean in to hear him. "You listen. I've kept my patience, sir. But I'm not going to sit here while you dishonor the young men and women who put on this uniform." The man tilted his earnest head and implored Remy with those electric blue eyes. "If you're not going to respect and support this young soldier's decision, I'm going to have to ask you to leave . . . before you disgrace the cherished memory of his father."

Remy laughed; the noise struck him as slightly psychotic. He wondered—*If I ran, could I make it past the soldier to the door?*—but the recruiter seemed to anticipate this and slid over a step. After a moment, Remy backed out of the office. Through the closed glass door, the recruiting officer stood with his arms crossed.

Remy turned onto the sidewalk, staring first in one direction, then the other. There was something about being presented with choices that he didn't entirely trust, so he hesitated, then began to walk away.

"Hey."

Remy turned. Edgar was standing in the doorway of the recruiting office, staring at his shoes as the recruiter watched nervously through the window, waiting to pounce if Remy did anything suspicious. Edgar stepped outside, the glass door swinging closed behind him. His black hair, which he'd always worn moppy, was too short to part now, just a thin buzz that wasn't enough to cover the pink of his scalp. "I just want you to know," Edgar began, "that I understand how you feel." He continued to stare at the ground. "I do. It's just . . ." He stared off to his left, a pose so familiar that Remy ached to see his boy again, wondered what this buzz-headed young man had done with him.

"It's just what?" Remy asked.

"Well," Edgar shrugged. "I've made so much progress."

"Progress," Remy repeated.

"It's not just me. Mom thinks so, too. And my therapist." He leaned in. "I've been through all the stages of grief. You can't want me to go back. What, to denial? Or . . . or anger?" He shook his head. "Anyway, I don't think I *can* go back. Not now. Not after I've finally accepted your death." Edgar looked up. He was as tall as his father now. But so different. "And really . . . someday, you are going to die. Right?"

Yes, Remy thought. *Someday.*

They stood on the mini-mall sidewalk, staring at the ground in front of each other. Edgar opened his mouth to say something else, but he shrugged instead. Then he pushed on the glass door of the recruiting office. And before Remy could say anything, or think of anything to say, the boy disappeared again behind—

THE DOOR was open a crack, and April leaned against it, her eyes red. "Please, Brian. You're torturing me every time you do this."

He was outside her apartment again, pleading through the tight chain. He closed his eyes, trying to shake the feeling that he'd already lived this moment. "April. I don't know what I did wrong. You have to believe me. I don't remember."

"You don't remember."

"No."

"You don't remember leaving me in a hotel room in San Francisco?"

"Did I do that?" He winced. "I'm sorry, April. See, my retina detached." He touched the patch. "My eye is—"

But she wouldn't look up. "And you don't remember leaving a

note that said you couldn't be with someone who was in love with a ghost?"

"Oh. I'm sorry." Remy closed his good eye. "I'm really sorry. I didn't mean that. Please." He looked again at the moving boxes, which were stacked by the door. "At least tell me where you're moving?"

She stared past him. "I gave the money away."

"What are you talking about? What money?"

"The settlement. The money you convinced me to get. I gave it all away. The lawyer got some. I gave some to Derek's parents. And I donated the rest. In case that's what you're here for."

"What?" Remy leaned against the door frame. "No, April. I don't care about the money. I never cared about the money. Look, I don't know what I did . . . but I'm sorry. I know I've been acting crazy, but I need you."

"You need me."

Remy was stunned by the flatness of her voice. He'd never seen this side of her. "Let's forget this craziness and just . . . go somewhere. We'll live in a hotel and . . . buy new clothes every day. Change our names—"

"You're unbelievable."

"Please. I'll do anything to get you back." He took her hand. "Isn't there something I can do?"

"Well." April pulled her hand away from his. Her eyes remained half-lidded, as if she were about to fall asleep. With those deep-set eyes, the effect was cool, intentional. "I suppose," April said, "you could stop fucking my boss." And then she gently closed the door in his face.

Remy stood there for a moment and then his head fell forward against—

THE DOOR of another apartment. He could hear laughter behind it. Remy lifted his head. He didn't know whose door it was. He felt dizzy, like someone bobbing on the ocean, looking around for anything to cling to. He could hear footsteps approaching, and although he didn't remember knocking, the door swung open, and there was Guterak, his hair neatly trimmed, a bottle of imported beer in his hand. "Hey, I knew you'd make it!" He turned and announced to McIntyre and Carey—"What'd I say? Didn't I just say this fugger would never miss my premiere. Now *this* is a friend. Pay attention, you ungrateful free-loaders. Hey. Come in, man."

Guterak looked thinner, mostly in the shoulders and chest, like he'd lost weight in all the wrong places, like a smaller version of the same bowling pin. His hair was different, too, styled and gelled into one of those intentional messes. A reed-thin woman with short black hair, also casually mussed, was setting up trays of food—seven-layer nachos and bread with spinach dip—on Guterak's coffee table, in front of Carey and McIntyre, who sat next to each other on the couch, work-ing their own beer bottles. They looked over their shoulders and nod-ded at Remy.

"Tara," Guterak said. "You gotta come over and meet this guy. This is Brian Remy I was telling you about. We used to be in a car, me and him. Worked The Boss's detail together before this fugger went and got a desk job, and then went and got himself a sweet disability. We went through some harrowing shit together that day."

"Yes, you've told me," she said, and Remy thought he caught just a trace of irritation in her voice. She came over, younger than Guterak by at least fifteen years, a girl on the border between cute and hard: laser green eyes and a stud in her right nostril.

"Remy," Guterak said, with as much formality as he could muster, "this is Tara. She works for the production company I signed with, and apparently she has an unhealthy attraction to old cops."

They shook hands.

"I've heard a lot about you," she said.

When she let go of his hand, Remy self-consciously touched his eye patch. He wondered why no one mentioned his eye.

"So how's early retirement, you lazy mutt?" asked McIntyre. He sat with a beer on Guterak's futon.

"Your back can't be too bad," Carey said, as a pile of dip fell from a tortilla chip into his thick hand. "You're still walking upright."

"My back's fine," Remy said quietly.

"Come on. I'll get you a beer." Guterak led Remy into the kitchen.

Remy looked around the kitchen of Guterak's apartment, and at the pictures of his kids on the small refrigerator. He took the beer and managed a long swallow. He leaned against the kitchen table. "Listen, Paul . . . I need your help. I'm wrapped up in something here . . . I don't know . . . there's some crazy stuff happening and . . . I might be on the wrong side of it."

"Yeah, you really fugged up, man. I talked to April. She told me you slept with her boss. What were you thinking?"

"You talked to April?"

Guterak leaned in close. "Who'd have thought we'd get these young women, huh? Like we got a fuggin' sex mulligan, ain't it? Tradin' our old broads for these babes. No, you should definitely go back. On your hands and fuggin' knees, man."

"No, it's more than just April," Remy said. "I'm losing track of everything, Paul. . . . I do things I don't remember. It's almost like there are two of me." He leaned in closer. "There was this thing in Miami, and then I went to San Francisco . . . there's this pecan dish and this duck, and this old Arab guy in a wool coat . . . and Jesus, I'm starting to think"—as the words formed in his throat, Remy knew the truth of this particular thought—"I'm starting to think that . . . this bad thing is going to happen no matter what I do."

"I'll call April tomorrow. I'll talk to her."

"This is not about April!"

"Paul!" Tara called from the other room. "It's on."

"Come on, man. You're gonna want to see this." Guterak walked into the living room and after a minute alone in the kitchen, Remy followed. He stood in the back of the room.

On TV was the cop show that was always shouting about being *ripped from the headlines*. The music played—*duh Duh*—and then the first scene: A deliveryman was pushing a handcart with a big-screen television on it, when he came across a dead body. In the next scene, the two regular detectives were crouched over the body. Remy knew the ritual: the body always came first, and then the detectives' job was to go to locations around the city and interview people quickly, asking one or two questions before moving on to the next interview, to make sure they caught the killer before the trial began in the second half of the show. The camera panned down to show the victim: a young Arab man splayed out on a sidewalk. The camera looked up to the window from which he'd tumbled, accidentally or, no doubt, otherwise.

Remy looked at Guterak, but he showed no reaction.

The show tramped along. The cops interviewed their witnesses; one, a social worker who lived in the building, told the detectives that she recognized someone on the sidewalk right after the man fell out of the window—a retired cop named Bruce Denny, who'd recently left the force because of back problems. The lab also had a footprint from a shoe at the scene and they wanted to compare the print to Bruce Denny's shoe.

Remy covered his mouth. He looked around, but no one else seemed to see anything strange in what they were watching.

Duh-Duh. One of the detectives picked Bruce Denny up at the airport to question him. On the show, Bruce Denny wore an eye patch. Remy touched his eye patch again.

"Jesus, Paul," Remy began.

"Shhh," said Tara.

The detective asked Denny his shoe size. It was twelve—the same size as the footprint at the murder scene, the same size Remy wore. Then Bruce Denny asked if he could confide in the detective. He may have been at the scene, Denny confided, but he couldn't remember. He said he was having some kind of problem with his memory, that he was having "gaps." And he asked the detective to follow him.

"Follow you?" the detective asked.

"Yeah. Follow me."

"Like . . . keep track of what you're saying?"

"No. Tail me. I think I'm involved in something and I want to find out what it is."

That's when the first commercial break came.

Remy looked down at Guterak in disbelief. "Jesus, Paul, did you . . ."

"Shhh—" Guterak raised a hand and pointed at the TV. "Here it comes."

The TV cut to commercial and Remy saw how seamlessly this happened, one world to another and the detectives were gone and two kids were standing in a clean suburban living room—*just like Carla and Steve's house,* Remy thought—staring out a window as emergency lights rolled across their faces. "Cool!" one of them said. As the rousing music swelled behind them, the camera moved outside to settle on a firefighter and a cop standing in the street, talking and gesturing toward some unseen emergency, a blur of police tape and swirling lights. The cop was Guterak. He and the firefighter turned to the camera, shot and lit from below, like superheroes.

"When trouble comes—" said the firefighter.

"And it will—" said Guterak.

And then they both pointed to the camera and said in unison: "You need to have a hearty breakfast! The breakfast of heroes."

And cut to a sunny breakfast table. On the table were two boxes of cereal, at perfect angles; behind them were the kids in soft focus, devouring their cereal as if they hadn't eaten in months. Each box looked like an American flag; the firefighter was on one, Guterak on the other, looking serious, staring off into space. Through the magic of television, both men winked from their boxes of cereal.

The camera returned to the photogenic kids, their spoons overflowing with hearty oat goodness.

"I got the flakes!" said one, and Remy thought he sensed just the slightest disappointment in this boy, who also had slices of bananas in his cereal.

"I got marshmallows!" said the other kid, with no reservations.

And then the deep-voiced narrator said: "First Responder. The cereal of heroes."

When it was over, McIntyre, Carey, and Tara applauded. Remy didn't know what to do.

"Baby," said Tara, "you're a star."

"So what do you think, Brian?" Guterak asked nervously.

But before Remy could answer, he felt the moment slipping and—

AT DAWN, joggers circled the kidney-shaped lawn. Their footfalls echoed softly against the retaining walls surrounding the edge of the park. Remy sat on the steps leading to the park, above the dewy grass. He had an open book in his hands, but he was staring past it toward the damp field. He was getting used to seeing out of one eye, to seeing around corners. In some ways, he wondered if this wasn't a more accurate view of the world, without the gap between his eyes, that little bit of distance that the brain corrected and covered. And he wondered about blind spots, if there weren't things that only he could see now, things the binocular missed.

In the park, a woman walking a little dog looked both ways before allowing the animal to shit in the bark surrounding the red jungle gym. Closer, a homeless man slept at the edge of the grass, parting the flow of runners as smoothly as a rock in a river. Remy counted six joggers in a lap, five men and a woman, and in the next lap it was seven, and then nine, and twelve, as if he were seeing in crackled time-lapse. Sunlight began to wash over the park. Nearly all the joggers wore tiny head-phones, listening to music only they could hear, as alone in the world at that moment as it was possible to be. Soon the first commuters joined the joggers, slowly making their way across the park toward the finan-cial district, like blood cells to a wound.

Women in dark pantyhose and tennis shoes carried huge bags; men in suits strode purposefully, barking into cell phones. Remy thought of that other morning, distant, urgent, end of summer, a glimpse of cool fall, primary day, people stopping to vote, dropping kids at schools and daycares, just getting to their offices, sitting at desks, arranging photos, looking through call sheets, and he imagined April, her recently returned husband gone to work, humming around the house, thinking that her life was back to some semblance of nor-mal, then finding his cell phone, listening to the message and calling her sister at work, and March, crying at her desk—both of them be-lieving that morning was the worst of their lives, *no idea,* until a low roar cleaved the morning air—

The homeless man rose in the park. He was a chunk of a black man in grease-stained jeans and a parka. He stretched and immediately went to work—even the homeless have to be ambitious down here, Remy thought, Type A panhandlers—and his outstretched hand only drove the flow of passersby further afield. Most held a single hand up to stop him from asking, though a few shook their heads and eventually one man was distracted into kindness, digging in his pocket absentmind-edly as he talked on his cell, as if the beggar were a tollbooth.

Two more rejections, and then the homeless man hooked another

one, a young Middle Eastern man. Remy raised his head. The man . . .
was Kamal, Assan's brother, Subject Number One. He was sure of it.
Wearing a blue blazer and tan slacks, Kamal seemed like a thinner version of Assan . . . like a higher branch of the same tree. He was carrying a brown package, wrapped like a sandwich. He glanced nervously
around the park. Kamal tried to shake off the homeless man, who
grabbed his arm and seemed intent on telling Kamal something. Finally
Kamal nodded and continued walking, until he reached a park bench,
where he sat stiffly, as if waiting for someone. He set the sandwich on
the bench next to himself. Remy checked his watch. It was three minutes to eight.

At eight sharp, a second figure approached the bench where Kamal
was sitting. It was Bishir, the agency's man inside the cell. He was
wearing a windbreaker. He sat down and pretended not to speak to Kamal. After a moment, Subjects Number One and Two stood up, moments apart, and began walking toward the street. This time, Bishir
was carrying the sandwich. They walked next to one another, but
moved stiffly, trying so hard not to draw attention that they looked
ridiculous.

Remy scrambled down the steps and fell in behind the men. They
walked slowly across the street and paused at a grade school, arguing
about something in front of its fanciful brick and iron fence. Kamal
gestured at the section of fence that looked like a ship on gently rolling
seas, and Remy touched his pirate's eye patch and felt himself go cold.
Not a school. They wouldn't try a school . . .

They began walking and Remy moved behind them again. As they
turned a corner, he saw the agent Dave sitting in a parked car with another man he didn't recognize. Was the agency in control of all this?
Did Remy need to follow Kamal anymore? A moment later, Kamal and
Bishir disappeared down the stairs of a subway station. Dave and the
other agent hurried behind them.

Was that it? Had Remy done his part? Perhaps it was possible after all—that if he just went with events as they presented themselves, things would work out. Traffic was beginning to pick up. Maybe he could even get some breakfast—

Then Kamal came out of the subway entrance across the street. Alone. He walked quickly down the sidewalk, breaking into a kind of skip-run. Remy looked around in vain for Dave, and now Kamal was rushing down the block. Remy ran across the street, trying to look like someone late for a bus, and stayed half a block from Kamal, whose head swung regularly as he moved, like a lizard. Remy felt frantic with confused adrenaline. Was he supposed to stop Kamal? Was something happening? Would he recognize it if it did?

He stayed behind Kamal, keeping an eye out for Dave, but the agent was nowhere to be found. Had Kamal lost him? Subject Two turned north, then west, south, and finally east again—a completed circle around the block. Remy stayed back at least a half block, trying to look nonchalant, which was difficult at the pace Kamal was setting for him. He paused here and there, ostensibly to check his watch, and kept moving down the block.

Kamal hurried toward a cluster of public buildings. Remy felt a surge of angry hopelessness. Everything here was a potential target. Cupolas and arches and pillars, the breathless neoclassical mass at the end of the block: Any of them would work, Remy thought, all of them packed with people and symbolic weight. He thought of a map of downtown tourist attractions he'd seen once, and he thought: The whole city is a target. Ahead of him, Kamal stopped suddenly, looked back over his shoulder, and took a sharp left, disappearing into an ornate building Remy had never really noticed before, wedged between all of these larger structures.

Remy hurried to catch up, but he didn't know if he should go inside, and he didn't want to lose Kamal, who might come right back out.

Instead, Remy drifted into a small park across the street, where he could
see the whole building. He stood behind a tree and took in the face of
the grand building, which he noticed now was like a kind of coded
map. Three arches on the first floor gave way to a row of three-story
columns and then a wedding-cake topper lined with statues of men—
famous men Remy didn't recognize, men looking down on him in judg
ment, men waiting for history to occur. Even towering over the street,
the men seemed real, down to the wrinkles in the sculpted folds of
their coats. Above the statues, gaudy dormers poked from the roof,
home to cherubs and eagles and shields, a symbolic, indecipherable alphabet that sparked in Remy an old wish for more education, enough
to illuminate the significance of the ship's prow, or the soldier and
maiden on one side and the Indian and Pilgrim on the other, staring
down at him with a sepulchral patience that was as terrifying as anything he'd ever felt.

Something buzzed at Remy's waist. He patted himself down and
found a cell phone on his belt. He opened it and put it to his ear.

"There's a game show I'd like to pitch," said a familiar voice on the
other end of the phone. It was the old Middle Eastern man in the wool
coat. Jaguar. "Name That Sacred Text: *Slay them wherever you find them.
Drive them out. . . . Idolatry is worse than carnage.*"

"Where are you?" Remy asked. He looked around the park and his
eyes went back to the statues on the building before him.

"Here's another one," Jaguar said. "*Thou shalt not make unto thee any
graven image, or any likeness of any thing that is in heaven above or that is
in the earth beneath.* Okay, so which is which?" He made a buzzing noise.
"No, I'm sorry. The correct answer is that there is no difference, except
maybe over whether we were created from dirt or from a blood clot."

"Where are you?" Remy asked again.

"And speaking of graven images, here's something I don't understand," Jaguar said over the phone. "All those people who genuinely *believe*

they saw Satan in the smoke that day. Don't you find it just a little bit demoralizing, to be fighting ignorant, dark-ages zealotry when half of the people you're fighting for believe the devil lives in a cloud of smoke and ash?"

Remy put his hand on his gun again and edged around the park, looking behind trees. "Where are you?" Remy asked between gritted teeth.

"I'm right where you told me to be."

"Where?"

"Right here."

Remy spun around. "*Who* are you?"

"Please," he said over the phone. "This isn't the best time—"

"They said you're organizing and funding a cell here. That you are buying explosives."

"Ri-i-ight," the man said, as if this were obvious. "With the money you gave me. I'm sorry. Did you need a receipt?"

"The money *I* gave you?" Remy began to feel off-balance again. He recalled the envelope of cash. "But . . . they said you were . . ."

"That I was what?" he asked.

". . . Jaguar," Remy said quietly.

"Jaguar? No. Really?" The man scoffed. "That's awful. God, is the entire agency made up of morons? Look, I appreciate that you don't want to endanger your work by telling those amateurs about me. . . . But come on—*Jaguar*? How could you let them do that to me?"

Remy slumped against a tree.

"What about Iceman. Or something that reflects my education— Doc, for example? Tell them that I find Jaguar culturally and racially offensive. Tell them you're worried that I'll file a civil rights complaint. That ought to scare those officious assholes."

"I don't—" Remy touched his forehead, trying to put it together. "Are you saying that . . . you work for us?"

"Us?" He laughed. "I'm sorry, but your idea of *us* tends to be a little bit fluid, my friend. *Either you're with us or . . .* what? You switch sides indiscriminately . . . arm your enemies and wonder why you get shot with your own guns. I'm sorry, but history doesn't break into your little four-year election cycles. *Are you with us?*" The man laughed, winding down. "May as well ask if I am aligned with the wind."

"Look. I just need to know—" Remy squeezed his good eye shut. "Are you . . ." He couldn't find the words. ". . . trying to hurt people?"

"Which people?"

"Innocent people," Remy gritted.

The man laughed. "That doesn't exactly narrow it down."

"I'm going crazy," Remy said.

"Yes . . . I used to think that," said the man on the phone. "The sorrow would come over me. Like a fever. And I would scratch at my own face, tear at my skin until the pain and the rage felt like one thing . . . then, I used to wonder if I'd gone crazy. But other times—" There was a rustling, and then he said, "Okay. Your boy picked up the package. He's on the move again. Your turn."

Remy spun around the tree and saw Kamal leave the ornate building, this time with a larger package, in a shoulder athletic bag. Remy began following him again on foot, though he was unsure what to do. He still had the phone at his ear.

"Other times," Jaguar said over the phone, "don't you wonder if *they're* all crazy? With their stone pilgrims, and their marble soldiers, with their virgins in paradise and their demons in smoke? Sometimes I think I'm the last sane person on Earth."

And then—

REMY SPRINTED down an alley, around a pile of cardboard, a bicycle rack, and some plastic garbage cans. He came out on the narrow street, between the fire escapes of two old tenements with glossy new entryways. He stopped and looked around. Was this where he was running? Something, the activity, his racing heart, caused the flecks in his good eye to swarm like bees. His left eye—black as a painted window—throbbed behind the gauze. Remy stared around at the street in front of him, panting. He looked left. And then right.

And then Kamal burst around the corner to his left, looking over his shoulder as he sprinted down the sidewalk, carrying the athletic bag like a huge football. As Remy watched, the man darted between two parked cars and ran into the street. Remy stood tensed on the sidewalk, in the middle of the block, unsure what to do—until he saw Markham dart around the same corner, waving a gun and sprinting twenty paces behind Kamal, but losing ground on him. Remy stepped around a parked car. Kamal saw him and tried to veer, but Remy jumped, hit Kamal full with his shoulder, and knocked the smaller man to the street. The athletic bag skidded beneath a car. Kamal started to get up, but Remy was on him, pushing him facedown to the blacktop, a knee in Kamal's back. Remy grabbed Kamal's wrist, and he said calmly, "Give me your other arm." Beads of sweat clung to his cheek. Kamal pulled his other arm out and Remy wrenched it behind the man's back, causing him to groan.

"Nice work," Markham said as he came up, panting. He pulled a plastic pair of zip-ties from his pocket and flipped them to Remy, who put them over Kamal's wrists, pushed the ends through, and zipped them tight. Markham reached under the car and pulled out the athletic bag. "What do we have here? A little present for the great Satan?"

"You are making a mistake," Kamal said, his face pressed against the street.

"The only mistake I made was not shooting you in the ass when you ran away from me," Markham said. "And I heard you throw like a girl."

"A mistake," Kamal repeated, pushing his lips back over his jutting teeth.

And then Remy heard tires screaming and a car barreled around the corner and squealed to a halt in front of them, bucking like a horse before it finally stopped. It was a dented silver gypsy cab with brand new tires. Remy watched as two thick guys in sweatshirts and ball caps climbed out of the car, guns drawn, white wires dangling from their ears. One of the guys was the greasy homeless man from the park.

"Get the fuck off of him," said the other man—the familiar agent with the crooked mustache and the BUFF ball cap.

Markham was still in the street, holding the athletic bag. "Who are you?" he asked.

Buff held up a small wallet for Markham to read. "Why don't you tell us what you're doing hassling our CI?" he said.

"What?" Markham looked dumbfounded. Remy almost felt bad for him. "He's a bureau informant?"

"Goddamn it, Remy," Buff said. "We're this close to penetrating this group of lunatics and you come along and nearly fuck it all up."

"You know this guy?" Markham asked Remy.

"So help me," Buff said to Markham, "if you endanger our operation, you'll be pissing through a tube the rest of your life. Do you understand me?"

Remy, for once, felt ahead of events. You can't beat this thing, he thought. You can *want* to do the right thing; you can vow to pay attention, to focus, to connect the dots. But once you start down this path, it really doesn't matter. Every path leads to the same place, events like water circling toward a drain. Without the slightest hesitation, Remy got off Kamal, cut the plastic handcuffs off his wrists, and helped him off the ground.

Kamal's eyes were misty. "These animals killed my brother," he muttered to Remy. "I wouldn't help them, so they killed Assan. These are not Muslims. They are animals. I would do anything to stop them."

And that's when Markham finally caught up. "Oh, for Christ's sake." He threw his hands in the air and spun away, like a pitcher who has just walked the tying run. "Is there anyone in this cell who happens *not* to be a government informant?"

THE CUBICLES were empty, the lights off. Remy checked his watch. It was after ten—*must be nighttime*—and the filing room staff was apparently off duty. He stepped up onto a chair and saw that he was in the center of this vast room, with only the pillars every fifteen or twenty feet breaking up the maze of cubicles. At each corner of the room a doorway led out, and above each doorway was a billboard-size inspirational sign quoting The President.

Remy stepped off the chair and looked around. He was standing in a cubicle. There was a desk with a computer, two filing cabinets, and a wastepaper basket. A frame containing a studio picture of a young man in a flannel shirt with two children was magneted to the desk, next to a stack of paperwork.

Remy took a document from the stack. This particular piece of paper wasn't scorched or wrinkled. Like the paper in the airplane hangar, it was more recent, a credit card statement for a woman in Sandpoint, Idaho. There was an entry outlined with a yellow highlighter—a donation to a charity called AfghanChildRelief. Remy thumbed through the other pages, most of them recent receipts.

Remy folded the credit card statement, put it in his pocket, and continued moving through the cubicles, each identical except for the photos on the desks. Eventually, he came to the end of this big filing room and found himself beneath one of the doorways. Overhead was a quote from The President, calling on his countrymen to "draw your strength from the collective courage and resilientness." Remy pushed through the door and found himself in long corridor leading to his office. He walked down the quiet hallway, past each dark office. A faint light glowed at the far end of the corridor. He walked past his office and kept going, until he got to the last door in the hallway, the one marked *SECURE*. A light was on inside, coming from a back room.

Remy took a breath and opened the door.

The outer office was dark and empty. It was a reception area, ornate, with a couch and a round desk and walls papered with framed magazine covers, certificates, and photos. A door to the back office was open a crack. Remy moved through the reception area and pushed the door all the way open.

The Boss was sitting behind a desk as big as a queen-size bed, lecturing his young ghostwriter, who was nodding and taking notes as he droned about "the best examples being the military and organized crime . . ."

The Boss looked up. "Hello, Brian."

"What are you doing here?" Remy asked.

The Boss consulted his watch. "What do you mean? I'm right on time. You're the one who's late. Which reminds me—" He pointed his finger at the ghostwriter. "The first rule of effective leadership is to manage your time better than your money. Anyone can make money. Only leaders can make time." The ghost took it down.

"How'd you get in here?" Remy asked.

"How did I get in . . . where?" The Boss looked from the ghostwriter to Remy and back. "How did I get into my own company?"

Remy took a step back. He looked around the office. There was a treadmill and a couch, a television and a DVD player. The walls were covered with photographs of The Boss posing with world leaders and touring The Zero with celebrities. In one photo, the Queen was knighting him. Next to that picture was a photo of The President and The Boss shaking hands, above a framed certificate from the Office of Liberty and Recovery lauding Secure Inc., for its "invaluable assistance in the War on Evil."

"What's the matter?" The Boss stood. "Are you sick or something?"

"Something." Remy fell into a chair. His mind scrambled back through his previous meetings with The Boss, trying to rewind fragments of dialogue, to find some hint of what he'd known.

The Boss waved at the ghostwriter, who pushed his glasses up on his nose, gathered his things, and left the room.

When they were alone, The Boss leaned over his desk toward Remy. "Are you sure you're okay?" he asked. "You're not working too hard, I hope."

"I work for you."

The Boss just stared.

"I'm not . . . working for the government . . . on some secret case."

"Are those agency bastards trying to steal you away from me? Or is it the Bureau?" he asked. "Look, Brian. I know you must be nervous because this job is ending, but this is not the end. After this, we'll have plenty of other jobs. This is only going to create more opportunity. And I'm not going to forget your contributions, if that's what you're worried about. There is no shortage of opportunities for someone with your unique . . ." His pause seemed long, intentional. "Skill set."

Remy pulled out the credit card statement he had taken from one of the cubicles. "We make money on this?"

The Boss sat up straight, stung. "You and I serve our country, Brian. We stepped in to do work that the government couldn't." The Boss tried another tack. "It's just like we said in our proposal, Brian: in today's world, there is no separation between civilian and soldier, between business and government. The private sector is the ultimate covert ops. We won't win this war without using our greatest weapon—our free market economy. You said it yourself."

"I wouldn't say that," Remy offered weakly.

The Boss waved him off. "It doesn't matter who said what. Things were said. I'm sure you said something." He sighed. "Look, I know how you feel. I do. Your work is coming to an end. Everything has been set in motion, and when it plays out the credit will go to other people. We will fade into the background again. I understand how that feels. But you and I will know, Brian. You and I . . . we'll always know what we did." The Boss reached in his breast pocket, pulled out an envelope, and slid it across the desk at Remy. "Here you go. Last of the seed money." The Boss stood and began pulling on his coat.

Remy opened the envelope, saw the bundles of hundred dollar bills. His mouth was dry. "What if I quit?" he asked.

The Boss had turned to take his briefcase from the desk. He smiled.

"What if I don't do anything else?" He thought of April. "What if I just . . . leave."

The Boss considered him for a long time. "What's this about, Brian? Are you asking for a raise?"

"No, I'm not asking for money. I'm quitting."

"You're going to quit your own operation, just as it's coming to fruition? I don't believe that." The Boss smirked. "You're free to do that, of course. You've done your part. But ask yourself this, Brian: If someone gets hurt because you failed to see this through to the end . . . can you live with that?"

Remy felt sick. He thought about Jaguar, about Markham and Dave and Buff. He thought of Assan on the boat and the way Kamal blamed that on the terrorists, al-Zamil on the sidewalk and how Dave blamed that on the terrorists. His head fell into his hands.

The Boss was at his ear, speaking in an insistent whisper. "I know this has been hard, Brian. I know you've second-guessed yourself . . . but do you honestly believe for a second that either one of us would be involved in anything that wasn't entirely necessary? I'll ignore for a moment the implication that you don't trust me. . . . Surely you trust yourself."

Remy didn't say anything.

"Come on. What are you afraid of?"

"That I'm causing something bad to happen."

The Boss laughed. "That you're *causing* it? That's a little grandiose, isn't it? Look around you, Brian. We live in a divided world. You and I didn't make that up. We didn't make up the hole in the heart of this city, or the people who want to see our way of life destroyed. Whatever is happening now was going to happen whether we were involved or not. We've always known that another attack was inevitable."

"But these guys all work for—"

"These *guys* . . . are our enemies. These guys have all engaged at one time in anti-American actions or thoughts or they wouldn't be where they are," The Boss said. "These *guys* hate our freedoms. You didn't *cause* the seditious letters these men wrote or the conversations they had. We owe it to the people who died in this city to find animals like this, animals capable of this kind of barbarism, and stop them before they even think of it." He seemed to be searching for a way to make Remy understand. "Look, a hunter can't flush birds without sending a dog into the brush. My firm was hired to flush the birds. We provided a dog. A dog doesn't ask questions. He doesn't worry about causes. He runs where he's told. He barks. And then . . ." The Boss pulled on his coat. "He waits for ducks to start falling."

The Boss shook his head as he buttoned his coat. "You want to know what caused this, Brian? All of this? I'll tell you." He looked around the ornate office, as if noticing it for the first time. "Ask yourself this: What causes hunger?" He didn't wait for an answer. "Hunger."

THE GUINNESS fit perfectly in his right hand, the red shuffleboard stone in his left. Remy looked around. "I don't think I'm supposed to be here," he said.

"Where you supposed to be?" asked an old man leaning against the shuffleboard table. Remy stared at him—it was Gerald Addich, the old man whose planner he'd found in the rubble. His head was dominated by those huge ears and by the spit of gray curly hair lapping his forehead. He spoke in grave, third-generation Irish, his head bowed slightly forward, as if the goddamn thing were too heavy to hold up.

"I don't know," Remy said. "But there's something happening . . . and I should probably be . . ." Be what? Remy was stumped.

"Always something happening," said the old man. "But if you don't know where else to be . . . this place is as good as any. Your throw, Cap'm Hook." The bar was small and crowded, and Remy was playing shuffleboard with this ancient little man, so pale he was nearly translucent in his vintage suit with a ruffled white handkerchief and gold-crested slippers. "Anyway, you can't leave till I answer your question," the old man said.

"Okay." Remy slid the stone across the cornmealed boards.

"Hey, now, that's got a chance," said the old man as the disc spun and slid to the end of the boards, hung there for a moment, and finally fell. "On a planet with more gravity. Ah, you greedy old pirate," said the old man. "You do realize that you don't score any points if it flies off the end. I've explained that, right?"

Remy took a drink of his Guinness.

"Okay, then," Addich said. "What did you ask? Oh, right. You wanted to know how a man knows if he's done the right thing? Boy, that's a doozy." The old man stuck his bottom lip out and his chin slid away into his neck. "I'm going to venture that he doesn't ever know." The old man leaned forward. "But while he may never know if he did the *right* thing . . . I'll tell you this: He generally knows when he's doing the *wrong* thing. But that isn't what you were really asking."

"It's not?" Remy asked.

"No. I think what you're really asking, if I'm not mistaken, is about this city."

"The city?"

"Not just *the* city," said Addich. "*This* city. Listen: I know that arrogant shit bird you work for thinks he invented the place, but he didn't. I worked for Lindsay when he was Boss and every goddamned day was a disaster would've broke that bully you worked for. Sixty-six in Browns and the east, Negroes fighting the PRs fighting the Guineas, it was a war in there. A goddamn war. This little three-year-old, little Russell Givens—you remember Russell Givens?"

Remy didn't.

"How could anyone forget Russell Givens? See, that's the problem: We got institutional memory like a whore on her fourth marriage. This poor Russell, he gets shot one day from a balcony. We send fifty cops in and it's like a tickertape parade on these poor flats, 'cept with bricks and shoes and flaming beer bottles."

The little old guy skidded a stone down the boards and it came to rest squarely in the threes. "Look at that! Two more thick ones here, Mona!" he yelled, waving his beer. "For me and my troubled young friend—what's your name again?"

"Remy."

"Freddie. You know what just struck me, Freddie? Russell Givens, he'd be, what, forty-something today?" The old guy shook his head. "'Bout your age. Course everyone stays at the age they die. Russell will always be three. And I'll always be old."

Addich stared off for just a second. "So, yeah . . . Sixty-six? Transit workers go on strike . . . you wanna see a city shut down, put the bus drivers and subway workers on strike. Garbage men two years later, mounds of trash all over the Lower East, rotting peels, smells like the whole place died—the teachers in O-Hill, every union in the city woke up the same day and said, 'Let's shut this son-of-a-bitch down.' Rockaways, Bushwick, South J, Corona—everyplace bubbling and melting in the heat of summer and it seems like every block got poorer and more racist and more violent every day—city was burning up. And we had crazy Muslims then, too, the Five Percenters killing Jews up the heights, till someone shot their boss." He grabbed Remy's arm. "City was a tinderbox. Your turn, kid."

Remy slid a stone and again it rode the cornmeal to the end, hung on a little longer than the first throw, and then fell.

"Firemen had to carry sticks and guns to fires. People would set fires just to get a crack at beating a fire crew—used to steal their equipment, their pants, their trucks. We send in cops to protect the fire crews, and then we gotta send more cops to protect the cops we sent to protect the firemen we sent to put out the fire. We're gettin' three, four fires a day, and before too long the trucks just stop going to some neighborhoods . . . whole blocks burning down, and right in the middle of it, like some stupid weather girl telling you it's hot in August, goddamn Kerner comes along to tell us the one thing we know: We got racist cops and crowded ghettos."

The old man stepped forward and threw another stone, gliding it along the boards until it came to rest against his first throw. Just then a waitress arrived with two more beers. "Pay the girl, Bluebeard. And tip her like you had a chance with her."

Remy handed the waitress a ten.

"And the hippies!" The old guy shook his head and looked up at Remy, his eyes like tiny polished stones. "Village looked like a goddamn circus. Radicals at Columbia running around yelling, 'Against the wall, mothers—' protests every day, protesters protesting protests. And not like today, these ladies in jogging suits marching on their lunch hour. We had ex-cons with bricks. Honest-to-God agitators. Cops didn't know whose heads to crack, so they just cracked 'em all." He shook his head. "Cracked every goddamn one. Your throw."

Remy concentrated so that this stone wouldn't go off the edge, and threw it about halfway, along the right rail. It drifted off the boards, hung a moment, and dropped.

"You have got to be the worst goddamn shuffleboard player I ever seen," said the old man.

"Bottom line, I suppose it was garbage that killed Lindsay. And in the end it all turned to garbage. The whole city was garbage—schools bad, services bad, crime up, parks and subways a horror show, corrupt cops, and everything we did made it worse. Pay the sanitation workers more to get the garbage, and the teachers strike. Send cops to stop the protests and they beat the protesters, which causes more protests, so we gotta send more cops."

He turned, grabbed Remy's arm, and spoke in a low growl: "This city—is a big goddamn place, kid. A monster. You can't imagine all the stuff that can go wrong here in a day. This was the city Lindsay ran, the city I had a part in running. For ten goddamn years this place was un-livable. It was a sinkhole. An ungoddamnlivable sinkhole. And then you know what happened? Do you?"

Remy waited. The old man got even closer, so near they could've kissed. "It got *worssse*," he hissed. "Seventy-six . . . seven? Bottom rung of hell. Drugs. Gangs. Bankruptcy. I almost moved myself, four, five times." Then the old man leaned back and thought a moment. "But then something happened. Something . . . unexpected. A miracle."

"What?" Remy asked.

Addich took a long drink of beer. "I went . . . for a walk. One night I couldn't sleep. I got up early, before dawn. Got dressed. And I went for a walk. It was spring. Air was fresh and clean. And it was amaz-ing . . . the shopkeepers misting the flowers, kids delivering papers, and there was this couple standing on the stoop next to my building, hold-ing hands, on this date that neither one of them wanted to see end. And it hit me. This is a hard place. God, it's a hard place. But it wakes up every morning. No matter what you do to it the night before. It wakes up."

The old man backed away. He stepped up to throw, but turned and considered Remy's face. "When I saw those lunatics in the Middle East on TV . . . jumping up and down celebrating because some nut jobs had murdered three thousand people, you know what I thought?"

Remy shook his head.

"I thought, *Fuck you*. We used to kill that many ourselves in a good year. This city, it doesn't care about you. Or me. Or them. Or Russell Givens. This city cares about garbage pickup. And trains. That's the secret . . . what the crazy assholes will never get. You *can't* tear this place apart. Not *this city*. We've been doing it ourselves for three hundred years. The goddamn thing always grows back."

THE MOON was just a shaving, a bright sliver of lemon peel hung between two buildings. A tuft of cloud drifted below the moon, underlined it, and then skidded away. Remy was standing at the bedroom window of his apartment, staring out between fire escapes at the buildings across the street. He stepped away from the window and let the curtain fall. He rolled his neck, pulled on a pair of jeans, and checked his watch. It was quarter to four. He sat on the edge of the bed to tie his shoes, checking first to make sure there was no blood on them.

So he would take a walk, to the one place where he might still be able to make sense of things. Remy grabbed his coat off a chair and left his apartment, walked down the hall, down the stairs and out onto the stoop. He looked down the block. It was empty; sidewalks glistened in the dark. The air was cool and clear, as if a new shipment had arrived by truck this morning, the old stuff flushed and packed in garbage cans. From the street, Remy looked up at his apartment window. It was dark and implacable, and he had the odd feeling that he might never see his apartment again. He started walking. The streets shined as from a fresh rain, but the sky was icy clear. He breathed in the morning smells: truck exhaust, sewage, bagels—but he didn't find that smell, and he was surprised that he couldn't come up with the odor. When had that happened? He had assumed the smell would never leave him. Now he had only a vague memory of it, but the odor itself was different from its memory, the way melancholy proceeds from sorrow.

Remy stepped between two parked cars and crossed the empty street. He paused when he saw a familiar car parked a block from his apartment, illegally, next to a hydrant. Remy made his way over to it and looked down, to the driver's seat, where Paul Guterak was leaned back, asleep, snoring lightly, his mouth slightly open. He wore a puffy winter coat, lined with horizontal seams, and binoculars around his neck. Across his lap was a notebook. Remy could see writing on the open pages: "0212: Subject BR returns to apartment. 0224: Lights out." Remy let his hand linger on the windshield for a moment, then tapped lightly on the window.

Guterak started, looked around, and then up at Remy, confused. Finally, he lowered his window. "Oh. Hey. I was just—" But he couldn't think of anything.

Remy crouched by the window. "Can I see that?"

"Oh." He handed Remy the notebook. "Sure. You know . . . you asked me to—"

"Yeah, I remember," Remy said. The log went back months, although it skipped days at a time. Each page had a date written on top; beneath the date were three columns, showing in military time where and when Remy went and where and when he left. Remy flipped through the entries and saw April's apartment, Carla and Steve's house ("stayed in car"), trips to the library and the courthouse and any number of bars and lounges. He saw Nicole's apartment and the office of Secure Inc. Twice Paul tracked him to the airport, but didn't follow him inside. It was strange seeing his life like that, and it was far less mysterious than Remy had expected. He found he remembered just about everything on the log, and he was surprised at how useless it was, seeing the places and times without any context, without any *why*.

Paul yawned. "I'm sorry it's not more complete. I did the best I could. I'm pretty rusty. I lost you a lot and I kept forgetting to do it."

"No. It's fine," Remy said. He handed it back through the open window. He looked down on his friend. "Did I tell you how much I liked your commercial?"

"You did? Thanks, man. That means a lot to me."

"You were great."

"You didn't think I looked fat compared to that smoker?"

"No. You looked good."

"Thanks." Paul sat up in the driver's seat and shook his head, as if trying to clear his mind. "Hey, can I ask you something?"

"Sure." He leaned against the window frame.

Paul looked around, as if worried that someone was listening. "Do you ever feel like things got away from you?"

Remy smiled.

"I was sitting there the other night, with Tara, watching myself in that cereal commercial, and I swear to fuggin' God, I couldn't for the life of me figure out what happened. I mean, I should be as happy as shit. But the one person I wanted to see it with . . . was Stacy. Of all the people . . . that ungrateful cow. But I swear to God . . . it was like . . . I had this moment . . . I honestly didn't know how I got where I was. Do you know what I mean? Does that ever happen to you?"

"You should go home, Paul," Remy said quietly.

Guterak nodded. He looked down at the steering wheel, but then looked back up at Remy. "Tara left."

"Why?"

"I don't know. The commercial aired. I ran out of fuggin' hair gel. Who knows?" He shrugged. "Maybe I talked too much about that day again."

"I'm sorry."

"How come you never talk about it? Every other cop I know talks about it, even if they weren't there. But you . . . you never talk about it."

"I don't really remember."

"Nothing?"

"No." But it wasn't entirely true. Remy did remember something from that day. Paper. He remembered smoke and he remembered standing alone while a billion sheets of paper fluttered to the ground. Like notes without bottles on the ocean, a billion pleas and wishes sent out on the wind. He remembered walking beneath the long shadows and watching the paper fall as a grumble rose beneath his feet and—

Guterak was staring at him. "The last time I saw you that morning, you were going in. Do you remember that at least?"

"No."

"We couldn't get anyone on the fuggin' radio and it seemed like the evacuation was slowing down. It was just smoke up there, and people falling, jumping . . . and you said you were gonna go in and get a visual, see where they stood with the evacuation. You were gone fifteen minutes or so . . . when everything went to shit. I thought for sure we'd lost you, until I saw you that night."

Remy searched his memory, but there was nothing.

"Sometimes I wish I'd gone in," Guterak said.

"What are you talking about?"

"When it all started coming down, there was that fire probie . . . stupid kid ran toward the thing. I passed him—he's running in while I'm running away." Guterak's eyes glistened. "Sometimes I hear people use that word—hero—and I feel . . . sick."

"Go home," Remy said. "Go see Stacy. And your kids." Then he stood and patted the roof of the car. "And don't follow me anymore."

Paul rolled up his window. Remy watched Guterak drive down the block and then he began walking, his shadow growing in the streetlight before him. He moved steadily down the dark sidewalk, careful to stay in the shadows. Above him, the fading rind of moon tailed him down the narrow street. Remy walked south and then east through neighborhoods he'd never seen on foot before, quiet, precise neighborhoods bordered by rows of businesses—copy companies and juice bars and cell phone sales, their façades covered with cages and bars and garage doors. He caught a glimpse of an avenue and the storefronts on it seemed to stretch forever. These had been cobblers and butchers at one time, and printers and razor salesmen and soul food restaurants and record stores and pawnshops, and one day they would be genetic splicers and pet cloners and jet pack distributors. *This city.* Yes, everyone believes they've invented the place, that their time is the only time, and yet the truth was—

THE GROUND is where history lay. They didn't put the Gettysburg memorial somewhere else. They put it at Gettysburg, or some version of that place, of that ground. They were the same: ground and place—plowed and scraped and rearranged, sure, but still you knew that in this place the soil was tamped with bone and gristle and bravery. That was important. The ground was important, imprinted with every footfall of our lives, the DNA of the profound and the banal, every fight, chase, panhandle, kiss, fall, dog shit, con game, stickball hit, car wreck, bike race, sunset stroll, fish sale, mugging—the full measure and memento of every unremarkable event, and every inconceivable moment. Remy turned from side to side, taking the whole thing in, feeling incomplete, cheated in some way, as if they'd taken away his memory along with the dirt and debris. Maybe his mind was a hole like this—the evidence and reason scraped away. If you can't trust the ground beneath your feet, what can you trust? If you take away the very ground, what could possibly be left?

And yet that's what they had done. He stepped back from the fence line and stared out over the place. They took it away. Nothing left here but a hole, a yawning emptiness fifty feet deep, football fields across, transit tracks cutting through the hole like hamster ramps, roads climbing the walls, excavation trails scratched across it, earthmovers and dump trucks, spotlights shining into the emptiness. God, they scraped it all away. No wonder they couldn't remember what it meant anymore. No wonder they'd gotten it all wrong. How can you remember what isn't there anymore? Remy leaned over the railing. He looked down the fence line, at rows of dying flowers, at notes of encouragement and defiance left by visitors. It looked like any other place now, like the site of a future business park, or a mall parking lot.

He imagined for a moment that he was in the wrong place. *Was this really it?* Christ, it seemed so small. Before, it had been vast enough to contain every horror (falling and burning and collapsing) . . . but that was all gone now. Everything was gone: the silhouetted steel shapes, half-buried I beams, berms of window blinds and powdered concrete, mounds of rubble and jagged window frames, gray undefined *rubble*, hills and pits of gypsum and cloth and . . . and steel! Steel forming itself into cathedral walls and sheaths and arches and caverns and trunkless legs of stone, like perfect ruined sculptures.

He had expected to feel something. But what can you feel about a place when that place has been scraped away? What was beneath all those piles? Nothing? No one?

It was just a deep tub now, a concrete-walled construction site, like any of the other sockets in a city that lived by creating such holes, cannibalizing itself block by old block to make way for the new, smoking sockets surrounded by razor-topped construction fences, waiting for buildings to be screwed in—and this the largest socket, a cleaned-up crater ringed by American flags and dead bouquets. Waiting for cranes. Above, the sky was washed out, colors faded like an old movie, everything the dull sallow of new concrete. *What's left of a place when you take the ground away?* Is the place even there anymore? If you scratched away the whole island and moved it somewhere else, would the city be where it had been, in the widened channel of opposing estuaries . . . or would it be in the new place, where you'd moved the ground?

Remy felt the man next to him even before he spoke.

"Aptly named," he said. "Don't you think?" Remy turned and really wasn't surprised to find Jaguar. In the first light of dawn, he got the best look at him he'd ever had. The man was in his sixties, intelligent looking, with a thin, craggy face and close-cropped gray beard and hair. He pulled his long wool coat up around his shoulders, and nodded at the epic construction site before them. "The absence of all magnitude or quantity."

"What?"

"Zero. The absence of all magnitude or quantity. A person or thing with no discernible qualities or even existence. The point of departure in a reckoning. Zero hour—that sort of thing. A state or condition of total absence. The point of neutrality between opposites. To zero in: to concentrate firepower on the exact range of something. That's a good one, too, although it's a bit literal."

Remy felt in his coat pocket and found two things. His handgun. And the thick envelope from The Boss. His hand moved from one to the other.

The man continued. "But I tell you the best derivation, for my money: *zero sum*. That's what we've got here, if you ask me. Gains and losses coming out equal. No possible outcome except more of the same. And yet . . ." The man shrugged. "No. Say what you will. It is a fitting name."

Remy looked up and saw the edge of moon again, faint now, about to disappear for the day. For the next fifteen hours the moon would be invisible, though of course it would still be there, driving tides and bipolars and the births of babies. And yet they insisted on saying each night that the moon *came out,* like superstitious men scratching their fear onto cave walls.

"It's an Arab word," the man continued. "Zero. From the word *sifr*. Means empty, like cypher. The world had no concept of zero, of nothingness, until we brought it west. Of course, we stole it from the Hindus. But it had never occurred in the West that there could be a number before one." He scoffed. "*Civilization.* They couldn't even get their minds around the concept of emptiness, of infinity, the circle completing itself. If you can't count nothing, you can't conceive of everything. Without zero, you can't comprehend negative numbers. So you can't see infinity. There's no sense to the universe. No negative to balance the positive, no axis on which to turn, no evil to balance the good. Without zero, every system eventually breaks down."

He nodded, as if convincing himself. "No," he said again, "it's the right name."

Remy swallowed. "What are you going to do?"

"I'm doing what we agreed to do, what you told me to do."

Remy felt for the gun in his pocket. "I'm not going to let anyone get hurt."

Jaguar stared at Remy with those implacable eyes. "I am on your side, remember?"

"Is that good or bad?"

The corner of Jaguar's mouth rose in a smirk. "Point taken." He cocked his head and seemed to be reading Remy for the first time. "For just a second there you looked like you couldn't decide whether to pay me or shoot me."

It sounded like he was joking, but Remy's hand remained in his pockets, between the gun and the money The Boss had given him. "Does it matter?" Remy asked.

"It matters a little to me," he said darkly, holding out his hand.

Remy had no idea what to do. "Maybe I should shoot myself," he said.

"You tried that," the man said without looking away, his hand still out.

Finally, defeated, Remy handed over the money.

As he counted, Jaguar said, "I'd better not see anyone there."

Remy said nothing.

"I mean it. No one moves until I'm gone. Right?"

Remy said nothing.

Jaguar looked up. "Look, if I so much as see a patrol car while I'm making the drop, I'm out of there. Do you understand?"

"No . . . Not at all."

Jaguar continued: "I sure as hell better not see *you* there."

"See me where?" Remy asked quietly, already sensing the answer.

"Good," Jaguar said. "That's more like it." He stuffed the money in his wool coat, tipped his finger to his head, and walked away.

Remy glanced over his shoulder, toward Wall Street, and saw the first tourists edging their way in, mouths open, cameras up. They posed for pictures on either side of a plastic American flag, which had been zip-tied to the railing. Remy watched this for a moment, and then he fell forward, his fingers locked in the wire fence surrounding the hole where the world had been.

THE WIRE room hummed with activity, translators pitched forward, agents coming in and out with printouts, computer screens registering the levels of voices. Remy edged in, breathless, as if he'd just run over here. The room was long and narrow, like a cheap motel conference room, with one bank of windows looking out over the river, the other long wall lined with bookshelves covered with bound books of transcriptions, and on either end of the room a station equipped with a computer registering the levels of digital recording. Translators sat next to technicians, headphones over their ears. Over a speaker, Remy could hear an Arabic drone in the background—*"Bism-allah—al-Wadud. Ar-Rahim"*—while two other men argued in whispers.

"Name of God loving . . . and merciful," the translator said.

"Where have you been?" Markham whispered. "You almost missed it.

We got three targets in a hotel room waiting for Jaguar. And then they're gonna go. We're listening to Kamal make his suicide videotape. It's . . . cool."

The agent Dave was standing, his head pitched forward like a vulture, looking over the shoulder of the seated translator, a man in his fifties with a dark tangle of black hair, who was concentrating on the drone in the background. He translated in a consonant-heavy English punctuated by pauses and hums: ". . . as . . . uh . . . commanded by Allah . . . um . . . something infidels . . . those who would enslave and uh . . . what's the word . . . seduce . . ."

"Rape," yelled the other translator from across the room.

"Right," said the first translator. "Uh . . . rape . . . the Land of the Two Holy Places . . . the infidel wolf . . ."

Above the chanting Arabic was the sound of the other two men, whose whispered English was picked up by the wire.

"This is crazy," said one of the men on the wire, above the background drone. "I am not going to do this." Remy recognized the voice. It was Mahoud, the restaurant owner.

"Look, just say some crazy shit on the tape," Bishir whispered back. "You don't have to do anything after that. Just cover your face, hold the machine gun, and say infidels and wolves and shit like that."

"No. I can't do it."

"Do you see that guy?" Bishir whispered. "Does he look like he's fucking around? He'll have us both killed if he thinks we're backing out."

In the wire room, Dave was chewing his thumbnail. "Come on, come on. Hold him."

"But I never intended . . ." Mahoud began.

"Look, it doesn't matter what you intended," Bishir said. "We're here now. Just make your tape, and then you can run. But if you leave now we're both dead."

"That's right," said Dave. "Keep him hooked, Bishir. Don't let anyone out of that room."

"He's good," Markham said in a low voice. "I wish we could've afforded someone like that."

Remy felt the ground spinning.

The translator droned on: ". . . guide me in the straight path . . . not the path of those who have incurred the wrath of . . ."

"We've got to stop this," Remy said.

Markham reached out and grabbed Remy's arm.

"Is that Remy?" Dave asked. "Look, this is not the time, Remy. We're trying to work here."

"Somebody stop this!" Remy yelled.

Dave took a drink of the largest iced coffee drink Remy had ever seen, a pail of coffee and whipped cream. "No one does anything until Jaguar gets there with the bomb."

"They have a bomb?" Remy asked Markham. He watched as agents and translators moved around the room like ants on ice cream.

"It's not much of a bomb threat if they don't have a bomb," Markham said under his breath.

"We gave them a bomb?"

"The detonator isn't real," Markham said.

"This is crazy," Remy said. He yelled again, "Look! You've got to stop this! Right now!"

"All right! That's it. Get him out of here!" Dave yelled, pointing at Remy without looking back. "You had your chance, Remy. Now leave us alone and let us do our jobs."

"This is insane!" Remy yelled.

Markham began pulling him by the arm out the door.

"And the seas shall boil," the translator was saying, "and . . . uh . . . every soul shall know what it has done."

"Wrought," said another translator.

"Right, *wrought*," said the first translator as the door closed behind them.

In the hallway, Markham held Remy by the arm. "What's wrong with you?"

Remy felt sick. "They're all our guys."

"Technically," Markham said.

"No. They're all moles. Every one of them."

"Ye-e-eah," Markham said, as if Remy had just mentioned that the sun had come up.

"They all work for us."

"That's what makes it so perfect. What can go wrong?"

Remy pushed away from Markham and began running down the hallway.

"Brian!" Markham called. "Come back."

Remy turned the corner and still he heard Markham's voice. "You're gonna miss the raid!"

Remy ran out the door, into a long, empty hallway. The door behind him had a name that Remy assumed must be for a phony business—*All Field Transit*. There was a stairwell on his right. He crashed through it. An alarm went off somewhere, but he kept running down the dark stairs, taking two at a time, down three flights to the first floor. He burst out into a lobby, past a napping security guard, through the revolving door and out onto the street. He stood on the curb mid-block, eyes darting from building to building. Listening posts were often set up nearby; the cell could be meeting in one of these buildings.

It was a rainy morning, cabs jostling for lanes with delivery trucks and limos. He ran down the street. At the corner he stopped and looked both ways, glancing up at windows as if he might see a familiar face in one of them. Then, right in front of him, he saw the silver gypsy cab. The passenger door opened and Buff got out, a cord dangling from his ear, his middle finger on an earpiece.

"Jesus, Remy, should you be on the street? We're expecting Iceman any minute. You listening to this shit?" he asked, like a teenager who's found a peephole into a girls' locker room. "We got three bogies in this hotel room saying prayers and talking crazy. Just like on TV."

"You need to stop it!"

"Stop it? We got our CI in there and we got people all over the building." He waved at the buildings. "We got enough snipers for fifty guys. Soon as the last guy shows up, we move."

"No, no. What if something goes wrong? What if the bomb goes off?"

"No worries. They got a phony detonator."

"Other way around!" called the other agent from the car.

"Oh, right," said Buff. "The detonator's phony. Bomb's real."

"No. It's the other way," said the other agent from the car again.

Buff ducked his head so he could see inside the car. "Real bomb, phony detonator?"

"No," the voice said from the car. "You keep saying it the same way. It's the other way around."

Buff shrugged. "Anyway, don't sweat it. We got it under control. Soon as Ice Guy gets here, we move. Fuckers at the agency are gonna shit their pants when we raid their deal." He hit Remy in the shoulder. "Thanks again, man."

Remy rubbed his brow.

Just then, the agent in the car leaned across the seat and hissed, "Ice on the pond!"

Remy's eyes drifted across the street, to where an older Middle Eastern man, face and head clean-shaven, wearing new rectangular glasses, was walking toward the brownstone. He carried an athletic bag over one shoulder and had his wool coat under the other arm. The sidewalk traffic parted and Jaguar reached for the door of the building, his eyes darting about.

"Look natural," Buff said, and he grabbed Remy in the most unnatural hug Remy had ever felt.

As Jaguar entered the building his head turned a few degrees, his gaze narrowed, and Remy wasn't sure, but he thought, for just the briefest moment, that Jaguar might've seen him.

"Target is inside. Move into positions," Buff said into his wrist. The other agent eased out of the car and began wading into traffic, as Buff let go of his smothering hug and stepped in behind the other agent.

Remy was left on the sidewalk, his feet glued to the spot. He turned to his left and saw, in the building he'd just left, Dave and Markham and another agent from the wire room emerge on the street. They began crossing the street in the middle of the block, and then Dave turned to look up the street, to where Buff was crossing at the corner, his head bobbing above the cab line.

"Come on. You've got to be kidding me," Dave yelped. He began moving faster.

Buff turned, saw Dave and began running for the building.

"Wait," Remy said helplessly. He looked up to the building Jaguar had gone into and saw two men suddenly appear in the top-floor windows, wearing black Kevlar jackets, rifles strapped across their backs. They began rappelling down the face of the building. "This is crazy," Remy muttered, to no one. And that's when the phone at his waist buzzed. He reached down and saw the number. April—

"HELLO?" REMY stood in a crowd, breathing heavily. He was covered in sweat, as if he'd been running. "Hello?"

"Yes?" asked a confused man in return. "Do I know you?" The man had a long burn on his face, like a baby's footprint. He was sitting on a wheeled trunk.

"Oh. No. I'm sorry. I was just, . . ." Remy looked around. "Talking to myself."

"You said 'Hello' to yourself?"

"I guess I did." Remy tore his eye from the man's face and looked around. He was standing at the gate of a subway station, between MetroCard machines, in front of a map encased in Plexiglas. Remy moved past the confused man to the wall map, which showed subway lines snaking toward the bottom of the island and then going hard left—red, blue, orange, green, and brown—like the plumbing schematic for a high-rise. A huge piece of pale green chewing gum was stuck to the map. After a moment, Remy pulled the gum away and saw the *You Are Here* arrow. He was at a subway stop at the train station.

Remy turned away from the map. He put his hands to his head, as if he could locate his memory manually. *April had called.* Yes. Remy pulled his cell phone out, but there was no service down here. His breath shortened; he felt a twinge of the same creeping claustrophobia he'd felt that helpless morning *(standing on the street . . . paper raining . . . no-service message on his cell . . .)*

Remy looked around wildly. He tried to concentrate, but there was nothing. She had called. Was she leaving on a train? She'd be going west, home to Kansas City, or maybe to San Francisco. Perhaps a bus? The bus depot was only a block away. No, she wouldn't take a bus. Maybe the train to one of the airports; he remembered there was a line to Newark Airport. The platforms would be across the terminal, two underground blocks away. He tried to remember: Was it New Jersey Transit or Amtrak that went to Newark?

Remy ran down the stairs and sprinted along the tunnel that ran beneath the street. He bumped people at the end of the hallway and was leaping up another set of steps, head clouded with memory *(moving slowly up the hot stairwell . . . coughing stragglers with smoke-stained faces going the other direction)* when he spun around a group of soccer players and crashed into a kiosk—like a machine gun nest of consumer goods. And he had the strangest thought as he tried to put the things back that cascaded down around him: magazines and candy bars, pistachios and gum, cigars, razors, pain relievers, batteries, film, pens and pencils (how long could a person survive on the contents of a single kiosk?) "Hey asshole!" said the clerk, but Remy was running up the ramp.

He came into the great terminal, but here he was slowed by the crowd, by streams of subway riders with backpacks and bags and crosscurrents of rail riders with briefcases and rolling suitcases, their faces flipping past his good eye like snapshots. Though he'd grown used to having a blind side, now and then he still bumped someone and mumbled his apologies. He stopped in the middle of the huge terminal for a moment, surrounded by travelers, their voices low and humming, like droning bees on a nest. Something felt wrong, and familiar *(turning back suddenly . . . stopping on the stairs . . . trickle of people moving down . . .).*

The crowds thinned and Remy ran across the terminal toward the ticket windows for the commuter trains—NJ Transit and LIRR and Amtrak. A handful of people were waiting on lines at the ticket windows. A woman was wrangling two boys in matching Giants jerseys. One of them looked up at Remy and covered his left eye.

(emerging into the empty plaza . . . white paper and smoking pieces of steel and bodies . . . and for the briefest moment he was alone, paper falling . . . he'd never heard the city so quiet . . . and then: a deep, low moan . . .)

He bounced from window to window, reading the train schedules, the list of departures: Trenton and the NE Corridor. Dover. New Brunswick. The Acela Express.

"Where the hell is Newark?" he yelled. People on line turned and stared at him. Finally he found the gate number, and was turning to run when he heard a familiar jingle.

April! He had service again. Remy nearly dropped the phone pulling it out.

"Where are you?" Remy asked.

"Where do you think I am? Making myself scarce." It was Markham. "I assume you're shredding documents. That's what I'm headed to do. Obviously . . . any work you did for us no longer exists."

"What?"

"God, what a mess that was. The bureau and agency are gonna say it was some kind of joint operation, but it was a clusterfuck is what it was. Twenty competing agents busting in doors and swinging through windows, dropping through vents. The crossfire was nuts. Two bureau guys got hit. They're lucky they were wearing vests and that the targets were the only ones . . . you know . . . neutralized—"

"You killed them?" Remy's head fell to his chest.

"Well . . . yeah," Markham said: another stupid question from Remy. "They were making suicide videos. They were holding a machine gun, Brian."

"You got all of them?"

"All but Jaguar. They figure he got spooked by something because he never made it up to the apartment. He got on the elevator but they think he got off on two, went down the stairs and slipped out a loading dock in the back. But they don't think he got far. I would not want to be that guy right now. It's only a matter of time." And then he paused. "You know, the more I think about it . . . maybe you *can* race time. But I don't think you can win."

Remy surprised himself by hanging up. It was as if his hand snapped the phone shut on its own—as if his hand had finally had enough of this lunacy. He stuffed the phone in his pocket. He felt the urge to leave. Find April and just go with her, wherever she was going. Maybe back to San Francisco. He edged his way through the crowd. Markham called again, but he ignored it. He moved through the station, watching the flow of people. And then Remy recalled Jaguar's stare. *All but Jaguar.* And then came an awful thought: *Soft target.*

Crowds. Major disruptions. Easy media access. Home videos and camera phones to maximize the horror. He stopped and looked around the train station.

He was here to find April—

Soft target.

—wasn't he? His phone was ringing again. It wasn't Markham's number. Or April's. He opened it and held it to his head.

The voice was slick and cold but didn't seem angry. "Did you follow me, Brian?"

Remy looked around the station again. "Listen—"

"No. You should listen to me." Jaguar spoke in his steady lecturer's voice, a tone that Remy recognized from their other meetings: *"For on that day there will be shining faces, blithe with joy, and there will be faces blackened with dust—the faces of the faithless and the graceless."*

"Look," Remy said. "I swear . . . I didn't—" But he didn't know what he had done, or what he hadn't done. "Where are you?" He scanned the crowd. "Are you here?" He spun around slowly.

A couple in matching sweatsuits, holding hands—

A woman with headphones pushing a baby stroller—

Two young men in scrubs, holding paper coffee cups—

"You know, it's ironic," Jaguar said over the phone. "I used to tell my students that there are a hundred ninety-two mentions of Allah's compassion in the Koran. And only seventeen instances of his vengeance. And yet, it is always the vengeance that seduces. Just like here. You claim to follow a simple prophet of poverty and compassion and build temples celebrating riches and power."

"Where are you?" Remy asked again.

"It occurred to me when I saw you talking to that agent on the street, when I realized that I was being betrayed—"

"No—" Remy began, but Jaguar kept talking.

"It occurred to me that I've been wrong all these years. Maybe power and vengeance . . . are exactly what we should build temples to.

We marvel at the zealotry of a man who would blow himself up for a cause. But imagine, too, the desperation. The fear. And maybe even something alluring—something . . . primal."

Remy continued to spin slowly.

"Isn't this what you wanted?" Jaguar asked. "This?"

Two girls in Catholic jumpers—

A fat man in custodian's coveralls—

"Let's go somewhere and talk. You and me."

"You and me," Jaguar said. "Yes. We had interesting talks. Here's something we can talk about: Does a man ever realize that he has been the villain of his own story?"

Remy wasn't sure which one of them he meant.

"Perhaps on his deathbed?" Jaguar asked. "Does he realize it then?"

Remy looked over his shoulder:

An old couple wearing matching silk coats—

A banger in a Bulls jersey—

"All along," Jaguar said, "I was the target?"

Remy started to say that he didn't know. But he was tired of saying that. "I'm not sure it even mattered," he said finally.

"And the others?"

"They all worked for us. None of them knew about the others."

Jaguar was quiet for a moment. Then he asked "Why?" quietly, without bitterness.

Again, Remy wanted to say that he didn't know. But that just didn't seem true any more. "Hunger," Remy said.

The phone went dead. "Hello?" Remy rubbed his cheekbone. "Hello!" He spun again. He was standing in the heart of the station terminal, at the center of this swirling maze of faces, all of them looking to him—and, finally, he had nothing left. His arms went to his sides and his head fell back.

And that's when he saw April.

She was wearing a pea coat and a woolen cap, straining with two heavy wheeled suitcases, moving down a ramp toward the waiting area for the New Jersey Transit trains. And if there was nothing else, he thought, perhaps there was escape.

"April!" Remy ran toward her, jumping a railing, following the line of departing trains. But he couldn't see where she'd gone.

He ran down the stairs toward the outdoor platforms. He caught a glimpse of her two platforms away, separated by two sets of rail lines, stepping into a shelter. She pulled her suitcases in behind her. "April!" he called again.

He ran up the stairs, back down the ramp and down the other stairs, his hand sliding down the railing. When he reached the bottom of the stairs, he paused for a moment on the narrow platform. The glass shelter was fogged; he couldn't see inside.

He looked down the track—no train yet—then made his way toward the glass shelter. The automatic doors slid open. There were only a handful of people inside, sitting on plastic chairs, reading newspapers and paperback books. One man was talking on a cell phone.

April's suitcases were stacked in front of her. In one hand she was holding her ticket up, as if it might be collected any time. In the other hand she held a train schedule she was reading. Her pea coat was pulled up tight around her throat. She looked up slowly, taking him in with her dark, imploring eyes. The ticket slipped from her hand but she didn't seem to notice, and her hand remained raised, graceful, half-open, as if she were awaiting a dance partner. Then her eyes shifted a few degrees, so that she was looking over his shoulder.

Remy turned to follow the path of her vision, and through the open door he saw Jaguar coming down the steps to the platform. His face was wet and lined. His gray wool coat was bunched up around him, as if he had something bulky beneath it. And there was something in his hand, a phone, maybe.

Remy turned back to April and opened his mouth to say

something—but she was staring at him with such a look of . . . forgiveness that it took his breath away and he only wished he could stay forever in that moment.

"You came," she said—

NOTHING MORE than air at first. And it wasn't so bad. He'd read somewhere that buildings, too, were mostly air. Maybe *that* was the truly dangerous part: air. Maybe the rest was manageable, the steel and paper and people. Maybe it was the air you had to watch out for. It sucked inward, Remy with it, and then thrust out, like a bellows, the way the ocean gathers water for a crashing wave. When it came, the blast at Remy's back wasn't hot or cold. It had no qualities other than sheer insistence; noise filled every space, concussive and sharp, not a boom but a crack, heavy with glass, and accompanied a split second later by the deep thud he'd expected, a resounding bass thunder like someone trying to frighten him to death, and a blinding flash and then *finally*, when he could stand the noise no longer, the heat came—searing—and he was airborne, free, light . . . like paper, tossed and blown with the other falling bits and frantic sheets, smoking, corners scorched, flaring in the open air until there was nothing left but a fine black edge . . . then gone, a hole and nothing but the faint memory of a seething black that unfurled, that lifted him and held him briefly on the warmest current—

IT WAS dark. No flashers or floaters. Nothing. Brian Remy dreamed or imagined that he was dreaming: He was on his stomach, staring down from the sky as great seams opened and people vanished into the rips. He dreamed that people ignored the tears in the sky and went about their business, filed their taxes, and that every once in a while one of them would fall up, disappear into the cracks, like falling into a man-hole, and the rest would just go on with their lives. And he dreamed that people paused on the street, looked up and spoke to him in muffled voices, asking how he was doing and if he could hear them.

He dreamed that a woman sat next to his bed and held his hand.

April?

No, it's me, said March Selios.

You got out?

I was the last one.

Where are you?

Here. We're all here. We've always been here.

Is April . . .

But the woman's voice changed. "This is going to hurt a little," she said, still holding his hand. And in the dream he was lowered into a scalding bath, and the pain broke him and later, in the darkness, he dreamed that he was spread out on his stomach on a board, and that people moved pins in and out of his back, perhaps marking the move-ments of armies in battle. He dreamed that people jabbed him with needles and poured liquid fire on his skin and then asked if he could feel it. He knew better than to answer questions in dreams and so he lay there, dreaming that they tugged on pieces of skin from the backs of his arms and legs, and that they removed tiny squares to sell to tourists. It wasn't bad, this dreaming . . . the gaps were fluid and he no longer lurched, but skipped from moment to moment with no anxiety, no ex-pectation of comprehension.

He dreamed of Edgar as a baby, but with a tree trunk for a neck.

And the dreams became even more outlandish: hushed conversa-tions and bedside ceremonies, imaginary doctors offering absurd treat-ments. In one dream, they rolled him onto his back, just long enough to pin some kind of medal on him, before rolling him over again. In an-other dream, they moved him to a new room, and people rolled him from side to side, and he dreamed that they gave him a roommate, a man burned in a truck fire, and that they put a television on for them both, a television that turned its own channels—slipping insanely from one reality to another, so that just as he got interested in the sound of strong men lifting kegs of beer a gap would interrupt things and he would find himself on the other side listening to an argument about gay adoption between a minister and a transvestite. And he dreamed that the man in his room, the man burned in a truck fire, told him to "Holler if you hear something that sounds good." But Remy knew better, and the television skipped happily from rising poll numbers to the winners of ballroom dancing competitions, from a double date between teenagers to men worrying about the rate of inflation. And Remy recognized that this had been his condition. This was what life felt like. This.

The televised dreams were especially clever the way they could skip away from anything unpleasant, go from death to music videos, and pass on information without informing. The way they could jump from channel to channel, from site to site, from wrenching tragedy to absurd comedy, with only the laugh track to differentiate them. One day he dreamed two men debating whether the recent bounce in The President's popularity was entirely due to the recent victory over a terrorist cell, in which four of the five members were killed and only one bomb was detonated . . . on a mostly empty train platform . . . killing only six . . . including the bomber . . . and severely wounding a retired police officer—

And when the dream television was off, Remy imagined that people came to see him—Guterak talking about his new job as spokesman for a tear gas company; Edgar shuffling his feet and mumbling that he had to get back to his base; The Boss pausing during a cell phone conversation long enough to ask if Remy was going to make it.

Dream trays of food came and went, and people asked if he needed anything, and through it all Remy clung to sleep. He knew that if she were right, and this had all been a kind of fever dream, that he should just stay in it and she would have to come. Life skipped along— snowboard races and cooking competitions and manatee rescues. "Holler if you hear something that sounds good."

And one day he dreamed that his roommate was sent home. A window was open and he could smell burning leaves, and hear horns outside and the sounds of grinding traffic. The TV that day was offering a particularly insane dream in which grown-up child stars ate insects in an allotted amount of time. A nurse was laughing as she carefully removed the tape and gauze from his face. "That boy is crazy," she said. "I used to love him on the TV. You ever watch that show he was on?" When the last of the gauze came off, Remy could feel the light behind one eyelid, and he could see the old flecks in his good eye. It was the most heartbreaking thing he'd ever seen.

"Okay," she asked quietly, "Do you want to try to open your eyes now?"

But he squeezed them as tight as he could, waiting for her to come.

Acknowledgments

I AM DEEPLY INDEBTED to a number of friends, editors, agents and writers who believed in this novel from its first pages and gave it valuable reads: Cal Morgan, Judith Regan, Warren Frazier, Bill Reiss, Dan Butterworth, Jim Lynch, Danny Westneat, Sam Ligon and my lovely wife, Anne Walter.

This book is fiction. To those people whose real pain I witnessed five years ago, I hope there is real peace.

Insights,
Interviews
& More . . .

Meet Jess Walter

Dan Pelle

JESS WALTER is the author of four novels and one nonfiction book. *The Zero* was a finalist for the National Book Award and the Los Angeles Times Book Prize, and winner of the Pacific Northwest Booksellers Association Book Award. His previous book, *Citizen Vince*, was a finalist for the ITW Thriller Award for best novel and winner of the Edgar Allan Poe Award for best novel. Walter has also been a finalist for the PEN Center USA nonfiction award and the Pulitzer Prize for spot news reporting. His essays, short fiction, criticism, and journalism have been widely published, and he is coauthor of Christopher Darden's bestseller *In Contempt*. He also writes screenplays and appeared in an independent movie in which he displayed the full range of his acting skills by growing a mustache. Raised in a family of failed cattle ranchers, Walter lives in his hometown of Spokane, Washington, with his wife, Anne, and his three children.

> 66 [Walter] also writes screenplays and appeared in an independent movie in which he displayed the full range of his acting skills by growing a mustache. 99

A Conversation
with Jess Walter

Jess Walter discussed The Zero *with
Amy Grace Loyd, literary editor at* Playboy.

Amy Grace Loyd: In arguably the most
visualized event in American history, the
attacks of 9/11, what's left for the writer?
And for the fiction writer in particular?

Jess Walter: It's exactly the pervasiveness of
those images—jets dissolving into buildings,
people dangling from skyscrapers—and their
power within our collective unconscious that
makes them such vital subjects for fiction. We
all witnessed the same event, but we didn't
see the same thing. Where some people saw
leadership, others saw opportunism; where
some saw victims, others saw heroes; where
some saw a crime, others saw an act of war.
Fiction's freedom allows us to rearrange and
reorder, to synthesize, satirize, and make
thematic connections between disparate
images and movements.

The closest parallel might be the
assassination of John F. Kennedy and the
televised shooting a few days later of Lee
Harvey Oswald. Most Americans can
probably close their eyes and still see the
Secret Service agents chasing the limousine,
see Oswald doubled over, as if cradling the
bullet. And yet no moment in our history
has created more speculation, more paranoia,
more conspiracy theories. Ask five people
what they saw and they'll describe the same
moment. But ask what Kennedy's death
meant and you'll get five very different
answers.

Sometimes I think fiction writers are ▶

A Conversation with Jess Walter *(continued)*

the only ones who *can* make sense of what has happened to us since 9/11. We were attacked by religious zealots hoping to start a war in the Middle East and we responded by starting a war in the Middle East. We have blindly traded civil rights and privacy for the illusion of security. We have responded to an increasingly serious world by becoming surreally superficial. We live in a world that could only have been dreamed up by Graham Greene and Franz Kafka on a weekend bender, with George Orwell along to write slogans.

AGL: What particular access did you have not only to the event but to its aftermath that might give you a vantage that other novelists who've written about 9/11 did not have?

JW: I was at Ground Zero on a writing assignment, and had fly-on-the-wall access to a broad swath of public officials, cops, rescue workers, firefighters, and ordinary people trying to deal with the horror and tragedy. Real people inform the novel but it's not about them. It's satire about *us*, about the collective post-traumatic stress that we've suffered and the way we've retreated into a cocoon lined with real estate listings and 401(k) updates while truly frightening measures are undertaken on our behalf. From the first day I began writing I knew this wouldn't be a 9/11 novel. It's more of a 9/12 novel.

AGL: You recently won the Edgar Award for your novel *Citizen Vince*. You are a literary writer but have used genre to frame/structure your work. Are you doing that here?

66 I was at Ground Zero on a writing assignment, and had fly-on-the-wall access to a broad swath of public officials, cops, rescue workers, firefighters, and ordinary people trying to deal with the horror and tragedy. 99

JW: I think suspense should be like any other color on a writer's palette. I suppose I'm in the minority but I think it's crazy for "literary fiction" to divorce itself from stories that are suspenseful, and assign anything with cops or spies or criminals to some genre ghetto. As one of the characters in *The Zero* says, "History has become a thriller plot." When the newspapers every day are filled with stories of surveillance, torture, and suicide bombings, I don't think it's in the novelist's best interest to ignore these things or make them mere backdrops to some domestic story about middle-aged rich people coming to terms with their mortality. ("The parties that season were especially grim.")

AGL: There's a lot of hilarious satire here (the officials in this story will be recognizable to some) as well as Kafkaesque fragmentation and almost dream-like sequences; but there are also acute realistic descriptions, and throughout you manage to remain empathetic and affectionate toward your characters. Was that balance important to you?

JW: That was certainly what I hoped to achieve, the dizzying balance between the real and the surreal, between vivid description and dreamy inexactitude that I first experienced at Ground Zero. I wanted the reader to feel the same way the characters do, especially Remy and April. And they, in turn, had to be real enough to register that what happened wasn't just surreal, but truly awful. The best indication I have that this balance might've worked is how many people ask me if the agency Remy works ▶

> ❝ The best indication I have that this balance [between the real and the surreal] might've worked is how many people ask me if the agency Remy works for, the Department of Documentation, is real. ❞

for, the Department of Documentation, is real.

AGL: Your protagonist, a cop called upon to join a special investigative team, is a complicated hero: he's losing his eyesight and has gaps in his memory, often blocking out his own bad acts. How are you playing with our notion of a hero and with his and the reader's complicity in events surrounding 9/11?

JW: There was a real conflation of hero and victim in the wake of 9/11, in our perverse desire to create a triumphant myth out of pure tragedy. I wanted Brian Remy to be an unwilling hero, blinded in every way, to his own acts and to the motivations of others. Most of all, though, I wanted him to feel what I think most of us feel: confused and frightened, a helpless man of the very best intentions.

As for complicity, I don't personally subscribe to the belief that we were in any way to blame for the attacks of 9/11, that American policy somehow led to a terrorist response. I think that's insane. These were irrational and criminal attacks, entirely unprovoked.

Our complicity begins with our country's reaction to that attack and our failure, in my opinion, to debate the response honestly. The war in Iraq, the abuse of detainees, electronic eavesdropping, Guantanamo Bay—these things were all done on our behalf and they may turn out in the end to have created *more terrorists*. The way espionage and law enforcement have worked in American history, it could be decades before we begin to tabulate the price we paid to feel this phony sense of security.

AGL: What do you think 9/11 failed to teach us?

JW: I doubt the terrorists saw 9/11 as a teaching opportunity. And we're not really a culture geared toward anything as humble as "learning." But I was disappointed in how quickly everyone wanted to *get back to normal*. It was as if we watched terrorism on TV for a while, then got bored and turned back to *American Idol*. ∾

The *Zero* Journals

I KEEP A WRITING JOURNAL *full of notes and observations that often find their way into my novels. In these journals I record the reflexive highs and lows that most writers suffer, alternating between thinking a piece of work is brilliant and that it is unreadable, mood swings so drastic they seem like the diary of a man living on the coast who has no understanding of tides ("The water is disappearing!" "My God, it's a flood!").*

More than anything I've ever written, The Zero took shape from these journal entries, as I struggled to find a narrative shape for an allegorical satire about the aftermath of 9/11, about what I described to myself in 2003 as being like "collective insanity, a post-traumatic break from reality." What follows are excerpts from the six writing journals I kept over the four-plus years that I worked on The Zero, beginning with notes from my first trip to Ground Zero (September 17–23, 2001), and including a trip back to the site two years later. I lost one journal, which is the reason for the big gap in 2002 and 2003. Also, I've weeded out the endless notes about characters and ideas and the thousands of story dead ends I first tested in my journals. So this represents a fraction of the entries that deal with The Zero.

Thumbing through these notes, I was surprised, and not just by my bad penmanship and the many working titles I had for the book (Six Days After and Eight Days After and Days After and Dry White Rain and White Rain). I was also shocked to find that so many elements— the paper, the character of Remy, and most of all, the feel of the book, of a fractured and sorrowful reality—were there from the very beginning.

9-11-01: Oh God.

9-18-01: [*From Ground Zero*] Rubber burned off wheels. Twisted and melted metal. Rivets popped, girders bent and curled . . . No big pieces . . . dust, rubble . . . orange body bags. . . . Dogs smelling for remains. . . . Miles of cable and wire. Frustration. Expect to see someone alive. But not there . . . so quiet. A moonscape . . . across 6-story mounds of rubble. Quiet, listening for tapping. Quiet. Scorched cars picked up and stacked 3 deep.

10-1-01: I am empty.

> ❝ Expect to see someone alive. But not there . . . so quiet. A moonscape . . . across 6-story mounds of rubble. Quiet, listening for tapping. Quiet. ❞

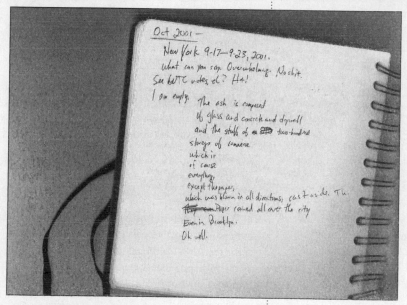

The ash is composed
of glass and concrete and drywall
and the stuff of two hundred
storeys of commerce
which is
of course
everything,
except the paper ▶

The *Zero* Journals *(continued)*

which was blown in all directions,
    cast aside. The
paper rained all over the city
Even in Brooklyn.
Oh well.

10-5-01: Saw a sign: God Bless America. New Furniture Arriving Every Day.

10-18-01: A New York book about the paper? He drives across the country. NY people did what they do—celebrated their uniqueness, fought and stole and wrote and sold and held press conferences and one-man plays and sold photos and analyzed their response and the response to the response—the biggest ant hill in the world, epic scurry and flight.

1-20-02: He comes to the hole to replace the paper that rained on every part of the city, pooling in corners and alleys.

4-12-02: The end of such a book must be sorrow and fatigue—a reckoning, a breath before action, an inevitability.

4-21-02: This is about our inability to register events. We want simple narratives; we don't want our presumptions messed with. . . . We all suffer from this malady, this affliction, and this is what I want to name.

7-16-03: Woman fakes her death? NY business people in for . . . what?

Gaps in my thoughts, now—in my confidence, in my life. Where am I going? Who am I?

8-24-03: What do you do? Where do you go? Faith moves too in patterns like weather.

Everything moves like weather, fronts and storms—things pass.

9-5-03: The names, the world—all pointing toward a specific symbolic meaning and yet, like Kafka, I think pain and meaning are general. Vast. . . . Character. He is trying to connect with these places—why?

9-6-03: [*In New York*] . . . the profound and the mundane . . . wakes up in a panic in his hotel room.

9-8-03: [*At the James Q. Wilson Lecture at the Manhattan Institute for Policy Research*] Four times as many people die in suicide attacks as in other forms of terrorism . . . False that money and education will "cure" terrorism . . . Terrorism increased as [Middle East] economy improved. [Terrorism is eradicated not by] by arresting the perpetrators but by eliminating the cause. But what if the perpetrators are the cause?

9-9-03: [*At Ground Zero*] Jesus, it's gone! They took it all away. It's just another construction site now, a parking lot for a business park. Something is wrong. . . . Flags on fencing and . . . it's like we've suffered some collective insanity, some post-traumatic break from reality.

9-19-03: BLAM. A man's face. In the background, sirens. "Mr.——? Mr.——? . . . lying on his side, big hole in his head. "Mr.——?" He dully answers the door. "I was cleaning my gun."

Psychiatrist: So what do you feel your life is missing? ▶

> **"** [*At Ground Zero*] Jesus, it's gone! They took it all away. It's just another construction site now, a parking lot for a business park. Something is wrong. . . . **"**

The *Zero* Journals *(continued)*

(Man): Specifically?

Psychiatrist: Yes.

(Man): Life.

11-23-03: Iraq . . . we've flushed our freedoms to 'defend our freedoms.' We've given up that great thing we were to protect its name.

11-25-03: Started today on *Eight Days After / A Dry White Rain* . . . the biggest story I know . . . we aren't even supposed to think the wrong thing. . . . White Rain, the fullness of America. Where is she, the sister . . . She's seeing a married guy. She's 31. Remy sees his dead brother's kid . . . the kid tells the truth. Amazingly precocious kid . . . fascinated by the detail.

11-30-03: Distraction, national distraction. We've let it get away from us. There was a moment of purity, of clarity. Sorrow and tragedy are lessons and we ignored them. The honor of sorrow, of sadness, of redemption. This is what we forgot. . . . Where are we going? What do these flags have to do with it?

12-3-03: Remy finds a day planner. . . . "What do you do?" "Tours." "What's it like?" "People describe it as a moonscape. Or hell." "Both places they've never been." "Yeah."

12-13-03: Are we fighting [in Iraq] for an economic system? Is that all we have left?

7-7-04: Starts with Remy. He goes to work for this guy. Putting paper back. Woman escaped with the paper. Must gather her, too. WWVD—What Would Vonnegut Do?

7-22-04: *Days After:* The ground beneath my feet. Concrete . . . the verticality of NY. But what happens when it becomes a horizontal city. The ground has every imprint ever put on it . . . registers every footfall, every streetfight, kiss, dog piss, stickball, car wreck, footrace, stroll, fish sale, mugging, panhandle, con game, speech, cracked sidewalk bike ride. Just keep digging because the ground is ten storeys down now.

Move past cold war irony and sarcasm to . . . what?

8-19-04: *Eight Days After:* . . . need to connect that idiocy to us. Céline, maybe, is a better comparison than either Vonnegut or Heller. Absurdity—in the face of absurdity.

10-20-04: Browning—"Our interest's on the dangerous edge of things/the honest thief, the tender murderer/the superstitious atheist." . . . Remy was sitting in the lobby of a Best Western. He knew it was a BW because he could see the sign turning. The skyline was no help to him. . . . Was he staying at this hotel?

11-13-04: There is a Japanese word that translates roughly to mean *aware*. This is the feeling that life is both wonderful and awful. . . .

11-18-04: . . . those emotional moments between characters . . . with Guterak and Edgar mostly. End of the play he wants to go see his kid. Damn it he wants to. [But] Next scene he's in bed with girl. Then surveillance. Bomb threat. How quickly we forgot and how stupidly we remembered.

11-19-04: Sent [my agent] Warren and ▶

> ❝ The ground has every imprint ever put on it . . . registers every footfall, every streetfight, kiss, dog piss, stickball, car wreck, footrace, stroll, fish sale, mugging, panhandle, con game, speech, cracked sidewalk bike ride. ❞

The *Zero* Journals *(continued)*

[my editor] Cal 25,000 words of *White Rain* today. Exhausted. I think it might be great. I'm about to send Remy to Kansas City.

12-8-04: If this [book] is nothing more than a flash of awareness about our mortality, is that really profundity, or is it a selfishness, a glimmer, nothing more. Joyce [wanted to write] about a man hit by a streetcar, suddenly his every action has deeper meaning. Then he wanted to take away the streetcar. What if, instead, you took away the MAN? Just streetcars barrelling down roads. Luck. Chance. Raw fucking deal. That's what the world looks like, streetcars barreling down roads.

12-13-04: Days pass. Faith returns. Lost day today.... Randomness, cruelty of moment and—time settled for Remy. But why? Flushing out terrorist? Engineering them? Who are we chasing? Which side are we on? Are there sides?

12-27-04: Longest gap in a while. Remy's gaps like my journal, gaps in the measurement of life, not in the life. The novel is a measurement of that life ...

1-5-05: Just sitting here while *White Rain* moves in that lurching way toward, what ... Remy's death? Blindness?—It's one thing to deny our vulnerability, quite another to deny our culpability.—

1-7-05: The challenge with *White Rain* is to make the story move given the narrator's inability to track.... What exactly am I trying to do? Describe the way we are ... trading liberty for security, demanding our own propaganda. Party to our own deception.

> ❝ Joyce [wanted to write] about a man hit by a streetcar, suddenly his every action has deeper meaning. Then he wanted to take away the streetcar. What if, instead, you took away the MAN? ❞

The propaganda of distraction, of triviality. Endless process of moment, overcoming, forgetting, nostalgia. A nostalgia factory.

1-17-05: Tough day. Stopped believing in some of the new book. Fearful that I haven't done enough, that I can't write this book . . . all of which might be okay because who knows if I'll even get a contract. . . .

1-21-05: We have chosen to forget. We have chosen to be a party to our propaganda. We are all living half our national lives, allowing some side of ourselves to do the dirty work.

2-18-05: There was a moment when we realized this hadn't happened to US. That WE were okay.

2-26-05: Hunter S. Thompson committed suicide—so sad. And yet . . . I'm amazed that he could DO that—that he could think about it and just decide—I AM DONE. That's the thing I can't imagine—the plane plummeting, the heart stopping, brain sparking and fritzing, finally going out— and what is the thing that is so sacred, so valuable—which minute, breath, thought is this all for? We've lost our isolation . . . innocence.

3-6-05: I realized what I need *White Rain* to do—Answer who is doing this? The Life behind the Life—the prisoner behind the wall. Torture. To have a war without all the TV and sacrifice that is usually accompanying a war. To take away rights without ever letting people in on the fact that they had them.

3-8-05: The first test of history is that it make sense, which is the first problem, too, ▶

> **❝** I realized what I need *White Rain* to do—Answer who is doing this? The Life behind the Life—the prisoner behind the wall. **❞**

The *Zero* Journals *(continued)*

that it doesn't make sense. We imagine a world governed by rules that we do not really abide while the truth is all sex and power and the nightmares of children.

3-20-05: Haunting displays of airbrush artistry.

4-5-05: Had the dream again last night where I'm guilty of some horrible crime and I'm not sure if I did it or imagined it—woke with that in my subconscious and I couldn't shake it, couldn't seem to get my arms around whether it had happened or not.

4-6-05: Saul Bellow died yesterday.

4-11-05: Remy's getting used to the oddness, but what is out there? Blood on his clothes? Or his hands? Can't get it out . . . No. His shoes. That's chilling—blood on his shoes!

4-12-05: There is infinite hope—but not for us—Kafka. We watch *American Idol*. Brad and Jen. The Dow.

4-16-05: Part II Everything Fades. Scenes— eyes getting better. Odd, barely keeping it in domesticity. [Remy] comes to believe that April is still in love with her husband. Blood on his shoes. Drumbeat behind him rising. The Boss's company. Paul falling apart. Remy thinking he's better and then—BAM.

4-17-05: What if the great 9/11 book comes not from there, but from here, one of those fuzzy places that doesn't exist to them, just lakes of light from the air. Just stay with it.

4-17-05: Everything fades. We go back to where it was before, but the colors are

❝ What if the great 9/11 book comes not from there, but from here, one of those fuzzy places that doesn't exist to them, just lakes of light from the air. Just stay with it. ❞

different. Everything is washed out, the way they do memories in Hollywood. Everything fades. The people mostly. They fade . . . Rushdie says terrorism is murder. Plain. Simple.

4-23-05: *White Rain*—"What was it like before?" That is the important question. No one remembers. Maybe it was different.

No, it was just like this.

Capitalist culture eats everything, even this.

4-25-05: "There is infinite hope—but not for us." Remy is in a coffee shop.

4-28-05: *Herzog* (Bellow): . . . "I'm not even greatly impressed with my own tortured heart. It begins to seem another waste of time."

5-1-05: On my way to San Francisco. . . . So, *White Rain*. . . . Skipping like a stone. . . . Ship wakes like chalk scratches on the slate surface of the bay. The city like transistors, rectangles. Gray and white, reflecting bits.

5-4-05: Alone in a city again . . . San Francisco, the people tumble down hills, to the creases, Market and the Wharf—always a homeless willing to show you to your bar and hotel . . . a union of homeless. This. Is. What. I. Do. . . . The only response to an insane act is to act in kind.

5-7-05: We have buried what happened, the way it rent a hole in our fabric—we go on, blithely, because it is the only thing we know to do. We move the furniture around, cover up the hole—but it's still there, a long tear in who we are. ▶

The *Zero* Journals *(continued)*

> Maybe Remy is a good man . . .
> He counts the stairs
> and steps between rooms
> waiting for that day
> when blindness
> comes.

5-10-05: The path is through the characters, always through the characters. That quality of living a transparency, animated by the looks of others. And you wonder, do I exist when I'm alone? There is infinite hope. There is infinite hope. There is . . . There is. With Kafka, the government bears down on the individual. Now—it is us. We are culpable.

5-12-05: Part II is about real estate. All about the land beneath the . . . trade center, beneath every house.

5-21-05: 45,000 words.

5-22-05: Almost no sleep. Self-absorption, fatigue, impatience . . . clouds piled at the ends of the horizon great stacks and piles, thick and black rising to blinding whiteness . . . it's not all in Remy's mind, not exactly, but he'd allowed himself to not question it, to allow it to be somewhere else. Blood on his shoes . . . Real estate! April is in real estate!

5-26-05: [New title:] *The Zero.* Go into the future. Time screaming by. Picks up son. . . . All he's been through. *The Zero.* So when Remy goes to *The Zero* and when the war starts, it's a surprise that it's gone, that we're in Iraq. The speed with which the country moves on, digests even this.

6-7-05: Remy goes across country. To S.F.

" The path is through the characters, always through the characters. That quality of living a transparency, animated by the looks of others. "

Streaks and floaters out of control—he can barely see—and then the explosion and he's strewn. . . . March: I'm here. We're all here.

6-12-05: Translucence in the writing. Make Remy more connected, who he is, let the story guide you, not the other way. What this is about—steel and brick, drywall and sprinkler heads—

It's like a self-defeating army, a suicide army. . . . You can't win this way. Use them to defeat themselves—to create the enemy themselves—to respond by creating a real war. Wars are declared. Like intentions.

7-15-05: Remy is the Zero.

7-18-05: Nice up here in my office, cool and surrounded by books, by my work. *The Zero.* . . . Never been so unsure of a book before.

8-8-05: A national disorientation. We call things what they're not—everything is an invention. Peter Jennings died two days ago of lung cancer. . . .

8-11-05: Got to 60,000 words of *The Zero.* . . . No one knows where the people went. They just disappeared. Pressure and then dissolved. Cells. Chunks. Fragments, bits, dust. Mr. Selios doesn't know what happened to March. This is the worst part. April longs for one of those voicemail messages . . . and now this war, more young people missing limbs.

8-19-05: Read with Sherman [Alexie] tonight. We were funny. . . . A good point, not to get down on America too much, to remember humor. Vonnegut's humor and humanism ▶

> " Read with Sherman [Alexie] tonight. We were funny. . . . A good point, not to get down on America too much, to remember humor. "

The *Zero* Journals *(continued)*

combine, a good example, love your
characters, even the villain. Even
The Boss.

9-7-05: This novel, with its disorientation
and jerking point of view is tough to work
on for that reason—I'm off balance so
much of the time. . . . Combed through
75,000 words yesterday. . . . The odd
helplessness of being complicit in this
delusional policy and world view. We
make four mistakes at once, every
possible mistake, mutually exclusive
mistake, contradicting mistakes—and the
whole universe of fuckups and fallaparts.

9-12-05: Rolling on *The Zero*—nearing
80,000 words, turning back on itself . . .
getting around to the climax, that sense
of no matter what we do we're fucked.

10-30-05: *The Zero*—This national condition,
a kind of slipped consciousness, the ones who
do the best are the ones who had it before,
who had slipping ethics, or whose brains
worked this way before, drifting in and
out of reality. Remy moving inexorably.

11-15-05: It was us. We tortured. We
bombed. We waged war. We reacted with
fear, and fear, God, is the worst thing. . . .
The most destructive thing in the universe.

12-3-05: Glorious goddamn morning. Wrote
the ending yesterday. Think it's getting better.
Also had a vision for what it is. . . . It tries,
and that's all you can ask of it.

Let them sell it. That's their problem now.
Tom Waits on the stereo. Coffee gurgling.
Snow frosted trees. Cool air.

1-12-06: [*Rewriting*] We create our enemies. It's all in there. . . .

1-22-06: Don't know if I can finish . . . here I am—a week or so away from when I'm supposed to get it in and I don't even know what it's supposed to do.

2-8-06: Done. Finished with an exhausting collapse, sick for a month, office disgusting. Everything collapsed at the end, any energy I had went to writing. And the book? Today, it's good.

2-10-06: Taking one more pass. Meanwhile, Bush says the terrorists' aim is to weaken governments, so they can foment civil war and create a situation in which they can take over. No greater ally than Bush.

2-24-06: So I sit here in my sun-lit living room, staring through windows smudged by little fingers, staring out at the late winter sky, all of this so real, so un-literary, not the shadow of a great day or the representation of it—but a day, a goddamn great day. *The Zero* is away. (~~)

> **❝** Done. Finished with an exhausting collapse, sick for a month, office disgusting. Everything collapsed at the end, any energy I had went to writing. **❞**

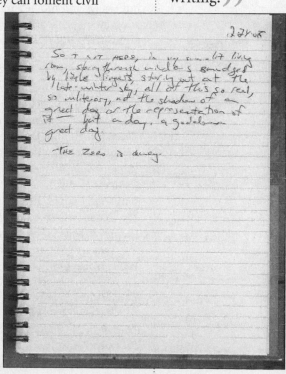

Author's Picks
Grim Inspiration

THESE ARE A FEW of the books I read, reread, or reconsidered over the years I was working on *The Zero*. There are nods to some of these books in the novel, for instance, the names of all the doctors (Dr. Destouches is the real name of Céline; Dr. Rieux is the protagonist of Camus's *The Plague*; Dr. Huld is the lawyer in Kafka's *The Trial*). Many of these books are social satires, some are allegories, others are stories of fractured or distorted consciousness. A few are nonfiction. Like any writer, I am also indebted to countless other books (including several about Islam) and interviews and movies and magazine articles and newspaper stories and conversations and nightmares, but this, I suppose, is a start:

The Secret Agent, Joseph Conrad
Hunger, Knut Hamsun
Catch-22, Joseph Heller
One to Count Cadence, James Crumley
The White Album, Joan Didion
Being There, Jerzy Kosinski
Slaughterhouse-Five, Kurt Vonnegut
Concrete Island, J. G. Ballard
The Trial, Franz Kafka
The Plague, Albert Camus
Journey to the End of the Night,
       Louis-Ferdinand Céline
White Noise, Don DeLillo
Time's Arrow, Martin Amis
Three Farmers on Their Way to a Dance,
       Richard Powers
The Music of Chance, Paul Auster
Bel Canto, Ann Patchett
Cloud Atlas, David Mitchell

*102 Minutes: The Untold Story of the Fight
to Survive Inside the Twin Towers,*
Jim Dwyer and Kevin Flynn.
*American Ground: Unbuilding the World
Trade Center,* William Langewiesche
Step Across This Line, Salman Rushdie

I didn't read any novels about 9/11 prior to
finishing *The Zero,* but since then I have read
three that I greatly admire:

A Disorder Peculiar to the Country, Ken Kalfus
Falling Man, Don DeLillo
Saturday, Ian McEwan ◠

Have You Read?
More by Jess Walter

CITIZEN VINCE

Winner of the Edgar Allan Poe Award for best novel, *Citizen Vince* is an irresistible tale about the price of freedom and the mystery of salvation—a darkly hilarious and unexpectedly profound book by a writer of boundless talent.

Eight days before the 1980 presidential election, Vince Camden wakes up at 1:59 a.m. in a quiet house in Spokane, Washington. Pocketing his stash of stolen credit cards, he drops by an all-night poker game before heading to his witness protection job dusting crullers at Donut Make You Hungry. This is the sum of Vince's new life: donuts and forged credit cards—not to mention a neurotic hooker girlfriend.

But when a familiar face shows up in town, Vince realizes that his sordid past is still close behind him. During the next unforgettable week, on the run from Spokane to New York, Vince Camden will negotiate a maze of obsessive cops, eager politicians, and assorted mobsters, only to find that redemption might just exist—of all places— in the voting booth. Sharp and refreshing, *Citizen Vince* is the story of a charming crook chasing the biggest score of his life: a second chance.

"This terrific book . . . is smart, funny, dark, and moving, and Jess Walter is clearly a writer to watch."
  —Nick Hornby, *Atlanta Journal-Constitution*

"It's been a long time since I read a book as compulsively, indeed greedily, as I read *Citizen Vince*."
  —Richard Russo, author of *Empire Falls*

OVER TUMBLED GRAVES

Rich with the darkly muted colors of the Pacific Northwest skies, *Over Tumbled Graves* established Jess Walter as a novelist of extraordinary emotional depth and dimension. During a routine drug bust, Spokane detective Caroline Mabry finds herself on a narrow bridge over white-water falls in the center of town, face-to-face with a brutal murderer. Within hours, the body of a young prostitute is found along the riverbank nearby. What follows is a novel that confronts our fascination with pathology and murder and stares it down: as Caroline and her cynical partner, Alan Dupree, are thrown headlong into the search for a serial murderer who communicates by killing women, they uncover some hard truths about their profession . . . and each other.

"Exceptional . . . transcends the mystery of crime and takes a courageous look at an even more profound mystery—the mystery of what it takes to continue living. Totally absorbing."
—Ursula Hegi

"Riveting. . . . Without ever taking the easy way out, the book explores the battle of good versus evil on very human terms."
—*Washington Post Book World*

LAND OF THE BLIND

In this fiendishly clever and darkly funny novel, Jess Walter speaks deeply to the bonds and compromises we make as children—and the fatal errors we can make at any moment in our lives.

While working the weekend night shift, Caroline Mabry, a weary Spokane police detective, encounters a seemingly unstable but charming derelict. "I'd like to confess," he proclaims. But he insists on writing out his confession in longhand. In the forty-eight hours that follow, the stranger admits not ▶

just to a crime, but to an entire life: a wry and haunting tale of poverty and politics, of obsession and revenge. And as he writes, Caroline pushes herself to near collapse, racing against the clock to investigate not merely a murder, but the story of two men's darkly intertwined lives.

"Intelligently written, bittersweet, and thoroughly absorbing . . . an affecting meditation on friendship and the price of betrayal."   *—Seattle Times*

RUBY RIDGE: THE TRUTH AND TRAGEDY OF THE RANDY WEAVER FAMILY

What went wrong at Ruby Ridge? Why was Randy Weaver's son fatally shot in the back? How could the FBI justify shooting a woman as she held her infant child? Why were the Weavers given a $3.1 million settlement by the U.S. government? Was there an FBI cover-up and how high did it go?

Ruby Ridge answers the critical questions that cut to the heart of the most explosive issues in the United States today.

The Weaver family took to the woods to escape what they believed was a sinful world on the brink of Armageddon. But Randy Weaver's indictment on a firearms violation escalated into a deadly shootout at his northern Idaho cabin. Before it was over, a federal marshal, Weaver's wife, and his only son were dead.

In this edition, featuring exclusive interviews with key figures on both sides, Pulitzer Prize finalist Jess Walter objectively reconstructs all the riveting events surrounding this controversial case.

"A stunning job of reporting."
    —New York Times Book Review

Don't miss the next book by your favorite author. Sign up now for AuthorTracker by visiting www.AuthorTracker.com.